Love Thicker Than Blood

Cassandra Diviak

LUCKY ACE PUBLISHING
FROM THE HEART TO THE PAGE

Contents

Dedicated to my mother for making me prove that romance doesn't need to be Hallmark to be worth reading. Romance can be smart, witty, and mostly, so filled with imperfect pieces.

Content Warnings

Dear readers,

Thank you for choosing this book. *Love Thicker Than Blood* is meant to be a contemporary romance with mostly humorous overtones, but I would be remiss if I neglected to outline the possible content warnings invested in this book. The following subjects are mentioned in the story, so please be advised:

- **dealing with the loss of a sibling; grief**

- **on-page anxiety disorders**

- **abusive family situations**

- **physical aggression/violence from a former partner**

These topics are not ones that I treat lightly or without the proper lived experiences in my personal life. They apply largely to our protagonist, Nina, and I ask that you take care of yourselves. If reading this story would harm your mental health, then please preserve your mental health first.

Additionally, this book does contain several instances of open-door sexual content. Several chapters (**21 and 25**) include mild to explicit sexual content per the standards of the adult romance genre. If these scenes make you uncomfortable, please feel free to skip them with little impact on comprehension for the rest of the story.

Happy reading!
Cassandra

Love Thicker Than Blood
Playlist

- **Suneater**
  Leanna Firestone

- **Fun While It Lasted**
  Ashe

- **lust to love**
  renforshort

- **Attention**
  Charlie Puth

- **Blonde**
  Maisie Peters

- **Washing Machine Heart**
  Mitski

- **Feel Alright**
  JoJo

- **Slow Hands**
  Niall Horan

- **Shower With My Clothes On**
  Ashe

- **doomsday**
  Lizzy McAlpine

- **Million Dollar Man**
  Lana Del Rey

- **Don't**
  Ed Sheeran

- **mine**
  Kelly Clarkson

- **Going Home**
  The Aces

- **Sunday Crossword**
  J Maya

- **11:11**
  Ben Barnes

Chapter One
Cole

Despite his status as "junior associate," the word *busy* perfectly described Cole Yearwood's professional life. Working at the city's most reputable estate law firm should be a cakewalk for him, but some days tested him more than others.

"Alright. Have a good day, Mr. O'Brian . . . thank you, sir." Cole clapped the phone into its spot and slumped back into his plush office chair. He pinched the bridge of his nose between two fingers, but he should consider himself lucky that a mild headache was the only aftereffect of dealing with a fussy client.

Cole checked his watch for some good news with his ten A.M. call wrapped up later than he expected and a mandatory meeting with his associate mentor at ten-thirty. Ten-twenty-five taunted him for ditching breakfast, stoking the hunger pains gnawing at his sides. *Fantastic.*

Cole hustled out of his office without a second to lose. Five minutes should be enough time to swing by the break room and fight any of the interns for the last cup of liquid sludge the Richmond and Sons office called coffee.

Elliot would understand.

Cole's brisk walk to the break room shaved off a minute from his few minutes of downtime, but he entered the room expecting more people. However, finding it empty made Cole's miserable morning ten times better. *One coffee coming right up.*

He spotted a filled pot attached to the machine and hovered his hand over the glass, feeling the heat radiating off it. A fresh pot, too? His luck doubled on the walk from his office, huh.

"It's my fucking lucky day," Cole sang like a classic jazz crooner and grabbed one of the disposable paper cups out of the cupboard overhead. He poured himself coffee to the brim and raided the fridge nearby for creamer. He would prefer half-and-half but could settle for a flavored creamer.

He squatted to check the bottom shelf when he spotted Taylor, the college student who worked at the front desk for extra cash, guiding someone down the hall. The stranger appeared to be a client, dressed in all black, besides her soft, honey-blonde hair curtained around her face. Her hair covered everything beyond a slight glimpse of the soft peak of her nose.

Taylor dropped the client off at the conference room, where Elliot, his mentor, lounged in one of the swivel chairs. She lingered outside the door until the woman stepped inside the conference room behind the glass walls, visible to any observing party.

Cole turned away for a moment and finally found the creamer shoved against the back wall of the break room's fridge. That would be the third time someone moved the creamer from its convenient spot in the door, but whatever.

He grabbed the creamer and added a splash to his coffee, accepting the hint of salted caramel. Not his favorite flavor, but he would manage for one day.

He grabbed a stirrer and turned back toward the open archway, seeing two of his colleagues there where they weren't before. Fellow junior associates Scott Goodwin and Mollie Cardenas appeared transfixed by Elliot's conversation with the client.

Cole stepped in between them and sipped at his coffee. But he gasped when Mollie tossed him a small paper bag that smelled like sugar and something fresh from the bakery's oven. "I owe you my life."

Mollie shrugged. "You covered a couple of cases for me these last few months, so I'm the one who owes you." Her eyes met his but playfully danced away.

Cole almost missed Scott's scoff of "get a room" under his breath or the defensive slump of his shoulders. Anyone with a working pair of eyes could see them and deduce Scott and Mollie shared a complicated past. But he avoided coworkers' drama for the sake of his sanity. If he wanted free entertainment, he would bother his brother, Dean.

He and Mollie were friendly, while he and Scott gave each other the occasional nod when they passed in the hallway or shared an elevator. *Friends* would be too strong of a word for either relationship.

"So, what do you think they're talking about in there?" asked Cole, tearing open the paper bag and finding a warm, buttery croissant inside. He tore off a bite with his teeth and chased the mouthful of butter down with a sip of scalding coffee.

"My money's on a young, new widow to an old rich guy," Scott snorted behind his coffee as the three watched Elliot reach for a box of tissues behind him. He offered them to the woman, who first shook her hand with a polite dismissal. But her tune quickly changed, and she ended up with several clenched between her fingers. "Maybe she killed him, and these are the crocodile tears to take all his money."

"Why does your first instinct always go to murder? You should've gone into criminal law." Mollie leaned against the archway, sounding so over Scott's theory.

"Alright then, genius. If you know it all, share your theory with the class."

"Look at her. Those tears seem genuine enough to me. I would guess she's like our usual clientele—a mourning child whose parent passed away, and now she has the unfortunate job of handling affairs."

Cole stared through the glass at the woman's posture. She looked defeated, thoroughly exhausted in the slump of her shoulders and how she curled into herself. Elliot hesitated with a heavy pause. It didn't take a genius profiler or a lip reader to agree with Mollie's assessment.

Whatever brought the woman into Richmond and Sons clearly distressed her. It sounded like an obvious statement to make when death typically was involved, but some people jumped for joy when they heard the assets they'd receive upon their "loved one" passing.

Scott appeared unimpressed with Mollie's assessment, which he asserted with a loud, "Maybe I'm morbid. But you have no creativity. You're perfect for estate law."

"Shut up."

"That's all you've got? Typical."

Cole sipped his coffee while regretting his choice to stand in the middle of the snippy argument between Mollie and Scott. He focused on the conversation between Elliot and the client and how Elliot led the discussion heavily.

"Cole?" Mollie waved her hand in front of his face. "You still with us?"

"Yeah. Repeat the question?" Cole glanced down, realizing he'd eaten half his croissant without thinking about it. He chewed another bite as Mollie and Scott stared at him expectantly.

"Why do you think she's here? Whichever of us is closer to your guess wins," said Scott. A competition explained the hungry gleam in his and Mollie's eyes, but Cole wasn't sure he wanted to be their tiebreaker.

"Honestly, no idea. We've seen both options, so I'm not in a place to speculate," he remarked calmly and drank his coffee in the sweet silence of a disappointed Scott and Mollie.

"I still think she killed her rich husband-"

"We don't even know if she had a husband!"

"Cole, doesn't your brother do criminal defense? You could probably hook her up with a discounted rate since you have an in."

Cole rolled his eyes at Scott. "No. Dean transferred to civil law and opened a firm with his fiancée months ago." He stepped back into the break room with the sneaking suspicion that he required more coffee to tolerate that morning's challenges.

However, all three quickly sobered up when the door to the conference room opened, and Elliot stepped into the hallway. His face fell as soon as his back faced the client seated in the conference room, eyes screaming for help. Cole spotted the "I have to turn down a client" thousand-yard stare painted across Elliot's face.

"Would any of you happen to know some pro bono lawyers?" asked Elliot. Cole, knowing his mentor well, understood that Elliot was the type of guy who wanted to help everyone who came into the office. But their firm's policy on payment was strict, with no sliding scale in sight. "Preferably ones who have experience with wills and family law equally."

Cole raised his hand, "I might know a guy or two . . . hypothetically."

"Okay, hypothetically speaking, would these referrals be able to be prepared to fight for custody of a minor specified in a will if there are any contests?"

"Yes. I definitely know a guy."

Elliot gestured at the still-seated client behind him, "Then, would you mind doing the honors because I'm going to crumble if I have to see her cry?"

Cole stepped up and clapped his mentor on the shoulder, "I've got this. Grab yourself a coffee because you look like hell." He watched Elliot stagger toward the coffee machine, and Mollie and Scott stared after him, eyes wide.

Their eyes snapped back to Cole, but he had one foot in the conference room door before they could speak. He slipped inside and made sure the click shut sounded behind him.

He approached the seat Elliot used, directly next to the client, but her head hung low until Cole sat in the chair. She tipped her head back, and Cole caught a glimpse of her face for the first time—*oh, she was young and pretty.*

Young felt like a relative term for someone who appeared close to his age, if not a year or so younger than him, but pretty barely scratched the surface. The soft starlet curls of honey blonde framed high cheekbones and startlingly big green eyes rimmed with red from lots of crying.

She shrank away from him, tucking her hands deep into the sleeves of her black woolen cardigan. "Um, hello?"

"Hello there," Cole offered his hand and kept every movement gentle, careful not to spook her. "I'm one of the junior associates. Can I have your name?"

"My last name is Byndel."

"Nice to meet you, Ms. Byndel. I understand that you've come to us in some dire circumstances. Is that correct?"

Ms. Byndel wiped at her eyes with a broad smear of her sleeve, "Yes, I would say so. I already told Elliot that I don't know where else to go to prepare for this . . . I don't even know what to call it."

A twinge yanked hard on Cole's heart, but he held onto his composure by the skin of his teeth. Who could blame Elliot for wanting to help when a pair of sad eyes begged someone to intervene? He remained firm in his promise.

Cole scooted his chair closer. "Miss, I hate to be the bearer of bad news. However, our firm exclusively focuses on estate planning and the execution of wills and trusts. Once the wills are figured out and read, our work finishes unless the client requires the management of long-term assets."

"Oh, I see." Ms. Byndel swallowed hard and sank further into the cardigan, which appeared ready to envelop her slim frame whole. "I apologize for wasting your time. I had seen a card for this office in my sister's belongings and assumed she had already retained representation here. Elliot couldn't find any past client files, though."

"It's not a waste of time, miss, I assure you. But I can help you in some other way."

"You can? I don't understand-"

Cole pulled out his cell phone and scrolled through his contacts until he found the one he wanted. Then, he gestured toward the legal pad and untouched pen sitting next to Ms. Byndel on the table. "May I?"

Ms. Byndel scrambled to push it to him, and Cole wrote down a name, number, email, and office address from the contact on his phone. He tried his neatest writing, so every letter was readable and within the lines.

He pressed the notepad into her hand, "On that is someone I consider a friend. He works for a legal aid organization, which means they do pro bono or reduced-cost legal aid. As long as I've known him, he's been involved in custody cases. If you need a lawyer to help in a custody matter, he's the man you want, and I can vouch for him."

Ms. Byndel stared at the information. Her hands started to shake, but she nodded hard. "Thank you. I appreciate the referral to something that won't break the bank."

"No need to thank me, Miss." Cole was relieved. Some potential clients lost their cool when the firm rejected their cases, driven by their emotions. A calm and gracious response made things smoother. "If you'd like, I can call him and give him a heads-up that I sent you his way sometime today."

"Please, I would appreciate that, too."

"Of course. If there's anything else I can get you, like water or some more tissues, let me know. If not, I'll escort you to the front."

Ms. Byndel hesitated but eventually shook her head. She grabbed the legal pad and her purse from the floor. "I don't require anything else, so I'll head out." She stepped out of the chair and peered up at him.

Cole nodded but gestured for her to go ahead. He held the door open for her, as his mom raised him to do, and followed her out. Scott and Mollie had enough decency to pretend to be busy from their perches in the break room, and Elliot tanked his coffee behind them.

He escorted Ms. Byndel to the front desk with a hand hovered over the small of her back, planning to leave her with Taylor to handle some logistics. But she caught his wrist before he turned heel.

"Thank you." Ms. Byndel's voice never scratched above a whisper, and the crackling over two words almost hurt him. Yet, Cole held it together by a thin thread. He hoped for the best for this woman, whatever happened to her. "You've been such a help."

"I try my best, Miss. You have a good day, and be safe out there."

Cole melted into the background when Ms. Byndel turned away to speak with Taylor. He returned to the break room and poured himself a fresh cup of coffee.

Elliot's hand clapped his shoulder. "Thanks for stepping in, Cole. I know that was for the best, but I can't imagine how stressed she would've been if we agreed to take that on."

"Yeah. I will place some calls with my friend, and he'll happily take on the case, so I'm sure it's in good hands." Cole shrugged. The job required them to be discerning with their cases, and the firm had its rules for upholding the Richmond and Sons standard.

He and Elliot brushed past Scott and Mollie, who had gone quiet since their earlier spat, for the conference room and settled into different chairs. The heaviness in the air dissipated after a moment of silence beyond the slurps of hot coffee until Elliot yelped.

"Burned tongue?" asked Cole.

Elliot waved a hand around his mouth and nodded fervently, eliciting barely suppressed laughter from Cole. He wisely set his coffee down and observed unabashedly as Elliot curled his fist and narrowly avoided cussing.

Cole had met Elliot on his first day of work, hired immediately after passing the bar. He expected to have some awkward experiences, cautioned by his dad and Dean about a newbie lawyer's first-day mistakes, but Elliot stepped in to show him the ropes. The two were friends.

After a moment of theatrics, Elliot simmered down and set his coffee to the side. "Okay, that needs a break. No more hot coffee. We're here to talk about you, Cole. So, let me ask: How are you handling the new caseload?"

"You know, I was worried about it at first. But I'm finding it isn't too much for me to handle, which the partners will be happy to hear."

"Yeah? I'm glad the cases aren't killing you because I like having you around this place. You keep things interesting during lunch hour take-out runs and prevent Scott and me from falling asleep in meetings."

Cole snorted, "Mollie takes some credit for that second one. Any excuse she gets to kick Scott in the shins under the table is a win in her book."

Elliot let out a half-chuckle. "Do you ever wonder what the deal with those two is? My money has always been on a hook-up gone sour or former class rivals. Something as daytime television drama as that."

Cole nursed his coffee and shrugged. "Honestly, yes. However, I like minding my business because the last thing I need is to turn into the chew toy for their weekly game of verbal tug-o-war."

"You're a stronger soul than I am, man," Elliot smiled. "Speaking of that, I remember that your new apartment is supposed to be ready soon, right? Are you ready to move off your brother's couch?"

"You have no idea. I've been sharing the couch with a dog named Socks for the last three weeks and can't wait for my own bed. I fall off the couch constantly in my sleep."

"How bad is it? Living with your brother again?"

Cole thought about it. Truth be told, he liked the experience most of the time. Dean and January, his future sister-in-law, offered him a place to stay since he got caught in a tricky move. His lease ended while his new apartment building was being renovated, leaving him needing a place in the city. So, Jan offered him their couch until he could move into his new home.

He sighed, "Okay, so I love Jan. She's one of the best people to hang around with, and I love enjoying the closeness of family. It reminded me of when I was younger. Plus, I like seeing my brother in a happy and fulfilling relationship. I could've done without the occasional but obnoxiously loud pre-marital sex."

"No! They didn't!" Elliot wheezed and almost choked on his coughing from laughing too hard. Cole was less amused.

"Oh, yes, they did. At least Jan pretends to be sorry when I accidentally overheard them getting it on. Dean just wears a shit-eating grin and walks around like the king all next morning. I have never wanted to know that my brother has a robust, functioning sex life."

Elliot collapsed into laughter, and Cole soaked it in while drinking his coffee. Moments like these are why he stayed loyal to Richmond and Sons. In his friendship bubble with the coworkers he connected with, he felt like he fit in.

He wasn't Cole Yearwood, son of Stephen Yearwood or younger brother to Dean Yearwood. His work stood for itself, and so did the results. He brought something meaningful to the table all on his own. No more living in anyone's shadow for him.

He finally got to create a legacy.

Chapter Two
Nina

Nina sat inside her SUV, parked outside her sister's apartment building, alone with grief in her throat. In the backseat, a stack of moving boxes and a tube of bubble wrap protruded into the view of the sun visor's mirror. The items sat next to an empty child's car seat.

Her eyes flicked toward the stoop outside the apartment building like she expected to see her sister, Naomi, step through the giant front doors. Her sister's dirty blonde hair would be pulled back into a messy bun, wearing a shirt stained by some unknown substance after a long day with a rambunctious daughter and her sweet brown eyes twinkling as Nina arrived as on-demand babysitting.

But Naomi would never walk down those steps again.

Nina's eyes burned, and she stared into the rearview mirror to see tears gathered on her lashes, dripping off the damp ends. Her breath shuddered in her chest, and the car's walls threatened to come crashing inward. She knew that was an irrational thought, yet she couldn't stop.

"Pull yourself together," she hiccupped into her hand, even as it clapped hard over her mouth, and leaned into her wheel. She only managed to shape up and hold the tears back when her forehead pressed too hard into her steering wheel. The honk disturbed the silent block, and Nina slumped back.

She couldn't break down at a given moment anymore. She had new responsibilities, ones that took precedence over anything else imaginable. She was beyond the stage of taking care of herself.

Nina cut the engine of her car and climbed out. She grabbed the boxes in her hands, light for the moment. She dreaded having to return with packed boxes alone, but she should have enough space in the trunk, backseat, and maybe for a box in the front passenger.

She climbed the stoop and let herself into the apartment building, having memorized Naomi's code after years of coming over. Nina couldn't see well over the boxes, so she stepped loudly with her sneakers against the linoleum floors of the first floor to alert any poor resident of her presence.

Naomi's apartment resided on the second floor, but the elevator appeared closed with construction tape and a big sign that read "OUT OF ORDER" over its doors. So much for easy access to the higher floors.

Nina started on the stairs and shuffled up them, careful to take her time. If she rushed, a broken ankle seemed the least of her problems. She was more likely to earn herself a fractured neck or worse from a tumble.

All she could think about was the next steps, robotically combing through the motions. After packing all the boxes, she needed to stop by the grocery store to pick up dinner. In her current state, cooking dinner from scratch sounded like a disaster waiting to happen.

Nina pushed up the last stretch of stairs to the second floor and its narrow hallway. Her shoulders brushed against one of the walls as she inched to the side, hearing another pair of footsteps. A disgruntled maintenance man slipped past her with a grumble muffled in the crook of his elbow like a sneeze.

Nina's nose crinkled hard at the odor of cigarette smoke and half-dried paint lingering in his wake, but she knew picking a fight would be a waste of time. Sadness slipped into anger with the frightening speed of a runaway train barreling down the tracks.

She set the boxes down when she approached the door to Naomi's place, Unit 209, and knocked on the door. She overheard the ambient noises of television inside the apartment but was otherwise quiet.

The door pried open after the click of the locks and the sliding of the deadbolt. Nina smiled and nudged the boxes to the side with the tip of her sneaker. She couldn't be bothered to dress up for the occasion, sticking to some high-top sneakers and baggy jeans over the tank top she fell asleep in.

"Nina, I'm glad you made it." The woman who opened the door, Penelope, smiled and held it wide for her. "Do you need any help with those boxes?"

"I can manage, but thank you. Has Brooke been alright?"

"She's been wonderful. She asked when you'd come, so I know she's happy to see you."

Nina felt a slight skip in her heart. "I came as soon as possible from buying a storage container for leftover things and grabbing some boxes to pack everything. I'll take her home after this, but thank you for staying with her."

Penelope's face softened, and she reached out to Nina. Her streaks of gray through copper curls showed a fully-lived life, and the crow's feet at the corner of her warm brown eyes comforted Nina. She reminded her of her grandmother, who passed away when Nina was sixteen, but Penelope was way younger.

Naomi always spoke fondly of Penelope whenever she came up in conversation, which happened frequently. Penelope showed up at the hospital when Nina called every contact in her sister's phone, carrying Brooke with her, and that's when she learned that Penelope covered for Naomi as a babysitter during unexpected errands.

Nina appreciated her presence during the worst days of her life.

Penelope held the door open and led Nina inside the apartment once she grabbed her boxes from the floor. She ensured the door shut with a light kick and set the boxes on the kitchen table.

On the floor, curled up on the rug, Brooke kicked her little legs and scribbled into a coloring book. A pile of mismatched, stubby crayons sprawled on the floor beside her, lined up next to a small plastic princess bowl. Nina leaned over and saw sliced green grapes as a mid-day snack.

Brooke was only five, so a small snack would keep her attention.

On the television, brightly colored cartoons played decently loud, but Brooke appeared preoccupied with coloring neatly in the lines of her coloring book. In some small part, the quiet comforted Nina, but she knew Brooke couldn't truly understand the permanence of death.

She was only five. Still a sweet baby.

Nina waved goodbye to Penelope when the older woman stepped out of the apartment and shut the door behind her. She went to sit down on the floor next to Brooke and whispered, "Can I have one of your grapes?"

Brooke lifted her head up and gasped, "Auntie Nini!" She squirmed off the floor and climbed on Nina's lap with all the energy a five-year-old could muster. Nina hugged her niece and buried her face into Brooke's blonde hair.

Naomi had been a blonde, but she used to joke that Brooke looked more like Nina's baby than hers. Nina and Brooke shared the green eyes that skipped Naomi; she had brown eyes with green flecks instead. She also had freckles all over her face, spread out across her nose and cheeks, while Nina didn't have any.

"Hi, Brooke. How's my favorite bug feeling today?"

"I feel okay. I was hungry, but Miss Penelope made me a snack."

"She did. I love green grapes, but my favorite is usually blueberries or strawberries." Nina bounced Brooke on her lap until she wrangled her into a comfortable position. She turned the volume of the cartoons lower. "Want to show me what you've been coloring?"

Brooke squealed, making grabby hands at her coloring book. Nina picked it up for her and gave it to Brooke. "I colored a flower, some kitty cats, and a princess riding a unicorn!"

Her chubby little hands flipped the pages of bright, colorful pictures done by a little girl's generous hand. Nina looked at all the pictures with a smile and pointed to the one with a princess with blonde hair and bright green eyes.

"I love that one the most. Is that supposed to be you, bug?"

"No, I think it looks like Mommy. But I didn't have brown for her freckles."

Nina nodded because her throat went dry, but she kissed her niece's hair. "She looks beautiful. Is it okay if we have a talk about big things? Can we do that?"

"Okay," Brooke mumbled. "I don't like big thing talks."

"I know, and I'm sorry. But I wanted to tell you that the nice Child Protective Services lady asked me to take you to my house. I'll pack your toys, clothes, and other things in a box to take home."

Brooke didn't respond at first. Instead, she fiddled with the crayons on the floor and picked a pink one. Her silence and scribbling didn't help the lump in Nina's throat disappear, nor did it inspire confidence.

She had no idea what she was supposed to do.

At twenty-five, Nina never expected to become a mother figure. She wanted to spend a few years on her career and settle into married life before considering having kids. She watched Naomi's hardships as a single mother to Brooke and the toll it took on her through the years.

Nina tried to be there and help out as the cool aunt. Naomi wanted Brooke to know that she was loved and had a family, although an unconventional one. Child Services couldn't locate Brooke's biological father in the aftermath of Naomi's accident since his name wasn't listed on the birth certificate.

The CPS worker explained the process to Nina while at the hospital when Naomi had been touch and go. Since there was no lead on the sperm donor who abandoned her sister when she discovered the pregnancy, Nina would be the next of kin. Naomi listed her as her emergency contact for all things, and until she had a will reading, Nina was responsible for taking care of Brooke as the closest relative.

Apparently, will readings were supposed to happen after the funeral. But that was another thing that Nina had to arrange on her own.

Nina never expected her sister to have a will in place, but she shouldn't be so surprised. After everything the two experienced in the last few years, her sister likely planned for the worst-case scenario. They had no family to rely on besides one another.

But Nina had gone through life without ever considering the off chance that something could go terribly wrong. And it did.

Naomi, the big sister she looked up to, died in a car crash. In the span of five seconds, a truck collided with her sister's sedan at an otherwise quiet intersection, causing Nina's life to spin out of control and fall apart. Within hours of the crash, Naomi never made it out of surgery.

Nina expected hard questions over the last few weeks and struggled with the unknown. However, the worst question came from Brooke herself. She asked what people meant when they said, "Her mommy went to see the angels," and Nina never had an answer for her.

How should she explain death to a five-year-old? She was supposed to tell Brooke her mom was gone and wouldn't return. She couldn't even wrap her head around Naomi's death.

She tried to rationalize it or juggle the plentiful "thoughts and prayers" for her during the grieving period. But the world continued to move on, and she couldn't keep up, not with everything frozen around her. Nothing made a lick of sense.

"Brooke," Nina whispered, gently leaning into her niece's vision. She took in the sullen frown and her downturned eyes. "Talk to me, bug. It's okay to have some big feelings about moving from the house."

"Do we have to move?" asked Brooke.

"Yes. But you have a bedroom all to yourself at my place, and I promise we can decorate the walls in whatever color you'd like. Plus, I will keep all the toys that you want to keep. We'll put them in special boxes for safekeeping."

"Any color I want?"

"Of course," Nina promised. "We can stop by the hardware store today and pick the color you want for your walls. But Auntie Nini has to pack up some boxes first. So, keep coloring those pretty pictures while I handle all the packing."

"Okay!" Brooke scrambled off her lap and plopped onto the floor. She lay on her stomach and grabbed a fistful of crayons from her little pile. Her pigtails swung whenever she kicked her legs and scribbled inside the lines.

Nina stood up, brushed off her knees, and headed to the boxes stacked on the table. She grabbed a black marker from inside the box alongside a large packing tape roll. She singled out boxes and sorted them into three groups.

TO KEEP FOR BROOKE

TO DONATE

NAOMI STUFF

She glanced around the room and surveyed the studio apartment, all its furnishings, and the pieces of her sister's life. According to the building manager and his curt email to Nina yesterday, the rooms come fully furnished. So, most of the items belonged to the apartment and would stay behind.

She started with the pictures mounted on the wall of her sister and Brooke throughout the years. Each one depicted a different period; within them, they told the story of Brooke growing up and Naomi's happiness as a single mom.

Nina gently laid them inside the box with extra padding to keep the glass from breaking. She would save those for Brooke when she got older. She grabbed Naomi's old college hoodie hung on the rack by the front door, next to Brooke's sparkly fairy lunch pail from the discount store.

She folded it up and stuffed it into the box. The mementos that Nina thought to keep seemed the easiest to find around the apartment. It was Naomi's favorite pair of fuzzy socks or the assortment of magnets she used to collect from every state she visited during road trips on breaks from college before she got pregnant with Brooke. The little pieces of her sister's life that would belong to Brooke one day all went into a cardboard box.

She filled two of them to the brim with the mementos and sealed them shut. Nina set the boxes by the door, stacked on one another.

Nina sighed and pulled her hair back from her face. She held the marker clenched between her teeth with occupied hands but set it down before she went to raid the drawers near the bed set. Inside those drawers, she unpacked the hand-me-down clothes picked up from consignment stores or yard sales.

Naomi splurged on Brooke's things but never went all out for herself. If Brooke wanted toys, new clothes, or anything else her heart desired, Naomi went out of her way to give her the world. She was the greatest mom.

Nina worked through the piles of clothes. Everything that belonged to Brooke went into the keeper box, while Naomi's clothes piled into the donation box. She had plans to swing by a thrift store later in the evening.

Soon, the drawers appeared empty, like no one had occupied the apartment. The more things she packed away—dolls for Brooke, necklaces belonging to Naomi, and a small collection of plastic cups and cheap silverware in the kitchen cupboards—the sparser the apartment became.

Brooke stayed put on the floor in front of the television. Nina swore she overheard the off-key humming from her niece during commercial breaks. With every layer of items loaded into the box, she checked that Brooke stayed distracted with either the television or her coloring book.

"Bug, before I pack your stuffed animals into the box, are there any of them you want to take on the drive?"

Brooke scampered with her coloring book tucked underneath her arm like a rolled-up newspaper and peered up at the box, too high to see. Nina scooped her up and held her over the box.

"The pink cat! Her name is Glitterball!"

"Didn't I buy you Glitterball for Christmas last year?" asked Nina, recognizing the stuffed cat she picked up from the mall.

Brooke gave her a cheesy grin. "Nooooo! Santa Claus brought me Glitterball," she explained so casually that Nina couldn't help but laugh. She had addressed the present from Santa Claus with Naomi's permission.

The memory tasted bittersweet, yet Nina chewed on it for a moment longer, desperate to feel a small twinge of shared happiness. She still remembered the scant mini tree Naomi hauled home in the backseat of her car, where she had been cleaning out pine needles for weeks afterward, and her car smelled like a forest.

Nina shook her head, "Well, you can take Glitterball for the ride to keep you company. I'm almost done with the boxes, so we'll drive home soon."

"You mean to your house?"

"You're right."

Brooke quietly exchanged her coloring book for Glitterball, only to return with her crayons gathered in a loose fist. Nina held her hands open and poured the crayons into a plastic baggie instead of its usual box. She stuffed those items into the box to take home with them.

Nina carried the final box, the seventh one, to the door and added it to the stack. She looked at all of them to guess how many trips she required down to her car. The thought of leaving Brooke unattended, even inside the apartment, stirred discomfort in her stomach.

Maybe Penelope could return for a moment until Nina finished her trips to the car?

Nina sealed the final box with packing tape and a few added inscriptions about the contents' fragility. She had a few porcelain items like jewelry boxes and some plates Naomi bought with her first paycheck at her summer job when they were teens.

She made sure Brooke stayed in front of the television, watching the cartoons with Glitterball before she stepped into the hallway. But she almost yelped when she noticed several men gathered outside the door.

Penelope rounded the corner and waved. "Nina! I was about to knock. These lovely gentlemen—Marcus, George, Jon, and Ryker—live in the building on different floors and have volunteered to help with moving boxes. They all knew Naomi, and we all appreciated her presence in the community."

"Sorry about your loss," the guy Penelope identified as Jon mumbled, moving his shaggy dark hair out of his face. The others looked sad at the mention of Naomi's passing, and Nina felt comforted.

Nina propped open the door with her foot. "Thank you, boys. I only have seven boxes, and my car is parked out front. Please load them into the trunk, the seat on the opposite side of the car seat, and the front seat if needed."

"Sure thing!" Ryker beamed and grabbed the first two boxes from the door. The other guys grabbed boxes and followed after Ryker.

Penelope held out her hand, and Nina took a moment to realize she wanted her keys.

Nina handed the keys over and saw Penelope walk after the boys with the boxes. Since she turned over Naomi's keys a few days before, she could head home with Brooke with all the boxes.

She headed into the apartment and scooped Brooke off the floor, ensuring she held onto Glitterball nice and tight. "All the boxes have been loaded up by very nice boys from the apartment building, so let's say goodbye to the apartment, okay?"

Brooke whispered, "Okay. Goodbye, apartment."

Nina carried Brooke with her little head resting on her shoulder to the door frame, lingering between the hallway and the studio apartment. Something felt indescribably out of place and uncanny valley without the items distinguishing the space as Naomi's and Brooke's.

She headed down the hall and moved carefully when she descended to the base floor. Nina walked through the front doors and down the stoop to her car, where Penelope and the boys waited.

"They managed to get all the boxes in the trunk. The two in the front seat are meant for donation or thrift stores!" Penelope beamed, and Nina wished for her optimism or energy. She hadn't slept much these days with too much planning to handle.

"Thank you, Penelope. I appreciate you . . . and the help."

"Of course. Naomi was one of us, and we will miss her. Be safe and take care of the little one."

Nina nodded but stepped to the side. Her eyes observed traffic, more so than she used to before Naomi's accident. But she couldn't cross the road anymore without a nagging voice screaming at her, *Don't stop looking at the road.*

She could barely drive her car without the sudden, unrelenting worry that a drunk driver would strike her. Naomi never saw it coming, and Nina refused to let herself be too vulnerable.

Nina pressed against the side of the car, opened the door to her backseat, and set Brooke down. Brooke held Glitterball to her chest while Nina buckled her into the chair, green eyes heavy with a sleepy look.

"M'sleepy," she whispered. "Can I take a nap?"

"Of course, bug. I promise that I'll be here when you wake up." Nina kissed her head and watched Brooke close her eyes, snuggling deeper with her cat plushy. Her eyes lingered on how Brooke crashed in the backseat of her car, her chest rising and falling with a soft exhale.

Nina's fingers brushed Brooke's pigtail over her shoulder and sighed, "Sleep well, bug. Sweet dreams." She closed the door and ambled around the car to her side, retrieving the keys from Penelope on the curb.

Nina offered a smile, although half-hearted and shy. Penelope returned to stand with the boys as Nina slid into her car. She locked the doors, and through the rearview mirror, she admired her sleeping niece.

She had no clue how to be a guardian, but she planned to do right by her niece and Naomi. Life decided to throw her a challenge, and Nina knew better than to let it keep her down.

Chapter Three
Cole

Cole's hands raked through his hair, alone in the upscale bathroom of Hare and Turtle Brewing Co. Dripping water slithered down the sink bowl to a steady pulse in an otherwise silent bathroom. Movement and noise echoed beyond the door from the ongoing event, but Cole knew he would be out there soon.

Dean and January favored the brewery as their venue for social events related to their firm. That evening was reserved for one of their largest events since opening Yearwood, Quinn, and Associates.

He studied himself in the mirror and clicked his tongue at his reflection, "Looking sharp, handsome."

With a final tuck of his turtleneck into his jeans, he felt ready to plunge into the crowd and mingle. Even with an established career, networking events never hurt to attend. Besides, Jan and Dean put on some of the best events for the local legal community, opened their doors to students for reduced rates, and never skimped on the drinks or dinner.

Cole reached for the door and slipped out of the bathroom. He heard the sea of conversations before he rounded the corner of the hallway where the bathroom was tucked away, out of view from the rest of the patrons. People in different stages of business casual, carrying glasses of champagne or the house brew and chatting about many things, appeared through the main foyer. Cole couldn't see the side garden yet but had a different target.

He wanted to find Jan and Dean.

A passing waiter held up a tray with champagne flutes on the verge of sloshing over the gold-tipped rims, weaving through the crowd with a narrow edge of luck on his side. Cole reached up and snatched one of the flutes from the tray before the waiter vanished into the crowd.

He kept the champagne close while he traversed through the crowd, on the hunt for either January or Dean. He imagined he would find them together since the two often spent their days attached at the hip. In time, they became a far cry from their old ways.

He paid slight attention to the snippets of conversations in the crowd while looking for his brother and future sister-in-law. However, he gravitated toward the center of the room where all the action seemingly took place and found them.

Cole noticed January first with her dark hair pinned back from her face and the bright smile shared with her audience. She held her champagne and offered some to Dean, who stood vigilantly beside her.

His brother's arm looped around Jan's waist and kept her close to him. Dean whispered something against the shell of her ear, prompting laughter from his fiancée. The two waved to the small group gathered before them as the people shuffled into the crowd, intended for other conversations or a place at the open bar.

Cole spotted his opportunity and strode over, catching January's eyes. She stepped forward to greet him, and the two collided into a welcoming hug.

"Cole!" January beamed. He greeted her with a respectful cheek kiss and leaned down to let her reciprocate the gesture. He and January often teamed up to make fun of Dean.

"Hi, Jan. You look lovely this evening."

"Thank you. Did Dean mention the navy memo, or did we all manage to match?"

Cole glanced down at his navy slacks, then noticed how January and Dean color-coordinated their outfits with navy blue and soft ivory accents. Total coincidence on his part, but he knew Dean and Jan loved to color match during events.

He laughed, "Living with you guys rubbed off on me. I still get up at five A.M. like I expect Dean to come waltzing in the living room with nothing but swim trunks on."

January burst into laughter, "I hope that hasn't deterred you from wanting to stay with us in the future. Our couch is always open to you, and I hope to keep your brother walking around with missing clothes to a minimum." She squeezed his hands.

"Appreciate that, Jan."

"Make sure you eat something? I assume you forgot because of the move to your new place."

"Don't have to tell me twice. You guys ordered catering from the best Italian joint in the city, and I could eat a whole cow after all the unpacking." Cole noticed his brother from over Jan's shoulder, approaching the two of them.

Dean pretended to scowl, "Hey man, I'd like my January back. Stop hogging my fiancée." He scoffed, but Cole knew his brother meant no harm. That's how they teased one another over the years.

January snorted, "Dean, honey, you're the last person to complain about hogging. Let's not mention that you and Socks currently are in the running for who steals the covers more." She winked at Cole, and the two snickered at Dean when he broke into grumbles.

"Which one of us are you engaged to again?"

"You, dear. But Cole is the little brother I always wanted and never had."

"And you, Jan, are the daughter our parents wanted but had to settle for Dean."

Dean groaned, "You two become demons when in the same room. This isn't fair." His complaints were discarded when January squished his cheeks between two fingers. She pulled him down, and Cole averted his eyes politely as his brother and Jan shared a loving kiss.

When she pulled back, Cole dared to look over, but he choked on a laugh. One of his hands clapped over his mouth, and he wheezed.

"Dude," he raised his brows when taking in Dean's lopsided smile. "Red is so not your color."

January giggled when Cole gestured to the lip region as January's kiss left the smear of bright red lipstick across his lips. Dean reached for the pocket square neatly folded into the breast of his suit jacket and cleaned off his lips.

"You should let me help out. You have it all over." January took the cloth from Dean's hand and gently dabbed at his mouth to clear the lipstick away. Cole observed the tender scene for a moment but recognized when his presence overstayed its welcome.

"Have either of you seen the parents?" asked Cole.

"Not since the party started," Dean remarked between wipes of the pocket square from January's hand. "Didn't you see them earlier, baby?"

"Yes. I saw them around the food table while the caterers laid out the dessert section. Haven't seen them since, though."

"Alright, thanks. Keep up the good hosting, you two."

Cole dipped into the crowd, moving with the flow of people, and kept his eyes peeled for any sight of his parents among the guests. He sipped at his champagne for the taste of celebration that Jan and Dean's life seemed to exude.

The last year took plenty of effort from those two, worried they'd try to strike out on their own and land on their faces. But the worries about a rocky debut vanished when the plans came together—Jan's meticulous planning and Dean's charismatic pull created something people wanted to succeed.

Cole admired the risk they took, seeing how life rewarded their efforts and bravery. He watched from the sidelines as their life took off and their thirties promised nothing but success.

His eyes drifted through a gap in the crowd to see the outdoor section of the venue, all tall green shrubs and string lights tethered to metal poles overhead. Fewer people gathered out there, but everything seemed peaceful compared to inside.

There, tucked into the corner, Cole spotted his parents. His dad held his mom in a warm hug and rested his head on her, speaking to her where Cole couldn't make out the words on his dad's lips. But whatever it was, his mom's smile stretched across her cold-bitten cheeks as they basked in the September evening.

Cole turned from the window. He could find them later so as not to interrupt their moment. Would it be too late to extend his unused plus-one invite to Elliot or Mollie? Probably.

His hand brought the champagne up, and he greedily chased relief at the bottom of the flute. The world around him continued to move, but Cole rooted into his spot. His thoughts circled back to the inevitable.

He was the odd man out.

Not that long ago, he and Dean were single. But out of them, Cole always thought himself the closet romantic, while Dean avoided the confines of any exclusivity. Some part of him assumed he would find someone first, but Dean beat him to the punch. His parents and Dean and Jan reminded him he was the last to find a committed relationship.

It left a conflicted taste in his mouth. He wanted nothing but happiness for Dean, who met someone to challenge and encourage him to be a better man. Yet, a small drop of envy tainted what could be selfless.

Cole abandoned the champagne flute on the tray of another waiter when he passed, stacked high with empty glasses. He stared into the heart of the crowd and moved through the shifting bodies for somewhere to sit.

He ended up in the corner of the main room, closest to the bar yet across from the front doors to the street. Cole sat in one of the leather armchairs lined against the wall with a small end table between every pair of chairs. The lively crowd quieted when Cole sank into the cushions of the armchair.

The quiet soothed over the wounds he opened with his own overthinking—his own worst enemy half the time. He watched the faces of guests and waited to see Dean and January making their rounds through the room, or maybe he'd catch the sight of another member from their firm.

He knew Esther, Sabrina, and Mason decently well. He swung by the building with pizza once or twice during the renovation phase and met the team. Were they friends? He wouldn't say so.

Cole expected the evening to pass by in a long dredge of watching conversations and the occasional moment where he might rub elbows, but his assumption faded quickly when the grinning face of Rudy Hawkins, a colleague of his, emerged from the crowd.

"Yearwood! Hey! I didn't expect to see you here." Rudy made his way over, and Cole got out of the armchair. The two clasped in a firm handshake, and Cole looked his friend over. He looked like he came straight from work in his dark pea coat and red knit scarf, dressed for the colder weather.

"I wouldn't miss Dean and Jan's function. They never skimp on catering choices and good drinks." Cole shrugged.

"Right! I noticed you sitting over here all by yourself and figured I owe you a drink as a thank you."

"Ah, you don't have to do that."

"Maybe not," Rudy shrugged but gestured to the bar with a slight grin. "But you tossed me a killer referral the other day, so I wanted to honor the favor. She's in my capable hands."

As promised, Cole referred Ms. Byndel—the woman from his office—to Rudy's legal aid organization. He worked as one of the lead attorneys in their family law division, and Cole expected he would handle the situation with the needed expertise.

Cole looked him over and shrugged, "Referrals are all part of the game. There's no need to thank me, man."

"Okay, what about for the time that I asked for a personal favor with the mess of my parents' estate and all that legal paperwork that required untangling? I promised you drinks the next time we went, but I haven't been able to catch you out since then."

"Okay . . . but not too many drinks. Dean would kill me if I got sloppy at his event, and I need to be coherent enough to call a cab to take me home."

"Good man. I promise you that you won't regret it. To the open bar!"

Cole allowed Rudy to escort him to the bar and signaled for the bartender to slide over when she could. She nodded in acknowledgment, and Cole slid into a seat, ready to enjoy the house tap and leave an evening of silent discontent behind.

Cole regretted it the following day.

Underneath the scalding, steaming torrent from the shower, his headache showed no signs of leaving. He had woken up that morning and immediately wished to crawl back to sleep, confronted by an almost violent pain between his eyes.

Cole braced his hands against the damp glass walls on either side before he plunged his face straight into the water from the showerhead. He spluttered when the water got into his mouth and nose, but the rush pushed out some lingering haze.

However, a hot shower only equaled part of the equation to a successful hangover cure. The other two pieces, hot coffee and something to eat, wouldn't be found in the apartment since Cole hadn't unpacked his coffee machine or stocked the fridge.

Cole tipped his head forward and let the water run down his spine, circling the drain underneath his feet. He waited for a minute more before he turned off the water. Steam and water droplets caressed his skin when Cole reached out of the shower for a towel and departed with it.

He didn't spend too much time in front of the bathroom mirror to size himself up. Instead, he grabbed a dress shirt and boxers from the bedroom floor and a rogue pair of sweatpants he packed in a duffle before moving out of Jan and Dean's apartment.

His keys rested on the end table, and Cole snatched them with a passing hand. He picked his wallet up closer to the front door, set on top of the shoe rack, and traded bare feet for a pair of loafers. In his haste, he nearly left the house without shoes on.

Cole locked the door behind himself despite how the jangle of keys poked at the pain settled in his temples. He ambled down the hall and its bright white walls that felt blinding for such an early morning hour. He crawled into the elevator, halfway packed, and nodded to the others inside the carriage with him.

Sure, he felt their eyes on his back when he turned to face the doors and dodged the heat creeping along his spine.

The short elevator ride spat him into the lobby, and he crossed through the fancy foyer of the apartments. He strode into the tenant's parking lot and spotted his car in his assigned spot, never more thankful for the fresh air than at that moment.

Cole slid into the driver's side of his sensible, four-door sedan and grabbed a pair of sunglasses from a compartment overhead. The air conditioning blasting his face woke him from his hangover stupor, but the glasses helped dim the world around him. Everything was too bright.

Cole should've planned a destination before he got behind the wheel of his car, but the open road called out to him. He drove slowly, earning a fair share of horns and middle fingers from other drivers.

That's why he stayed in the right-hand lane and barely drove five over the speed limit. Not his fault some people wanted to act like the road belonged to them.

He surveyed the newer part of town. He moved closer to the office than his old place used to be, but he saved a few paychecks to afford the new apartment. So, some of the roads were unfamiliar, and he should find time to explore soon.

Cole spotted a grocery market, a few restaurants for takeout or sit-down dinner, a park, and two different schools for an elementary and junior high. The quieter side of the city, closer to the outskirts than downtown, carried an air of comfort. Cole lacked a better word to describe the sensation of seeing people on the sidewalk smiling and the close-knit buildings compared to the spacious, modernized backdrop of the downtown cityscape.

Part of him forgot that he had left his apartment searching for coffee and something to fill his empty stomach until he noticed a small coffee shop on the corner of the upcoming street. The bright colors of the window art stole his attention, and the people loitering outside the building screamed art students or hipsters.

"Might be an arm and a leg, but artisanal coffee sounds stupidly good right now," Cole mused and checked the street both ways before he whipped into a smooth U-turn. He spotted a parking spot snugly between two smaller cars and an open meter in the green. Maybe it was his lucky day.

Cole lapsed into silence when he started to parallel park until he marched inside the coffee shop. Fresh coffee grounds and an assortment of baked goods hit him like a ton of bricks, cocooning him in the aroma of the morning and the promise of a hangover cure.

A few people gathered around the room at tables or the high countertops overlooking the coffee bar stared at him. Cole expected an untucked dress shirt and loose gray sweats to give a conflicting fashion statement, but like them, he wanted some damn coffee.

The lengthy line would've been an issue, except he spotted several tablets lined against the wall for self-service orders. *Bingo.* Cole beelined for the unoccupied tablets and tapped on the screen, squinting behind his glasses because the screens were still too bright.

He skimmed the menu but quickly stopped when he saw a section labeled "frequently ordered," the third item happened to be called "HANGOVER CURE." A light snort escaped him as he added it to the cart and picked out a classic cinnamon roll. The transaction moved smoothly, better than if he had waltzed up to the counter and stared at the menu behind the colorful-haired barista for a minute.

He slid over to the newly opened countertop and hoisted himself into his seat, content to stew in silence while waiting for his coffee and pastry. But the chime of the bell over the door borrowed his attention from studying the empty countertop.

His attention stayed there, however, when he spotted the familiar figure of Ms. Byndel entering the shop. She had her hands tucked into the back pockets of her mom jeans, rolled cuffs at her ankles, and the cozy sweater swamping her frame. She appeared mid-conversation with a man and woman on either side of her, but her face turned at a slight angle, and her eyes met his.

Cole witnessed her whisper something to her companions before she stepped forward... and began walking over. He sat taller and raked his eyes over her comfortable attire, settling on her lips twitching like she was trying not to smile.

"Hi," she whispered. She teetered on her heels, swaying side to side, and Cole lowered the sunglasses onto the bridge of his nose. "I thought that was you, but I wasn't sure."

Cole couldn't help smiling either, "It's me. I look a little rougher than when we last spoke, but there's only one guy as devilishly handsome as me in the city," he joked.

Ms. Byndel giggled, "I think that's an understatement . . . no offense, but you look like you got into a fight with your bed, and the bed won."

"Hangovers will do that to you. So, what brings you to this lovely coffee shop on such a bright Saturday morning?"

"I had some business at the church across the street, and Beth and Aaron offered to buy me a coffee for my troubles."

"That's nice of them."

"Oh yeah," Ms. Byndel reached for the stool beside Cole's, and he watched her claim the seat for herself, hesitant like she expected him to refuse her. Quite the opposite, he wouldn't mind if she sat beside him while they waited. "What about you? Is this your usual coffee joint?"

Cole's hands flipped his glasses onto his head and gestured to his face, "Well, I'm still painfully hungover and recently moved. So, my fridge is empty, and the area is a tad unfamiliar. I decided to explore and found this place."

"That makes sense." She hummed and leaned her elbows on the counter. With her hair pulled back from her face and a less emotionally fraught meeting, Cole got a chance to study her features from the delicate slope of her nose, how her lashes brushed against her cheek whenever she blinked, and the corner of her lips turned upward.

He eventually mimicked her lean on the counter with his elbows and chin tucked into his overlapping hands, "You know, I only know you as Ms. Byndel."

"Funny, I don't have your name at all."

"Well, if you give me yours, I'll give you mine."

"That's alright with me," she murmured, head cocked to the side, and a stray hair fell out from her loose ponytail. "My name's Nina."

Cole paused. Somehow, the name suited her, and his undergraduate minor in linguistics buzzed in his head with useless name-related facts. Instead, he offered his hand to her.

"A promise is a promise. My name's Cole Yearwood. It's nice to officially meet you, Nina," said Cole.

"Same to you, Cole," Nina grasped his hand in hers, and the coldness of her hands shocked him, causing him to hold onto her for maybe a beat too long. But Nina didn't comment on it, or she might not have noticed it.

Regardless, it happened, and Cole noticed.

His focus broke when he overheard a shout from one of the baristas, "Order for Cole! One Hangover Cure and classic cinnamon roll! For Cole!" They set the paper bag on the small section of the counter reserved for to-go orders.

He glanced back to Nina, who was studying him, and she smiled, "That's you. Go ahead. I'm a big girl and can wait for Aaron or Beth to find me."

"If you're sure, then it was good to see you. Take care, okay?"

"I'll try my best. Have a good day, Cole."

"Maybe we'll see each other around," Cole's thought never reached his lips beyond a nod, reciprocated by one from Nina. "Thanks, Nina."

He slid from his stool, wallet and keys in hand, and grabbed the bag from the counter. Then, he was gone from the coffee shop.

Chapter Four
Nina

The worn walls of the small chapel on the graveyard grounds could crumble on top of her, but Nina wouldn't care. She had marched through Naomi's funeral on autopilot, choked her way through a half-written eulogy to her sister that probably sounded pathetically short, and stood at the lectern with faded green carpeting underfoot.

She choked back the tears whenever her eyes began to burn.

A crowd of faces she didn't know watched her every move, and the small voice inside told her to be brave. One pair of eyes mattered—Brooke's—and she refused to let the little bug see her lose her cool.

Nina swayed on the heels of her feet in a slow, tight circle and took in the sight of the chapel. Dark wooden pews occupied either side of the narrow aisle to the pulpit, meant for parishioners of the deceased. A solitary, dirtied glass window hung on the wall at the back of the lectern, shining the light of day on the spot where a priest conducted rites.

A sleeping Brooke lay in her arms with her head buried into Nina's shoulder and her little body limp yet warm. The little one had loose arms tossed over her shoulders, and Nina swore she reminded her of a doll with her stillness. Beyond the sound of her breaths through her mouth, Brooke silently dozed.

That morning, Nina barely managed to de-escalate a meltdown from Brooke because she wanted her mommy and asked when she would return from seeing the angels. The answer of *Mommy can't come back* wasn't appreciated.

Nina was trying, racked with enough guilt to drown her under emotional turbulence.

But beyond the simple act of providing food, a roof over Brooke's head, and being there, she hadn't the faintest idea of how to explain the permanence of death to an elementary school-age child or how to be a mother. There wasn't a manual for these things, much to her inconvenience.

I wish you were here, Naomi. Nina's eyes climbed the walls until she settled on the cross mounted over the window. *I don't know how to fill the shoes you left behind, and Brooke needs you. Hell, I need you. I stopped believing in heaven, hell, and all the little things in between years ago . . . but I need a sign that I'm not alone. Can you hear me, Naomi?*

None of those words left the safety of her mind while she stared through the window for a sign. She listened for something to prove her sister didn't vanish after being lowered into the ground. The minute she accepted Naomi was gone, she expected the weak denial to snap and let the world crush her underneath its weight.

The chapel simmered in silence despite the chilly autumnal morning outside its walls, taunting Nina's naïve hope for a miracle.

Her eyes walked up to the ceiling and noticed the splotches of water damage to the surface, all browned puddle shapes against the creamy white paint chipping off in flecks. They reminded her of puddles on the sidewalk that she and Naomi used to jump through after rainy days at school. The echo of laughter accompanied the damp splashes of pink polka dot rainboots into deeper waters.

Nina stared into the pews and imagined the sight of her and Naomi, their blonde hair pulled into double braids with their mother's worn scrunchies from her college days, racing home after a long day at school. They used to live two blocks away and always walked together once the dismissal bell rang.

Naomi looked out for her, even as kids, like older sisters were supposed to. But who was looking out for Naomi? Not any God that Nina knew.

She blinked, and the vision of her and Naomi when they were young vanished. She stood among empty pews in the dilapidated graveyard chapel, begging for a sign never meant to come. Grief held her head below the waves, but she only needed to tread water.

Nina remained quiet while pacing the altar from end to end, aware of Brooke asleep in her arms. She and Brooke could sidestep the grief that hung over their heads like dark clouds in their sleep.

In any other situation, Nina's first call used to be Naomi. Her big sister always dubbed herself a "fixer," able to piece together solutions to seemingly impossible dilemmas. She'd pinch Nina's cheek with that knowing smile and a soft promise that everything would be alright . . . Naomi had it handled.

Nina thought about railing against the unfairness of it all. Naomi deserved a lifetime with her daughter—Brooke needed her mother—and half of Nina's heart guarded the bargain she might offer in a heartbeat: *Naomi's life for hers.*

Naomi would hate it. She would refuse until she went blue in the face or Nina recanted, whichever came first.

"I need to stop before I lose my stomach." Nina shivered. Her thoughts easily slid into memories, musings, and various stages of grieving. She moved past the denial but ended up stranded somewhere between bargaining and anger, destined to stay for a while.

When her thoughts circled back, she found herself stuck on the idea of young parenthood. For all intents and purposes, the world saw her as Brooke's parent and looked to her to guide her through life. Nina wasn't prepared.

Was anyone ever truly ready to be a parent?

"Nina! There you are, sweet pea." A voice carried across the pews from the front doors, and her head snapped up to meet the face. She recognized the black skirt and cozy turtleneck emerging from the shadows as she saw Joy, the worship leader of the church Naomi attended. "I was worried when I noticed that you disappeared."

Nina dropped her eyes, whispering, "I needed a moment of space from everything. You understand."

"Ah, I do. I've presided over many funerals for my parishioners over the years, but the feeling in your chest never gets easier when seeing grief tear families apart. But the Lord is merciful; he shall care for you two through the hard times."

The hint of a southern accent slipped out, reminding Nina how Joy left her family's Southern Baptist community for a non-denominational church thousands of miles away. She told her story at the pulpit, and Nina appreciated the touches of humanity in her sermon, even as someone who only attended a few sessions at Naomi's behest.

Nina mutely nodded. She stared at Joy, tall and striking with sharp features and box braids in a rich caramel color, who stroked the top of Brooke's head. Upon first glance, she and Joy appeared the same age, but Joy radiated wisdom from decades ahead of Nina.

Nina adjusted her hold on Brooke, careful not to wake her, and sighed. "I'm ready to head back to the others. I should thank people for coming."

"We were more than happy to come and support you today. No thanks are necessary. But I remember Patrick, one of the members of our congregation, asked me to find you. He said he needed to speak about something regarding Naomi . . . He said it was urgent."

"I'm right here!" A male voice joined the fray, and Nina glanced toward the front to see an older gentleman with a cane and a worn black suit draped over his withered figure. He offered a tentative nod as he hobbled over.

"I can leave you and Miss Nina alone to speak."

"That's alright. I might need you as a witness." Joy helped Patrick onto the altar on account of a bad knee and grabbed a chair from the dusty back corner for him to sit. Nina stood and passed Joy a thankful smile as she headed to close the doors at the front, preserving a sense of privacy.

She and Patrick lingered in silence until she noticed him remove a manilla envelope from inside his coat. Her eyes skimmed for any identifying markers, but *Naomi Byndel* in dark ink sat on the front.

"I'm sorry, sir," Nina shook her head. "I don't understand what this is about. Naomi never mentioned you before."

"That's alright, miss. Naomi got into contact with me when she started coming to services after Joy's invitation. I'm an attorney, planning to retire soon, but she had asked me years ago to help her draft an official will."

"She did?"

"Yes, she did. I'm so sorry that I'm not long gone when this is getting unsealed, but her passing means that whatever she directed in these documents will go into effect once I read the will."

"Oh."

Patrick waited until Joy returned from the doors to unseal the envelope. A lump of nausea wormed into Nina's throat while she waited for the information to hit her. *She had no idea what to expect in the will and testament.*

"It says that I, Naomi Byndel, in case of death or life-altering circumstances that render me invalid, appoint Nina Byndel, my younger sister, as the executor of my estate," Patrick fixed the large bifocals on his face to read the fine print. "I gift all my belongings and custody of my daughter, Brooke, to Nina. She will inherit all my monetary assets and physical property in my name to do as she sees fit. Additionally, I stipulate that none of my personal effects or custody of my daughter should be awarded to Thomas and Vera Byndel or Maxwell Byndel, as we are estranged."

Thomas, Vera, and Maxwell. Father, mother, and brother.

Nina curbed any rush from hearing the names of their parents and brother. Naomi had been disowned years before, so she disowned them back. Nina chose low to no contact with them throughout the years, but escaping them seemed impossible. Her mother had ways of tracking her down.

She swallowed. "Patrick, this may be a stupid question, but can they contest the will if she leaves them nothing? I thought attorneys left one dollar to people otherwise disinherited as a petty trick to stop them from legal action."

"Some attorneys are favorable to that trick, but many attorneys find that even the slightest amount added to the will can cause more issues long-term. Besides, the cost to inform them of their one-dollar sum and the potential for problems isn't worth the momentary satisfaction of a petty jab. That should be the strongest deterrent to any legal action since Naomi was smart enough to acknowledge them and explain why she left nothing in her will."

Nina wasn't a lawyer, so she would put her trust in Patrick's word. Although Cole Yearwood's face flashed in her mind as a potential second opinion on the strength of her claim against any contests of the will.

"I see. Can I take the document, or will I get an official copy?"

Patrick handed her the envelope and the papers stating her claim over Naomi's entire estate. "Your sister was a smart woman, Nina. She took every consideration and protection to secure a future for you and that little girl." Joy helped him out of his chair until he managed to lean on his cane.

"I know she was," Nina agreed and clutched the papers tightly in her hand, focusing on Brooke. Naomi trusted her enough to establish a future for Brooke, leaving little to no guidelines on handling the items. That level of trust should feel heartwarming, but it made Nina ache for her big sister like a child. "Thank you for helping her, Patrick."

"Of course." Patrick tipped his head and hobbled down the narrow aisle for the doors. Joy bounded behind him with long strides to catch up quick.

Nina followed behind them, a suitable distance away. She focused on the rush of emotions thundering in her head like a drum line in a marching band. Brooke's legs swayed and knocked into her ribs with little jolts of pain to remind her that she was alive.

She emerged into the light of day and sucked in a greedy breath of autumn air, spiced with fallen leaves and loneliness. She stared at her sedan parked beyond the graveyard's limits, and the long line from her popped trunk.

Nina's mouth dropped when she saw those who attended the funerals stack different sizes of Tupperware and other boxes into her trunk. She spotted fresh cookies, cakes, soups, and casseroles, among other non-perishable food items.

A presence materialized next to Nina, and she glanced to the side, seeing Joy holding an envelope in her hands. A smile adorned her face like sunshine after a thunderstorm relented its grip on the world.

"For you," Joy murmured. "A small collection passed around while you stepped aside, and many of our congregation brought you supplies to hold you over. Cooking can be difficult when life gets tough. Food nourishes your stomach and your soul in equal parts. I hope this second gift is enough."

She cracked open the envelope flap, but Nina grappled with the urge to cry at the sight of money. She counted several dozen crisp twenty-dollar and ten-dollar bills tucked into the envelope. Any support pushed her buoyant above the uncertain waters.

"Joy, I can't pay you back for this-"

"Family doesn't leave one of their own stranded. Please, this is from the graciousness of our hearts. You only need to keep Naomi's memory alive and care for Brooke. That is what she would've wanted."

Nina tightened her arms around Brooke, who wiggled deeper into her embrace for warmth, but her eyes turned to the crowd. The last observer loaded their offering into the trunk of her car before they closed the back.

All eyes landed on her, and she struggled to find the words to explain herself. But she felt Joy slide the envelope into her hand with Naomi's will. She snapped back to reality with the crowd's watchful gazes.

"Thank you all," said Nina. "I feel so lucky that Naomi got to know you over the last few years and that you brightened her life. I can't stay much longer, but I am grateful for your support. Thank you. Thank you."

People parted when she stepped forward and lined her walk from the graveyard to her car. Someone kindly opened the back door for her to buckle Brooke into her car seat, and another held her driver's seat door open.

Her purse and car keys waited in the front passenger seat, and Nina set down the cash collection and the copy of Naomi's will. She waved and watched as the people from the church moved out of her way at the roar of her engine.

Nina kept her eyes on them while she pulled away from the graveyard. Tears gathered in her eyes when their figures retreated the further she drove down the gravel road toward the city. Those tears threatened to fall, but Nina forced herself to hold.

It wasn't the time to cry. She couldn't let anything distract her from safe driving.

On a bench at Haddsworth Park, a special place to her and Naomi for wildly different reasons, Nina paid attention to the happy world around her. She and Brooke sat off the main path, but people passed them on their way to the playground in sight or a shady spot on the grassy hills.

Bright-colored clothes, kites flying high, and the laughter of families nearby added small pops of vibrancy to the world. Yet, Nina swore her funeral garb sucked the joy out of life. It was a beautiful day, but she couldn't bring herself to enjoy it without guilt.

In her hands, she checked her phone for any messages or missed calls. She half expected to receive one at any moment with some lame excuse about why he wouldn't show his face. A public park meeting was the third time, anyway.

"Are you okay, bug?" asked Nina, meant for Brooke.

Brooke nodded from beside her on the bench, having woken up from her nap no more than five minutes ago. Nina expected her to stay half-asleep through the errand she needed to address at the park. Yet, Brooke grasped her hand from their seat on the bench and stared at the duck pond.

She loved ducks.

Nina scanned the park before she glanced back at her phone. She planned to go home if he didn't show up within five minutes of their agreed-upon time. He was the one who insisted on the meeting anyway. If it were up to her, Nina would never see his face again.

Her eagerness to leave needled down her spine and the growing ache screamed at her to get the emotional toll over with. It was all too much.

She waited, keeping her purse clutched in her other hand for a quick getaway at the chosen time. But, as she started to stand up, her eyes caught sight of him. He looked out of place for such a casual park in a designer polo shirt and wearing sunglasses more expensive than the cost of some people's rent, yet none of that diminished the tumbling ache in her chest.

His curly blond hair flopped over his eyes, and he brushed his hand over a five-o-clock shadow. Until that moment, Nina had never seen him look unkempt like that. Some part of her felt unsettled by the strangeness of her ex-fiancé.

"Zachary," Nina greeted him. She shoved down the rush of memories tethered to Zachary Piker, but the reminder of early mornings tangled in the sheets, swapping laughter through kisses and collecting sweet nothings before the day began irked her. Even though those memories weren't old, life changed so quickly for an unsuspecting heart. "Thank you for meeting me."

Zachary's hands rested at his sides, but Nina took notice of the scrunch of his fingertips against his pants. "Yeah, it's cool. We should probably get this over with, huh?"

"We should. Anything you want to say before we part ways?"

"No-I mean, is there something you're expecting from me?"

"If you have to ask, I'll take that as a no." Nina let go of Brooke's hand but checked on her. Brooke's eyes stared at Zachary, and she waved at him after a moment. She smiled, kicking her legs, too small to touch the ground.

The blank stare on Zachary's face while Brooke was genuinely adorable stirred up a bitter taste in Nina's mouth. She barely held back the urge to spit it out with a comment to fuel angst.

She pulled off the thin, silver chain around her neck and slid it into her hand. She admired the ring—a small diamond in a classic cushion cut and a silver band—in the palm of her hand. *The last piece of their engagement would be removed from her possession, all the better for her.*

Nina tossed Zachary the ring, and he caught it. The slightly affronted gleam in his eyes challenged Nina to start an argument, but she only wanted to hand him the ring back and clean her hands of their history.

In the immediate aftermath of their broken engagement, Zachary demanded she return the ring to him so he could fetch a "refund for his wasted time." Nina almost exploded at that shining comment, tempted to keep the ring. But, knowing he might stoop low enough to cause legal issues over it, she decided against being petty.

"If that's all, then I'll be heading out," said Nina, taking Brooke's hand.

Zachary's eyes jumped between her and the ring, stammering, "Wait. Hold on. Nina, I don't think that we have to end this way."

"Oh? Is that so? Why's that?"

Zachary's attention dropped from her face, and she followed the line of his vision to Brooke. He lowered his voice to a whisper, "Do you not regret how things transpired between us? What about how we ended? Be honest."

Nina paused, swallowing hard. Regret felt too simplistic of a term to describe the spectacular implosion of a three-year relationship. "No. I wasn't the one who tossed an ultimatum on the table."

"That's not fair-"

"It isn't?"

"No, it's not. You're being unfair."

"You broke up with me days after my sister died. When I pressed you for a reason, you told me that you weren't ready for the responsibility of a kid . . . even though you were the one of us that kept mentioning children."

Zachary's face turned a shade paler than before, but Nina continued pressing the wound. She needed him to explain himself because she still didn't understand how he could betray her like that.

After Naomi passed, CPS placed Brooke with her, and she mulled over her options about taking Brooke in more permanently. She knew Naomi would feel betrayed if she let CPS give Brooke to the family that abandoned her all those years ago. Instead of being a supportive partner and weighing their options together, Zachary turned into a toddler with temper tantrums about how she was ruining their lives.

She grieved her sister and the death of her relationship all at once.

Zachary's Adam's apple bobbed hard when she stared at him. She demanded an answer before she left him in the past. "I do want kids."

"He speaks," Nina hissed. "So, why wasn't Brooke an acceptable member to add to our hypothetical family? Is it because she isn't your blood, and you have some fucked-up notion that blood is all that matters?"

"I want my kids to be mine, Nina. That's not a crime!"

"No, but it sure is a damn shame. You're a selfish prick, Zach . . . jealous of an orphaned child."

Nina noticed how Brooke put her hands over her ears, and she softened. Zachary wasn't worth her time to argue with. She had arrangements to handle so he could wax poetic about the good times he walked away from. *He left her, not the other way around.*

Nina leaned down and scooped Brooke into her arms. She kissed her forehead and murmured, "Are you hungry, bug?"

"Yes, Auntie Nini."

"Okay. How about I make you lunch, and we'll get into PJs afterward?"

Brooke fervently nodded and buried her face in Nina's neck, holding her tight. Nina supported her niece in her arms and glared at Zachary, who gaped with his mouth wide open like a beached fish in desperate need of rescue.

She stepped past him without a second glance or a word. Zachary Piker represented the last failure of her past; after today, she left him behind. She gave him endless chances to figure out his grievances, but he chose to play games.

He ran out of chances.

Chapter Five
Cole

Finding parking outside the closest grocery store to his apartment proved a worthy challenge for Cole, but he managed to nab a spot sandwiched between two minivans. He laughed when he noticed the cliché decals slapped against the back window.

With a fridge needing food to fill it, Cole headed inside the name-brand supermarket chain to the ringing of his cell phone. He couldn't subsist on coffee and takeout unless he wanted to fall behind on his recent improvements. He rummaged through the deep pockets of his sweatpants for his phone and slid it between his ear and shoulder.

"Cole Yearwood speaking," he greeted as he nabbed a grocery basket from the stack by the automatic doors. "May I ask who's calling?"

Dean snorted on the other side of the conversation, "Don't you have caller ID on your phone?"

"I do, but I didn't check it. I'm grocery shopping at the moment, so what's up?"

"Hey, are you upset I almost dropped the bar on you earlier? Because that was an accident; you have a problem holding grudges."

Cole rolled his eyes while he slid the basket into the crook of his elbow. He wandered into the fresh produce section to grab enough for the next few weeks. "That feels a mild understatement, you asshole."

"Hey! I got distracted!"

"I'm aware. Every time January walks past in a pair of leggings, your tongue flops out of your mouth, and you suddenly get butterfingers. I've met dogs with better self-control."

Cole noticed a few stray looks his way and forced his voice into a whisper, embarrassed. He loaded some bananas into his cart alongside fresh celery, carrots, an onion, and bushels of greens.

"My fiancé is stunning," Dean protested despite the rustling in the background. "I didn't injure you, so no harm, no foul."

"Dean, are you antagonizing your brother again?" January's voice cut through the stammering of his brother, and Cole felt his mouth twist hard into a laugh. "Play nice."

"Jan, please."

"Dean, please nothing. Stop being a little twerp to Cole and apologize for being the worst spotter in the gym."

"A TWERP? Jan, what are we? Eight?"

"I can use a more colorful adjective if you're inclined, babe. But Cole's right, and you're not, so you should apologize." January laughed while Dean scoffed loudly. Meanwhile, Cole leaned against the stand with the fresh, off-the-vine tomatoes silently wheezing.

He loved January so much.

Dean mumbled a quiet, half-serious apology, but Cole overheard movement in the background to make his eyes roll. He moved through the produce section with a few more pitstops in a few seconds.

Even while on the other line, he became the third wheel in the Jan and Dean show. So, Cole pulled off to the side and said, "Alright, I've overstayed my welcome. I'll talk to you two in a few days."

"Bye, Cole," Jan took over Dean's side of the call, and Cole heard some garbled comments from his older brother. "We're still on for family dinner on Friday, yeah?"

"Sure are. I'll bring the appetizer like I promised."

"Mmm, I love your cooking."

"I know you do. See you later, Jan." Cole hung up, smiling still. Over the last few months, he took cooking lessons at a nearby rec center to the Yearwood-Quinn apartment and picked up needed skills. He had a natural talent for culinary arts when he applied himself.

Cole picked up some fresh herbs in their little pots, shallots, a few potatoes, and a carton of mixed berries before he rounded the corner to the dairy and meat aisle. A draft from the industrial freezers inched up his bare arms, left unprotected by a sleeveless tank top after the gym.

Part of the bi-weekly routine encompassed trips to the grocery store for meal prep materials and extra in case he wanted to cook something. He started those small milestones while living with Jan and Dean, promising to continue to take care when he moved into his new apartment.

He needed to be a tad more put-together as a man in his late twenties.

Alright, I need chicken, fish, or shrimp. Mostly chicken, he mentally counted down his checklist, regretting not writing down everything he needed on his phone or somewhere like a sticky note. "Let's see what they've got."

As he perused the giant, freezing shelves of raw meat, Cole caught a few stares meant to be discreet. When they passed, women around his age or significantly older ran their eyes over his figure. The most flagrant of the looks came from a girl standing beside a tall guy wearing glasses and a graphic t-shirt of some comic book hero. The guy's hand tucked possessively into the back jeans pocket of the girl, sending a crystal-clear statement.

Cole met her eyes, and the bite of her lip sent him scrambling to grab the first package of chicken breasts without checking the prices of other containers. He shuffled further away and snatched up some shrimp as he fled.

Somehow, he sensed her disappointment when he nearly ran toward the dairy fridges for eggs, milk, and creamer for his coffee.

Cole shook out his shoulders to chase away the unease of stares. People on the outside saw a cocky flash of bravado and a tendency to joke about flirtation, missing the true him. Keeping the outside all flash and humor distracted from the shortcomings of his discomfort in matters of the heart.

He caught his reflection in one of the glass doors and turned away from himself. He loaded his cart and wandered down one of the aisles for a last check in case he forgot something from his list. Since his apartment lacked the basics, he welcomed additional supplies.

Unlike other parts of the store, the first hallway he chose appeared mostly empty beyond one woman pulled off to the side of the road. Cole kept his place slow for his wandering eye, jumping between shelves on either side for anything he might want.

However, his attention soon became consumed when a little face peered from around the woman occupying the aisle with him. Bright green eyes blinked through blonde hair loose over her face, staring at him.

Cole watched how the little girl, who sat in the upper section of the half-full shopping cart, would hide behind her parent before peeking back out to peer at him down the aisle. After the first two times, Cole found it hard to resist a smile. *What a cute kid. She couldn't be more than six at most.*

Playing along, he pretended to cover his eyes and jumped in surprise when he removed his hand and found her staring. She giggled whenever he pretended to be spooked and immediately moved out of his vision.

Cole continued that while he approached one of the shelves, finding some jars of peanut butter and honey bears stacked at the topmost row. He dropped them into his basket and moved closer to the little girl and her parent, standing in front of the cookware section of the aisle.

"Excuse me, miss," he cleared his throat when he stepped up behind her, more focused on the different silicone spatulas and their patterns. He wasn't expecting the variety but narrowed down two multi-colored, patterned ones from the shelf as potentials. "I need to reach past you here."

"Oh! Sorry, I didn't mean to get in your way-Cole?" Nina's eyes widened, but Cole saw how his presence painted her gentle features in a surprised pallor. "Small world, huh?"

Cole chuckled when Nina pushed her shopping cart back enough to clear a space. She leaned on the cart, and he plucked two spatulas off the shelf, holding them up for her opinion.

Nina pointed to the one in his left—polka dots covering the silicone spatula head—and Cole dropped it into his cart, humming aloud, "We've got to stop meeting like this."

"And by 'this,' I assume you mean like in ways perfectly encapsulated by cheesy romance movies?"

"Yeah, something like that . . . um, is this your daughter?"

Nina glanced over her shoulder when Cole tipped his head to the little girl in the shopping cart, who had a small fistful of Cheerios from a snack cup. However, he noticed Nina's throat bobbing with a rough swallow.

"Uh, no," Nina shook her head. "This is my niece, Brooke. Brooke, this is Mr. Cole. Can you say hi to Mr. Cole?"

"Hi, Mr. Cole!" Brooke offered a sticky hand with Cheerios in it to him. While a sweet offer, Cole would be okay.

"Hi there, Brooke. It's nice to meet you. How old are you?"

"I'm five!"

"Whoa, five! You're so big, kiddo." Cole tried his best to squat a little, ending with his hands resting on his knees and the basket filled with groceries tucked at his feet. Brooke's face brightened, and she giggled, turning her face away from him like she suddenly became shy.

His eyes darted to Nina, who watched the exchange quietly and pretended to be fixated on the shelves of cake mixes directly across the aisle from them. Cole straightened back up and leaned into her view.

He lowered his voice, "What else do you need to pick up?" He didn't know how much Nina had going on with Brooke or the whole situation. Call it a hunch, but he suspected the custody question sat in the shopping cart.

"Um, some shampoo, detangler spray, snacks for her daycare lunches, muffin mix, and some deli meat from the counter." Nina listed off with a frown and nodded toward her cart. "I'm shopping for two, and one of us is a tad on the picky side."

"Ah, I remember those days. Dino nuggets are a staple for picky eating."

"Dino nuggets!" Brooke shouted and clapped her hands, almost spilling her Cheerios onto the floor. Nina lunged and caught the cup before it tumbled or turned over to lose the Cheerios to the grocery store floor.

"I'll add that to my list. Do you suggest tater tots or French fries?"

"Both."

Nina giggled and began pushing the cart down the aisle toward the frozen foods, two aisles down. Although she hadn't officially invited Cole along with them, he followed behind her when she glanced over her shoulder at him with a hopeful look.

Soon, he fell into step with her and the two moved through the store while Brooke babbled and munched on her Cheerios. Cole noticed the small things like how she and Nina held hands over the shopping cart handle or the exhaustion Nina let show whenever Brooke became distracted.

He leaned over. "Between you and I, how are you holding up?"

"Not well," Nina whispered, head tipped toward the floor, and Cole studied her face. "I'm trying to hang in there for her, but every day seems like an uphill battle. I miss my sister. She was so young and had her whole life ahead of her . . . and now she won't be able to see Brooke grow up. Where's the justice in that?"

She lost a sister and had new custody of her niece.

Cole swallowed. He tried to imagine losing Dean, but the idea of his older brother being gone, even though the two fought and bickered as often as they got along, made his stomach jolt uncomfortably. His sympathies ran deep as a man who loved his brother.

"I know you've probably heard this a million times, but I'm sorry for your loss. I'm sure your sister was an amazing person and an even better mother."

"She was the best mother in the world."

"I don't doubt that. Brooke is lucky to have you in her life, though."

Nina shrugged. "I'm trying my best. I don't know how to do the mother thing . . . I always assumed I would have more time to figure it out."

"You say you don't have the mom thing figured out." Cole reached around her and pulled out a giant bag of dino nuggets from the freezers. They'd collect things on the way. "But your mindset already makes you a better mother than some out there."

Nina's eyes softened around the corners, yet she shrugged. The two waltzed a few aisles over for the hair stuff to load into her cart. Cole caught her biting her lower lip a few times like she wanted to say something.

So, he went first.

"What's on your mind? I've been told that I'm a good listener," he murmured.

"My sister, Naomi, was my best friend. We'd always been close as kids, closer as teens, and stayed close as adults. With her gone, I feel empty. I never was one for meeting people and going out, so the last few weeks have been so lonely . . . sorry, I'm rambling." The tips of Nina's ears flushed red, but Cole shook his head.

"Whoa, there's no need to apologize. I asked because I wanted to know. Besides, the season amplifies loneliness. I feel it too, all the time."

After a short stop at the deli, he, Nina, and Brooke gravitated toward the shortest line since they exceeded the amount for self-checkout. Cole gestured for Nina to go in front of him, and they worked together to load the conveyor belt filled with groceries.

"How are you doing today?" the cashier behind the counter asked, but Cole wasn't sure if he meant that for him or Nina . . . or them together.

"Good, thank you-"

"Can't complain-"

Nina and Cole shared a look when the words tumbled out simultaneously, and neither spoke again, even while Brooke babbled and waved to the cashier with a giant smile on her little face.

However, when Nina turned her back to grab the first paper bag of her groceries to load into the cart, Cole swiped his card down the pin pad. He relished the little chime signaling the paid balance, but Nina's gasp had Cole fighting a pleased grin.

"Cole, you didn't have to do that-" she whispered.

"Maybe, but I wanted to." Cole rubbed her back but dropped his hand after a beat too long.

"I can pay you back later. Do you have an app for money transfers?"

"You don't have to pay me back. You don't owe me a single thing. I've got more than enough to cover yours and mine."

Even while she loaded the other bags into the cart, Nina stared at him, but Cole could tell she wasn't entirely convinced. She had a hard enough time as is. "Okay, what about some other means of payment? Dinner? Coffee?"

"You don't owe me anything, and I mean that." Cole counted his groceries while they moved across the conveyor belt, enough to hold him over for a while. "Besides, what kind of gentleman would I be if I didn't help people when I could?"

"Gentlemen are hard to come by these days," Nina remarked, and it almost sounded like she was speaking from experience.

Cole tipped his card back to the pin pad to pay for his groceries, neatly stacked into two paper bags, "Chivalry isn't dead yet, not if my mom has anything to say about it."

He and Nina grabbed their bagged groceries and walked out together, stepping into the light of the late morning. The middle of September boasted the scent of fallen leaves and a hint of spices in the air. Even when the days were hard, he loved the season.

From her spot in the shopping cart, Brooke looked on the verge of falling asleep. Her head lolled to the side, and she almost dropped her Cheerios for the second time, only stopped by Nina's quick reflexes. For being a new guardian, she already had mom superpowers.

Nina tugged his arm, "Would you mind walking me to my car? It's okay if you've got somewhere to be-"

"Hey, it's not a problem at all. Lead the way."

"Thank you."

Cole followed Nina to her car, parked close to his. He loaded his two bags into the shopping cart but kept them away from Nina's items. While she carried Brooke into the car seat before she fell asleep entirely, Cole loaded the groceries into the trunk.

He made quick work of all the bags by himself and stacked them in clusters from lightest to heaviest. He felt Nina's gaze on his back but glanced over his shoulder, spotting Nina fixing her purse's strap and smiling.

The smile eased her features from the strain of exhaustion. Nina leaned on the shopping cart. "It's not so bad we keep meeting this way. I appreciate the company of someone who understands."

"I get that," Cole chuckled. He tucked his hands into the pockets of his sweatpants. "I'll make sure to plan something more swoon-worthy for our next meeting, yeah? Any requests?"

"Oh, I don't know. A park? Out to dinner? Surprise me." Nina stifled her laughter behind her hand, and Cole found himself drawn to the brightness of her eyes. Had anyone ever told her that she sparkled when she laughed?

"Consider one surprise in order." Cole moved the cart out of her way and closed the trunk. "You're ready to go. Anything else you need from me?"

"That should be everything. Thank you again . . . for the groceries and for walking me out. You can never be too careful these days."

"Anytime. Promise me you'll drive safe?"

"Promise."

Cole nodded and moved the cart out of the way. He'd put it away after he loaded up his car so she wouldn't have to worry about anything but getting Brooke home for a nap. He stepped to the side and stood on the small curb beside the parking space.

He waited while Nina started her car and pulled out of the spot, careful and focused. Cole watched as Nina and Brooke drove off, but he spotted a smile in the rearview mirror before she got too far out of sight.

I need to get out more often, Cole thought with a smile, thinking about how lucky Brooke was to have someone like Nina. *Maybe I'd meet more people like her.*

Chapter Six
Nina

Beyond the soft tick of the clock mounted onto the wall, Nina lingered in the silence of her condo with her eyes on the door to Brooke's bedroom. What once was a spare guest room turned into her niece's personal space, and Nina went to great lengths to reflect the décor tastes of a five-year-old.

That meant a patterned bedspread, soft pastel colors, and lots of room for her toys and new favorite tea party set Nina bought last Christmas. She distinctly remembered that Santa Claus took the credit for that one, but buying Brooke another year of childhood meant everything after all she experienced.

She put a crabby Brooke down for a nap after her third meltdown of the morning, and Brooke didn't fight when Nina tucked her underneath the covers. She fell asleep fast and hard from all the crying.

Nina felt like a mess.

She raked her fingers through her hair to tie it back with the scrunchie on her wrist. A loose ponytail managed for the casual workday she planned, even before Brooke woke up on the wrong side of the bed.

In a pair of sweatpants, stained with bleach spots from years of washes taking its toll on the fabric, and an oversized shirt that belonged to an old fling who ghosted her before she could return it, Nina imagined she looked awfully cozy for her work.

She had her laptop propped open on the kitchen counter, next to the unopened juice box she snatched from the fridge and a cuerno sweet bread from a nearby Mexican bakery. With a pre-lunch snack, Nina searched for the energy to finish her current piece for work.

In college, she discovered a latent talent for writing when she joined her school's newspaper and realized her ability to crank out articles under tight deadlines. She became known as the paper's pinch hitter, able to meet deadlines if someone else's story flirted too close to the deadline without being finished.

These days, despite a journalism degree, she freelanced her talents. From monthly articles to various newspapers as a guest columnist to the occasional novel ghostwriting, Nina did it all like a modern Renaissance woman. The workload moved flexibly to suit her needs, but money became directly dependent on how many projects she took on. Hence, the skill of writing fast turned into her greatest asset.

Nina chose projects indiscriminately in the past and moved through them with little standing in her way. But her progress hit a dead end in the wake of losing Naomi.

Her typically speedy turnaround ground to a crawl as grief cast a looming sense of writer's block over her brain. Every sentence was tainted with an agonizing rush of disappointment, unease, and every other negative emotion she could discover in the pages of a dictionary.

To her, nothing sounded right. She second-guessed each choice until she became unassailably convinced she had screwed up somewhere and needed to start over.

Luckily, her bosses on the current projects offered their condolences and an extension of her deadlines for a week or so. But Nina faced the worry that their sympathies wouldn't carry her to her next paycheck. She needed to finish today.

"Alright, brain," Nina mumbled while opening her email inbox. She already had the screen split, with one page on her email and the other half sitting on her incomplete news article about the best drugstore dupes for name-brand makeup. "I need you to work with me today, and we can go back to being depressed later."

Nina cracked her knuckles and set off on a frantic sprint. She skimmed across the keyboard with her freshly done nails in peach pink, churning out a few sentences she didn't immediately hate. *A good sign.*

Nina gave herself a break between every paragraph to check one offer in her inbox. She would read the offer's requirements first and usually found the pay a few lines down. The ones she liked got a golden star and were saved for later determination.

For every project she took on, she completed one first.

She hovered over the fourth one of the day, and her lips pulled tightly into a thin line. The price immediately jumped out to her with many zeros tacked on at the end, but everything made sense when she peeped at the deadline. A pinch-hit article for *Sunkissed Magazine,* one of the most famous women's magazines internationally.

She sensed a golden opportunity if she could break through her writer's block with a sledgehammer of inspiration.

She kept the tab open on that specific email while she pumped out another three sentences on the second to last product in her draft. If for nothing else, she wrote to collect the check waiting for her at the end.

Sure, she had Naomi's nest egg of savings and donations from the kind folks at Joy's church. However, it would be irresponsible of her to slack off and shirk her responsibilities as a provider simply because she could rest for a few months.

When she reached eighteen, most of that money belonged to Brooke; whatever remained would go toward putting a roof over her head or any unexpected emergencies. Everything else would be her responsibility.

Nina caught a stride and decided to run with it, held back for too long by self-doubt and exhaustion. She got less sleep than in college with a fussy little one, often stricken by nightmares and sleeplessness.

She had notes she took ages ago when she first picked up the article and crossed them off with a glittery green pen. Green was her favorite color, even more so with a splash of glitter. Maybe it was childish to be so fond of glitter pens, but the giant tub on her living room bookshelf never ceased to make her smile.

Between the notes and what she had written on the page, Nina's attention had its work cut out for her. Her hands moved fast over the keys. However, she barely reached the end of the article before her concentration broke at the ring of her phone, charging at the kitchen outlet.

"Great, I wonder who the fuck that is." Nina didn't want to interrupt the healthy pace she set up after such a writing drought, but the incessant ringing might wake Brooke from her needed nap. She slid off of her stool and switched off the phone's ringer.

Unknown number, the screen read.

That could mean several things—a telemarketer, a blocked number, or a genuine unknown, like a potential client—so she answered the call.

She barely slid the phone up against her ear before she heard a voice that sent an unwelcome shiver down her back, "Ah, you finally answered."

Disapproval slithered off Vera Byndel's tongue with enough ease to make a snake jealous, but Nina had other choice names for her long-estranged mother. She worried about receiving a call from her, but doomsday came sooner than expected.

"I believe most people start conversations with 'hello' or 'how are you.'" Nina's response would've earned her a lecture if she were much younger. "Is there a reason that you're calling?"

"I need a reason to call my children?"

"Seeing as you always have a reason when you call me, yes. So, come out with it because I'm on a tight deadline."

Nina started seeing a therapist when she went away to college. While she no longer had access to the free services hosted through her university, the time spent there taught her all the wonders of low-contact communication and establishing boundaries. Those came easy to her as the often-forgotten middle child.

Vera huffed loudly, "Fine. I was calling because I heard through the grapevine about Naomi's accident. Ladies from the crochet club wanted to give me their condolences, but I hadn't the faintest idea what they weren't talking about." She sounded annoyed that she wasn't the first to know, not distraught about losing her eldest daughter.

Even her choice of words, *accident* instead of *passing*, screamed that Naomi was dead to their mother before she was lowered into her grave.

Anger blistered on her tongue. She chose the pain of holding back over the nuclear fallout if she exploded on her mother's nonchalance. "I thought the crochet club knew better than mentioning her name in front of you."

Her wicked sarcasm appeared lost on her mother, who breezed past her little comment like she hadn't heard her. In sheer frustration, Nina considered tearing off the wallpaper in her kitchen when she heard, "Anyways, I wanted to invite you to dinner. Feel free to bring Zachary if his schedule permits."

The mention of Zachary burned Nina further. She and Zachary's broken engagement remained between them, but she could expect him to break the news to his family and how it eventually would circle back to hers. Apparently, nothing in their social circle stayed a secret for too long.

"I don't think that's a good idea. I'm swamped."

"Then, you should tell me a date when you're free. Your father and I insist that you come home."

"You aren't going to take no for an answer, are you?" asked Nina, knowing her mother's stubbornness. As much as her mother swore that she hated Naomi, the two used to be painfully alike . . . only Naomi knew how to stop being a bitch.

"I won't," her mother sighed exasperatedly, like Nina's reluctance tired her. "I have dinner this Sunday at six P.M., and I would like you to be there at five-forty-five at the latest."

"I can stop by for a little while. That's all I promise." Nina said, despite the sinking feeling puncturing her chest with the velocity of a bullet. Worry blossomed outward until her hands began to shake so much, struggling to hold her phone.

"Five-forty-five. Don't be late."

The call ended from her mother's side, eliciting a disgusted noise from within Nina. She set her phone down and stepped away, tempted to dial her mother back and give her a piece of her mind.

A few breaths pushed through her clenched teeth while she paced across the kitchen floor, going in circles. Her hands flexed with every jolt threatening to make her vomit all over the floor. *Her mother knew about Brooke.*

She had no proof to substantiate that, but her gut screamed at her to take cover. After everything that happened when Naomi was pregnant with Brooke, the thought of her estranged family taking notice of Brooke choked her up.

Her hands fumbled for her phone, and she dialed the number for Rudy, her attorney, to ask for some advice. She listened to it ring but couldn't stay still while the dial tone rattled in her ears. She walked to her bedroom's en suite and tossed open the medicine cabinet built over the sink.

She pulled out a weekly pill box and opened the Wednesday top slot. She forgot to take her morning dose earlier with Brooke's meltdowns and faced the prospect of being unable to function for the rest of the day.

"Fluoxetine makes the world go round," Nina whispered, and she dry swallowed, too preoccupied with the ringing phone in her hand to juggle a cup of water. "Rudy, please pick up."

Unfortunately, she hit his voicemail, "This is Rudy Hawkins of The Kinsler Legal Aid Foundation. I'm sorry to miss your call. Please leave a name, number for a call back, and a message, and I will contact you as soon as possible."

Nina chewed on her lip. "Rudy, it's Nina Byndel. I don't know if I have anything technically, but my estranged family called me. They asked me to come to dinner, but I think they know about Brooke. I won't take her with me for her safety, and I promise to try and be careful. If you can give me any advice, I'd appreciate it. My number is (468)-994-0134."

She hung up after an awkward beat of silence between her and the answering machine on the other line. The ripple of her reflection in the mirror caught Nina's eyes, and she stared at the woman before her. Haunted eyes sank into dark bags, and the paleness of her skin had her ready to schedule a doctor's visit.

"Hold yourself together," she murmured while gripping the edge of the sink. "You know what they're capable of, so you won't be caught off guard if they try something. For once, you have the upper hand. Don't play happy family with the demons."

When the headlights of her car pointed down the street of her childhood home, Nina prepared for a fight. No, she didn't expect a physical scuffle or an immediate threat but a psychological one. In her family, words were how they waged war.

What a lovely sentiment to share about her blood relatives, but a mixed bag of status chasers, socially conservative and judgmental of those they perceived below them, was how a kinder person might describe them.

She, on the other hand, had some choice words to make the priests from her old parochial school turn red in the face.

Nina drove until she found a parking space directly across the road. She stared at the white picket fences and small yard meticulously gardened by a landscaper in front of the blue-roofed, white-walled house.

The engine cut out, and, in silence, Nina waited. She counted a few breaths in and out until she tempered the race of her treacherous heart. She grabbed her tote bag and stepped out in comfortable wedges. She plucked the dress she wore from the back of her closet for the occasion—black with a square neck and a knee-length skirt.

She was still in mourning, after all.

She locked the car behind her and brushed off her dress while approaching the unlocked front gate. Soft footfalls on the pavement met the crunch of stray leaves blown into the yard from the neighbor's tree.

Nina reached the porch steps and used the knocker, a little more forceful than strictly necessary. But the rush of defiance seeped out in small acts to relieve her. The door swung open rather quickly, and Nina faced her father.

Thomas Byndel's stocky frame occupied the doorway, and his thick mustache boasted a hefty amount of gray. From the wrinkles on his forehead and the way his skin sagged, the years had not been kind to him. Neither had he, so call it retribution. He still wore a suit from all his years in investment banking, and his choice of attire appeared stuck in the eighties.

"Nina, glad to see you made it home." He offered a one-arm hug, and Nina chose to not reciprocate at first. She patted his back with a firm hand, and he let go. Good old Thomas never knew how to connect with his kids, so he stayed long hours at the office, where he probably fucked a secretary or two in his heyday.

Soon, her mother hustled into view. She appeared a Betty Crocker dream with her blonde hair pinned back and a plaid blue apron tied around her waist over a long-sleeve blouse. She lifted Nina's face with perfectly manicured French tips, clicking her tongue.

"You dressed up, good. Although, you could've done without the gloomy eyeliner. It makes you look like one of those freak show rock performers that Maxwell pretended to like for a while," she chided, and Nina considered the ethicality of burning the house down.

"You always know how to compliment a girl, Mother," said Nina.

Unlike their phone conversation, her sarcasm translated enough to draw ire from her mother. Then she shouldn't launch into her unwarranted opinions if she wasn't interested in people returning the same viciousness.

"Well, don't just stand there." Nina was pulled inside by her arms and heard the door shut behind her. Her mother's nails latched onto her wrist while her father lumbered to the dining room. "Since you showed up late, help me with the finishing touches. Everyone else is waiting."

"Everyone else?" asked Nina, knowing she should've prepared for unmentioned guests to conveniently pop up at dinner. Surprise ambushes always were the Byndel approach.

Her mother ignored her as she shoved a stack of her finest china into Nina's arms, gesturing to the forks, knives, and cloth napkins on the counter. "We need to handle the place settings. You can manage that, I'm sure."

"Yeah, I guess."

"Good. Hurry up and get ready."

Nina rolled her eyes when her mother turned her back and pulled something hot from the oven. The blustery rush of hot air caressed the back of Nina's neck, and she leaned against the counter to escape it. She focused on the silverware, and her hands moved quickly. Muscle memory retained the nightly ritual where she and Naomi would help with dinner while their father and brother sat around the television expectantly.

She set each bundle on an individual plate, but she barely set down the last one before she felt her mother's presence looming over her shoulder. For such a small-statured woman, she knew how to domineer over people.

"So, where's Brooklyn?" asked her mother, and Nina's eyes snapped toward the wall.

"Who?"

"Brooklyn."

"I've never heard of Brooklyn before." Nina knew that she might sound pedantic, but she didn't know a person named Brooklyn. Brooke wasn't short for Brooklyn. Not technically a lie in her book.

She bit on the inside of her cheek hard to avoid smiling when a disgusted scoff from her mother signaled a small win. Every inch of leverage counted.

"See, one of the ladies from the crochet club brought your sister's obituary when I asked for it. In there, it's mentioned that she's survived by you and someone named Brooklyn, yet it never specifies who Brooklyn is. I don't know who wrote that damn obituary, or I would demand answers."

Nina held her tongue because she had written the obituary and intentionally shielded Brooke's identity from nosy people. Her mother stumbled right into her trap.

"And you think I'd know?" Nina grabbed two plates, preparing to set them on the table and leave the conversation. However, her mother stepped in her path.

"I do. Tell me, is Brooklyn what she named her child? You know how your father and I felt about her keeping the pregnancy as a personal rebellion of our beliefs-"

"Then, why concern yourself with if she had the baby? Ever think about that?"

Nina watched how her mother chewed on that momentarily and grabbed the plates as intended. She tipped her head and allowed herself an eye roll for the downright self-centered characterization of the unexpected pregnancy of her sister, who had been happy to be a mother.

"Anything else you'd like to ask before we eat dinner?" Nina rolled her neck and stared at her mother, waiting for her to be ridiculous. She'd rather take the comments about her life than her mother dragging a dead woman's name through the mud more than she already did.

"Where's Zachary? We were hoping to see him tonight."

"He's working. You know how it is with finance guys and their jobs—they're married to them first and foremost."

"Well, I hope he comes next time. He's a good young man to settle down with, and you need a good man to provide."

Nina's jaw locked, and the annoyance palpitated in her chest louder than her heartbeat. Her mother met Zachary twice during their relationship. *Twice.* None of those times had been her choice, but what happened was out of her control.

"That's a shame he couldn't show up tonight," A new voice chimed in from the doorway, and Nina slowly turned her head to face Felicity, her brother's long-time girlfriend. Her strawberry blonde hair, fresh from a box paired with the most horrendous curtain bangs, almost blinded Nina in rage. "He should join the celebration."

"I didn't realize today was a celebratory dinner." Nina almost snapped. She used to think Felicity was friendly when she first met her. Then Felicity outed Naomi's pregnancy to the family before she got the chance to process it, resulting in her getting disowned. Since then, Nina had harbored a grudge like a raging bitch.

"Why wouldn't it be?"

"I think you know why."

"That's not what she meant, Neebs." Nina's eyes flicked to where Maxwell, the youngest but golden Byndel child, sauntered into the room with his hands tucked into his dark jeans and his dirty blond hair slicked flat on his square head. "She meant that she and I will take the rush to the altar off you and Zach's hands since . . . we're fiancé and fiancée now."

Felicity held up her hand to flash the sizable ring on her finger, and Nina heard her mother's overjoyed laughter from beside her. All she felt was her throat twitch. *Great . . . the last thing she wanted to hear.*

Nina grabbed the plates without a word and shoved past them with a more forceful than necessary shoulder check. She stacked the dishes in spots and hesitated when she saw Naomi's chair empty. She and Naomi sat together on their side of the table, and it used to be them against the world most nights, holding hands under the table while they ate.

Apparently, her staring caught the attention of everyone else at the table. Their hands clasped together for grace, but all eyes were on her. The rush began in her head as a low throbbing sensation but soon trickled through her ears and throat. She struggled to swallow or hear over the noise.

But she caught movement in her peripheral and saw her mother sit taller in her chair beside her father's at the head of the table. Felicity and Max filled the other side of the table, leaning in on their elbows.

"We were all discussing earlier your sister and how tragic the loss of any life is . . ." her mother prefaced, but Nina prepared for the rudest awakening in the next breath. Her mother knew no other way. "but we believe that there can be a blessing to come out of a tragedy like this."

"What are you talking about?" Nina considered herself more of a non-confrontational person, but Naomi had rubbed off on her. "Do you hear yourselves? Naomi died, and you can't even say her name. Yet you expect me, the only person who gave a damn, to find the silver lining in grief. What could possibly be your ingenious solution?"

Felicity dabbed at her lips. "The baby. I know that Naomi kept her pregnancy and carried it to term. She had a baby girl . . . I asked one of my friends to check her social media despite them being private."

Nina wanted to throw up right there, but she held firm. Her eyes jumped between the parties at the table, all equally guilty in the ambush. She bunched her hands full of fabric from her dress's skirt.

"We want what's best for that baby, and I see a way to save it from a life of sin. Felicity and Max discovered that they couldn't conceive, which seemed unfair. Since my granddaughter should know her family, we wanted to ask you to give up guardianship of the baby, so Max and Felicity may adopt her and raise her as their own."

Nina stood there, shell-shocked.

Max rose from his chair, holding Felicity's hand, and softened, "C'mon, you know the statistics say that a two-parent household is better for raising a child. You and Zach aren't married yet-"

"Neither are you and Felicity. What's your point?"

"It would be better for that girl to be with us where we can raise her right. Besides, Naomi would've wanted the best for her daughter if she was a good mother."

"Shut up. She was the best mother to that little girl until the day she died. You hadn't spoken to Naomi after your idiotic fiancée purposely outed her, and none of you wanted anything to do with her pregnancy when she lived." Nina roared louder than Max to shut him up.

He flinched a little.

"Nina, sit down. You need to act calmly," her father started, but she held her hand out to his face.

"No. I won't. Naomi knew something like this might happen and specified in her will that I would get guardianship of her daughter. She demanded that none of you be involved in her life after how you outcasted her because her boyfriend got her pregnant and dipped. I follow her wishes, not your pretend fantasy."

"Naomi—I mean Nina—" Her mother snapped, but silence blanketed the table awkwardly and swiftly. Nina hardened. She knew who they pretended she was, but that confirmed it for her.

Max stepped toward her. "This is in the child's best interest. If you continue to be stubborn, we have no choice but to pursue legal action for custody."

"Knock yourselves out," Nina scoffed, and she shouldered her purse higher since she never set it down. "I have a lawyer ready to go and will fight you every step of the way."

With such a statement, the gauntlet appeared thrown down. Nina stormed from the dining table and straight out the front door. She plunged into the night all flustered and marched toward her car, intending to leave that hellhole.

Behind her, the rush of footsteps slapped against the sidewalk until a pair of hands grasped her bicep hard. Nina whirled around and saw Felicity, who appeared on the verge of a tantrum too childish for her age.

"Nina, you need to be reasonable here! Give up the baby to me, please . . . I promise I'll take care of her. You can always have another baby if you want, but I deserve to have a baby. Don't be so selfish and not share!"

"Selfish?" Nina stared Felicity dead in the eyes. She felt unhinged at that moment. "No baby deserves a mother like you. You're not entitled to a baby."

Felicity's eyes welled up with tears, and the waterworks exploded belligerently. She wailed, sobbed, and beat her fists against her chest so loud it might disturb the neighborhood. At her cries, Max ran out from the doorway.

"What did you do to her?" he asked.

Nina bared her teeth in a smile. "Gave her a taste of her medicine. Now, fuck off and never speak to me again."

She stalked to her car with her middle finger held high for Max, Felicity, and their parents. They could outcast Naomi a million times over, but Nina would refuse a million times to give them the last piece of Naomi left in the world.

Chapter Seven
Cole

September slipped through Cole's hands, and he hadn't realized he made it halfway through the month until that morning. A glimpse at the calendar on his phone sidelined him hard. *Where had the time gone?*

The fall and winter seasons proved busiest for the office since the holidays made people turn their sights to the future. People got disowned from wills and inheritances. Others came into good fortunes after the passing of loved ones. The only people who worked as much as he did these days were probably doctors during flu season and insurance companies preparing for the misfortunes in the winter season.

During his drive out of the city, he stared at the orange-and-red-lined trees and rolled the windows down to embrace the chilly weather. Cloudy, overcast skies promised rain with wind, but Cole didn't mind a change in the weather. He left the congested heart of the city for the suburbs—returning home.

Cole rolled up to the half-empty driveway attached to his childhood home and parked in the spot belonging to his dad. When he got a call from his mom last night, she explained that his dad needed to head out of town on some business and couldn't help with heavy moving around the house.

Hence, he made the drive from the city to home. What kind of loving son would he be if he let his mom potentially injure herself throwing around heavy furniture?

Cole exited his car and brushed off the oversized t-shirt he grabbed from his closet, picking something casual he didn't mind getting dirty. The same went for the baggy sweats he uncovered from an otherwise untouched drawer.

He headed for the door but got as far as the front lawn before the front door swung open, revealing his mom. She ditched her usual style for a pair of grungy, paint-covered overalls, and her hair piled into a bun. She removed all her fancy jewelry beyond her wedding ring on a chain around her neck.

"You're earlier than I was expecting! Come in, my love," His mom beamed, and Cole hustled up the stairs to pull her into a hug. He laughed when he lifted her off the ground and felt her legs kick in the air. "Goodness, I've forgotten how strong you are."

"I've been lifting hardcore again." Eventually, Cole set his mom back on her feet and locked up his car before he headed inside. He put his keys in the bowl beside the door and turned to her.

"You can head upstairs. I have the paint all set up to the side and will be there in a few moments to help move the bookcases. Your dad helped with the rest yesterday, but we started late."

"Yes, ma'am."

He bounded up the stairs without another word and walked down the hallway, spotting the door to his dad's home office cracked open by a closed can of paint. Cole stepped inside and noted the plastic tarp tossed over the floor and taped to the white baseboard.

To the side, a couple of containers for paint and rollers waited to be used. Beyond the bookshelves, towering to the ceiling, the room appeared completely cleared for the new paint job. Yet, even without the furniture, nostalgia hit Cole in the chest.

For years, Cole and Dean knew they wanted to follow in their dad's footsteps as an attorney. They never hid their ambitions, so their dad allowed them to hang out in the office while he worked.

Cole remembered how he would sit in one of the corners with a book from school, and Dean sat next to him, back against the wall, while he texted people on his phone. Their dad would sit at his desk with reading glasses perched on his nose and a pen tucked along the shell of his ear while he read over cases.

Yet, that never stopped them from asking many different questions about the cases he worked on. He'd answer them with a knowing smile and raise a brow but still kept things confidential. No one came close to his dad.

Years later, he and Dean managed to honor those hours spent in the office with their careers. The Yearwood name held so much power in the city, and such a currency might lead to a big head. Cole tried to stay grounded in the opportunities he was given.

Footsteps creaked up the stairs, and his mom came into view, smiling brightly. "Ready to move the books?"

"Sure am," Cole hustled to one side of the bookcase and watched his mom grab the other. "On the count of three?"

"One-"

"Two-"

"Three!" Cole lifted up and handled most of the heavy lifting of the bookshelf. He faced the door and kept an eye on the top of the door frame. "We should be able to step through the door without hitting the top, but maybe move slightly lower."

His mom gave a breathless laugh, but she followed his instructions. The slight dip left enough room between the top of the bookshelf and the white doorframe to avoid collisions or scrapes. The two settled the first bookshelf in the middle of the hallway with the other furniture like his dad's desk chair, the various knickknacks, and his mug collection.

"One more to go, thank you." His mom stepped up to him and pinched his cheek affectionately. Cole swatted her hand away and crinkled his nose hard. *Oh, come on, Mom!*

"You know I'd do anything for you, even helping out with one of your many home improvement projects," said Cole.

Every mom he knew had a thing—something they enjoyed doing with their free time. Some moms loved brunch, gardening, crocheting, shopping, or baking. Others loved traveling and trips, education, volunteer opportunities, or reading. His mom's thing was home improvement projects. Nothing made her happier than breaking out tools and upgrading their home.

She built the deck in the backyard by herself, including the porch swing, and repaired the fences after Dean accidentally ran them over when he first started driving. She redid the kitchen more than once and designed the guest bedroom with all-new wallpaper and carpet flooring.

Cole wished he had half the repair skills his mom did.

The two headed back into the study and lifted the other bookshelf like they had the first one. Luckily, they again avoided scratches on the doorframe and deposited the second shelf next to the first.

"Now, some paint? What color did you get again?"

"I forgot the name, but it's a stormy blue color, like a mix of blue and gray. Your dad requested this shade for the office since it's muted but a nice change of pace from the white walls. I offered to paint it as my anniversary gift to your dad."

Cole couldn't help how he cooed. His parents raised the bar impossibly high for him and Dean to follow in their relationships. Yet, he appreciated the standard being set so high. He would work to find someone great.

He observed how his mom swapped the paint can propping the door up for two heavy books and cracked it open with the ease one might pop open a cold beer. Paint leaked into the tray in a stormy blue color, as his mom aptly described, and he waited for her to coat two of the roller brushes in the paint.

She handed him one. "Here you go! I'll take the left wall if you get the right?"

"Sounds like a deal." Cole accepted his task and approached the wall, ready to smear paint onto its blank canvas. "You made sure to add tape to cover the edges at the top, right? Unless you want the ceiling painted blue, too."

"I want the ceiling blue, too. I prefer it uniform."

"You're the boss."

Cole heard his mom laugh somewhere behind him and he grinned to himself, lower lip tugged underneath his teeth to stall any laughter of his own. Hearing his mom laugh was one thing but knowing that he caused it boosted him slightly. Family meant the world to him.

"So, do you already know what Dad planned for his anniversary gift?" asked Cole as he laid the first streak of blue paint against the wall. The roll satisfied him with a perfect stroke, so he chanced for another one.

"Oh, your dad is an excellent secret keeper. I do know, however, that he enlisted the help of January with his. I've tried to bribe answers from her, but that girl knows how to keep a secret. Not even Dean can get her to break!"

"Hah, I'm sure he's not happy about that. He hates being left out of the loop . . . drama queen."

"Be nice to your brother."

"He's not even here!" Cole gasped. He almost smeared a wobbly streak across the wall when his hand slapped against his chest in mock offense. "You would take his side over mine?"

"Moms should never take sides . . . but you know I love you both," his mom assured, and they glanced at one another over their shoulders. A few lines of blue paint on each white wall showed their slow progress, but they had the day to work.

Cole chewed on those words when his mom cracked open the window to let a rush of fresh air in. The fumes would mess with him if he lingered too long without release.

She loved them both . . . even though he hadn't caught up with his brother? Cole paused when the little voice piped up with its unwarranted opinion. He focused on the wall needing paint and rolled a few streaks to cover the white spackle, already primed for color.

His silence clashed with the gentle humming from his mom on the other side of the room, dancing to an unknown tune on the verge of vague familiarity. Cole knew she meant well, but the nagging feeling of his inadequacy resented his avoidance.

Sighing, Cole put the brush into the paint container and stepped away from the wall. "Mom, I need to ask you something. Be honest with me, okay?"

"Of course. What's on your mind?"

"Are you disappointed that I haven't settled down yet? I moved into a new apartment, an upgrade from the shoe box I used to live in. But Dean and Jan have their lives full speed ahead, and all I have is a lack of progress."

"What? No!" His mom dropped her brush abruptly mid-stroke. "Why would I ever be disappointed because of that?"

"I don't know." Cole shrugged.

His mom walked away from her wall and the paint container she had burned halfway through. Her hands cupped his face between her hands, squishing his cheeks lightly. She made Cole look at her. "You can always tell me how you're feeling. You might be all grown up, but I'm still your mom."

"I've been thinking a lot these days. New lifestyle changes have opened my eyes a little bit."

"All I've ever wanted is for you to be happy. Same for your dad . . . and we thought the same about Dean not that long ago."

Cole nodded. "Has that changed at all?" He caught onto the past tense in her statement, keen to untangle the external expectations from those all his own.

"I know I used to be harder on you and Dean about settling down with someone, but seeing Dean with January changed my mind. My approach wasn't working, and it made me see that you two can handle yourself fine without my interference. You are intelligent, confident young men with plenty to offer a partner."

Cole stayed quiet, but he said, "Thanks, Mom."

"Are you ready to tell me what brought this on?"

"It's nothing. I'm the last man standing, so to speak. You have Dad, and Dean has January with so many exciting things in your lives. I've got my work and some potential dates, but I haven't found much luck. I want to feel like I'm not falling behind or letting anyone down."

His mom frowned, "Cole. I never realized this weighed on you so much. You're always bantering and treating the situation lightly, so I assumed you meant everything in good fun."

She sounded hurt. Guilt ached in his throat like a secondary heartbeat, and the light thump dragged him toward the verge of tears whenever he breathed. He should talk about those things more, but sometimes the words refused to come easily. How should he explain that being the second son slightly envious of his older brother's successful turnaround bred its own type of inferiority complex?

Instead, he said, "I don't blame you, but those jokes don't mean I'm not hurt or upset with myself."

Although he cast his eyes down at the tarp-covered floor, his mom's thumb caressed the length of his cheek until he decided to look her in the eye again. Softened eyes and a quiet frown greeted his bravery.

"Thank you for being honest with me. I haven't told you enough, but I'm proud of you. Your dad and brother are, too. So, if not having a partner bothers you, I promise we won't bring it up anymore."

"Thank you."

"Of course. Besides, there's a chance you've already met the young lady that you'll make your forever person. Your dad and I didn't start dating immediately and were friends first," his mom murmured.

Cole pulled her into a close hug and rested his chin atop her head. His mom's arms looped around his waist as the two swayed from side to side. No one gave hugs quite like his mom.

Behind his closed eyes, he tried to imagine what his dream woman might look like. He couldn't quite pick one idea or feature from his imagination—not the color of her hair or her smile—but that wasn't what mattered.

He knew how she would make him feel. She would make him into a fool, full of jokes and laughter, who would do anything to elicit a smile from her. He would wake up to her soft snores and breaths while their limbs tangled around one another recklessly. He could feel at ease with her after a long day. But, most importantly, she would remind him that he was good enough to stand behind.

Cole's blissful thoughts screeched to a halt when something cold smeared against his cheek, and his eyes snapped open. "Mom, what was that?"

"Nothing," his mom tried to sound innocent, but the sensation against his skin reeked of paint. Then, he noticed the paintbrush sneakily grabbed in her hand, dripping with the paint meant to be on the walls.

Cole snatched the paintbrush from her hand, and he watched his mom scurry away from his reach. He howled with laughter and chased after her to exact his revenge. Time with his mom never hit a dull moment.

Chapter Eight
Nina

A pop of blue among a sea of neutrals, Nina stared at the shifting faces belonging to the employees of *Sunkissed Magazine.* Every monthly magazine release earned a small soiree for the writers, editors, and designers who worked on *Sunkissed's* newest edition.

Since Nina guest wrote several articles for *Sunkissed* in her career, she knew the head editor, Teagan, quite well. Every time she contributed, Teagan invited her to kick it with the rest of the crew.

But Nina, more of an introvert than the social butterfly type, accepted the invitations with a grain of hesitance. She tried to put herself out there and sometimes rubbed elbows in shallow conversations with strangers.

From her corner, Nina observed the conversation between colleagues in the rented-out restaurant. With an open bar and a catered buffet, people ate, drank, and made conversation. She noticed Teagan float through the room, draped in taupe and cream. Her dark curls bounced when she spun around to the applause of her staff.

Nina lifted the Manhattan she ordered from the bar to her lips and sipped away in her reserved corner. She was merely a guest of Teagan's generosity or her interest in retaining Nina to clean up her potential publication disasters.

A smattering of applause diverted her attention away from Teagen until she spotted the buffet table with an assortment of gourmet desserts. The kind that would break Nina's bank for a single spoonful.

People flocked to the table with their plus ones on their arms, and Nina stayed on the sidelines. She wasn't an employee of *Sunkissed* and was the only person at the party without a date to accompany her. If things were different, she would've applied for a steady position at the company. She also would have a fiancé who could make good small talk and knew the fancy names of the desserts on the table or what fancy cocktails to order to seem more sophisticated.

Come on, girl, her inner monologue emerged from the silence. *Hanging around them never made the hoity-toity types likable, and dating Zach never changed that. Stop throwing a pity party over a man unwilling to fight for his future wife.*

Her chest burned with embarrassment. There she was, at a party she had no interest in being at, reminiscing about her crummy ex like she could undo reality with the power of wishful thinking. *Try not to be delusional.*

Nina leaned into the corner with her back lined against the wall and nursed her Manhattan close to her chest. Hair began to slip loose from the lazy updo she pulled together before rushing to the restaurant, and thus started the urge to slide out the back door with the last drop of liquor on her tongue and a few desserts smuggled in her purse while no one noticed.

So, Nina downed her Manhattan in a few sips and laid the empty glass on a table with other drinks left partially unattended. She carefully moved through the crowd so as not to bump into anyone and draw attention to herself.

She snatched up two plastic boxes with what appeared to be a salted caramel brownie and a lemon cheesecake shot to take home with her. Brooke liked brownies, and Nina found herself partial to cheesecake and lemons. Win-win for everyone involved.

As conspicuously as possible, Nina crammed the boxes into her oversized purse and cringed at the crinkle of the plastic boxes. However, she was smart enough to carry herself confidently, knowing that someone appearing unbothered would draw less attention to her departure than a hypervigilant, nervous wreck.

Nina pushed through the side door and directly into the alleyway behind the restaurant, close to the bathrooms. She stepped around two restaurant employees sharing a smoke where the small burst of orange from the end of the cigarette illuminated their features from the dark.

A shiver pressed along her spine while she walked onto the main street from the alleyway, not keen on lingering. But she gasped a few greedy breaths of the fresh fall air; the cusp of October would dawn on the city within a few days.

Once in the view of streetlamps, Nina checked for the time. *Seven-forty-five.* Late but not quite time to relieve Penelope of babysitting duty. She offered to come to Nina's and spend time with Brooke there, who had been ecstatic to see Penelope again. Penelope was the closest person to a grandma for Brooke, and Nina refused to get in the way of their bond.

She needed a village until she got on her feet with the guardianship thing, however long that would take.

Nina grasped the purse she brought a little tighter once she slid her phone away, content to stand in the nighttime. Fresh air cleared her jumbled thoughts, and the urge to order another drink so she could forget left with clarity on its heels.

She stared around the crowded commercial area with businesses open to the public and plenty of people enjoying the evening. Conversations floated out from open doors and tables loaded on the patios of some buildings. The air thrummed with the welcoming atmosphere, filled with laughter and the twinkle of movement.

If Nina wanted to go home early, she'd need to walk a short distance to the shared parking lot. She could've parked closer to the restaurant, especially since she wore a pair of slingback pumps, but the parking lot had free parking after six P.M. Otherwise, the metered spots still required payment for every thirty minutes spent.

Nina wrapped her arms around herself as she walked, slightly wishing she had brought her knit cardigan for extra insulation. She passed a few buildings—a restaurant, a pottery studio, a flower shop—before her pace slowed in front of a bar.

A chalkboard propped outside the door with bright neon colors and doodles drawn on the dark surface caught her attention. The board read *Single Mingle Speed Dating*.

Her eyes drifted through the open door and at the different "singles" in semi-formal attire, wanting to look their best on the hunt for potential partners. Nina stepped a little closer, a few paces, and watched the interactions of shaking hands, hugs, and even the swapping of drinks.

Nina's interest jumped when a loud buzzer echoed from inside the bar, and people scattered into new pairs without a pattern from Nina's perspective. However, her presence on the outskirts managed to snag some attention.

Soon, a woman gripping a clipboard with manicured nails appeared in the doorway, and her eyes landed on Nina. She strode down the steps, and the next thing Nina knew, the woman towered over her.

"There you are," she remarked coldly and glanced at her watch. "You're forty-five minutes behind schedule, but better late than never, I suppose. Head inside, and I'll give you the name tag we reserved for you."

Nina should've interjected and told the woman she had been passing by on her way to the parking lot and wasn't the person she was waiting for. However, her tongue stopped working as the woman forcibly ushered her inside and handed her a sticky name tag.

She exhaled exasperatedly, "Well, put it on. You'll have to wait until the next buzzer to find a partner. You should be able to get at least three rounds in, so pick wisely. Good luck, Iris."

Again, Nina should've handed the name tag back and explained that she was a random passerby on the street. Yet, she slapped the name tag onto her chest and scurried away with a nod.

She vanished into the crowd to dodge the judgmental gaze of the organizer, and within a moment, she ended up on another side of the room. She found the nearest chair and took it, wanting to rest her feet and observe the crowd. She planned to head out during the scramble for new partners and head home, exhausted from enough social interaction for the day.

She planted her roots and relaxed into a wallflower state, content to focus on everyone else and the senses working in overdrive to take it all in. Sure, Nina noticed a few interested eyes from some guys who already had dates. She refused to engage despite a fleeting moment of eye contact.

However, when the crowd shifted a little, Nina's line of sight found a new and delightfully unexpected target. Cole Yearwood.

Although his tan coat treaded on the more subtle side, Cole radiated vibrant energy from how several women in his vicinity eyed him like their last meal. Perhaps unbeknownst to their eyes, Cole nursed a chilled soda and nodded at his current partner. The peppy redhead appeared to be chattering a mile a minute and gesturing with her hands, eliciting a flash of a smile from Cole.

Nina focused on their interactions, too curious to pull her eyes away and be polite. Cole interjected a word or two but appeared to take on a more passive role and listened. He kept eye contact and leaned on the tall table with an elbow, chin tucked into the palm of his hand.

As she observed, she lost track of time until the loud buzzer sounded off, and the conversations halted accordingly. Beyond a few good-byes and exchanging numbers between hurried hands, people moved on to the next match.

Nina fumbled for her purse, and with it, her exit plan commenced. However, she stumbled onto her feet and glanced toward Cole one last time, only to find him staring at her. No doubt about it, she was noticed.

Cole stepped through the people in the crowd, moving toward her. Nina half expected either another guy to intercept or one of the girls eyeing Cole before jumping over and grabbing him. But he approached her undaunted.

"Hello, stranger," said Nina. She offered a shy smile to the man who continued to crop up in the most unexpected places. "One time is a coincidence. Two times is suspicious. But three times, and I think the universe wants us to be friends."

Cole laughed and raked back his hair with a smooth push of his hands, giving Nina a perfect view of his eyes. She couldn't ignore the amusement and how flecks of green pulled from the warm hazel whenever he appeared on the verge of laughter.

"So, Iris? Care to elaborate on the name change?"

"Uh, would you believe me if I said that the organizer mistook me, standing outside the bar and watching curiously, as a late speed dater?"

"Surprisingly, I would. That sounds too outlandish to be made up on the spot. So, either that's the truth, or you're the best liar with an even better imagination and poker face than most people I know," Cole remarked.

Nina saw the wiggle of his brows, and trying not to laugh, she focused on fixing her dress. "Wherever Iris is, I hope she's doing alright . . . but that'll be the last time I borrow someone's identity."

"I thank Iris for her service." Cole looked into her eyes, but not before he gave the slickest once-over of her outfit. "So, before the mistaken identity, what brought you to the area?"

"Work, technically. I was invited to a dinner party for *Sunkissed Magazine*."

"I feel like I've heard of that one before. It's giving me this sense of déjà vu, you know?"

"Oh, I do. *Sunkissed* has been one of the biggest fashion magazines since the early nineties, and it's got a hold on the market space. They write primarily on fashion, makeup, and travel. It's for the material woman," Nina explained.

"Oh, that makes sense. I've probably seen it at the grocery store or on a newsstand while on the way to work. I didn't realize you were a writer for the company?" Cole sipped his drink and gestured to her, a question in his eyes.

Nina realized he had offered to grab her a drink but shook her head. She needed to drive home, and one Manhattan seemed enough. Getting behind the wheel worried her still after Naomi.

She shouldered her purse a little higher. "I'm a guest writer, actually. I freelance and take on several gigs at one time for the best flow of cash. I prefer the flexibility offered by being my own boss."

"That's awesome. You clearly have the skills to sustain yourself long-term, so more power to you. How's Brooke doing?"

"She's hanging in there. Some days are easier than others . . . but enough about us. I'm wondering about you."

"Oh?" Cole's voice twitched into a higher octave, betraying any semblance of nonchalance. He almost squeaked when Nina flipped the tables on him, and smiling became impossible to avoid.

"See, I have an excuse to be here. But what are you doing here? I never expected you to be at a speed dating night in some trendy bar." At the first inklings of an ache in her feet, Nina leaned on the nearby table to alleviate the pressure.

Cole's face pinkened from the tips of his ears to his neck, teasing Nina with a glimpse of a shy side to Mr. Yearwood. "About that . . . you're going to make fun of me."

"I wouldn't dare!"

"You promise?"

"I promise. So, spill."

Cole glanced around like he expected someone to listen and leaned closer to her, "My older brother, Dean, signed me up without my knowledge. His fiancée, January, told him that he shouldn't do it. Older siblings never listen, so I was dragged here and dropped off without a ride."

Nina burst into giggles and clapped a hand over her mouth. Her side quivered when she attempted to hold in her laughter, but Cole covered his face behind his hands with embarrassment.

"That is such a big brother move. I'm the middle child of my family, and Naomi would maybe pull something like that. She had a mischief streak when we were in our teens, a little rebellious," said Nina.

"God, she sounded like my brother," Cole's laugh came a little quieter, a little more breathless than hers, but he seemed to be taking it like a good sport. "Dean was the heartthrob when we went to school together while I could barely talk to a girl. Being the debate club president wasn't attractive to the ladies."

"You did debate club? I always wanted to do it, but I had prior commitments to a sport that conflicted with practice times."

"What sport, if you don't mind me asking?"

"I don't mind at all. I took ballet for years but didn't want to pursue it as a career, so I switched to my school's varsity dance team."

Cole's eyes lit up. "Dance? Now that you mention it, I see it. You carry yourself like a dancer, especially with how you walk. You move with elegance."

"Thank you. I've never heard that one before . . . but I'll take it as a compliment." Nina could've sworn Cole's lips twitched up at the corners with an unspoken *it was* conveyed through the subtlest of moves.

"Have I foiled your escape enough, or can you spare a little time?" he asked, and Nina reached for the chair she used while studying the crowd.

"I don't have anywhere to be if you don't." She sat, and Cole mirrored her by finding an unoccupied chair to drag to her table. "Is this the part where we exchange cheesy, first-date icebreakers until the buzzer sounds?"

"I thought we were already doing that, but you tell me?" Cole replied, chewing on the thin black straw of his drink. A flash of his canines made Nina sit taller in her seat.

"Alright, you mentioned debate. Is that what drove you to become an attorney?"

"No, it was more like a logical step in the sequence. I knew I wanted to be an attorney since I was a kid. My dad's an attorney. So are my brother and his fiancée. I joined the debate club to practice my skills and get scholarship offers.

"Did you?" Nina asked.

"I did. A hefty sum to a good undergraduate school got me a double major in economics and history and a minor in linguistics. Then, I headed straight into law school on the heels of Dean's graduation." Cole set his empty drink on the table and laced his hands.

Nina's lips parted open from shock. Of course, she expected Cole to be intelligent for passing law school and the bar. Yet, she hadn't been prepared to learn of his extensive education. She almost wilted because her bachelor's in journalism felt underwhelming next to the stature of his degree collection.

Cole's head cocked to the side with an air of innocence, and she cleared her throat, "I'm impressed. You impress me."

"Consider it mutual?"

"I'm not anything to write home about-"

Cole shook his head, and Nina's voice faded, wanting to hear him speak, "That's not true. You have an established career as a freelance writer with the kind of flexibility people dream about from their nine-to-five office cubicles. Not to mention, you're brave."

Then, it was Nina's turn to flush as warmth slithered up the back of her neck. "You think so?" She probably sounded surprised, but who wouldn't be?

"I do."

Nina forced herself to keep eye contact with Cole and not skitter away, even as the heat pressed under her collar. When did the room heat up?

Cole leaned a little forward to rest on his arms atop the table. "Let me ask you . . . Why did you leave the magazine party? Was it boring?"

"Honestly, yes. I'm not one for huge social gatherings, especially those filled with strangers. I've guest-written for that magazine dozens of times and gone to similar wrap parties for each edition I worked on, yet I haven't made any friends. Part of me didn't want to go, but I needed an excuse to wear this dress somewhere."

When she mentioned it, Nina noticed Cole's eyes dropped on her dress, and he appeared to soak in the details. She chose something classy but with a touch of unexpected in the one long-sleeve and the over-the-shoulder sleeve in a soft baby's blue. The silhouette clung to her frame straightly and capped at her calves.

"I noticed this part and the asymmetry first, but I like the dress." Cole traced the shape of the dress's top through the air, and Nina pretended to take a bow. Maybe she had the chops to be a fashionista after all.

"Writing for a fashion magazine has started to rub off on me, it seems."

"I should probably grab one for more tips . . . you've got to be kidding me."

"Is something wrong?" Worry sobered Nina up from her good time, and noticed Cole's face scrunch into a half-scowl.

"Dean's come to check on me and ensure I'm playing along. He and January are outside if you want to look over your shoulder." Cole groaned. He grabbed the straw from his empty glass, fiddling with it between his fingers like he might do with a pen.

Nina glanced over her shoulder and spotted two people peering into the bar. A gorgeous woman sporting killer curves in a body-con dress and glimmering sapphires in her ears and around her neck brushed back her dark hair while her male companion grinned. The man had a neatly trimmed beard and loomed in the doorway in a turtleneck over jeans.

She met their eyes and took in their expressions. The woman she assumed to be January waved politely, and the man, Dean, flashed an eager thumbs up. He appeared seconds away from bouncing on his heels and breaking into laughter.

Nina watched them turn and hustle down the street as quickly as they came but checked on Cole. His hands covered his face, and he whispered, "Did they leave yet?"

"They're gone," Nina assured him, and Cole lowered his hands from his face. Nina understood the younger sibling's plight a little too well and reached out to rub his shoulder. But her hand retracted when the buzzer went off overhead. "That should be my cue to leave."

"Want me to escort you to your car? I think I've had my fill of speed dating for the night." Cole offered, and Nina, although curious, held back. Instead, she grabbed her purse and stood up.

"I'd love that."

"Great."

Cole offered his arm, and she slid her hand into the nook. They waltzed past the organizer, who appeared pleased at the sight of a match made. Oh, how wrong she would be.

Nina and Cole spilled onto the sidewalk, heading toward the parking lot where she parked her car. She shivered when the evening air kissed her bare skin, so much that Cole leaned over.

"I've got a long sleeve under this. Did you want to borrow my coat?"

Despite the chatter of her teeth, Nina shook her head, "I'll be okay. My car isn't far from here, and I have seat warmers."

"The greatest invention to man, right?" Cole laughed, and Nina followed his lead. Seat warmers did bring use to her life; she couldn't deny that. But beyond that, silence comfortably surrounded her and Cole alongside the September air.

Eventually, her car came into view, and Nina unlocked it once they were close enough. Cole hung back as she opened the door and slid into the driver's side, becoming a pattern for them.

"Before you go," Cole reached into his coat pocket and produced something small and square. He offered it to her, and Nina realized it was a business card when she took it from his hands. "Since we keep meeting like this, we might as well be friends."

"I agree. I'll text you with my number later?" Nina smiled at the card before sliding it into her purse in the passenger seat.

"Sounds like a plan. Have a good night, Nina. Drive safe."

"Good night, Cole. I'm glad I ran into you."

"So am I." The two stared at one another. Nina expected to turn on the engine and head home for Brooke, but she glanced at her passenger seat. She hesitated as she turned the ignition, and the car roared to life.

Cole stepped back from her car, but Nina leaned out the window as soon as she closed her door. "Didn't you say your brother and January were your ride home? Want to hitch a ride with me instead? I'll drop you off."

Cole's brows raised, but he settled on a soft grin, "You know what? I'd appreciate that," he said, and Nina tipped her head toward her passenger side.

"Get in."

Chapter Nine
Cole

The shift from September to October proved busy enough for Cole to use as a shield, hiding from Dean. Since the speed dating night and seeing Nina, Dean spent the last week bombarding Cole with prodding texts about his mystery woman.

Cole took every chance to avoid answering questions about Nina or providing his brother with any information to tease him with.

Speaking of Nina, the two exchanged maybe five texts after she dropped him off at his apartment. They swapped numbers while they sat in the car outside, listening to the song on the radio dialed down to mute. But Cole expected she was busy with Brooke.

Cole shifted on his heels while waiting for the court clerk and tucked the manilla folder with his papers deeper under his arm. Even inside the courthouse that afternoon, the coldness seeped through his woolen coat and sweater to prickle along his skin. He tightened his coat by fiddling with the buttons lined down the lapels.

Around him, people seemed wrapped up in their little bubbles, and he ventured back into his. He checked his phone to pass the time and spotted a message from January. He almost avoided it, convinced Dean might steal Jan's phone to pry. But his brother knew better if he valued sharing the bed with his fiancée.

Cole clicked it open, and it appeared harmless, much to his relief.

JAN: Hey! I hope you enjoyed the lasagna from the other night. We couldn't fit all of it into our fridge, and I know you've been working late the last few days. Wanted to make it easy on you :))

Cole softened because January somehow managed to be the sweetest person he'd ever known. The same woman allegedly terrorized his brother for years before they fell in love, but he assumed Dean played a large part in his misery. To him, January deserved her flowers for putting up with his goofy older brother and all his antics.

She made him stupidly, obnoxiously happy. Cole couldn't deny how those two were well-suited for one another or how excited he would be when the two finally married.

COLE: I did. I appreciate you two thinking of me. I've been a tad overwhelmed with life.

JAN: You're welcome to come over whenever you want, have dinner with us, and even stay the night. Socks misses you, too.

COLE: I miss him and his little boots more than Dean, that's for sure.

JAN: That'll stay between you and me.

COLE: Good. I don't need another reason for him to spam me with texts. I like not answering questions about what you two witnessed at speed dating.

JAN: I can protect you until the next family dinner. I suspect that Dean will recruit your mom to pull information out of you, so there's not much I can do there.

COLE: Yikes. Thanks for the heads up.

Cole groaned as he stepped up to the next open window at the clerk's office. Behind the glass, he watched red envelop the face of one of the clerks. Dani struggled to pull off her pastel blue, horned glasses and fluff out her vibrant copper curls from a sensible ponytail, trying to appear seamless.

"Hi, Cole!" She leaned on the counter with her chin tucked over her folded hands. "How can I help you today?"

Dani couldn't have been older than twenty, which showed in the youthful glow around her cheeks. But, more noticeably, she tended to break out into a stammer and avoided eye contact whenever he came to her window. The crush was obvious after Dean pointed it out to him.

He wouldn't confront her about it since it was harmless at the end of the day. Cole was significantly older than Dani, so there was no chance of anything coming of it from him. But he refused to embarrass her since it didn't interfere with her work or his filings.

Everyone had an embarrassing crush at least once in their life. Cole counted three in his, so he understood.

He tipped his head, "Good to see you, Dani. I need to record some client documents and already have the signed authorization on file."

"Alright! Show me the documents, and I'll set that up for you." Dani scrambled to clear her desk and nearly knocked the microphone stand onto the floor. Her face deepened in red, and Cole waited for her to collect herself before he pulled any documents from the envelope.

He laid the deed and other asset paperwork for one of his client's living trusts onto the counter, sliding them through the thin slot in the window. Dani accepted them from his hand and skimmed through them, although her hands trembled lightly as she did.

"Everything alright?" asked Cole.

"Yeah! Totally! I drank too much coffee this morning. I should probably cut back."

"Understandable. Coffee makes life more bearable."

"Right! Especially with early work hours and late evenings. But you probably have more of those than I do. I'm just in undergrad."

Cole nodded and set down the manilla envelope, prepared to be there for a while. His eyes wandered when he glanced over his shoulder, not expecting to find anything interesting in the movement behind him.

However, he stilled when he spotted none other than Nina in the hallway. She appeared turned away, but he caught the unmistakable sight of her profile. She wore a dark suit—billowy black pants and a dark blazer layered over a white dress shirt—and tied her hair back into a sensible bun. She appeared court-ready, somber, and prepared for anything.

Beside her, Rudy pulled out his cell phone and showed the screen to her. Nina nodded, and Cole noticed the slight twitch of her jaw when she accepted his cell phone. She handed it back just as quickly.

Cole's eyes followed them up the escalator and their slow walk down the long hallway on the second floor. They eventually settled on a bench outside one of the courtrooms, and Nina downright slumped to seated. She scrunched into herself, forcing Cole to turn back to Dani.

She hadn't finished his documents, but he felt awkward staring at Nina from a distance. If she caught him staring, he'd probably weird her out. *He hadn't known that she planned to come downtown today, let alone stop by the courthouse . . . not that it was any of his business.*

Dani glanced up from the paperwork and looked anywhere but his eyes when she noticed him looking at her.

"Everything okay?

"Yes, I'll need you to add some signatures and fill out any boxes for exemptions to waive the fee. Let me grab those."

Cole sighed, "Great. Thanks, Dani."

"Of course," her voice squeaked out with a smidge of confidence. "Um, did you have a good weekend?"

"I did. I was supposed to hang out with my brother and his fiancée, but the weather ended up storming too hard to drive. So, I spent the time with Netflix and binged a couple of shows I'd meant to watch for a while." Cole checked over his shoulder for Nina and spotted her, still accompanied by Rudy.

He turned back to Dani, who held a stack of blank papers in hand and accepted them when she slid them through the open slot.

"I'm going to need your signature on the lines marked on each page and to fill out the check boxes for any necessary exemptions or disclosures," said Dani.

"Sure thing," Cole cleared his throat. He accepted a blue ballpoint pen from Dani's eager hand. He started down the forms, marking all the necessary spaces and adding his signatures to the paperwork. "I hope you had a good weekend, too."

"Oh! I got out of town before the bad weather, so a few of my sorority sisters and I went up the coast on a road trip in this cute RV!" Dani verbally bolted into a story about how the girls got trapped in a mud pit and had to manually push the vehicle free. Cole was sure that the story was probably funny.

Yet, he couldn't help himself from sneaking another glance toward Nina. He first noticed Rudy's missing presence as Nina sat alone on the bench, arms crossed over her chest. Even from a distance, the shaky bounce of her knee told him that something bothered her.

Nina started to fidget, further proving to Cole that something remained amiss. He focused on his paperwork once more but moved faster than before. Nina wasn't one of his cases, but nothing in any professionalism handbook said anything against checking on a friend.

Nina believed the universe wanted them to be friends, and he agreed. So, they were friends.

His handwriting became a little less perfect in his haste, yet still looked plenty legible. Even with his concerns, he couldn't do a shitty job on his cases.

Dani went silent after a moment, and Cole might feel guilty about tuning out her enthralling story about her weekend road trip later. Right then, he fought against the urge to bolt for the escalator. Call it intuition, but he never allowed anything to keep him from trusting his gut.

"Is this everything for the paperwork?" Cole asked, and he tried to curb the audible impatience in his tone. He slid the finished paperwork through the slot and watched Dani comb through them. While he appreciated her thoroughness, she could speed it up a little.

"Almost. I have to fax these into the system, and then you'll be ready."

"Alright."

"Thanks." Dani neatly stacked all the papers and loaded them into a scanner. Cole counted each as they appeared on the screen to the impatient humming on his tongue.

He chanced another glance toward Nina. However, she wasn't alone like the last time he looked over. Instead, four people stood over her while she remained seated, and Cole didn't need to see their faces to understand. *Danger.*

Nina's face lost color while she scooted until her back hit the wall, leaving her nowhere else to go. Her eyes dropped to her lap when one of the women got in her personal space, and that was enough.

Cole whirled around and grabbed the manilla envelope off the counter when the final paper scanned through on the screen. He hurriedly slid the originals into the folder, "Is that everything?"

"Yes, I think so-"

"Thanks. Have a good day."

"You too . . ." Dani stammered nervously, but Cole sped toward the escalators. He dodged around slow walkers and wedged through uncomfortably close spaces in his beeline for the escalator, earning a few grumbles. Usually, he'd be over-apologetic, but the rush in his ears drove him forward.

He climbed the escalator's steps to the second floor, not content to ride leisurely. People going down on the opposite side tossed him a few stares, but Cole brushed them off.

At the last step, he marched down the long hallway in the same path Nina and Rudy walked earlier. He spotted her ahead with those people still surrounding her. *Suffocating her.*

Cole didn't think. He moved. His brisk pace pushed him ahead of any remaining walkers, and he stepped forward, breaking through the circle around Nina. He heard a few gasps and a man raising his voice, but he hugged Nina.

Nina's breath caught, yet her arms locked around his waist like she refused to let him go. He paid close enough attention to the slight tremble in her shoulders, preceded by a shaky, tear-filled exhale.

"I'm going to keep my voice low so they can't hear us," he murmured against the shell of her ear, purposely close. "But, if you can't speak, nod your head for yes and shake it for no, okay?"

Nina nodded, and her hands bunched into the woolen coat he wore, tugging hard. She burrowed into his arms deeper. Cole glared when he caught one of the women lurking in his peripheral, and she backed away when their eyes met. He tried to be polite, but he sensed sharks circling for blood.

"Are you overwhelmed?"

Nina nodded frantically, and Cole's jaw set. He'd seen his fair share of nasty legal battles, and intimidation was the lowest form of legal strategy—reserved for those with little intellect or standing.

He rubbed her back in small, soothing circles. Her nails dug into his skin through his coat, and Nina's weight buckled into his arms. But Cole held her up so no one could see the weakness in her knees. *Come on, sweetheart, stay with him.*

Cole dipped his head closer until his lips pressed flush against her ears, "Are they threatening you? I can grab security."

Nina nodded but flexed her arms to hold Cole still, "Don't."

"Security will handle them, but I'm listening. Tell me what's going on."

"They're . . . this is my estranged family. They want to challenge me for custody of Brooke. They were the ones I worried about."

Nina's voice cracked hard, sounding on the verge of tears, and Cole swore red streaked his vision. Her family turned on her like a pack of hungry wolves, but they should learn to fight fair before it bit them in the ass.

"I've got you now," Cole promised, and Nina's shallow breathing heightened when someone tried to reach a hand around. "Tell me their names."

"My parents, Vera and Thomas, and my brother Maxwell and his fiancée Felicity." Nina spilled while she shied away from the hand, falling deeper into Cole's arms. He eclipsed her in height, so hiding her came easy.

Cole nodded and stepped in front of Nina, shielding her body with his. Her arms held around his waist as her lifeline, but Cole's eyes coldly swept down the line of four. He identified the older woman and man as Vera and Thomas, finding Felicity and Maxwell easy to figure out afterward.

"I suggest you back up and give Nina some space," he remarked, choosing to stay deadly calm with his tone. But no one should mistake his calmness for the absence of anger burning white hot in his chest, prepared to rain down on whatever poor soul crossed him next. "Harassing an opposing party isn't a good look, especially for such self-righteous folks."

"Are you talking down to us, man? Who the hell do you think you are?" Maxwell snapped, and Cole mirrored his movements when he tried to square his shoulders back like he wanted a fight. Cole had the height advantage, which sent Maxwell a step backward. The bravado fled to reveal cowardly colors.

So, he would be willing to get in a woman's space and throw his weight around until a man stepped up to the plate? Typical.

Cole flicked his eyes over Maxwell and turned to the others. "My name is Cole Yearwood. You can consider me a friend of Nina's, and I'm warning you to leave her alone. No judge will appreciate your underhanded, conniving tactics to harass a respectable young woman like Nina."

Felicity scoffed, "You're warning us? Is that a threat?"

"No. I don't make threats. Unlike you, I'm above that."

A few immediate reactions jumped out, but Cole swallowed the urge to smile with teeth bared. He needed to send them packing, but they seemed itching for a confrontation. They would find it in him, not Nina.

"This is ridiculous," Vera scoffed while fanning her face with a folded instructional brochure from the information desk. Of everyone, she appeared the most indignant in the stiffness of her face and her red lips painted into a scowl. Cole swore it made her look like a clown, though. "Do you know anything about the law, young man? Because I doubt you do."

"You're right, ma'am . . . I only graduated from law school at the top of my class and currently hold licenses to practice in three states, including our jurisdiction. But I'm sure that years of schooling and passing three bar exams means absolutely nothing to your twenty-minute internet search about the law, hmm?'"

Vera's face twitched slightly, but Cole turned toward a belligerent Maxwell. "But my education isn't the issue here. My issue is that you'd rather harass Nina instead of fighting on the merits of your custody claim, and thus, I know you have nothing of substance. Instead of bothering her, maybe you should figure out how much you're about to acquire in legal fees for your baseless custody suit."

Thomas's face flushed a dark red bordering on purple, and the veins in his forehead added a nice touch. "She can't afford to keep fighting if we keep pushing."

"See, that's where I disagree. I know plenty of attorneys willing to take on pro bono work, and the court will find it in its heart to award an equitable settlement, including covering all legal fees incurred by Nina. So, make wise choices."

Nina's arms around his waist shifted, tearing Cole's eyes away from the shocked and angered faces of her family. He lifted his arm when Nina stepped out from behind him and let go, able to stand on her feet.

Cole looped his arm to rest comfortably around her hip. The hand placement might look suspicious to his title as "a friend," but he couldn't change the perceptions of the stuck-up imbeciles before him. How someone like Nina came out of a family like hers baffled him.

"I asked you to leave me alone earlier. Cole is asking you again to leave, and I want you to leave. I will report the harassment attempts." Nina remarked, and Cole didn't hear a single strain in those words. She meant every word.

"You're not a fit parent to that little girl. You'll come around eventually," Felicity scoffed, but Nina stepped forward. Cole had his eyes on her alone.

Nothing prepared him for laughter. At first, Nina let out a few breathless huffs strung together by a thin thread of mockery. But soon, her laughter spiraled out of control with the kind of laughs to cause aching ribs and fill the space in its strength.

Nina wiped at her eyes where tears sprung from laughing. "What would you know about parenting, hmm? I would sooner fling myself into the ocean than let you take Brooke from me. She deserves the world, and you wouldn't love her as she is. She is like Naomi, and we all know how much you hated Naomi."

"You heard the lady. She suggested quite nicely that you leave. I won't be as nice when calling security." Cole interjected.

He waited for anyone to make a move or start another argument until Rudy came around the corner, pulling his phone away from his ear. Nina's family wordlessly scurried down the hall with the good sense to pretend to be busy elsewhere.

Cole, however, had a few choice words for his friend.

"Cole, I didn't know you'd be here . . ." Rudy's eyes darted between him and Nina, mired in confusion, and he lingered a beat too long on Cole's arm around Nina. Even with her family gone, she stayed pressed to Cole's side.

"I was downstairs at the recorder's office. But I saw you two up here and came over to find that Nina was alone. Her family started harassing her."

"What?"

"Not to step on your toes, but why didn't you bring a victim advocate for extra protection? This is a high-risk situation, and the family showed that they're not above playing dirty to get their way."

Rudy rubbed his face with an exasperated sigh. "We've been short-staffed on victim advocates, and those we have are swamped with cases. All are on high priority and couldn't spare the time."

Nina, rubbing her arms, caught Cole's attention. Maybe she wasn't a high priority to Rudy's firm, but she was to him. He would do the whole confrontation a thousand times over without hesitation.

"I see. Just be careful with leaving her alone," said Cole.

"I'll see if any of the interns at the office are willing to take the requisite training and come along. I can spin it and label it dispute resolution and mediation practice." Rudy relented, but Cole knew that he couldn't ask too much of Rudy.

So, he turned to Nina and checked her face. She looked cheated out of sleep and ready for everything to end before anything started.

He kept his voice soft when he said, "Hey, you."

"Hey," Nina whispered and finally stepped out of his arm. Cole didn't fight it, letting his arm rest along his side. "Thanks for the rescue back there. I wouldn't let them intimidate me, but they tried it."

"I'm sorry that happened. Do you want to talk about it?"

"Maybe? It seems like so much to explain, and we should be called back at any moment . . ."

"Then, I can wait. If you'd like, I can stay nearby, and you can come and find me after the hearing. I'll have my phone, and you know my number," Cole offered.

Nina perked up, "You'd do that for me?"

"Absolutely." Cole rested a hand on her shoulder. "Friends can be listening ears, sounding boards, and bodyguards all in one. We're friends, aren't we?"

"We are. I'll find you after all of this is over." Nina reached up and took his hand between hers, squeezing tight. Although her eyes remained soft ponds of green, diluted by unshed tears, Cole took comfort in the fiery gleam underneath.

She was a fighter.

Chapter Ten
Nina

Hours slipped away from Nina while she sat in the courtroom, and she wondered how people like Cole managed to stand it. She studied the blank walls while Rudy handled the preliminary matters with her family's team of attorneys.

Her family hired a luxury firm and brought three attorneys to represent their interests. Their willingness to show off their disposable funds punched a dull pain in her chest.

But when Rudy rubbed her shoulder and told her, "We're done for the day. Head home safe and tell Brooke I said hi, okay?" Nina gathered her purse with a sweep of her arm and beelined for the door. Her family hadn't noticed her departure, and she hoped to keep it that way.

She walked toward the escalators and grabbed her phone from her purse, remembering her promise to Cole before they parted ways. Her fingers punched *C* in her contacts, and he popped up at the top of the list, despite their limited texts since exchanging numbers.

Nina waited on the dial tone, accompanied by ringing, but the call switched to Cole's voice rather quickly. "Hey, you alright?"

"Yeah, I'm okay." Nina leaned on the escalator railing as she stepped onto the first stair. "I finished and snuck out before my family could corner me again. You still up for that talk?"

"Way ahead of you. Look through the glass doors."

Nina's eyes lifted ahead and spotted Cole, standing outside the glass doors at the front of the courthouse. He waved, still holding the phone to his ear and smiling knowingly. Yet, that smile became the most reassuring thing to happen all day.

She had a few people ahead of her on the escalator, so she whispered into the phone, "How long have you been out there?"

"Ah, a while. That isn't super important," Cole laughed while the sounds of foot traffic and the rush of cars chimed in behind him. "I promised I would be here, and I'm a man of my word."

"You are."

Nina waited for the last person ahead of her to clear the escalator before she walked the rest of the way down, not wanting to have Cole wait out in the cold for too long. She gripped her purse tight as she jogged toward the doors. She needed to get out of there.

The automatic doors parted at her approach, and Nina strode into the clear, seeing Cole ahead by the stairs descending into the plaza. He waved and cut the call from his end.

Nina fumbled to put her phone away while she met Cole halfway. After hours of high stress and being around her family, his presence soothed over the wounds like a balm. She couldn't remember the last time she had a friend who wasn't Naomi.

"I hope I didn't keep you from anything important," Nina breathed out, looking him over. He appeared at ease, especially in how soft his hazel eyes were.

"Not at all. I called up my office and one of my coworkers was nice enough to bring some things I left behind. I holed up at the coffee shop across the street from the plaza and worked at a table there, focusing on paperwork."

"Law sounds like a lot of paperwork. Does it ever get tiring?"

"Sometimes. I'm not litigation-focused, so I handle be-hind-the-scenes transactional work unlike Rudy or my brother when he worked in criminal defense. Paperwork can be tedious if there's a lot to do, but it balances nicely with a more flexible work schedule and remote options if needed." Cole remarked.

Nina understood. Freelancing wasn't as lucrative as law, but the flexibility made up for any deficiencies in earnest. She glanced around him at the plaza filled with people heading home from their serious jobs as the first inklings of the evening streaked across the sky. It should be getting dark soon.

"Thank you for waiting for me," said Nina. "I don't know if I've said that already, but I don't know how to handle all this. My family can make me miserable, but I don't understand why they think they can push me around."

Cole's once upbeat demeanor flattened into the ghost of a frown, and he offered his arm, "If you're not ready to talk yet, then maybe we should head and grab something to eat. I pre-ordered a hot drink to go, and if you want anything, I'm happy to cover it."

"I could use a drink, maybe a tea or something to wind down," Nina agreed, walking alongside Cole down the stairs. He switched sides so she could use the railing and moved when she moved, a perfect mirror for her.

Nina felt the ache in the soles of her feet become an unavoidable burning sensation, a far cry from an annoyance. She chewed on her lip hard to stifle a groan and focused on getting down the stairs safely, paranoid that one misstep would lead to disaster. Anxiety buzzed around her head like flies as of late.

She descended the stairs and made it most of the way through the plaza to the crosswalk leading to the coffee shop before a sharp hiss escaped her. Red hot pain blistered along the soles and balls of her feet, all from her unfortunate choice of heels.

Cole immediately stopped and offered his arm to her, "Hey, what's going on?"

"My feet. I've been wearing these heels all day, and they've started to hurt." Nina gestured to the closed-toe pumps and their thin, stiletto heels. She probably sounded pathetic to whine about something that was her fault, but Cole appeared pensive.

"Let me try something," he guided her to a bench near the planted trees lined at the front entrance of the plaza, next to the metered parking. He pressed his phone into her hands, and Nina's eyes widened when she noticed he had unlocked it. "Stay here for a minute, and I'll be right back. Go ahead and place your order for a drink to-go."

"I can transfer you the funds later—" Nina started to say, but Cole, shaking his head, stopped her. Her cheeks puffed, and she stared at him, unaccustomed to such generosity. She hated owing people.

"It's okay. I get reward points for every purchase, so you're already helping me. I'll be back soon," Cole promised and jogged down the street toward a row of cars parked along the meters. She noticed him lean against one of them and reach into his pocket for his keys.

Nina glanced at his phone and scrolled down the app for the coffee shop, one of those popular chain stores. She picked out a large cup of Earl Grey to add to Cole's decaf coffee, satisfied with a drink on her empty stomach.

She would have to make dinner for Brooke anyway.

She looked up at the approaching sound of footsteps to see Cole back quicker than expected. In his hand, a pair of sneakers dangled from his fingers with the laces undone. But his smile promised something more than a pair of ordinary sneakers.

"Alright, we have a couple of options," Cole stopped in front of her and lifted the sneakers up for her inspection. "You can take these sneakers and replace your heels with them for a while... or I'll give you my dress shoes to replace them, and I'll wear the sneakers."

"Sneakers, please." Nina reached out toward the sneakers and kicked off her heels, flooded with relief. Cole kneeled down and slid the sneakers over her stockinged feet. He even tied up the laces on the shoes, which were too big for Nina.

"I'll take these," Cole held her heels in one hand, dangling in a loose grip, and offered his other one to help her off the bench. Nina accepted the help, and her aching feet thanked Cole for quick thinking. "Now, we can grab those drinks, and I'll walk you to your car. I assume you parked in the parking structure close to the courthouse."

"Actually, I ordered a cab to drive me to the court. I had to drop my car off for routine maintenance, and they were backed up even with an appointment. I'll have to pay for a few stops since Brooke is at daycare."

"She's in daycare? I don't know why I assumed she was in kindergarten."

"She was supposed to be. But with Naomi's accident and everything, I was advised that we hold off for another year before putting her into kindergarten. Professionals recommended I allow her time to grieve before I burden her with traditional schooling. Not to mention, I missed the deadline for registration, and no school in the area will grandfather her in late."

Nina slowed her ramble as she and Cole stopped at the crosswalk, noticing the red hand and Cole's lips tipped downward. It wasn't quite a frown, but his expression danced the thin line between pensive and saddened.

She pressed the button to cross several times until the white walking figure replaced the stop signal. An apology sat heavily on her tongue; she never knew when to keep to herself, ever the chronic oversharer when given a chance.

"Where's the daycare?" asked Cole, speaking for the first time after her confession.

"It's about three blocks from here. It's on Arista Avenue, and the ahead cross street is Mayer Street."

"Hmm, I could take you."

"Cole, I can't ask you that—"

"You aren't. I'm offering to help out. Driving you three blocks isn't a burden on me, and dropping you two off won't be either," Cole assured her. Nina wished for the confidence to accept help so comfortably, but something inside her hunkered down at the thought of being a drain on a guy like Cole's generosity.

Or anyone's willingness to help, for that matter.

Nina swallowed hard. "You've saved my skin more than once, so I feel bad relying on you so hard. But I won't fight you because paying more for a cab wouldn't be ideal."

"I know this is easier said than done, but please don't feel bad. Friends help each other when in a tight spot, and I know you're not taking advantage. Don't let your head talk you into feeling bad for what isn't your fault," said Cole.

Frankly, hearing those words made Nina want to break down and cry. After all the emotional turbulence of the day, she didn't have the energy to fight when Cole offered help. She needed help to stay afloat.

"I'll try."

"That's all anyone can ask."

Nina and Cole slipped inside the coffee shop when another patron pushed the door open, and Nina embraced the aroma of ground coffee beans and sugary sweet caramel syrup. Coffee shops had been havens during her college years, and she never knew when that changed.

Cole guided her toward the counter and grabbed the drinks labeled with his name. Nina watched him sniff the cups and handed her a rich purple-colored cup with a lid slapped on top. "For you. My roommate in college was an exchange student from Europe, and he loved his Earl Grey more than life itself."

"Oh yeah? Naomi got me hooked on it." Nina cupped the tea between her hands, letting the warmth pierce her to the core. After a cold day, she needed something warm to keep her mind from the worst.

"I don't mind it half the time, but coffee is my go-to." Cole lifted his cup and tapped its lid against Nina's, a silent cheers for the day's ordeal. "Let's get Brooke before the daycare closes, hmm?"

Sitting in the passenger seat of Cole's car, Nina closed her eyes and basked in the brush of the car's heaters on high. Despite the long day, Brooke's incessant babbling to Cole softened whatever dread lingered after court.

From the moment they picked her up, Brooke had Cole's ear as she described her day in detail. Coloring, recess with snacks, and naptime made a filling day for Brooke. Throughout the conversation, Cole erupted into laughter more than once.

Nina would listen to him and Brooke talk about everything and nothing all at once, smiling so hard. Everything about the energy in the car wiped away the aftermath of the bundle of anxiety in her chest.

"...And then Lara told Kelly that she likes Alex, but Kelly got mad because she also likes Alex. Lara got mad and pushed her off the swing, so Ms. Gloria put her in time out!" Brooke squealed, covering her face with her little hands still speckled with finger paint.

"No!" Cole gasped despite him and Nina learning about these other kids for the first time five minutes ago. His eyes found hers through the rearview mirror, and Nina took in his quirked brows and the borderline hysterical amusement laced in hazel. "Then, what happened?"

"I heard that Ms. Gloria called Lara's mom. She's probably in big trouble." Brooke nodded.

"That's why we don't put our hands on other people unless it's in self-defense," Nina reminded, and Brooke clapped her hands. She had observed from the sidelines the lessons Naomi stressed for Brooke to learn and committed to keeping those alive.

Cole leaned over when the car rolled up to a four-way stop, lowering his voice to barely above a whisper, "I had no idea that five-year-olds had such drama."

"You and me both."

"This is easily the most entertaining thing I've heard all day, though."

Nina stifled her laughter when Cole proceeded past the stop, seeing the last turn before her condo complex ahead. Disappointment popped and fizzled out in her chest, but Cole probably had more important things to do than play chauffeur. *He had already helped her out more than she deserved.*

She grabbed her purse and cleared her throat, "You can drop us off along the sidewalk. I have my keys, and I'll put my heels back on before Brooke and I go."

"Okay, that sounds good—"

"Mr. Cole! You won't come to dinner with us?" Brooke interrupted from the backseat, and Nina turned over her shoulder so fast it handed her a heaping dose of whiplash. Brooke's hands fidgeted with the seatbelt drawn across her chest in place of her proper car seat.

"Brooke, he's probably busy with important work."

"But I wanted to show him my princess tea party set."

Nina noticed Cole staying silent, but his eyes followed her until their gazes met. She half expected him to agree with her and politely decline for another day. He likely had someone waiting at home for him to set up their own dinner plans.

Cole, however, pulled to a park outside her building and closed out the GPS instruction he inputted. "I don't have any plans beyond scrounging in my fridge for a late-night meal and scrolling through unread business emails to draft responses to in the morning. I couldn't impose, though."

From the backseat, Brooke flashed Nina the best puppy eyes she'd ever seen and turned her gaze downcast for further effect. *She put on an Oscar-worthy pout,* thought Nina while the car awaited her answer. She sensed the expectation heavy in Brooke and Cole's eyes on her.

Eventually, however, she caved.

"We're friends. It wouldn't be imposing when you're always welcome. Besides, a home-cooked meal is the first step in paying you back for all your kindness.

"Guess I'll be seeing that princess tea set, after all. I hope you have a spare tiara for me, Brooke. I'll be hanging out with the coolest princesses in the city."

"Yay!" Brooke squealed. Her little legs kicked hard from sheer excitement. "Thank you, Auntie Nini!"

"Thank Mr. Cole, not me. He's the guest of honor." Nina slid out of Cole's car with her discarded heels in-hand and a stretch for her stiff muscles. She needed a deep tissue massage and at least eight hours of sleep to fix the damage done.

She stopped at the backseat and lifted Brooke out of the car. Her niece clung to her with tight arms around her neck and legs gripping Nina's side. Nina balanced Brooke onto her hip and headed for the porch of her condo, knowing Cole walked behind her.

Nina reached into her purse and tried to fish out her keys, but she hadn't mastered the juggling act with an excited five-year-old on her hip and her hands focused on supporting her. However, a soft "May I?" disrupted her thoughts.

Cole appeared in her peripheral with his arms held out and Nina lifted the purse at first. However, Brooke reached toward Cole and jumped from Nina's arms. Cole caught her before Nina even thought to scream.

"I think I can handle Brooke for a moment," Cole spoke to Nina, but sharing an exaggerated wink with Brooke elicited a dozen giggles from Nina's niece. Relief washed over her, and Nina chose to hurry up with her keys.

She let them in, instantly hit with the worry that maybe she should clean up. The house looked *lived-in* with toys left out in unexpected places, hoodies hung on the backs of chairs instead of folded into proper drawers, and a pile of unread mail tossed onto the table.

Brooke squealed to be let down and thundered across the living room until she found a few stuffed animals. She grabbed them in her arms and looked at Cole and Nina. "Tea party time!"

Still by the front door, Cole took off his shoes and headed toward the carpet. He stood beside Brooke, "Alright, where's the party?"

"Right here! I'll get the table!" Brooke handed him the stuffed animals and ran into the other room. Light clattering filled the room when she returned, holding a plastic tea table with all the fake cups stacked on top.

Nina hung back and watched Brooke assemble the table with her stuffed animals holding court. She left two spaces open for Cole and herself before she ran to collect crowns for all the princesses at the tea party.

A laugh almost doubled Nina over when Cole, who sat at the table with several pastel-colored stuffed animals, let Brooke put a sparkly pink tiara on his head. He fixed it with a single hand and accepted a flower-patterned teacup from Brooke.

"This tea looks delicious." Cole pretended to slurp the tea loudly, and Nina wished she knew his secret to make Brooke laugh so hard. He was a natural. "Introduce me to the other princesses at this party?"

"Okay! This is Butterscotch, Glitterball, and Clover!"

Nina's eyes remained on Cole and Brooke while she stepped into the kitchen, watching them through the open space over the island counter. She grabbed a few glasses out of the shelves for drinks and unloaded plates from another drawer.

"Brooke, what do you want for dinner?" asked Nina.

"Dino nuggets, please!" Brooke clapped her hands so hard that her crown slumped toward one side, a little too big for her head. The lopsided angle and her pleading smile wrapped a soft hand around Nina's aching heart. She was so innocent, so optimistic for a world that stole flickers of joy too early.

Beside her, Cole's lips pulled a smile, and Nina remembered the grocery store conversation. Cole recommended dino nuggets, which became Brooke's favorite weekly meal for her picky palette.

"One order of dino nuggets coming up." Nina rifled through the freezer and loaded a tray with the dinosaur-shaped chicken nuggets in uniform lines. She preheated the oven and continued her observation of Cole and Brooke having their princess tea party. She sometimes turned her back for a split second, listening while tidying up the kitchen.

Brooke led the conversation, bounding from topic to topic with the ease of a butterfly's flight. She raised a toast once or twice for the silliest things, but Cole lifted his glass and played along without missing a beat. He even pretended to intervene when Brooke got into a one-sided argument with Glitterball about the flower centerpieces that Brooke chose.

Quite the imagination her niece had.

However, Nina's eyes snapped toward the tea party when Brooke jumped to her feet and excitedly danced, "Be right back!" She sprinted past the kitchen in full force and headed into her bedroom, closing the door behind her.

Nina raised her brow at Cole, who rose from his spot at the tea party table, and he joined her in the kitchen. His hands gently removed the tiara from his head but held it. "Hey."

"Hey."

"Can we talk? I know things are complicated, but I'm here to listen to whatever bothers you . . . especially your family."

Nina's hands reached for something to ground her, and she ended up with a faded blue dish towel drawn taut between her fingers. Any harder, and she might tear the cloth down the middle. "You want to know about my family?"

"Only if you're comfortable with sharing," Cole murmured, hanging underneath the open archway between her and the living room. He leaned in the door frame with a sparkly tiara in his hand and concern in his eyes.

Nina sighed, "This isn't where I expected to have this conversation, but life is funny like that. Naomi was the eldest, and my parents expected more of her than they did of themselves. Everything Naomi did wasn't good enough, even when she was straight As, president of three clubs, and constantly volunteering at the church on weekends and nights. On the other hand, Maxwell is the baby of the family, which means he was born to be the favorite child. He never worked for anything while Naomi struggled for our parents' approval. As for me, I was the forgotten middle between 'perfect' Maxwell and 'not-so-perfect' Naomi. I can tell you times when my parents legitimately forgot about my existence beyond a smile for family photos, but you didn't come here for my sob story."

Cole didn't interrupt, but Nina couldn't bring herself to check whether he paid attention to her while she spilled her guts atop the kitchen counter next to the baking tray of dino nuggets. She relinquished her hold on the dish towel, moving on to distract herself by putting away dishes from the drying rack.

"Naomi and I were always so close. Sometimes, she was the only one I considered true family. Even with the tense dynamics, Naomi valued family more than I could understand. However, when Naomi was in her last year of college, she discovered she was pregnant with her then-boyfriend. He chose to skip town and dump Naomi over text, leaving her with a decision to make. Before she could figure out what to do, Felicity, my brother's fiancée, snitched to our parents about the pregnancy and forced Naomi's hand. She said she would choose the baby and my family disowned her, except me. So, now that Naomi's dead, they've come around and want Brooke in their lives . . . but they want Max and Felicity to be her parents instead of me. Maybe that makes me petty, but I won't let them take the last piece of Naomi I have left . . ."

"Nina, stop," Cole's voice pressed against her ear, and a pair of hands removed a ceramic bowl from her fingers. She hadn't realized she was trembling, but her hands suffered worst. "Look at me."

"I'm embarrassed," said Nina.

Cole's hand tipped her face back to him when she tried to hide, "You have no reason to be. What you're doing isn't petty or some kind of revenge. You're protecting that little girl in the next room like Naomi would've wanted. Those people, the ones you share blood with, aren't family and they would destroy her identity or whatever ties she associated with her mom. You keep those memories alive. You're doing the right thing."

"I want to believe that." Nina closed her eyes when the burning stung at the edges, threatening tears. "But things are so hard. They're going to try and bankrupt me before they give up. It was easier to conceive the thought of being a parent when I was engaged. I can't give up, though."

She opened her eyes and caught the faintest frown on Cole's face. "I didn't know you were engaged." He sounded . . . sheepish almost.

"Keyword: was. I broke it off. He gave me an ultimatum—him or Brooke—and I chose Brooke in a heartbeat. I don't miss him per se because he showed me his true colors and made me question if I could ever be happy with choosing him. But I can't deny that the loneliness doesn't help during this time."

"I understand . . . and if it's any consolation, that guy is a fucking idiot. I hope he enjoys a lonely, bitter existence for being threatened by a child."

The thought brought Nina a small dose of catharsis to get all the festering feelings off her chest. She hadn't confided in anyone since

Naomi's death, and the lightheaded rush overwhelmed her. *It felt good to feel safe enough to share.*

She softened and straightened up enough where Cole's hand slipped away from her cheek, "Thank you . . . for listening and understanding. I should probably start on dinner for us since I don't think dino nuggets are up to your sophisticated palette."

"Are you kidding?" Cole grinned from ear to ear. "You never outgrow dino nuggets. Slap some for me on the tray, and I'll be happy. I'll be even happier if you add some box mac and cheese or fruit."

Nina's lips twitched and she resisted the urge to laugh at the goofy wiggling of Cole's brows and leaned around him to reveal boxed mac and cheese in one of the cabinets. "Guess we're eating like royalty tonight with dino nuggets and mac and cheese."

Much to her startled delight, Cole plopped the tiara onto Nina's head and winked. "A meal fit for a princess tea party, perhaps? We're missing the one more princess at our table . . . so I think you'll fit perfectly."

Nina opened her mouth to reply when she overheard the patter of Brooke's bare feet and spotted a blur of pink speed by. Brooke brought out her favorite princess gown to wear to the party. "You know what? I accept your invitation to the princess tea party."

Cole's grin deepened. "Excellent."

Chapter Eleven
Cole

Over a week had passed since Brooke's princess tea party, but Cole was still discovering flecks of glitter in his hair. No matter how many washes he went through, pink glitter appeared on his pillow at night or lined the collar of his most expensive dress shirts. He couldn't find it in himself to be upset, though.

He and Nina talked more after a dino nugget and boxed mac and cheese dinner with Brooke, exchanging easy chitchat about life.

Posted up at a countertop seat at Lone Tree Bar and Grill, one of the most popular drinking spots for other attorneys in the city, he signaled to the bartender for a refill. Although he usually grabbed himself a classic cocktail, he started with an Arnold Palmer or two.

Cole dragged the straw in his empty glass between his teeth and lost himself to the ambient noise around the bar. For a Friday evening, he expected the crowd to be a little rowdier to celebrate the end of the work week. But hey, he shouldn't complain.

He relinquished his glass when the bartender slid his way and leaned into his hand, propped up by his elbow on the bar. A long day at work left him ready to go home and close out his tab.

A hand clapped him on the shoulder, eliciting a sigh from Cole, "I was wondering if you were going to show up or if I had been ditched."

"You really think I'd ditch our plans without at least telling you?" Dean questioned, sliding into the seat to Cole's right. Dean shrugged off his coat to drape over the back of the chair and got comfortable. "I'll take a martini, please."

"Martini? What are we celebrating?" asked Cole when the bartender went to fetch his drink.

"Celebrating? What makes you say that?"

"Dean, you never order a martini unless you're in a celebratory mood. So, I'm guessing another fat paycheck crossed your desk, or you retained a big shot client."

Dean looked him over and sighed, "Stop that! You freak me out whenever you do that."

"Do what?" Cole snickered. "Read you like an open book?"

"Exactly. A man needs to have a little mystery to keep things interesting. You should've been a shrink in another life, I swear."

Cole said nothing to further antagonize his brother, knowing how to toe the line between good fun and shit-stirring. After all, he was the "good Yearwood" growing up because he knew how to circumvent trouble, unlike Dean.

He graciously accepted his Arnold Palmer and sipped at it. "What took you so long to make it? You tend to leave work on Fridays at five-thirty sharp and not a moment later, so something kept you behind."

"I was catching up with a friend . . . and here he comes." Dean pointed toward the door as the bartender delivered his martini. Cole glanced over, spotting Rudy heading their way. Huh, he had no idea that Dean and Rudy knew one another, much less that they were friends.

"Cole, hey." Rudy gave a two-fingered salute and a welcome grin, sliding into the seat on Cole's left. "I can't stay long, but Dean mentioned you two were meeting up."

"He and I try to hang out every other week. He's a busy man with his firm and a lovely fiancée who puts up with him."

"I detest that characterization. Jan loves me."

"Shockingly, she does."

Cole laughed when Dean looped his arm around his neck and squeezed into a light chokehold. His hand gripped his Arnold Palmer as he slipped from Dean's grasp, shoving his older brother away.

Dean's pouty scowl further incentivized the urge to laugh and prod his ego a little more, but Cole watched Rudy nurse two fingers of scotch. *Uh oh.*

"Rough day?" Cole asked, tapping next to Rudy's glass of fine scotch.

"You have no idea," Rudy laughed, but it was a bitter and draining imitation of one. He swirled the scotch around the tumbler, and Cole's eyes circled the waves created in his wake. "Nothing kills the mood of a good day faster than a custody battle."

Cole's chest tightened, and he sipped at his drink, hoping to dispel the choking sensation he suddenly discovered in his throat. The slow crawl of nausea forced him to set down his glass, pushing it back toward the other side of the bar. *Brooke and Nina.*

"Would this happen to be for Brooke and Nina?"

"Some days, I swear you have mind-reading powers."

Cole shrugged, but he worried. He couldn't reason through the situation after Nina gave him the rundown about her family and their motives. No universe existed where Nina would be in the wrong to fight, even if she second-guessed herself.

For people he met once, a well of hatred built itself deeper than any man-made reservoir, closer to the fathomless depths of the ocean blue. *The Byndels were awful people.*

"I know you can't discuss details of the case with me since confidentiality and all that, but is there anything I can do for Nina. I know she needs a lot of support—"

"Cole, stop," Rudy cut him off and plunged Cole into a pained silence, holding his tongue out of respect for his friend. "While I admire your interest and willingness to help, I have everything under control."

"Yeah, I understand."

"Nina will be more than fine in my hands since I've secured a victim's advocate pending further developments. I'm more than capable of handling it."

"I never said that you weren't." Cole's mouth twisted tight. His confidence splintered into pieces, which he searched for in his Arnold Palmer with every sip. He asked not because he didn't trust Rudy but because he and Nina were friends. He hoped that any of his friends would show up for him if he were in Nina's position.

Dean, who witnessed the exchange but remained silent, finally asked, "Who's Nina?"

"She's a friend."

"Whatever happened to that girl from speed dating the other night, the one Jan and I saw you with. The lady who organized the event mentioned that she saw you two leave early together."

Cole knew that would come up eventually, but he couldn't outrun the conversation anymore. So, he took another swig of Arnold Palmer and slumped back in his chair. "That would also be Nina. She's one and the same."

"Are you serious right now?"

"Completely."

Dean and Rudy stared at him, equally confused, and Cole figured he should start digging his grave. He got tangled in the web of coincidences if he thought about it too long. He and Nina had an unorthodox start to their friendship, but he liked their connection.

He brought his Arnold Palmer to his lips and drank to fill the silence. He'd rather not explain while stone-cold sober, but he drove there himself. No liquid courage for the evening, not for him.

Dean stayed with his eyes on Cole, even as Rudy threw down a wad for his tab and mentioned something about heading out. Dean tugged Cole's sleeve when Rudy left the bar.

"Alright, you need to explain because I know you're not dumb enough to get involved with a client," he remarked coolly.

"She's not my client. It's complicated to explain—"

"Try."

Cole swallowed and turned his face toward the multi-colored rows of liquor bottles stacked against the wall and illuminated by the lights on the bar's surface. Their fractured shadows and kaleidoscopic touch stole his attention for a moment.

He cleared his throat. "Nina came into my firm looking for representation in a custody dispute, which we don't handle. She was with another colleague, but I gave her a referral to Rudy as consolation. She and I kept running into each other, like at a local coffee shop or when I saw her at the grocery store with her niece, Brooke. Each time wasn't planned, and I recently saw her at the courthouse when she was there for her custody dispute. Her family was causing problems when Rudy left her alone, so I stepped in for a little while."

Dean gave him a once over, steeped in disbelief, and said, "You're not telling me everything. I can see it in your face . . . you're being overly selective about your word choice."

"Dean, that's absurd."

"Is it really?"

"Yes! Nina and I have become friends because all the coincidences made us laugh. She's a lovely person, and I am invested in her case being successful."

"Then, what about the speed dating night because you two looked awfully cozy. Jan and I had circled the bar several times that night to check on you, but none of your other potentials had you laughing or smiling as much as her." Dean pointed out.

Dean *may* have a point that he didn't connect with another woman at the speed dating event. But that wasn't a Nina issue. He failed to make a love connection because he wasn't eager to be there. Dean was the one who signed him up without his explicit permission, or had he forgotten?

So, Cole shook his head and went for another sip of Arnold Palmer. He used the time to compose himself enough for an answer. Dean looked for something that wasn't there.

"I didn't want to be at the event, and Nina showing up had been another funny coincidence. She had been at a restaurant a few doors down for a work event and unintentionally got roped into speed dating."

"But you also left early with her. Care to explain that?"

"She needed to get home to her niece and relieve the babysitter from their duties. I offered to walk her to her car since it was late and dark like a gentleman. You and Jan were my ride home, and I wasn't interested in returning to speed dating, so Nina nicely offered me a ride to my apartment."

Dean opened his mouth but closed it not long afterward. Although his eyes narrowed while he searched Cole's face, he circled back, "You're telling me that nothing is going on between you two?"

Cole shook his head, "Nothing. We're friends." He remarked, hoping to deter Dean with some sense of finality. Even when the flash of the princess tea party and dino nugget dinner crossed his mind, he chose silence. Dean didn't need to know about that to fuel any delusions about him and Nina.

"Okay, I'm going to trust you . . . but do be careful. Even if you don't intend anything beyond a friendship, I wouldn't be so cavalier that nothing could change."

"Dean—"

"Trust me on this one, Cole. Please." Dean rubbed his shoulder. At that moment, Cole understood that Dean meant well and had his interest at heart. Getting involved with someone like Nina would change the definition of his current lifestyle.

"I appreciate the wise words, but I can assure you with reasonable certainty that Nina isn't looking for anyone." Cole remembered their conversation when Brooke left the room, mentioning her ex-fiancé and how she chose Brooke. In theory, any good guardian would put a child first, but real life and theory didn't always jive.

Dean's skepticism melted out of his features, but Cole waited for the other shoe to drop. His brother, when he felt convinced of something, nothing could entirely change his mind. Simultaneously admirable and frustrating, Dean's dedication to his convictions worried Cole.

Dean quietly sipped his martini, which he hadn't touched in some time, and said, "Okay."

Cole nearly slumped back in relief into his chair. Finally, their evening could be peaceful; they would continue sharing a drink or two before heading home for the weekend. All the Nina speculation would stay behind them.

That was wishful thinking on Cole's part.

Dean nudged Cole in the ribs, and when Cole looked his brother's way, he noticed Dean's head tipped toward the other end of the bar. An attractive woman sat across the way, hands folded onto her lap and dark hair dramatically cascading around her face and all its sharp features.

"She's been sneaking glances our way for the last five minutes. You should see if she's interested in a drink since your speed dating night was a bust.

"Dean, seriously? For all we know, she could be looking at you and wanting you to make a move . . . not me."

"You need to have more confidence that when we're standing next to one another, an interested woman wants you over me," Dean groaned.

Cole bit his tongue hard. The urge to remind his older brother that had never been the case rattled him. Dating wasn't a competition, but sometimes it felt like a losing race to Cole. He shouldn't settle for being unhappy or okay in a relationship.

He shook his head. "No. It's not a confidence issue. I'm not interested in hitting her up, especially when I know you're in a scheming mood. I'm happy that you've been so lovestruck with Jan and finally believe in relationships, but setting me up with everyone you see isn't the key to me finding happiness. I have to find my own Jan on my own terms."

The last thing Cole wanted was to snap, but he felt the edges of his patience begin to fray. A slower temper always caused a bigger boom when he lost a grasp on his calm.

Dean mulled over his words, visibly taken aback, and relented with his hands up. "Okay. I'll ease back . . . for now."

"Good. If you had continued, I would've threatened to call Jan and ask her to pick you up."

"You wouldn't dare. Fridays are her Pilates night."

"Oh, I know. I would dare because the combination of you causing trouble and then her having to leave Pilates early would guarantee a cozy little spot on the couch for you."

Cole heard Dean grumble that he was evil and hid his smirk behind his drink. He preferred being a mastermind, but he knew what Dean meant. Besides, it was his solemn duty as a younger brother to torment his brother and then run to whoever would have his back—usually Mom or January.

At some point in the silence of enjoying his drink, Dean got off his stool and headed toward the bathrooms at the back of the bar. Past all the patrons and the giant televisions mounted on the wall playing highlight reels from ESPN, the distance felt safe enough for Cole to reach for his phone.

He opened his text messages, and Nina's conversation sat at the top of the list, having been the most recent text he sent. Dean believed something more swirled between him and Nina, but Cole wanted no room for doubt.

NINA: Brooke keeps asking me when you'll come for another tea party. She thinks you're infinitely cooler than everyone else she's met.

COLE: Yeah? What can I say? She's a clever little lady.

NINA: I think so, too. If you're ever in the mood for a home-cooked meal . . . just give me advanced notice so I can prepare adequate portions. Dinner seems to be the only way I can repay you for your help.

COLE: You don't have to pay me back.

NINA: Maybe not, but I want to. How about that?

COLE: Alright, you won this round. In another life, I could see you making a fine attorney. You're pretty persuasive.

NINA: Is that right? I learn something new about myself every day.

Cole searched for any sign to prove Dean's absurd theory and found no evidence. He liked to be a rational man and live his life by facts. The truth was he and Nina were friends, would continue to be good friends, and they had desperately needed friends for a while.

Chapter Twelve
Nina

S lumping against the door to Brooke's bedroom as she closed it, Nina wanted to give up and cry. Exhaustion weighed heavy on her shoulders, pushing what little energy she had left further into the grave she dug for herself.

Nina closed her eyes and willed herself to step away from the door, knowing that if she lingered around, her luck would cause more fires for her to put out. So, she headed down the hallway and stuffed down her guilt until it didn't cry out for her attention.

Brooke hadn't been easy that evening; she spent hours crying about different things, turning each inconvenience into a full-blown meltdown. Nina barely managed to fix one problem before a new one cropped up with cruel swiftness.

First, a stray piece of broccoli ended up in Brooke's dinner from the pasta bake Nina put together after a long editing day. Next, it was a fight while Nina tried to detangle her hair in the bath. Then, the final tantrum involved Brooke's protests of not being sleepy enough at her appointed bedtime. Eventually, the crying fits and half a melatonin gummy struck a winning combo and knocked Brooke out for the night.

Nina understood that gentle parenting was meant to be a process, but a constantly crying kid wore down her strained patience.

She wandered down the hallway with her hands tucked into the same sweatpants she had worn for the last two days, having lost the energy to change clothes. She wandered into her bedroom and shut the door as quietly as possible.

Nina entered the bathroom and ran the faucet to the hottest setting. She grabbed a washcloth from the nearby rack, dousing it in hot water. Stripped clothes fell to the floor in a pile, and Nina rubbed the washcloth over her skin. She scrubbed her skin raw and red to clean herself.

As she did, her eyes wandered to the pile of clothes on the floor. She spotted tear and snot stains streaking across the fabric of her T-shirt. *Great, another load of laundry.*

The chores heaped onto her already packed schedule, and Nina wanted nothing more than to crawl into bed and scream it out into her pillow. At times, the whole guardianship gig left her more frustrated than she could put into words.

Even when frustration knocked against her head, Nina knew to be better than how she was raised. With her and Naomi's father never around, all the punishment landed on their mother, and she made it her mission to strike the fear of God into her children. Screaming and physical punishment weren't uncommon, and Nina still had a few healed-over scars to prove it.

How could she be anything like her mother against a little girl, no matter how stressful her day was? Nothing about that seemed right.

Nina emerged from her thoughts when the water dripping from the rag ran cold against her skin, followed by a stinging feeling. She spotted a few darker red splotches on her skin where she had gone a little too hard. But she felt cleaner than before.

She twisted out the excess water from the washcloth and laid it along the rim of the laundry basket she kept in the bathroom. In it, the last remains of her clothes tumbled down when Nina tossed them afterward.

Nina plodded into her bedroom, colder than the bathroom, and shivered hard. She beelined for the drawers pushed against the wall and adorned with all the framed pictures, hosting all her clothes. She rummaged through the drawers from top to bottom for something new to wear.

She jumped into the first pair of sweatpants, struggling to keep them up and countering with a tank top tight against her torso. She pulled the drawstrings on the sweatpants until the waist held up.

Around the middle of the dresser, she pulled open a drawer she swore she had emptied out a while back. But she stopped when the supposedly empty drawer revealed a hoodie neatly folded in the middle. Embroidered on the dark green fabric, *Crestwood Community College* stared back at Nina.

Naomi attended Crestwood for two years before transferring, intent on saving money and avoiding potential loans.

Nina's hands shook as she reached into the drawer and pulled out the hoodie, folded perfectly like done by the hands of someone who worked summers in retail for extra cash. *Naomi's.*

She guessed that Naomi left it behind at her place, totally an accident until she shook out the hoodie and a white envelope tumbled out from the pocket. Unopened, the envelope hit the floor before Nina could catch it.

She leaned down and picked it off the floor, seeing "Nina" written in Naomi's handwriting on the front. She flipped it over and examined the flower indent of the wax seal, done in a soft rose gold wax.

"What's in here?" she murmured and hoisted the hoodie onto her body, immediately greeted by the leftover touches of Naomi's perfume. Jasmine, with notes of wild vanilla, enveloped her in a pair of ghostly arms while the softness of the hoodie's insides brushed against her damp skin, clinging hard.

Nina clutched the envelope addressed to her hard in her hand and left her bedroom, unsure of where to go. She wandered through her house until she ended up on the living room floor, knees tucked into her chest and her back pressed into the couch. Even seated, the ground beneath her felt ready to shift and pull the world out from underneath her.

The envelope sat unopened for a few minutes as Nina weighed the merits of opening it. *Its contents would haunt her forever—unopened and mysterious or opened and known—so she needed to choose.*

Whatever the outcome . . . she would live with it.

Here goes nothing. Nina bit on her lower lip so hard, she could swear she tasted the metallic hints of blood in her mouth but opened her mouth to no blood on her fingers when she checked.

She tore open the letter and fished out its contents to find a stack of lined paper with handwriting along every line. The words spilled into the margins of the red lines, vertically intercepting the dark blue horizontal lines, jumbled like alphabet soup at first glance.

Nina's hands shakily flipped through the pages, noticing the writing on the front and back of every page. Naomi's thoughts couldn't be contained onto a couple pages of college-ruled paper, and never had something pierced her so bittersweetly. The reminder cut her to the core.

She stared ahead before she dared to skim the letter.

Dear Nini,

I'm so proud of you. We got off the phone ten minutes ago, but you told me that Zach proposed. You're all grown up now. It's hard to imagine how much time has passed from when we used to walk home from elementary school together and spend our weekends watching Barbie movies in blanket forts.

But that's not all. You finished college with your bachelor's, and I know better than anyone about the gift you have. Writing is in your blood; it's what you were made for. God, I'm so proud of you.

Can you believe that you're getting married?

Nina's stomach turned too hard, and she couldn't bear to read another line, let alone another few pages of her older sister's sweet praises. Tears welled up in her eyes and streaked down her cheeks. With sadness, a hot flush pressed against her face until she struggled to breathe between hiccups and shallow gasps for air.

The letter sucker-punched the air out of her lungs without even trying.

Even though Nina was the writer of the family, Naomi's words hooked her heart and showed no signs of letting go. Her heart screamed for release, and the tears pooled down the bags under her eyes and along the apples of her cheeks. She wished she could've shared the reading of the letter with Naomi, not without her.

Naomi deserved to be there to see her tears but happy ones instead of ones chock-full of mourning thinly held together by her need to remain mentally stable for Brooke. Her responsibility to her niece came above all else, even herself. That's what parents were supposed to do, right?

Fuck, she missed Naomi so bad.

Nina set the letter on the couch and pulled her knees tighter into her chest. It started with trouble breathing, but the crushing sensation pressing down on her stomach would soon follow. Grief manifested in its worst form as Nina cried harder.

Every other breath turned into a choked hiccup, stuttering and cutting her air short. Panic set in when her hands laid around her throat and her nails dug into the skin. The burn barely registered through the dizziness swirling about her head.

She recalled how Naomi used to find her having panic attacks in the bathroom after a hard day at school and would sit behind her, holding her close. Yet, the act of remembrance worsened the sensation coiled so tightly in Nina's chest that she worried it might burst under pressure.

Nina tipped over, and her hands didn't move to catch herself or prop herself back up. Instead, she lay on the floor, knees tucked into her chest and head pressed into her kneecaps. She stayed still beyond a few tremors she couldn't hold back. She almost wanted to vomit at how hard her face buzzed with dizzying anxiety, blurring her vision already marred by unshed tears.

Had she taken her meds today? She never got this upset while on her medication, but she had enough near misses in the last week to worry over.

She hated the pounding in her head and how she wanted to crawl into bed for the next two days until the pain subsided. The sudden ringing in her ears caught her off-guard in the chaos of it all. At first, she assumed the ringing was a figment of her imagination until its persistence got her to look at the table.

At the edge of a nearby coffee table, her phone buzzed and vibrated around until it fell off the ledge. Nina managed to reach out and grab it off the rug after a harmless thud, checking the screen. She would've guessed a robot call or telemarketer due to the late hour.

However, her gasping cries stopped when she noticed *Incoming Call: Cole* on her lock screen, beckoning her to answer. She held her breath, cheeks puffed hard, as she attempted to collect herself before she answered the other line.

"H-hello?"

"Nina, hey. I know it's late, but I'm glad that I caught you," Cole sounded genuinely glad to hear from her, which tore her heart up. "Are you at your place right now?"

"Yeah, I am. What's up?" asked Nina, who pushed herself back to seated. She gravitated toward shorter answers if one word wouldn't suffice. She didn't trust herself not to break down if pressed for too long.

"I was supposed to meet over dinner with a few law school buddies, but we had to cancel at the last minute. I took home the leftovers I ordered before the plans fell apart. It's way too much for me to finish in the week."

"Yeah? Sorry about your plans."

"Ah, it's not a big deal. But I called to see if you and Brooke were up for some company tonight. If you're interested, I have plenty of food for the three of us. What do you say?" If Cole's canceled plans bummed him out, he was great at hiding the disappointment from Nina.

She wiped her eyes with the back of Naomi's hoodie, throat and eyes burning. Her first instinct was to pawn off some pitiful excuse and hide from the world, especially with how hard she bawled. She probably looked like a mess, unseemly to another's eyes.

But the growl of her stomach hit her as hard as the panic attack had. She thought back to her last meal and the hours racked up. She hadn't eaten since that morning.

So lost in her thoughts, Cole's soft whisper of "Nina, are you still there?" almost spooked her out of her skin. She forgot his presence, albeit on the other line of the call. He couldn't see her face or know that the hunger pains fed into the dizziness threatening to knock her over and let her grief spill out.

"I'm still here," Nina promised, yet her voice trembled. She bit her cheek when the burn crept into her eyes, refusing to cry while on the phone. "What kind of food?"

"Italian. I have classic spaghetti with marinara, ravioli, and garlic bread if that's your speed . . ."

"Sounds really great."

Cole paused on the other line and Nina could hear the pensive furrow in his brows. "Do you want to talk about what's upsetting you, or should we wait until another time?"

Nina knew she had been caught. A rogue sob pushed out of her mouth, and she clapped her hand across her lips to muffle it, unable to hold the tears back. Despite that, she whispered, "Not over the phone.

I can't be alone right now, and Brooke's asleep. She doesn't need to see me like this. Please, don't let me be alone."

"Alright, I'll be there soon. Wait for me," Cole remarked, and all Nina could do was nod.

Nina heard the quiet knocks on the door—three to be exact—and crawled off her sorry slump on the floor. She held the wall while she moved from the living room to the front door, not trusting her legs to keep her up.

She spent the gap between Cole's call and the knocks in tears about everything under the sun. Her life seemed to have fallen apart at the seams—broken engagement, dead sister, and single parenthood in her foreseeable future—and months ago, she had been looking forward to good luck in her corner.

Nina checked through the peephole to confirm Cole outside her door and opened the door when she saw him and the same coat he wore the night of speed dating. Funnily enough, she recognized the coat first since he had been preoccupied with his phone.

Cole snapped to attention at the opening of the door, and his smile dropped when he saw the state she was in. Nina almost wanted to apologize for the disheveled appearance, but Cole set down the takeout on the floor, its plastic bag crinkling.

He opened his arms wide and stared at her until Nina shuffled toward him, stopping shy of the full embrace. Cole's arms gestured again wordlessly, and Nina leaned into his chest. Her arms wrapped around Cole's torso while one of his hands rubbed her back. *Cole gave great hugs.*

His chin rested on top of her head, and Nina sank deeper. When was the last time she hugged anyone outside of Brooke? She couldn't remember.

"Let's head inside. We can settle down and talk about whatever's on your mind," Cole offered after a while, and Nina realized she stopped counting the moments since entering the hug. Her brain shut down momentarily, but she needed a breather from overthinking.

"Good idea. Come inside . . . I can grab us some plates and some forks, too."

"That won't be necessary. I grabbed extra at the restaurant, so we'll be good. Do you have a lactose allergy or anything?"

"Uh, no." Nina shook her head as she pulled Cole inside from the October night air. She had cleaned up a little since the last time he came over. She shut the door behind them, immediately locking the bottom lock and the accompanying deadbolt. "No allergies for Brooke or me."

Cole nodded and followed Nina to her spot on the floor beside the couch. She excused herself to the kitchen long enough to grab two water bottles from the fridge but returned to Cole, who had set out two plates of garlic bread and ravioli. It was a good guess on his part that she preferred ravioli.

Nina sat beside him and tucked her knees to her chest again. The two plates and waters formed a tiny wall between them, but it had nothing on the emotional wall standing to the ceiling.

Cole shifted around so his body faced her, even when his eyes already did. His undivided attention belonged to her. "What's wrong, Nina? I know grief works in unconventional ways, but you look like you're hurting."

"I had a small panic attack before you arrived. I think I'm fine now," Nina rushed the second part out when Cole pulled a face at the mention of a panic attack. "I found Naomi's old sweater and a letter addressed to me. It made me think about how quickly my life changed, not necessarily for the better. Months ago, I was engaged and had the best big sister in the world. My life was on track. Now? Everything fell apart for no good reason."

Cole scooted a little closer but still hovered outside her personal space cautiously. "Nina, you can come back from this. Yes, life won't be the same as before you lost Naomi. But I know that this low point isn't the new normal."

"I wish I had your optimism. But from where I'm sitting, with every day its own battle to be a guardian and keep Brooke safe from the world, I'm starting to lose myself. My best days are behind me, and my life is over."

"I don't believe that. Your life isn't over."

"Maybe it's not, but that's how I feel," Nina protested and stared into those warm hazel eyes beside her, captivated by their concern. There she sat on the floor of her condo, feeling sorry for herself and overwhelmed, but Cole tried to set her back onto her feet.

"Okay, and that's valid to feel as long as you recognize that you're far from done. I know there is so much more of you that the world deserves to see," said Cole. "So, I'll ask you one small favor."

"Which is?"

"Tell me what you still have that makes life worth living."

Nina hesitated, but Cole's eyes pressed her for an answer. He had a look that she couldn't fully describe, and she wondered if he could see right through her. Her heart raced faster, but her fingers curled into the carpet to ground her from another runaway panic attack.

She swallowed her traitorous tongue and whispered, "Brooke. I have Brooke."

"You have more than Brooke, but she's one of the pieces," Cole interrupted, but his voice never peaked with annoyance or anger like she was used to. "Keep thinking."

"I want you to tell me what you see then because you've got something in that smart mind of yours that I'm missing."

"You're a great guardian to Brooke, of course. But you're selling yourself horribly short, Nina. You've got your kindness, wits, and talent that makes you great at your job. You can write well, but it's how you speak to your readers with such personality. I read a few of your articles on the internet, and maybe I wasn't the target audience, but you write like you're speaking to a friend. That connection jumps off the page."

"You read some of my articles?" asked Nina, shocked. She ran her slick hands down the new pair of sweats, pressed into her thighs until the heels of her palms formed indents in her skin.

"A handful. I never knew how much I could learn about makeup and fashion from some articles." Cole smiled, and that broke through the fog. A tiny laugh escaped her, and she covered her mouth, but Cole pulled her hands away.

Nina cleaned her face and exhaled all the bad feelings. She glanced down when her stomach growled ridiculously loud; even Cole heard her, whistling with a borderline impressed smile.

Cole passed her a plate of ravioli and held up one for him, prepared to enjoy their quiet dinner. The two dug into the crunch of the extra garlicky garlic bread. A few bites in, Nina noticed how the dizziness muted.

All the crying wore her out.

She inhaled her plate, and Cole piled seconds onto hers without comment. He let her eat in peace, which she needed after the day she had. So consumed by hunger, she almost missed the soft patter of bare feet.

Brooke emerged from the bedroom, holding a blanket in a tight fist and rubbing her eyes. She stood in the doorway, still half asleep and wearing her bear-themed onesie. The little ears of the brown bear onesie appeared creased from her habit of sleeping in awkward positions.

Nina planned to set down her plate and see what Brooke needed, but her niece vibrantly jumped and squealed, "Mr. Cole!"

"Oh my goodness! It's a little bear!" Cole greeted as Brooke sprinted toward him, launching herself in a full jump. He caught her with ease and sat her on his lap. "Hello, little bear. How are you?"

"Hungry." She mumbled, peering into the plastic bag. Cole, with one arm down, fished out the tin of spaghetti. He held it up, and Nina watched as Brooke's eyes widened to the size of the moon. She made grabby hands at the spaghetti.

"Well, since we're friends, we can share," Cole remarked, grabbing a spare fork from the bag. He cracked open the plastic lid, and the warm aroma of marinara filled the living room, more so than with the ravioli alone.

Brooke accepted the fork from Cole's hands and stole some noodles from the spaghetti. Cole set his dinner aside to keep her from making too much of a mess. Nina set down her plate, prepared to take over.

Then, she caught Cole's eyes over Brooke's shoulders, and he winked at her. He mouthed, "I've got this."

Nina's shoulders slumped in relief. She took another bite and continued to witness Brooke calmly eat spaghetti as the sauce smeared across her cheeks, and Cole tried not to laugh at her mess.

The moment, although small, gave her hope.

Chapter Thirteen
Cole

The ache in Cole's neck would've bothered him more if he had woken up in his bedroom. A few blinks through blurry vision revealed sage green colored walls that most certainly weren't in his bedroom or any room in his apartment.

But, after a pause, Cole started to remember the night before. Flashes of an Italian dinner shared between three and the cozy atmosphere when rain began to pelt along every window and the roof. He was at Nina's place.

Cole's head lolled to the side, and his eyes landed on a still-sleeping Nina and Brooke curled up underneath a fuzzy blanket. Nina's face looked at peace while she slept, and her body submerged partially into the throw pillows and cushions lining the couch. Her blonde hair curled around her face and spread haphazardly over the back of the couch cushions.

Cole stretched out to the crackling and creaking of his body, brushing off the sleep from the corners of his eyes. Tiredness melted away from every joint when the urge for coffee nipped at him. He checked his watch for the time.

But the day, Saturday, hit him first.

I almost forgot that it was Saturday. Cole stared at the plastic and aluminum foil containers stacked on the nearby coffee table with the occasional smear of marinara against the aluminum foil. After dinner, Brooke asked to watch a movie, and Cole vaguely recalled her insistent clamoring for *Annie. At least I won't have to do the walk of shame at work.*

Although, could it really be called the walk of shame . . . unless someone's definition of shame included indulging in too much pasta and watching movie musicals?

Cole set the remote on the table, and the movement stirred the paused screen of the television, hovering over the scene menu. He lowered the volume manually, unsure if someone already clicked the mute button.

He remembered half of the movie... so he fell asleep in the second half. Brooke had been the first to pass out, but he couldn't remember when Nina fell asleep. Regardless, all three spent the night on the couch.

Cole moved silently toward the kitchen and surveyed its surroundings. He spotted a small coffee machine beside the stove and cabinets surrounding the fridge. Food and coffee, in that order.

But a quick search through the cabinets and fridge shelves revealed more scraps than materials for a hearty breakfast. He spotted half a loaf of sliced whole grain bread, three eggs, half a tomato, a small cluster of blueberries in a Tupperware container, and a half-empty bag of pancake mix powder.

"Uh, I think Nina needs some groceries." He murmured and patted his pockets until he found his phone. He scrolled through the apps on his home screen until he spotted one for their local grocery, which offered same-day delivery.

He scrolled through the options, picked out a little bit of everything—fruit, veggies, fresh deli meat, dairy, bread, and sweets—and changed the address from his apartment to Nina's. He might've hesitated before ordering, but the fridge was empty.

Cole budgeted his paycheck well, so he kept a small nest egg for spontaneous splurges. Spotting her groceries for a second time wouldn't break the bank. It would, however, make all the difference for Nina and Brooke.

But the issue of breakfast still sat on the table.

Looking at his choices, Cole had few options and fewer ideas for any substitutions when the inevitable came up. He could make scrambled eggs and toast, but Brooke may not be happy with the choice. The tomato and cluster of blueberries weren't enough of a meal either.

The thought of waiting until later for him to eat, picking up something on the way home, crossed his mind until a small hand gripped one of his fingers. Cole glanced down to find Brooke standing beside him.

Brooke rubbed her eyes. "Good morning." She yawned, and the drowsiness on her face had Cole concerned that she would find a way to fall asleep standing up.

Cole scooped her underneath her arms and sat her on the countertop next to him, seeing how her eyes snapped open. Brooke rubbed her eyes hard and stared expectantly at Cole.

"Good morning, Brooke," he kept his voice low, guessing Nina was still asleep on the couch. After the previous night, she likely crashed harder than the rest. "I was going to make some breakfast, but the fridge looks nearly empty. Do you like eggs and toast?"

Brooke crinkled her nose and shook her head fervently with the strong opinions of a five-year-old on display. "No."

"Then, what do you like for breakfast?"

"Can we make pancakes?"

Cole turned the bag of pancake mix to the side, reading along the ingredients for instructions. He saw one egg and some water as the recipe listed on the side of the box. Pancakes would work nicely on a stretched ingredient list.

"You know what? We can make pancakes, but I'm going to need your help. Will you help me?" Cole asked, but he didn't need to wait for an answer. Brooke gasped and pointed to one of the nearby drawers. Cole opened the drawer and pulled out a few measuring cups decorated with a flower pattern.

Brooke accepted the measuring cups and earnestly stared at Cole. "I'll hold the cups for you." Her legs hung over the edge of the counter, swinging them lightly. Cole couldn't fight his smile or hide how Brooke's puffed cheeks and eager giggles warmed his heart.

Cole handled the heavy lifting of gathering the ingredients and cracking the egg, but Brooke insisted on mixing the batter with how firmly she held onto the whisk. It allowed him to drop a few blueberries into the bowl to make blueberry pancakes.

Cole peered into the bowl when Brooke started to mix the ingredients together, pointing to a few air pockets where the powder mix might hide. "You're doing a good job. Make sure to eliminate those air pockets."

"Okay!"

"Have you and your aunt made pancakes before?"

"Yes, and my mommy used to help us, too."

Cole heard the sadness in her voice when she mentioned her mother, and he couldn't blame her. She was only five and already knew a profound sense of loss, although somewhat diminished by a lack of permanence.

"I'm sure your mommy made great pancakes. I'll try my best to be half as good," Cole promised, and Brooke's mixing slowed to a stop. She peered up at him and held out one of her hands with the pinky flexed up while the rest of her fingers curled loosely.

"Pinky promise?" whispered Brooke.

Cole linked their pinkies and shared a smile, "I pinky promise."

He let go first and let Brooke continue mixing the pancake batter until the mixture dripped off the end of the whisk. A few dark spots of blueberry floated around the bowl among the sea of batter.

Cole hadn't found any butter, so he pre-heated the pan on the stove without anything inside. As he listened to the sizzle, he watched Brooke play with the whisk and skim it along the edge of the bowl.

"Mr. Cole, can I tell you a secret?" she said, blinking up at Cole. She glanced from side to side to check that no one was listening. Her hands fidgeted with the flower-patterned pajama pants she wore. Something tipped off Cole's alarm.

"Of course, you can." Cole turned off the stove and walked back to the counter, squatting down to be at eye level with Brooke. "Did something bad happen?"

"No. A lady came to the daycare and tried to sign me out. She told Miss Gloria she was my grandma, but mommy told me I don't have a grandma like other kids."

Cole's blood ran ice cold, and he stared at Brooke. He didn't think Brooke's biological father would randomly pop up in her life, let alone his family. From what little he knew of Nina's family, they seemed the right type to pull a stunt like that.

"Did she say anything else to you, Brooke? Anything about what her name was or why she came to pick you up?"

"No. Miss Gloria told her that she needed to call Auntie Nini and ask her about something, but the lady looked scared, and she ran out the front door. She didn't come back."

Cole sighed, and he leaned on the counter. Brooke dodged his gaze and stared at her pajama pants like they were the most interesting thing in the world. "Brooke, have you told your aunt about this?"

"No."

"Why not? You won't be in trouble, and I won't tell her unless you want me to."

"I was scared. Auntie Nini has been sad since Mommy died, and I know she's always working hard. She cries when she thinks I went to sleep sometimes," Brooke mumbled, and her hands continued to fidget. In her silence, she meant well.

She's a good kid. Cole frowned and stilled when Brooke hugged him, holding his waist and pressing her head into his chest. He lifted a hesitant hand to stroke her hair. *They need support more than ever. Rudy has the legal angle covered, but everything else might be where I can help.*

Cole moved the pancake batter bowl away from the edge, and Brooke shrugged, pulling the hood of her bear onesie over her head. He squatted down a little more to catch her eyes, and Cole smiled. "Your aunt only wants the best for you. I promise she wouldn't be upset with you if you told her."

"She won't?"

"No, she won't. Your aunt knows you've done nothing but be a good kid. As I said, if you want me to tell her for you, I'll mention it."

Brooke said nothing to that at first, but her downcast eyes reached up to Cole's. Then, she nodded and played with her sleeves. "Okay."

Cole reached into his pants pocket and fumbled around until he uncovered his wallet stashed deep inside. He thumbed through the cards and cash until he found a few of his business cards hidden between the different cards.

He handed the card to Brooke, "I want you to take this with you, okay? If something like that happens again, I want you to call me on an adult's phone, and I'll come to help. I know you might be nervous to tell your aunt, but I want you to know you can tell me."

"Promise you won't be mad?"

"I pinky promise you. If you need my help or even want to call me, I will answer. Your aunt and I don't want anything bad to happen to you, so it's our job to protect and keep you safe."

Brooke took the card from his outstretched hand and held the it against her chest. "I'll put it in my backpack!" She wiggled toward the counter's edge, and Cole caught her before she fell off the side.

He set her onto her feet and watched as she sprinted toward the front door. He vaguely recalled a few hooks mounted on the wall for purses and backpacks. In the empty kitchen, he loaded the other eggs into a skillet for him and Nina to share.

While the eggs sizzled on the stove, he loaded the first ladles of pancake batter into another skillet on the opposite burner and turned to medium heat. Between the busy stove, Cole prodded at the buttons on the coffee machine until he switched it on.

The soft hums and groans of the machine would've woken him up if he had been curled up on the couch still. He expected to see Nina any moment, especially when Brooke ran back into the kitchen with a smile.

She stood beside him but backed up whenever he approached the stove. Looked like someone had taught her all about kitchen safety, which put Cole at ease. He snuck a few glances down at the streak of brown whenever Brooke raced behind him, eyes concentrated on the two tiny ears flopping with every bounce.

A half-forgotten melody and garbled lyrics to a song sprang up in his head while he cooked breakfast, but Cole hummed it regardless. In the liveliness of the surrounding kitchen, he missed the approach of footsteps and the creak of someone leaning in the archway.

"Oh, you made breakfast?" Drenched in the heavy gravel of sleep, Nina's voice sent a shiver along his spine. Although he expected her, she snuck up on him.

He watched Brooke squeal loudly and sprint across the kitchen, arms raised. She crashed into Nina's legs and wrapped around them like she wanted to climb into Nina's arms. She got her wish when Nina leaned down and scooped Brooke into her arms.

"Good morning, Auntie!"

"Morning, little bug. You haven't caused any trouble for Mr. Cole, right?"

"No trouble at all. Brooke's been an excellent help," Cole interjected, bolstering Brooke's insistent nod of her helpfulness. He smiled and prodded at one of the eggs. "Morning, by the way."

"Good morning. The food looks great." Nina smiled at him, shifting Brooke to sit on her hip. Brooke's cheeks pressed to Nina's collarbone, and Nina kept her close. She wandered toward the stove and peered over.

"We have blueberry pancakes. But I added some coffee and eggs for us," Cole said.

"Oh? Those sound unbelievably good right now, especially the coffee."

"Thank Brooke for the suggestion of pancakes. I added the blueberries since the container appeared almost empty. I might've ordered some groceries for the empty fridge."

Nina's eyes widened a little, and the pink flush to her cheeks spread down her neck. Even the tips of her ears brightened from the blush. "Thank you. I hadn't realized how empty the fridge and cabinets were."

"No problem," Cole flipped the first pancakes over to get the other side to the golden brown color of the first half. *Not half bad*. He patted the top of each pancake and admired the near-perfect cook on the upturned side. "Brooke, you might want to brush your teeth and wash up since the first pancakes will be done soon."

"Okay!" Brooke ran from the kitchen, and her footsteps thundered down the hallway, eventually fading once she vanished into her bedroom. Cole felt Nina's presence at his side as she peered at the stove.

With a few minutes to themselves at most, Cole seized his chance. He flipped the fully cooked pancakes from the skillet and set them on a spare plate nearby for the spare pancakes. He ladled the other half of the batter into the skillet and handed Nina the mixing bowl to put into the sink.

She accepted it from his hands, and their backs brushed together as she passed to the sink. He heard the rush of water from the faucet and waited for the water to cut out before he spoke up.

"Hey, please don't see this as me overstepping or anything, but I think you should consider talking to Rudy about seeking a temporary restraining order until custody is decided. I don't trust your family to play by the rules or leave you two alone," Cole remarked.

He paused when Nina returned to his side while he checked the new pancakes. When he looked at her, she appeared to be studying his face. "If you think so, I can ask about it."

"You trust my judgment, huh?"

"Immensely. You haven't given me a reason not to."

"Good," Cole heard the coffee machine chime, and he opened the nearby cabinet overhead, searching for two mugs. Nina closed the one he pried into, but she pointed two cabinets down and took the spatula from him. "Trade?"

"Go ahead. Make us some coffee." Nina laughed and nudged Cole over with a light hip bump. Cole did as she asked, two mugs ready for coffee. He grabbed a few sugars from the dish next to the machine.

He turned to ask Nina how she liked her coffee, finding her sampling a bite of one of the pancakes from the plate. She covered her mouth, but her cheekbones raised with her smile, and the cheeky glimmer in her eyes smoothed over any apology.

"How are they?" asked Cole.

"Delicious," Nina promised, producing three plates for them and Brooke. "The blueberries add a nice touch since we're out of maple syrup and butter. I need to be more of a functional human from here on out."

"We all have our moments."

"That's reassuring coming from a guy like you."

"Me?"

"Yeah, it seems like you have everything together—a nice apartment, a good-paying job, knowing your responsibilities and not struggling to meet them. If I have it wrong, please tell me now."

Cole shook his head as he filled the first mug with enough coffee to jumpstart the rest of the day. "I didn't think anyone saw me like that. So, I appreciate that . . . you."

Nina smiled sagely but let the moment be. A knowing look passed between the two before the return of footsteps echoed closer. The private moment fluttered by and left the space for a peaceful breakfast.

After a long breakfast, Cole returned to his apartment for a change of clothes and his plans to do nothing meaningful with his free time. Sometimes, a man needed to veg out on television.

Brooke had grabbed his leg and gave him a puppy dog pout, begging him to stay. Yet Nina managed to pry her off and gently explain that Cole needed to go. He promised to stop by again soon, a promise he intended to keep.

Rolling into his reserved parking spot, Cole cut his car's engine and sighed. The interior of his sedan smelled of last night's pasta, and he recalled more moments from the night before when Brooke and Nina would sing bits and pieces of songs from *Annie*. He hadn't known a single one, or he would've joined along with his off-key tenor.

Cole stepped out of his car, locking it behind him, and headed for the apartment complex's lobby. But as he approached the front entrance, he noticed a familiar face off to the side with her pup wearing his walking gear.

"Morning sunshine!" January waved and pushed her headphones off her head to rest around her neck. Socks, wearing his walking booties and harness attached to his leash, began to vibrate excitedly. For a little Frenchie, Socks had a whole lot of energy.

"Jan! I didn't know you were swinging by!" Cole jogged over to them. Yesterday, the three had lunch, close to the Quinn and Yearwood office space, at a new health market for its opening day.

Since she saw him the day before—or rather, what he wore then—January's expression jumped from merely pleased to see him to boasting a sly smile and knowing eyes. She gave him a once-over.

"Weren't you wearing that yesterday?"

"Yeah, I wasn't home last night."

"Care to share where you were?"

"Depends. Will it be getting back to my brother?"

"That depends." January's amusement melted away for a split second, opening her eyes to concern. "Are you alright?"

Cole rubbed the back of his neck, even when he stopped in front of her and Socks. Socks pushed onto his hind legs and pawed at Cole's pants for attention. He wasn't content with a few rubs between the ears.

He nodded after a moment. "I'm fine. More than fine. I ended up spending the night over at a friend's house. I crashed on their couch after some takeout." Cole knew as soon as he said *their*, January's ears would perk up.

One of the first things lawyers learned in school was that words matter, yet their meanings could turn on a whim with enough emphasis.

January looked him over again like she tried to unearth the truth through a silent, intensive stare down. That thousand-yard stare earned her an invaluable reputation as a prosecutor in her former career.

"I assume this friend is named Nina," she commented, casually leaning back on her heels. Cole had been caught.

"How'd you know her name?"

"Dean told me. My fiancé is a little gremlin for gossip sometimes."

"How much about Nina do you know?"

"A little bit." January's tone struck an evasive note, but she sighed at his tense shoulders. He assumed his discomfort stuck out like a sore thumb. "As far as I know, Nina is the name of the woman you met at the speed dating event. You met her more than once, and she's currently engaged in some legal proceedings that worry you. Other than that, I know nothing else."

Cole tucked his hands into his pants pockets, "Dean's concerned about my friendship with her. He seems to think there's something fishy going on, but Nina and I are strictly friends." He couldn't help how he placed extra emphasis on *strictly* like it might save him from more interrogation.

January hummed, "I believe you. Truthfully, hearing that you're meeting more people and making friends is exciting. If she's a good friend to you, then I'm happy you've found companionship in her."

Unlike Dean, January accepted him at face value. Trusting his judgment, she didn't poke or prod for a non-existent truth. The little things about January Quinn reminded Cole why she was the best.

"I'm glad that you believe me. Dean oscillates between thinking I'm harboring secret feelings for Nina and trying to set me up with someone on a date. I haven't been single for that long, have I?"

"Dean, for all his clumsy mistakes, wants you to be happy. Because we're getting married so soon, he wants you to find the same level of happiness. But he and I took years to collide, and you're still young. If anything, I'm rooting for your happiness whenever it comes."

Cole smiled and reached his arm toward her. The two shared a brief yet warm hug, with Cole towering over Jan. "Thank you."

"Any time," January promised, patting his shoulder before she let him go. "You should head inside, shower, and enjoy your day off."

"You sure you don't want to stay a little longer?" asked Cole.

"I'd love to, but I need to get Socks' workout in for the day at the doggie park, so he won't tear up the apartment when I go out later. I have a spa day booked with Esther, Isobel, and Sabrina to unwind after a long week," Jan explained. She pushed onto her tiptoes and pressed a sisterly kiss to his cheek.

Cole smiled. "Alright. Be safe, and have a good day. You'll have to show me your nails later . . . I know you're a sucker for a good manicure."

"You know me so well!" January cooed playfully and tugged on Socks' leash. But before she left, she met his eyes. "One more thing before I go. I remember seeing you and Nina at speed dating night, and I thought I should say that you two were chatting like the world didn't exist. I suspect that you two will be good friends for a while."

"You think so?" Cole raised his brow, but he smiled at the thought, nonetheless.

"Call it my intuition . . . which is rarely wrong." January laughed and jogged off with Socks, who eagerly scuttled behind her. Cole waited until they vanished down the street before he turned and headed to his apartment.

January was right about everything.

Chapter Fourteen
Nina

Nina pulled the front door to her condo closed behind her while Brooke gripped her hand, softened by the feel of woolen gloves swamping her tiny fingers. The late October evening brought a crisp wind to kiss their cheeks pink and tousle through their blonde hair.

The sun hadn't set yet, but Nina expected the sun to go down soon. Gold and fall orange pushed the overcast clouds away while the air carried a subtle aroma from the color-changing trees.

"Are you ready to go, bug?" asked Nina while she fumbled with her keys to lock up behind them. She listened for the click in the door and slid her keys back into the mini backpack she had grabbed for their trip.

"It's time for the fair!" Brooke exclaimed, bouncing up and down to where her twin braids swung wildly around her face. "I want to go see the petting zoo!"

"I'm sure we can stop by the petting zoo. What animals are you excited to see?"

"A cow! Rachel told me that they have fluffy cows!"

"Fluffy cows sound adorable. Let's see if we have the nice cows today at the fair." Nina helped Brooke down the stairs with slow turns between each step. Brooke had been borderline obsessed with the idea of the fall fair that came into town a week ago since hearing about it from other kids at daycare. She talked about it non-stop for the entire week until Nina agreed to take her.

The agreement came with the caveat that Nina needed to finish all her current deadlines for projects, and Brooke stayed as quiet as a mouse whenever Nina worked on her articles. Nina noticed, and she wrote faster than usual.

But she finished her deadlines, so she had the promise to uphold.

Nina and Brooke stepped off the stairs, and Nina kneeled down to fix the sherpa-lined coat Brooke wore, wanting to keep her out from the cold. Her hands tugged at the tiny beanie over Brooke's ears to warm her up. Nina kissed her forehead.

"Alright, fairground time!" Nina stood up and turned toward her car parked outside her condo. However, her eyes wandered past her parked car when she noticed a familiar sedan roll up to the curb.

The window rolled down, and Cole leaned toward the passenger side, whistling, "Look who it is. Hey, you two."

"Cole! Hey!" Nina beamed and waved to him. She watched him put his car into park and turn down the radio, blasting some unfamiliar rock music. She stepped closer. "I didn't know you were coming by."

"I didn't plan on it, but I was passing through the neighborhood. I saw you two outside and decided to swing over and say hello. Any plans tonight?"

"Yeah, we have something—"

Brooke broke out of Nina's hands and sprinted toward the car at full force. She started chatting cheerfully and hopped up and down beside Cole's car. Nina rushed to pick her up, helping her stand at Cole's eye level.

"Auntie Nini and I are going to the fair! They have a petting zoo, a pumpkin patch, and lots of rides! She promised that if she finished all her work on time, we would go today," said Brooke.

Cole smiled. "Oh, wow. The fair sounds super fun. I'm guessing that your aunt finished all her work and upheld her promise?" He caught Nina's eyes, and she winked at him. He guessed correctly.

"Yes. I'm a woman of my word, so Brooke and I have an aunt-niece date at the fairgrounds. What about you? I assume you've finished work for the day."

"I am newly off the clock, but I had no other plans besides going home. I need a day to recharge after all the networking events this week. A few hours where I don't have to be the professional version of myself is long overdue."

A small laugh blossomed between them, and Brooke wiggled in Nina's arms, reminding her that she and Brooke had plans and Cole had a night home ahead of him. But Nina sensed he might be waiting for an invitation.

"Did you need a ride to the fair?"

"You should come with us!"

Nina and Cole stopped mid-sentence, having spoken up at the same time. Their words overlapped, but so did their intentions. A shy giggle pulled itself from Nina before she composed herself.

Brooke, however, squirmed out of Nina's arms and grabbed the door's handle, "Can Mr. Cole come with us to the fair?"

"You'll have to ask him."

"Please, Mr. Cole? It'll be lots of fun, and we can go to the petting zoo together!"

"If your aunt is okay with me crashing your girls' outing, I'd love to come along."

Nina scooped Brooke into her arms, "Alright, you've won us over, bug. We will be heading to the fair for your fluffy cows." She glanced into the car window, and Cole unlocked the car.

"Brooke can keep me company while you grab her car seat . . . she does need a car seat, right?" asked Cole. He brushed his hair from his face, making Nina realize he wasn't wearing hair gel or pomade that evening. The wind had left its mark on the swoopy fluff hanging over Cole's eyes.

It would be so easy to lean over and brush his hair out of his face. Nina's breath hitched but forced herself to get a grip. She opened the door and sat Brooke in the front passenger seat.

"I'll be a minute. The car seat is one of those booster seats, so it won't take too long to untangle it from my car." Nina stepped back and listened to the faded tidbits of conversation as she ran to her car, parked along the same curb. She picked up Cole's question about what animals were at the petting zoo before she couldn't hear them speaking.

She grabbed the booster seat from her backseat and carried it to Cole's backseat, smiling at how Cole and Brooke got along like a house on fire. Sure, Brooke was a friendly little girl to most people, but she talked her little head off whenever she and Cole got into conversation.

"Looks like the backseat is ready," Cole's voice interrupted Nina's distracted hands, and she helped Brooke into the backseat after her niece decided the best course of action was crawling from the front. She buckled her in quick when Cole cleared his throat. "Front seat is yours if you want it."

"Sounds good," Nina agreed.

She closed the backseat door and slid into the front, buckling herself in. She double-checked her purse and locked her car before turning to Cole. She noticed the fairground address flashed up on the GPS screen in the car already.

Cole leaned his arm out of his window and turned the volume to a low level. "Here we go!" he whooped as Nina and Brooke clapped and cheered. With a smooth turn of his wheel, the three took off from Nina's condo.

Nina rolled her window down enough to smell the fresh air from the snow-capped mountains miles away. Her cheek pressed against the colder pane of glass. She closed her eyes, swept away by memories. Fall had been her favorite season many years ago, and it might reclaim its place.

The wind whistled in her ears so loud, missing Cole and Brooke's attempts to get her attention until she registered the sensation of fingertips sliding up her arm. Nina jolted, and her hand brushed over the other hand, far too big to be Brooke's.

"Everything okay?" Cole whispered, leaning into her when the two stopped at a red light. Nina blinked at the cross streets in shock. She assumed mere minutes passed from the departure from her condo, but they appeared on the opposite side of the city judging by the cross streets.

"Yeah, I didn't realize time passed. I closed my eyes for a moment."

"You looked tired, and I noticed you were asleep two lights ago, but the green flashed before I could wake you up. It says we'll be at the fairground in less than five minutes."

"Thank you for driving," Nina yawned and stretched. She had fallen asleep without even realizing it, more tired than she thought. "I think all the noise of the fair will help me stay awake."

"Oh yeah. Think about all the screaming children and loud noises from the rides." Cole chuckled while he drifted the car into the right-hand turn pocket as the light flashed green. Behind the wheel, he made precise moves even in moderate traffic.

Nina, by contrast, felt like such a nervous driver.

Up ahead, the bright lights of the fair stood out from the tall bales of hay and the considerably darkened skies. Brooke's thrilled squeals filled the backseat, and Nina reached her hand back to hold Brooke's while Cole figured out the parking.

He pulled the car into a dusty lot with an overabundance of traffic cones and white tape markings to designate open parking spots. The line of fairgoers stretched out along the fence with one large entryway.

The cries of excited children and families rose from the fair like smoke, filling the evening air. Nina stared through the window in awe until the car lurched to a stop in an empty parking spot.

"We're here!" Brooke screamed, rattling her fists toward the sky. The car couldn't contain her energy, especially with how fast she unbuckled herself and dove for the door handle in the backseat.

Nina, however, moved faster than her. She had already unbuckled and had one foot out the door before Brooke opened hers. She swore she overheard Cole's laughter from the driver's side but focused on wrangling Brooke in her arms. Wandering jumped to the top of her concerns.

"What did your mommy and I teach you about going to new places?" Nina softly chided, and Brooke whined.

"Auntie Nini-"

"What did your mommy and I always say?"

"Never go anywhere without an adult or run away in crowded places because it could be dangerous. Bad people might hurt me if I'm not careful," Brooke mumbled, and Nina set her down.

"You have to hold mine or Mr. Cole's hand wherever we go, okay?" Nina reminded Brooke and laced their hands together. "We'll go wherever you want us to, but ask us with your big girl words."

Brooke calmed down and nodded. She held Nina's hand while they inched around the car, looking for oncoming vehicles. Cole met them at the back of his car and offered his hand to either girl. Brooke accepted his hand, sandwiched between him and Nina for maximum safety.

Nina kept an eye on her as they joined the line of fairgoers waiting for entry, but she relaxed a little after catching Cole sneaking glances once or twice. Between them, they could have eyes on Brooke.

Surprisingly, the line into the fair moved faster than Nina anticipated, which brought her, Brooke, and Cole to the front gates within a few minutes of hopping into line. Cole whipped out his wallet before Nina could grab her purse and slapped some cash on the counter.

"I'll take the two-hundred-ticket package, please," he requested, and several people behind them let out a few murmurs. Nina gave them a cursory glance with an intended *mind your business* on her tongue but held back.

The overwhelmed attendant, with his pimple-flushed cheeks and greasy hair framing his face, slid over a handful of tickets per Cole's request and payment. He stammered, "Have a good time."

"Thank you." Cole stepped forward with the tickets and handed them to Nina and Brooke. "Go wild, girls. We have plenty for the rides, snacks, and games to last the evening."

"Mr. Cole, you're so awesome!" Brooke screamed, and her little legs kicked when the three passed the petting zoo. As Brooke promised, Nina spotted a pen with a brown, fluffy cow getting petted by little kids and their parents.

"Ah, I try. Promise me one thing, okay? We'll save some of these tickets for a funnel cake because I can smell them from here," Cole whispered, eliciting giggles from Brooke.

"Deal." Nina watched his head tip toward her, and she smiled at his pleased expression. "I love funnel cake. Do you only take yours with powdered sugar, or are you a man of taste?"

Cole proved himself a man of taste when he not only ordered a funnel cake with syrupy strawberries and whipped cream loaded on top but when he offered to split half with Nina. Strawberry and cream funnel cakes were one of the few desserts Nina would consider selling her soul for.

Nina wiped her lips clean with her napkin, catching leftover powdered sugar and strawberry syrup. "This was so good."

"You can say that again." Cole tossed his napkin down into the empty funnel cake dish alongside the two forks used by him and Nina. They'd devoured the funnel cake after three rotations at the petting zoo for Brooke. "How's your ice cream sandwich, kiddo?"

Brooke's cheeks puffed like a chipmunk's, and she held a partially melted chocolate chip cookie and vanilla ice cream sandwich. She smiled big with her mouth too full to speak, and a shot of nostalgia threatened to choke Nina up. *Naomi used to do the same thing.*

So many of Naomi's mannerisms transferred to Brooke, and they popped out more since her passing to Nina's haunted eyes.

"I want to go to the Ferris wheel, but the line looks too long!" she complained, her legs kicking under the table brushed against Nina's. "Look how bright and pretty it is!"

"You're right. The Ferris wheel does look pretty right now since all its lights are on. But we can occupy our time with other activities before we check on the line. How does that sound?" asked Cole.

Nina heard Brooke's gasp while she collected the trash from their sweet treat indulgence, needing to walk off the bloated feeling. She hadn't eaten a funnel cake in years, and the richness made her queasy.

"Sounds like you have a plan in mind. Care to share, Cole?" Nina leaned on the table and took in Cole's smile. His smile, a little lopsided with a secret, matched the twinkle in his eyes enough to tell her he had an idea.

"I suggest we check out some of those games on the outer edge of the fair. There's a dunk tank, ring toss, the duck game, and your standard fare for a traveling carnival."

"You're so on."

Cole and Nina grabbed Brooke to walk between them toward the game booths, throwing their trash out. She inhaled the scent of fried carnival food and the distinct touches of animals from the petting zoo while they walked underneath the large, bulbed string lights.

As mentioned, the games Cole pointed out appeared close to one another along with others, like water gun horse races and rows of basketball hoops. Her eyes jumped between booths to pick out something she liked until she spotted a shooting game.

"Cole, over there!" At the end of the row, second to last, Nina gestured toward the shooting game with laser rifles and moving targets like ducks. "I was so good at those games as a kid."

"Do you still have the magic touch?" Cole hummed, and his eyes danced with intrigue wrapped up in them.

"How about a friendly competition to find out?"

"State your terms."

"If I win, I get to pick the prize . . . and if you win, I'll sign up to be dunked in the dunk tank."

Cole let out a startled laugh, short but loud like a bark, and held his free hand to her, "Nina Byndel, I almost think you're a glutton for punishment. Dunk tank in this weather?"

"That's how sure I am that I won't lose," replied Nina, and she shook her hand with his. "Brooke will ensure we play fair, like our referee."

Brooke nodded, "I will! Fair and square!"

"Fair and square, that's right." Nina and Brooke high-fived and raced to the shooting game when the current players vacated their spots. Cole followed behind them and stationed himself at one of the toy rifles. Nina grabbed the other one and tested the heaviness in her hands.

She'd used a real one once or twice, learning from an article she wrote for one of her first pieces after graduating. But she preferred the game over the real deal any day.

"Three tickets per player," remarked the attendant at the shooting booth, a woman with bright aqua hair piled into a ponytail and wearing a black polo like the other fairground workers at every booth, ride, or food station. Cole forked over the tickets on his and Nina's behalf. The worker took them. "Good luck, and may the best shooter win."

Nina and Cole held up their rifles, and the bell chimed off, signaling the start of the game. The machine whirled to life with assorted noises and the painted scene of a peaceful lake where the targets would emerge.

At the first duck, Nina pulled the trigger, and the target turned from red to blue. Her rifle had a blue ring around the muzzle, which meant she tagged the duck first. Cole's rifle had a green one instead, so his prizes would turn green with a first hit.

But once the first duck flew, the rest came in dizzying succession. Shots fired off with the muted *boom* from the speakers attached overhead, yet Nina forced herself to tune all the noise out. She aimed and knocked down duck after duck, painting their targets blue with the barrel of her gun never dropping down.

However, when a golden target duck flew up the middle of the stage, Nina tagged the duck within seconds, and a bell went off inside the booth. She lowered her gun and noticed Cole do the same.

Unlike her, though, his eyes raked over her. The glimmer within them had a hot flush stirring underneath the heavy layers of her coat. He stared but lowered his rifle to the counter. "Nina."

"Yeah?" she asked, breathing heavily.

"Look at the score." Cole gestured with his head, and Nina glanced at the scoreboard. Cole got a respectable one-thousand, three hundred and fifty points for his hunting efforts, but she had almost tripled his score at four thousand and twenty-five. Each duck couldn't be worth more than 100 points. She turned back to Cole and found him smiling hard. "You kicked my . . . butt."

He censored himself for Brooke, who stood between them, and she appreciated that. She had kicked his ass, though. She won their friendly wager.

"That means I get my choice in a prize. Brooke, come here," she beckoned for her niece and scooped her up, pointing to the rows of toys at the top. "Anything you want from the two-thousand and up points row is yours."

Brooke examined the toys with a discerning eye, but in the end, the color pink won out when she spotted a fluffy pink horse. She pointed. "The horse, please!"

The attendant collected the horse as requested by Brooke, and Brooke squeezed the doll into her arms, burying her face into the horse's mane. Nina stepped back from the counter and walked to stand beside Cole.

"Where to now?"

"Well, seeing as the *Test Your Strength* game doesn't have too long of a line, I think it's time I redeem myself."

"I told you I have a killer shot, but I'll bite. Will you show off all your secret muscles for the crowd?"

"They're not that secret," Cole smirked and led her over to the *Test Your Strength* attraction with a hand hovered over the small of her back. Nina accepted the tickets from him in their tight bundle after he ripped off a few.

Cole handed the tickets over and conversed with the man behind the booth. The man handed over the mallet, and Cole waited his turn behind a young boy who seemed insistent on showing strength but fell short of the bell.

When the kid finally stepped aside after his two tries, Cole stripped off the coat he wore, revealing a medium gray long-sleeve. The shirt contoured to his upper body and arms, hiding nothing from view.

Nina's mouth went dry. She had been joking about secret muscles but took the opportunity to note how the sleeves accentuated the size of his arms and their perfect ratio between lean and jacked along a thin, golden line. But her eyes wandered to his torso when his shirt dared to stick and reveal the outline of his abs.

She snapped her eyes up when a whistle from him reached her ears, and saw him point to her. "You watching?"

"Oh, yeah. I'm all yours," Nina responded, and she assumed that women ogling him weren't out of the ordinary.

Cole grinned and swung the mallet onto his shoulder, studying the bell tower. He cocked his head where his hair fell over his eyes and cast shadows across his cheeks, obscuring him slightly. He moved a pace back and readied the mallet to swing.

Then, the mallet swung down and sent the small puck to ring the bell twice. Some spectators around the booth stopped and cheered. Cole, like a cheeky bastard, greeted his audience and took a bow.

He handed his mallet to the kid before him. "Have one more shot at it, kid. It's all about judging distance."

He beckoned Nina over with a smile. Nina moved through the crowd and approached Cole, whose eyes glowed with victory. He saved his pride after the shooting gallery. She turned to the rows of prizes as the bell went off behind them to the overjoyed screams of a happy child.

"So, what prize are you grabbing?"

"That depends . . . which one would you like?"

"Seriously?" Nina questioned and met his eyes, which brightened to tease the undertone of green from the hazel. "You're giving me your prize?"

"Why not? You or Brooke can have it." Cole reached to shrug back on his coat, and the move distracted Nina. Brooke's hand tapped her wrist, and she glanced down at her niece.

"You can have it!" Brooke chirped.

"Okay." Nina accepted her permission and scanned over the rows of prizes. She jumped around the options and eventually pointed toward the left top corner. "Those blueberry cows look adorable."

"One blueberry cow for the lovely lady, please," Cole remarked and presented the cow to Nina when the stuffed toy came off the shelf. "For you."

"Thank you." Nina tucked the blueberry cow into her purse and scooted closer to him as they walked toward the attractions.

"The Ferris Wheel line is still long," Brooke complained, burying her face into Nina's side with the impatience expected of a five-year-old. Nina sighed, rubbing her head.

"Well, how about the carousel while we wait? They're taking a new batch soon, and we have plenty of tickets for when the Ferris Wheel has fewer people in line."

"I like carousels."

"Good, and how about you? Do you like carousels?" Nina murmured, and Cole didn't answer at first. She almost tapped his arm when she saw his distant look and gently veered to check-in. But he shook his head, and the distance vanished.

He lightly poked Brooke's nose to her giggles. "I love the carousel. We should hurry." He and Nina pretended to run for the carousel, but it was more of a light jog through the packed fairgrounds.

The three got into the line and produced the nine tickets for them to ride, making it onto the next go-around. Brooke wiggled from Nina's arms and led her and Cole to a row of two horses and one stag painted in gorgeous colors.

"You get the horse on the inside, and I'll take the middle horse." Nina hoisted Brooke onto the painted saddle and buckled her niece in. "Hold onto the pole nice and tight."

"Okay!" Brooke grinned and wrapped her arms around the pole. Hers would move when the carousel started again, while Nina could take the stationary horse to watch her. Cole chose the stag on the outer edge and easily mounted it.

"I haven't ridden one of these in years. I probably look ridiculous," Cole whispered to Nina, who swallowed a laugh. Sure, Cole looked a little out of place since most riders were children with their parents standing beside them. But a few teenagers a couple of rows ahead proved that people of all ages deserved a moment of fun.

"I think you and the stag pair nicely."

"I'm naming him Hubert or something equally pretentious."

"You're ridiculous." Nina rolled her eyes, but her smile gave her away. A bell rang as the carousel began to move, and Brooke's delighted shrieks took over when her horse bobbed up and down.

Nina stayed stationary and held Brooke's hand across the slim gap between mounts, content to observe the joy written in every inch of her face. Her smile glowed, and at that moment, she became the spitting image of Naomi.

Her heart ached for Naomi, but the cure was her providing happy memories for Brooke to look back on when she grew older.

Nina's attention wandered to her other side, where Cole rode the stag, staring at the world with every go-around. He might've felt her eyes on him because he turned his face, eyes colliding with hers.

In her throat, her words turned into a lump of everything she wanted to say but couldn't. *Thank you for coming. You're one of the first friends I've had in years. I trust you. I needed a rock, and you've become it.*

Their eyes clung to the feeling brewing in the late October evening, but Nina's skittish gaze darted away when Brooke's hand squeezed hers tighter. The wind pressed against her face, and Nina let the heat gathered under her collar run off into the night.

The sentimental touch was fun while it lasted.

Chapter Fifteen
Cole

T hrowing open the doors to the courthouse, Cole stepped up to the empty line through the metal detectors. He offered the courthouse security a polite nod, falling short of a smile. He fixed his tie and laid his keys, phone, and wallet into one of the shallow buckets for inspection.

"Morning, gentlemen," he remarked and stepped through the metal detector, missing their garbled greetings. He cleared the check and picked up his belongings at the end of the line. "Have a good one."

Without missing a beat, Cole beelined for the escalator and checked his watch for the time. He had a standing appointment waiting for him and refused to be late, even if the traffic tried to hold him hostage two blocks from the courthouse.

The rumple of his sleeves caught his attention more than once, drawing his eyes down to the pristine fit of his new suit. He rarely treated himself to indulgences as big as a custom suit when a standard one and some minor tailoring worked best. Yet he couldn't find a single regret in what he wore, not in how perfectly it fit him or the crispness of its all-black layers.

In his hand, his phone burned hot with his anticipation for a text he expected to crawl in at any moment. He pushed his morning appointments to other days of the week and put in for some time off, only a day.

Midway through his journey up the escalator, the buzz pressed into his palms, and Cole checked his phone, prepared to either thank his luck or ask for forgiveness later. *Moment of truth.*

COLE: Hey, did you receive an email with my request for time off? I sent it a few days ago, but I understand how busy things get.

ELLIOT: I cleared it with the bosses, and they stamped off on it. Are you sure that everything's alright?

COLE: Yes. Thank you. I've been asked to help a friend and promised to be there.

ELLIOT: Good man. Besides, I don't know why you were nervous about your time off approval. You have the most time off, and you'll lose those days if you don't use them by the end of the year.

COLE: Hah, don't give me any ideas about a vacation.

ELLIOT: Besides the other day, you never call out of work. I still remember when you were putting together trusts and other documents at home while you threw your guts up and sweated out a one-hundred and three-degree fever.

ELLIOT: Knowing you, you cleared all your calendar appointments in advance or handled the paperwork days ago. Don't even sweat it.

Cole remembered the time in question and how his bedroom couldn't shake the vomit smell for two weeks. Such a buzzkill. He tried to save time off for the moments that mattered most, and three days ago, one of those moments landed on his doorstep.

January and Dean finally tied the knot in an intimate ceremony on a crisp November morning. January joked during her vows that although she already felt connected to his family, she had the legal paperwork to prove it. Dean was a little less eloquent when he sobbed that January better be prepared to be stuck with his heart for life. Yes, Dean had been the crier of the two. January had nice makeup she wanted to salvage.

Being the best man for the wedding was one of those "it matters" moments; no cash sum for a hard day's work could convince him otherwise.

His bosses' flexibility in their work policy made him a happy worker. It was a give-and-take that benefited everyone, especially him.

He liked Elliot's text once the escalator spat him out at the second floor, settled in the hallway he sprinted down last time at the courthouse. His head remained on a swivel for any signs of the Byndels as he walked down the hall.

Cole's eyes strayed ahead and spotted Nina standing outside one of the side rooms, dressed to the nines for the mediation.

"Speaking of, he made it!" Nina's voice picked up, and she waved Cole over eagerly, even while Rudy appeared exhausted by her excitement. But that didn't stop Cole from speeding and reaching him and Nina.

"Thanks for calling me, man." Cole shook Rudy's hand, giving him the proper due. The last thing he wanted was to step on Rudy's goodwill.

"Nina requested your presence today." Rudy cleared his throat, and neither could ignore the tension. Nina requested him, but Rudy dissented. "I told her this may not be the best idea to poke the bear, but she insisted."

"But his presence could deter them, too. They don't bother me when he comes. He scares them, so I would rather accept his help than do it alone."

"Whatever you want."

Nina turned to Cole and reached to grasp his hands, clothed by thin mittens. She smiled. "Thank you for coming to support me. I appreciate having you here."

"Of course," Cole murmured. His thumb stroked over her knuckles before they simultaneously let go, unsure who moved first. He watched her grab her purse from the bench behind her knees and clutch it close to her chest, protectively looping her arms around the loose straps of her dark tote bag. "How are you feeling?"

"I shouldn't be as nervous as I am. They can't do anything to me during mediation, but Brooke's being kept in another room, and they wanted to speak to her alone. I don't like having her involved, but she has to be."

"They wouldn't cause any distress to Brooke on purpose if that reassures you. Courts are intended to operate in the child's best interest, and her age will keep things simplified."

"That . . . is reassuring."

Cole nodded, observing Nina's worried fidgeting until her posture relaxed. Her shoulders dropped, and Nina forced an exhale, shaky. She blinked at him, and Cole coaxed another breath out of her to keep her calm.

After a few shared breaths passed between them, Cole offered Nina his arm like a gentleman and leaned into her. "Whenever you're ready to go, I'm with you at every step. They can't hurt you or Brooke."

"They can't hurt me or Brooke," Nina repeated in a soft whisper and curled her arm around the crook of Cole's arm. "Let's go."

When she wrapped herself around his arm, Nina stayed close to him, and Cole led her across the hallway. A glance over his shoulder spotted Rudy tucked behind them, on his phone, and he couldn't shake the feeling that Rudy preferred his presence elsewhere. But Nina's demands reigned supreme.

They piled into a room smaller than the average courtroom for mediation. However, Cole noticed the glass window peering into an adjacent room with an intercom speaker built into the wall. The layout reminded him of a police interrogation room down to the one-way glass window.

Through the glass, he spotted Brooke sitting at a small table in a dark dress. She appeared entranced by printed sheets from a coloring book and a plastic box of assorted crayons, some more worn down and duller than others. She wasn't paying much attention to the two women beside her, wearing badges from the court attached to their jackets.

With a pixie cut and cheekbones sharp enough to cut glass, one woman wrote something down on a notepad using an aqua blue pen. She occasionally glanced up, said something, and wrote down Brooke's response. Her eyes remained narrowed, almost scrutinizing every word of Brooke's babbling.

The other woman, boasting long strawberry blonde curls and a tailored charcoal suit, would pass Brooke crayons every few seconds. She stayed silent for the most part, interjecting during stretches of silence to prompt more conversation.

Cole didn't need the sound to understand that.

He turned to the others in the room, facing Nina's mother, brother, and future sister-in-law with one of their attorneys. A table with seven chairs resided in the middle of the room, and all eyes drew to it like the center of gravity.

"Nina. I'm surprised you came to mediation at all," Vera stared at her, eyes loaded with disdain, while she stiffly shoved her purse's strap higher onto her shoulder. All her movements exuded a robotic rigidity from the stick rammed so far up her ass, shrouded in designer-label clothes.

"The judge ordered it, and I'll play by the court's rules. We know it won't work anyways," Nina replied, chewing into the ensuing silence and spitting it out with an equal measure of contempt. Cole tightened his hold on her.

He grimaced. *Don't let them get the better of you, Nina. They're not worth it.*

Nina squeezed his arm when all parties whirled toward the main door at the slightest creak, and the final member of their mediation arrived. The mediator himself. A gentleman in a crisply pressed suit and a sun-touched tan shut the door behind him.

His tight-lipped smile presented as cautiously optimistic, but he opened with a warm, "Good day, everyone. My name is Hector Murillo, and I've been assigned to handle the mediation for . . . Byndel v. Byndel?"

"That would be us," Felicity remarked and stepped forward to shake hands, but Hector didn't react. "Thank you for your time."

"We should get started with the mediation, so please sit around the table." Hector grabbed the chair in the middle to be the dividing line, cutting the circular table into two halves—Nina versus her family.

However, the lack of seats became obvious when Cole counted seven chairs but eight people in the room. He pulled out Nina's chair and tucked her in while Rudy took the seat to her left, and Vera, Maxwell, and Felicity assumed their side of the table with their representation.

Nina glanced at Cole when she noticed him without a chair. "Cole, do we need to grab you an extra chair?"

"I'll be alright," he assured her. "I can stand for a while. I sit too much during work."

"Are you sure?"

"Positive. Let's get the mediation started with as few delays as possible. You have important errands to handle afterward, no?"

Nina hesitated, but she relented after a moment. Cole offered his hand to her to hold if she so wished, but Nina's fingers dug into her thighs through the fabric of her skirt. Cole's hand retreated to press into the back of her chair and rooted himself in the free spot to her immediate right.

His eyes wandered across the table to examine each opponent who sat down. Even between Vera, Maxwell, and Felicity, he noticed fractured demeanors, and those underlined their intentions.

Maxwell radiated an aura of smugness that wafted around the room like a cheap, watered-down cologne. *He wanted to win because he felt entitled to win.* Felicity reeked of desperation with how often she nitpicked at her clothes and jewelry. *She wanted to win because she wanted a child more than to preserve Brooke's happiness.* Finally, Vera continued to huff under her breath and glance at her wrist, probably for the silver wristwatch and the time. *She wanted to win as a final victory over her dead eldest daughter and punishment for Nina.*

Cole wasn't sure which of the Byndels equaled the worst offender if not all of them.

Hector gestured to the two attorneys. "Gentlemen, I appreciate you coming. I would like to facilitate a dialogue between all parties openly and reasonably, but if that cannot be handled responsibly, I will ask that you two proceed as the mouthpieces for your clients. Is that understood?"

"Yes," Rudy remarked first, and Nina squared her shoulders back. Her hand reached out to Cole's, and he switched his grip to lace their fingers together. The warmth from her mittens brushed against his cold palm.

"Good. Mr. Francisco, do you and your clients abide by those terms?"

Mr. Francisco, one of the attorneys for Nina's family, glanced up from his papers with his tortoise-shell bifocals ready to take a swan dive off the bridge of his nose with how low they sat. He cleared his throat. "My clients and I agree to the terms set. We are committed to the minor's best interest in this dispute."

Somehow, Cole could feel Nina roll her eyes without seeing her face. The harsh change in her grip on his hand told him about the rush of anger ringing in her ears. He pressed his thumb into the back of her palm instead of speaking.

They won't get away with it.

"Mr. Murillo," Nina spoke up, but unlike the rest of the room, Cole's body didn't tense like he expected a fight. No, she started off too soft-spoken and gentle to cause conflict unprovoked. "May I ask a question?"

"Yes, of course."

"Who is that in the next room with Brooke?"

"The woman with the shorter hair is Jodi Burke, the court child psychologist tasked with her evaluation, and beside her is Brooke's appointed minor's counsel, Holly Irwin. Minor's counsel represents the will of the minor, in this case, Brooke, related to custody arrangements and other matters. They're external, unbiased actors who gauge the child's needs."

Nina nodded, and Cole scooted closer to her, kneeling at eye level. She was worried about the process; he understood that. "Minor's counsel and child psychologists will keep things simple for Brooke and not overwhelm her with too many questions. They're ensuring that she's safe and happy living with you."

"She is," Nina whispered, tears threatening to fall. So, Cole started to rub soothing circles into the back of her hand until she sucked in a heavy breath. It would be okay.

Cole rose onto his feet and glared across the table, his eyes narrowed hard. He expected Hector to resume the negotiations as intended and reach the inevitable conclusion that neither Nina nor her family was willing to compromise. *All or nothing.*

"We will begin with opening the floor to whichever side wishes to speak first and allow you to state your interests, not your positions, regarding your dispute. Then, the other side will respond." Hector barely needed to wait before Maxwell and Vera exchanged looks.

"Our intentions are simple. We want to be a happy family and for little Brooklyn to live the most enriching life possible. If she lived full-time with us, then she would be happiest," said Vera.

"Ma'am, I strictly asked for your interests, not your positions."

"Apologies."

"Is that all you're claiming as your interests, then?"

When no one else answered, Cole heard Nina sigh loud in exasperation. The other side clearly did from how their eyes snapped over.

"If I may respond to that," Nina started, but her words sounded forced, like she shoved them through clenched teeth to avoid unnecessary fighting. "I don't think separating a five-year-old from the only family she's ever known and giving her to someone who won't keep her connected to her mother would be a mistake."

"How dare you accuse us of that," Felicity gasped, firmly out of line, and earned herself a warning stare from Hector.

"You want to adopt Brooke as your own, erasing Naomi from the records if you wish. I know you all, and you wouldn't tell her anything about Naomi because you hated her. You demonstrated a lack of care because you disowned her while she was pregnant with Brooke and left her to fend for herself. Naomi named me to be Brooke's guardian until the age of eighteen. I am looking out for her best interests and the wishes of her mother, who refused to let you know Brooke . . . and her name is Brooke, not Brooklyn."

"Nina, you're being bitter. The fact is that you can't provide for Brooklyn as a single woman compared to Felicity and Maxwell's dual income and the support of your father and me—"

"Actually, I can. I rent a two-bedroom condo in a relatively nice part of the city with enough funds to enroll Brooke in daycare when I can't stay home, purchase groceries, and provide for her necessities."

Hector waved his hands. "We are veering off-topic. Miss Byndel, I appreciate your insights into what you can provide, but how about we focus on your interests? What do you want coming to the negotiating table that you might share with your family?"

"I'm concerned about Brooke's health, her happiness, whether she knows the amazing woman that her mom was and maintaining the status quo."

"Alright, let's focus on that last one. Since both sides seem adamant about protecting the happiness and well-being of the minor, this dispute comes down to the execution of how best to support the minor's needs. What do you mean by status quo?"

"I would continue to have sole physical and legal custody per my sister's will. As my sister disowned them, none of our biological family would have visitation rights or a claim to her life. I'll pursue restraining orders to stop any potential interference or harm if necessary. Above all else, those ensure Brooke will have a better, more loving childhood than I had."

Vera scoffed loudly, and something in the air changed when her hand smacked against the table. "Stop being so dramatic! You had a great childhood and want to feel like a victim."

"Just because you mostly neglected my emotional and physical needs as a child instead of beating me often like Naomi doesn't mean I had a great childhood," Nina snapped back, and all hell broke loose.

"You can't talk to Mom like that!"

"I can't? Watch me."

"You should really consider therapy for the bitterness you're holding onto."

"How about you pay for those sessions and consider some for yourself instead of stealing a child from the dead woman whose life you ruined, Felicity?"

"You frigid bit—"

"Don't finish that sentence," Cole interjected and watched as Felicity clammed up, drawing the ire of Maxwell's eyes on him. Instead, he gestured to a frazzled-looking Hector. "The room's yours."

Hector got out of his chair and went to grab a bottle of water while the silence persisted, hushing the members of the Byndel family gathered around the table. His sleeve caught on a switch next to the intercom when he passed the window.

A soft crackle wheezed out from the intercom, but Brooke's voice carried through any static from the old machine, "-and I like hanging out with Auntie Nini and Mr. Cole!"

"Who's Mr. Cole, Brooke? You haven't mentioned him before." Jodi asked, immediately more interested in Brooke's words than scribbling on her notepad.

"He's Auntie Nini's friend! I met him at the grocery store, and he helped us with stuff. We went to the fair recently! And he and Auntie Nini play tea party with me all the time!"

"I got it. Do you like Mr. Cole?"

"I like him a lot! My friend at school, Millie, has a cool uncle who's a firefighter! I wish Mr. Cole was my uncle because he's a lawyer and super smart."

Brooke's words prompted a choked gasp from somewhere in the room, but Cole couldn't tell from whom due to the ringing in his ears. His brain felt like metaphorically running into a brick wall, at a loss for words.

Holly scooted closer to Brooke. "Sweetie, have Mr. Cole and your aunt talked about them being special friends or dating? Have they talked about getting married?"

"Nope!" Brooke shook her head and traded a crayon of dull blue for a bright green to color with. "But I want them to get married so I can be the flower girl—"

Hector switched off the intercom, and Cole realized he hadn't breathed since that little nugget of revelation. He assumed Brooke didn't seriously mean he and Nina should get married.

Yet, when he met Nina's eyes, his chest ached. Her eyes shone with something entirely unreadable, and she mouthed two words, *I'm sorry.*

Cole swallowed, still processing, and refused to relinquish Nina's hand. He caught glimpses of the shocked faces of Vera, Felicity, and Maxwell. None of them appeared sure of what to do or say.

He couldn't blame them there for once.

Hector sat back at the table and uncracked the lid on the water he grabbed. Cole listened to the crinkling of the plastic, doing everything in his power to push Brooke's words out of his mind. He needed to be present and focused on the mediation, even though it was destined to fail.

As he guessed, the mediation wasted two hours and went nowhere. Neither side was willing to budge on their positions, so they would proceed with more hearings before a judge. The custody battle was officially on.

Cole and Nina, who spent the entire time holding hands under the table, ambled out of the room. In the hallway, Cole caught up on the air that abandoned him at the mediation table.

Beside him, Nina's face retained a flush from when she raised her voice or held back tears during the talks. The pained gasp for breath escaping her when they crossed into the hallway yanked hard enough on Cole's heartstrings to leave a bruise.

She hunched over, one hand on her knees while the other still grasped his, and panted softly like she had run a marathon in the summer's heat. People levied awkward stares but gave them a wide enough berth and walked around.

"Nina," Cole murmured and lifted her to stand back up. "Breathe like this. You'll get more air in."

"Thanks," she shivered and tipped her head back. "That was the worst experience I've had in a solid minute besides breaking up with my ex-fiancé."

"I've had my fair share of break-ups, so I get it."

"He was my first."

"Oh," Cole wished his tongue stopped creating the most awkward entanglements to crawl out of. He wasn't a smooth talker like Dean. He would've spent more time drenched in the whole debacle of the mediation, but the next door down swung open.

Brooke walked out and looked around expectantly until she spotted Nina and Cole. "Auntie Nini!"

She broke out of Holly's hands and sprinted over in full force. Nina swooped down and scooped Brooke into her arms, kissing all over her cheeks. Giggles erupted from the aunt-niece duo loud enough to fill the courthouse from ceiling to ground floor.

"I missed you, bug. Were the ladies nice?" Nina scaled back all the kisses, but Cole spotted glossy lip marks on the little one's cheeks.

"Yes! Miss Holly colored with me, and Miss Jodi gave me a lollipop to save for home!"

"That's awesome!"

Brooke's excitement for Nina lasted approximately five more seconds before she wriggled in her arms, pointing directly at Cole. "Mr. Cole! Hi!"

"Hey there, kiddo," Cole beamed, and he offered her a high five. However, Brooke reached both arms out toward him in a silent demand to be held. He caught Nina's eye, followed by her nod of approval, and accepted Brooke into his arms. "How are you?"

"Do you want to see the pictures I colored with Miss Holly?"

"Of course! Show me what you made."

Brooke pointed to her backpack until Nina fetched the stacks of coloring sheets drawn on by Brooke's heavy-handed technique from its pocket. She passed them to Cole, allowing him to examine Brooke's art.

"The first one is a ladybug on a flower. The second one is a Halloween witch with her cat and a pumpkin, my favorite. The third one is a picture of the beach. The last one is supposed to be a fruit and veggie garden, but I didn't get to finish it." She explained each one with pride sparkling in the glow on her cheeks or how her eyes expressed every ounce of happiness she could hold.

Cole smiled, "Those are amazing. I might keep one of these."

"Really?"

"Really. Now, what do you want to do? I promised your aunt that I would owe the two of you lunch. Tell me where you want to go."

"Okay, but can we feed the ducks at the park afterward?" Brooke stared at him with those bright green eyes, not unlike Nina when she pleaded silently for something she wanted. Ah, he had the day off anyway.

"Alright, we can go feed the ducks. Now, where will we be going for lunch today?" Cole gestured to Nina to prepare to leave as the doors to the mediation room opened. Vera, Maxwell, and Felicity wandered out, and they all looked Nina and Brooke's way.

Cole's hand found a place pressed into the small of her back instead of the usual hover over the same spot. His fingers splayed out when Nina leaned into his touch. They spun around and walked out, knowing eyes followed their departure from the courthouse.

While Brooke writhed in his arms like a wiggle worm, Nina stayed painfully still beside him. Cole wanted to look her way, but he chewed on the nagging feeling that he shouldn't.

Even when the cold November afternoon slipped under the collars of the coats they wore or blew Nina's hair all around her face, neither said a word. Brooke's chattiness carried them to the car, where Nina accepted her niece from Cole's hands.

He hung back as Nina buckled Brooke into the backseat of her car and quietly closed the door, leaning on it. She stared at Cole. "I'm so sorry about what happened back there . . . with what Brooke said."

"Oh . . . wait, why are you apologizing?"

"I don't want to make anything awkward between us because we're friends. Ever since you've come around, you've been such a good presence for her and me . . . and I'd hate for you to think I've been peddling anything romantic between us."

Once she started, Nina took off in a ramble at full tilt. Cole witnessed her unraveling for a minute before his hands cupped either side of her face, stilling her one-sided dialogue with him.

"I appreciate your worries, but you don't have to apologize. Kids say things that either mean nothing serious or don't understand the gravity of their words. I wouldn't hold that against you or her," said Cole.

He waited for Nina to reply. His eyes skimmed over her reddened cheeks from the cold and how the flush stretched across her nose when he noticed the wideness of her eyes. Then, he thought about the intimacy of the gesture with his hands gently holding either side of her face.

Oh. Fuck. He made things more awkward again.

Cole dropped his hands and mumbled, "Sorry about that."

"No! It's fine. Let me drive you to your car at least, or I'll give you a ride wherever Princess Brooke decides for lunch," Nina assured him and scampered toward the driver's side of her car, quickly getting inside.

Cole jammed his hands into the pockets of his suit trousers and considered a nice smack of his forehead against the nearest concrete pillar. If he learned anything today, Brooke and Dean would get along amazingly, with their hopes for his and Nina's friendship becoming a little less platonic.

Chapter Sixteen
Nina

Sitting in the plush armchair of Teagan Batista's personal office at the *Sunkissed* headquarters, Nina's fingers picked at the chair's fabric while her bounding pulse thrummed in her ears.

She'd received an email from Teagan's assistant a few days ago asking her to come into the office for a meeting. While the email was vague, Nina guessed her recent article for the newly updated *Sunkissed* website needed some directional tweaks.

Nina had never been someone who embraced critique fearlessly. She understood it came with the creative territory, but she had long passed the day when she'd cry over comments or suggested changes. These days, critiques were expected in the writing industry, and she learned to co-exist with them and have self-confidence.

Yet, a woman like Teagan Batista intimidated her. Teagan ran one of the most prominent publications on the market, found in every grocery store, gas station, or newsstand worldwide. Who wouldn't be a little off their game if called to an unspecified meeting with her?

Nina's fingers raked down the arms of her seat, careful not to leave nail indents behind in the plush fabric. The office door behind her remained ajar, and all the ambient noises of a trendy but busy office space filtered through the crack. Phones rang while people's conversations meshed together to form a perfect symphony of connection that Nina missed.

Her writer life was a solitary endeavor, punctuated by stretches of silence to work and a back-and-forth email for editing or publication details.

The chair across the desk from her was empty, but the door behind her swinging open told her that Teagan arrived, albeit behind schedule. While Teagan expected punctuality, rumors alleged she favored the term *fashionably late* for herself.

Nina brought her hands into her lap to stop maiming her chair and locked them together, letting the tight sensation anchor her to the ground. "Morning."

"Good morning, Nina. Thank you for making time to meet with me." Teagan hung her burnt orange blazer over the back of her desk chair, adding another pop of color to the office. Nina envied the chic design of the office—not shy about its use of colors or modern décor—and how Teagan made vibrant colors and patterns the norm.

"I assumed it was important if you needed to speak with me. Is it about my articles?"

"Yes, I also wanted to talk to you about those."

As well. Nina wanted to swallow the urge to throw up all over Teagan's expensive desk. Since Brooke visited the courthouse for her evaluation a few days ago, Nina wobbled along the thin edge between coping and being ready to succumb to an anxiety attack. Every little strain promised to be the final push to send her over the edge.

She barely hung onto her sanity through meltdowns, mishaps, and the steep learning curve dedicated to child-rearing.

In a moment of foolish bravery, Nina coughed into her arm and asked through her aching throat, "Is there something wrong with the articles I sent in? I haven't received an email about them making the cut, but the check arrived in my mailbox."

"Oh, not at all!" Teagan waved her hands with all the breeziness Nina longed for, and some of her tension abated. "I want to commend you for the good work you've been producing for me. I don't know what it is this quarter, but my staff and normal pinch hitters have been dropping the ball."

"I didn't know that," Nina stammered, but she regretted how dumb she sounded. Of course, she would never know about the inner workings of *Sunkissed* simply because she wrote a few articles for them.

"I try not to publicize firings or other matters of my team, but let's circle back to you. We've established a good working relationship, and I'm never let down by your ability to adapt to assignments with tight deadlines and high expectations. Not to mention, your work ethic has been stellar despite your current circumstances."

Teagen sat back into her desk chair and rummaged through the desk drawers until she produced a colorful can of sparkling water, cracking it open with one of her manicured acrylics. She sipped at her drink, totally collected, but Nina stared at her.

How was she supposed to respond to Teagan?

Maybe she meant it as a compliment. Nina's brain scrambled to come up with a reaction, yet her tongue fell dead in her mouth.

Nina nodded quietly, shoving the clear memories out of her head about her hellish last few days. She was surprised that her makeup covered the bags under her eyes and the splotchy red spots all over her face from crying fits. Of the last two days combined, Nina ran on three hours of sleep, terrifying levels of caffeine, and a miracle.

"Thank you. It hasn't been easy . . . but what else did you want to discuss? Usually, we communicate through emails or the occasional phone call instead."

"Ah, yes. The main reason I called you here wasn't to sing your praises, but that provides a good segue into what I've been considering. I have a proposal for you, and I'd like you to hear me out."

"Oh, okay. Well, I'm all ears for whatever you need."

Teagan set aside her sparkling water and laced her hands together. "Your contributions to *Sunkissed* have all been welcome additions, and you've saved the publication a few times close to the deadline. I've learned that I can rely on you, so I thought about how I might help you more."

"Oh?"

"So, I've decided to bump you up on my roster. See, I usually kept you reserved for a pinch-hit in case of emergencies, but you've proved yourself a valuable writer. Some of your articles have generated thousands of clicks to our website, and I need that kind of talent in a more starring role."

Nina nodded, catching on slowly. "You want me to write original articles that are mine from the jump."

"Correct," If Teagan was impressed by her guesswork, she didn't show it. Nina's leg bounced underneath Teagan's desk from caffeine, nerves, or both. "Instead of being a last-minute call with a week-long deadline at most, you'd be offered the article first and have the option to take it or not."

"If I accept, how would my process change? Would there be more deadlines to meet before publishing? How about the choice of assignment?" asked Nina.

"Besides getting a first chance to pick up an article, I will offer you a bump in payment for every article that comes across my desk for publishing. As for the process, I would still set the general theme or subject of the article, but you have more creative freedom to write specifics. Let's say I give you a topic about summer fashion. You could write me a list of the top five influencers on social media to take inspiration from or a few examples of staple pieces in a summer wardrobe and where to find them. Are you getting the bigger picture here?"

"I am. When do you need an answer?"

"I was hoping to have your answer before you leave my office, but I can wait until the end of the week." Teagan stared at her with an unnervingly expectant gaze and drummed her nails against the desk.

Nina's leg bounced harder, even when she tried to stop herself. The pros and cons weighed on her mind, but she would've hesitated if Teagan asked her a month ago. While not what she initially looked for when she decided to freelance, more routine work came with a steadier paycheck for her and Brooke.

She had responsibilities to handle, and Brooke's needs topped the list.

Nina reached her hand out, "Deal. I assume a modified contract will come to my email before the end of the day?"

"Correct, and I'll have legal call you to go over any questions." Teagan shook her hand vigorously, and the nonchalance transformed into a serene, closed-mouth smile exuding an elegance befitting Teagan's status. "I'm pleased to offer you a more frequent presence here at *Sunkissed*, Nina. You've earned it."

"Uh, thanks. Did you have a specific direction for November's article, or would my next one be December?"

"I sense a go-getter in that question. No, I have something envisioned for November that requires your unique touch. I'm looking for an article about love and romance advice, so whatever comes to your mind will be appreciated. I look forward to seeing what you come up with for submission."

A sickening twist of regret punched through Nina's chest at the thought of love and romance. The healing process from breaking off her engagement had taken a backseat compared to her grief with Naomi, and she knew if she lingered over it, she might crack under pressure. Love would be her final push over the edge.

Her leg's bouncing resumed with a couple of rough knocks against the desk, pulling winces from Nina. She pushed one of her hands down hard on her leg to quell the shaking. She wasn't in the best headspace to write about love and all its enigmatic crap.

However, the words to request anything else fell short underneath Teagan's stare. Those eyes, almost hawk-like with intensity, undermined whatever confidence she might assemble to modify. *The paycheck, Nina. Focus on the end, not the means you used to get there.*

So, as much as she'd prefer to write about something as simple as beauty routines and fall color palettes instead, Nina sucked up her pride and collected her bag. She offered Teagan a thankful smile, pushing past the forced feeling, leaving phantom pains behind in her chest.

"Thank you for the opportunity. I assume the deadline is the last week of the month, per usual." Nina checked for her possessions as she rose out of the chair, ready to go home. She needed a solid hour of decompression in bed, bundled under a weighted blanket, and her mind taken off the task before her.

"Yes, of course. The Monday of the last week of November will be the deadline, so the editor can double-check and proofread. I'll contact you over the next few weeks to see your progress. Keep me in the loop, and I know we'll have another Nina Byndel hit on our hands." Teagan rose from the chair, gesturing toward the exit, but Nina already had one foot out the door.

Nina waved halfheartedly, yet the elevator called her name with a sharp whine when the doors opened. People poured out, spilling into the office and its open design instead of closed-off cubicles and restricted décor. Stepping around them and avoiding watchful eyes, Nina entered as the lone rider of the elevator before the doors closed behind her.

She shouldered her purse higher and clicked the button for the base floor, rocked by the shudder from the walls around her when the elevator descended. Her arms tightened around herself, softened by the fluff of her cardigan's sleeves, and her bag jostled against her hip with a few bounces.

"I need a coffee," Nina mumbled, glancing around despite no one else in the elevator. She knew of a coffee stand outside the building, but something frothy and flavorful might ease her writing woes. "I earned a coffee today."

The elevator doors opened on the lobby floor, and Nina headed out of the building, looking for the coffee cart. She spotted the checkered umbrellas covering the cart in a layer of shade from the oddly sunny morning for the first week of November.

Nina shielded her eyes until her vision adjusted to the brightness all around, blinking through the sunshine. She wandered toward the cart as the last three customers headed off with their drinks in hand, leaving the space wide open for her.

She hustled faster across the stone tiles and leaned forward, spooking the young woman refilling the chocolate syrup canister behind the counter. The girl almost hit her head against the metallic edge, and the poor thing let out a yelp as she nursed her scalp protectively.

"Sorry about that." Nina winced when the girl turned around and noticed her. "Can I get a salted caramel latte, please?"

"Yeah, no worries. That will be four dollars and fifty cents."

"I have a five. Keep the change."

"Thanks. Your latte will be out in a second." Nina exchanged the five dollar bill with the girl and stepped to the side. She waited by the small counter across the cart from the register, where her latte would be set down once ready.

She stared at the downtown skyline from her vantage point outside the office space, thinking about picking up Brooke from daycare after her alone time and how she might brainstorm a suitable topic for a love and romance article. All the gut reactions that raced into her thoughts were downers.

She backtracked from those thoughts when a bright green to-go cup slid across the countertop. Her latte warmed her hands when she picked it off the counter, cradled between shaky fingers.

With her latte ready to go, Nina shouldered her bag the highest it could sit on her shoulder and took a sip. It was almost hot enough to burn her tongue, but she preferred her coffee close to scalding. She turned on her heel and headed for where she parked her car, having under twenty-five minutes before her meter ran out.

She barely made it back around the staircase outside the *Sunkissed* building when she overheard a voice all-too-familiar call out, "Nina! Stop walking!"

Nina's strides abruptly stopped, almost lurching forward and spilling her latte across the tiles. But her body seized up, including her hands, and prevented her from falling flat on her face.

She barely turned over her shoulder to see Zach barreling toward her, and nothing about his posture put him in a good mood. From his narrowed eyes and the bitter scowl twisting his features into hollow, ugly shells of what her memories remembered, Nina struggled to recognize him at first.

Falling out of love with someone hit like a ton of bricks.

"Zach, hello. Have you been well?" Nina asked, but she couldn't pretend to be too interested in his answer. Since their last awkward encounter after Naomi's funeral, she avoided thinking about him too much. When she told Cole that she hadn't missed Zach, she expected that she might miss him or his presence eventually.

But she hadn't at all.

Zach didn't answer her question, breathing hard from his brisk speed, and he stared at her. His eyes appeared darkened, drenched in anger, but Nina couldn't wrap her head around it. She hadn't spoken to him, much less reacted rudely when he called her name. She could've walked away when she heard him call or snapped back with how she didn't owe him a moment of her time.

She'd been nice . . . so much for manners.

Nina gave him a moment to say something—anything at all—and when he failed, she sighed, "Is there something I can help you with because I've got to go."

"Are you seeing someone new?" Zach demanded an answer, not asked. Indignation flustered under the collar of her cardigan wrapped tightly around her torso. *What the fuck?*

Nina gawked openly at him, not understanding why he acted like he had any right to question her. She hadn't thought about him, but maybe she couldn't say the same in reverse.

Nina raised her brow. "Are you seriously about to cause a scene? I thought we were adults about our split since we want different things."

"Are you?"

"Even if I was seeing someone new, it wouldn't be any of your business. I'm not seeing anyone, and we won't discuss the subject further."

Zach's jaw twitched, and Nina expected him to cough up some lame excuse. He averted his eyes. "You could've said no without being defensive."

"What are you? The love police?" Nina held herself back from snarking. She lifted her hand to cut him off when his mouth opened like he wanted to say something. "We went our separate ways months ago, which makes us not responsible for one another. I'm not keeping tabs on you, nor would I."

"We went our separate ways because of a choice you made."

"A choice *I* made? Last I remember, you made a choice, too. Actually, to be precise with my words, you made an ultimatum and forced me to choose. You may not like my choice, but I don't regret my choice."

Zach crossed his arms and huffed, a sound of sheer disbelief tearing off his lips, "So that's it. You're content with losing all the memories and years we shared?"

"Yeah. Unless you've suddenly had a change of heart about Brooke's place in my life, but even then, I wouldn't want to be back with you. I can't unsee the man you are. You took my blinders off, and I won't put them back on for you," Nina remarked.

A stare-down ensued, but Nina hunkered down and waited for a response. Zach loved getting the last word in, the last dig to push her over the ledge, and to be correct.

However, when Zach couldn't speak, she took her cue to spin around on her heel and leave. Frowning, Nina gripped her coffee and headed toward her car, thoughts consumed with a kaleidoscope of emotions. *Annoyance. Pity. Disgust. Sadness.*

Nina shook her head and forced another sip. *What a pathetic little man to be jealous of an orphaned child. Who could look at Brooke and dislike her? She was adorable.*

She slid her hand into her purse in search of her car keys, hooking them with her index finger. After encountering Zach, their twinkling jingle soothed the leftover itch between her shoulder blades. He approached her aggressively and asked too many questions, drawing her ire.

She would never understand what the old her saw in him. But she chose to walk away in Brooke's best interest. Zach would never work as a parenting partner. Nina wouldn't let just any man waltz into her life since she became Brooke's guardian.

She would wait for someone special, a man who would love Brooke and cherish her presence as much as they cared about her. She set the standard high, and until a miraculous man came along to leap over the tall walls, the castle surrounding her heart and her home remained guarded.

Chapter Seventeen
Cole

Clocking out after a long workday, Cole usually checked his phone for any last-minute errands and called it for the evening. Unwinding with either a box of that week's meal prep or some fresh takeout marked the norm for his bachelor lifestyle.

However, one rainy evening in mid-November—that evening, to be precise—hosted a different plan.

It was an average Tuesday at the office. Cole waved goodbye to Elliot, Scott, and Mollie once they exited the elevator into the Richmond and Sons' lobby. He had his damp umbrella in one hand while the other fixed his dark blue scarf, knitted by his mom a few years ago.

"How about you, man? You looked ready to bounce off the elevator walls for a second there," Scott called after him. Cole glanced over his shoulder, seeing him and Mollie still congregated outside the elevator's closing doors. Elliot managed to get a few paces away but paused too and pretended to look busy on his phone instead of eavesdropping.

Cole chuckled. "Elliot, you can put the phone down first. You're a terrible actor. But I don't have anything too crazy. My plans are all about Tuesday night dinner."

"What does that mean? You're being vague." Mollie cocked her brow, but Cole said nothing. He tucked the ends of his scarf into his collar and shook out his umbrella, preparing to sprint to his car.

"Tuesday night dinner seems self-explanatory to me."

"But with whom?"

"Have a good night, you three." Cole spun on his heel and departed from the office, stepping through the doors. The rain came down lightly, but he read a few weather reports about heavier showers later in the evening. Luckily, he'd be at Nina's place and hiding out from the storm.

Since the fair two weeks ago, he and Nina started planning a standing weekly dinner for Tuesday nights. Tuesdays worked best for their schedules, more centered around his packed work week than hers, but both agreed. Tonight would be the first time, and Nina offered to cook the first meal or order takeout if she couldn't find the time.

Nina said she appreciated the company and someone to help her clear through leftovers. Cole saw weekly dinners as an opportunity to check on Nina and Brooke, but the companionship couldn't be underestimated.

With his umbrella in hand, Cole sprinted out into the rain and dodged around puddles for his car. He parked closer to the building in pre-planning and slid into his car, tossing his umbrella into the backseat. He sat in the dark car and let the storm pour down on his windshield, struck by the rhythmic drumming of rain against the glass.

When his coworkers emerged from the office, Cole finally started his engine and peeled out of the parking lot.

If they asked tomorrow, he planned to stick with the "Tuesday dinner" line for as long as it took. He didn't want anyone to get the wrong idea, so he hadn't mentioned it to January or Dean either.

He told them that Tuesday evenings were busy for the foreseeable future and left them confused. Although, he suspected January might catch onto him with her prosecutorial intuition.

Cole drove down the slicked, rain-covered roads with his headlights on high and everything else turned down to avoid distractions. In the dreary weather, the streets appeared empty, with fewer cars than Cole could count on one hand.

He memorized the side streets leading him to Nina's condo, where muscle memory took over. Even after a tiring day, the road assembled like a puzzle for him to piece together after each successful turn. So, Cole enjoyed the peace of the evening and its drizzle of rain.

His fingers tapped against the wheel in a disjointed, uninspired rhythm. The distraction helped pass the time and a few red lights until he rounded the corner ahead of the condos where Nina and Brooke lived. He rolled past a few rows of gentle gray condos grouped in clusters before parking behind Nina's car, outside the group with her condo.

Cole cut the engine, and his phone screen flashed bright enough to illuminate the darkened car from front to back. He checked for a missed call or message from Nina, finding one waiting.

NINA: Drive safe out there tonight. Not to rush you, but I made some hot and creamy pasta and picked up a bottle of red for us adults. See you soon.

Cole's mouth watered at the thought of pasta because he, like most people, was a sucker for Italian food. He shoved his phone into his coat pocket and tightened it, preparing for the short jog to Nina's doorstep.

He tossed the door open, greeted by the cold winds and rain droplets skimming against his face. The rain bent toward him on the winds, and Cole hit the inner door lock a split second before bolting toward the tall trees for extra cover.

Nice leather Oxfords met the damp pavement of a winding path through the cluster of gray condos, but Nina's home was the third from the street and in perfect view from where he parked. Cole shook out his hair from any water like an over-eager dog and sheltered from the storm underneath the built-in porch.

He knocked on the door twice and rang the doorbell for good measure, breaths evening as he waited for someone to answer. In the blink of an eye, the rain poured harder behind him, and a distant groan of thunder cried out from somewhere in the layers of dark, dusky clouds.

The clicking of locks and a deadbolt caught his focus again, and Cole straightened his posture, ensuring he looked presentable, not like a wet cat. He couldn't picture his damp hair hanging into his eyes or his cheeks battered red by the cold to be the most attractive sight, but Nina and Brooke never caused too much fuss about how he looked.

They accepted him dressed up after a day of work or sweaty from the gym in equal measure, so the wet cat look shouldn't be a step too far.

He waited for the door to open, yet all noise from inside the condo ceased. Cole prepared to knock against the door again when he overheard approaching footsteps on the other side of the door, quickly dropping his hand. "Brooke, what did I say about opening the door without an adult?"

"Not to do it," Brooke's voice, although muffled, responded to Nina's admonishment without much shame.

"That's right. Go wash your hands since dinner is ready, and Mr. Cole is probably hoping to eat right away."

"Okay!"

Cole stifled a laugh when the door finally opened, revealing Nina with bags of exhaustion under her eyes but a rueful smile. Nina looked cozy in a pair of blue denim jeans with a knit turtleneck tucked into the belted waistband. All she needed was a glass of wine to complete the image.

"Now, I feel overdressed," Cole laughed and reached forward when Nina did. A brief hug filled Cole with warmth compared to the colder weather outside, and he glanced over Nina's shoulder to the inside. "I tried to aim for casual as much as I could."

"Please, don't worry. As long as you're comfortable, I take you as you are." Nina held him at arm's length and took the sight of him in, damp and flushed from a light run.

"May I come inside?"

"Yes, you may."

Cole stepped inside as Nina shut the door behind him. He noticed a large, blue plastic stool in Nina's hand, which he assumed Brooke used to peer through the peephole and see him on the porch. He watched her shove the step stool neatly against the corner and turn back to him, smiling.

She waved him to follow, and the two spilled into the living room area, seeing some couch cushions on the floor like little seats. The blissful aroma of hot pasta and garlic bread filled every corner of the room in its presence, bringing Cole's mouth to water. He was starving.

Brooke raced back into the room, her pigtails framing her soft, pink cheeks and sporting a matching pumpkin-patterned pajama set. She grinned in glee when her eyes spotted Cole. "Mr. Cole!"

"Hey there," Cole squatted and held his hands toward her, earning a high-five from Brooke. "How was your day, kid?"

"Good! Auntie Nini promised that we could play a board game while we eat dinner. Do you want to play a game with us?" asked Brooke.

"Yeah, of course. What are we going to play?"

"Candyland!"

"Candyland, huh? I remember playing that when I was younger," Cole mused while holding Brooke's hand, or rather Brooke held his index finger as the two headed over to the kitchen island. Nina moved past them and grabbed three plates.

She held up three trays with smudged markings written on the side in black marker. "Our options are chicken alfredo, chicken parm over angel hair, and classic spaghetti with meatballs . . . mostly for Brooke."

"You had me at chicken parm," Cole groaned and pretended to swoon at the thought of a meal. "Pairs nicely with a red."

"Which I have," Nina lifted the still-corked bottle of red wine up like a prize. She traded the chicken parm in her hand for two recently washed wine glasses. She poured them two half-glasses of red wine and set them aside.

Cole stepped up and loaded a child's portion onto a blue plastic plate and handed it to Brooke. He added a fork onto the plate, and Brooke raced over to the cushions on the living room floor.

He felt a wine glass pushed into his hand, and Nina snuck into his line of sight, "So, do you want to split the alfredo and chicken parm, or would you prefer to have one dish only?"

"Let's split? Sounds fantastic."

"A man after my own heart."

Nina clinked her wine glass against his before she split the chicken parmesan and chicken alfredo down the middle onto the two ceramic plates. She kept the two entrees separate with a gentle push of her fork.

Cole accepted his plate and walked with Nina toward the living room, spotting Brooke riffling through the Candyland box. She had one of the player pieces between her fingers and pretended to walk it along the edge of the coffee table. A plethora of sound effects escaped her lips, none quite as loud as the raspberry noise she repeated twice.

Cole sat down, choosing a pillow next to Nina, and let Brooke assign him his piece for Candyland. "Alright, I'll need you to remind me of the rules."

Brooke gave an exasperated huff but pulled out the rule sheet while everyone took their first bites of pasta and sheltered away from the rain pouring outside.

Candyland lasted an hour at most, or at least until little Brooke fell asleep on her half-finished plate of pasta. She had a considerable lead on Nina and Cole, but it wasn't enough to keep her head in the game.

Nina carried her off to bed and tucked her in, focused on Brooke staying asleep. Cole waited for her to return before the two adults topped off their wine, put their finished pasta plates on the coffee table, and traded Candyland for a good, old-fashioned game of Scrabble.

Two things to know about Cole: he loved competition, and he was a Scrabble expert. Yet, Nina strove to prove that he met his match with every turn she got.

"Quixotry is not a real word!" Nina protested, jaw slackened, and her hands tossed into the air while she ogled the masterful point-grabber Cole set on the board. He pulled together a sickening amount of luck to notice how she left an open "try" for him to steal, and he had the vowels left over.

"It is a real word," Cole leaned to the side, drinking his wine with his body propped up by an elbow against the couch. Amused, he soaked in Nina's flabbergasted state. He chuckled. "Your turn?"

Nina shook her head. "No way. I'm not convinced that *quixotry* is a real word because you're a master of persuasion, Mr. Lawyer. Use quixotry in a sentence."

"Alright. Honoré de Balzac once said, 'This feminine Quixotry is a sentiment which hallows love and turns it to worthy uses; it exalts and reverences love.' So, does that count as a sentence?"

"Is there anything you don't know in that big brain of yours? It's unfair that I'm competing against a certified genius."

Cole meant to crack a little laugh, but he couldn't help the small wheezes snowballing into a fit of laughter he muffled behind his arm. Nina sipped at her wine, and he used the sight of her scouring her tile rack for a new word to bring him back.

"Hey, don't sell yourself short," he adjusted the *q* tile he set for quixotry as it appeared slightly crooked. His eyes found Nina's when she tore her gaze away from her tiles. "You think out of the box, and that's genius. You can still beat me."

"You're right, and I think I have the word for the job. Boom!" Nina shook her hands together like a gambler who wanted to bless his dice before she added her tiles to the board. Cole's eyebrows shot toward the sky as he read the word.

Whizbang.

"Whizbang?" Cole coughed hard, stranded somewhere between a choke and a laugh, and Nina flashed him a pair of finger guns, pretending to have him trapped.

"Yes, whizbang. It's defined as the sequence of noises a firecracker makes; you start with a whizzing sound during launch, followed by a loud bang when the firecracker explodes. Whizbang. Is that not a word according to your fancy JD and linguistics minor?" Nina questioned, all too proud of herself.

"No, it's not a word. You're trying to pull a fast one on me because of quixotry."

"Look it up! I swear on my life that it's a word. Those seventy-something points are mine, fair and square!"

"Oh, I will look it up." Cole reached for his phone. He'd never found someone equally as competitive as him when it came to Scrabble. Not even Dean and brotherly competition could compel the sheer challenge Nina put up. He checked the board for the spelling as he opened his phone to verify Nina's claim. "W-H-I-Z-"

Boom.

For one moment, everything seemed fine. Then, an isolated clap of thunder rocked the condo's walls, and the lights went out. Darkness blanketed the room while the rain slammed hard against the windows, demanding attention from them.

Cole heard a soft hitch of breath somewhere beside him, and he tilted his phone so the light from his screen captured Nina's face. Panic painted her features, but she stayed put and lit up her phone.

"The condos run on a backup generator, so it should turn on any moment now," she whispered when her phone's screen darkened again, pushing her back into the dark. Cole switched off his phone, comfortable waiting until the generator switched the lights back on. "It hasn't stormed so bad to cause a power outage in years."

"Have you lived here since college?"

"Yes. I started as a tenant to a nice older lady who needed company in exchange for her renting out her extra room. But when I got steady work, I saved my funds until I could afford to rent a condo myself."

"I'm impressed. You had a plan figured out and made it happen." Cole whistled and scooted closer to the couch, able to feel the plush cushions where his eyes couldn't see them. Although his vision adjusted to the sudden darkness, the world adopted a murky hue of shadow.

He listened for Nina's movements while they waited for the backup generator to kick in. However, nothing happened for a solid while.

Cole fidgeted in the dark, and he had the suspicion Nina was too. The restlessness settled in the room with them. He fumbled for his phone and switched on its flashlight, and Nina followed after him.

"Maybe it's raining too hard for the condo manager to go out and fix the box . . . the generator is located outdoors by their property at the end of the block. I would go, but I need a security key to access the generator, and the key is set by the condo manager. I'll grab some candles," said Nina.

She gathered the leftover plates and carried them in a loose stack to the kitchen. Cole waited for her but didn't need to spend too long alone in the dark before Nina returned. She grabbed a giant glass candle jar and kept a matchbox underneath her armpit.

Nina set the candle down, and Cole shone a light on its half-charred wooden wick buried among sage-colored wax. She struck a match and lit the candle to the instant and palpable scent of citrus and herbs like basil.

Cole turned off his phone's flashlight as the glow from the candle filled the room in a delicate sunset vibrance. The candle burned brightly enough for Cole to see Nina's face, and the phones disappeared.

She scooted closer to him as her back pressed against the couch. "You don't have to stay until the power comes on. It could be hours; I know you have work tomorrow," Nina murmured, tucking her knees to her chest.

"Yes, I could." Cole knew she had a point about the lateness of the hour, but leaving during the storm's peak while she sat alone in the dark felt wrong. "But I'd rather wait until the power comes back."

"I'm a big girl, Cole. I promise I can handle myself for a while."

"I know you're capable, but do you want me to leave?"

Nina shook her head. "No. I like your company." She locked her hands over her knees and glanced at the empty spot beside her. Cole moved the board with their incomplete Scrabble game onto the coffee table next to the partially filled glasses of wine.

He moved closer and rested his back against the couch, too. He stared into the candle while the storm raged outside, banging on the windows for his attention. Then, he said, "I like your company too. It's nice."

"You're the only person who knows the whole picture of what's going on with my life. Not even Brooke understands what's going on with the custody battle, and I don't think it's right to tell her. She's still a baby to me."

"She deserves to be a kid, but you need someone to be there for you who understands and who you can lean on. The custody process, parenting, and life aren't meant to be done alone."

Nina rubbed her eyes, unable to look at him. "Why aren't you with someone?"

"Excuse me?" Cole swore he misheard her, but Nina didn't rephrase her words or apologize. *Why wasn't he with someone?*

"Cole, someone like you is a rarity out there. You've got a well-paying job, friends, a welcoming family, and a great personality, and you lucked out in the looks department. If anyone were a perfect romance candidate, it would be you. So, why hasn't anyone made an honest man of you yet?"

"You think all that about me?"

"Yeah. So, unless there's some major red flag I'm missing here, I don't understand how you haven't been snatched up by someone for keeps. Any woman in their right mind would see you're unlike anyone else."

Nina finally turned to look at him, and a shiver pressed against Cole's spine at how earnestly she believed her words. Authenticity shone in her eyes brighter than any star Cole could point to in the night sky. *She thought so highly of him.*

"The truth?" He shrugged. "I've been searching for someone who makes me happy. My brother had this strict criteria list about what he wanted and needed in a woman, which I remember teasing him for. But he landed his fiancée, who makes him happier than anyone ever has, and that set off the metaphorical lightbulb. I've dated before and tried to do the long-term thing when I got comfortable, but I decided to try and chase happiness. I'm looking for something that can't be explained or narrowed down to an exact specification like my brother, but something that inexplicably changes how I feel."

His eyes wandered to Nina again, taking in her features bathed in candlelight. Cole noticed how her hands moved from around her tucked knees and raked down the rug next to their feet. A slight tremble rocked her knees, where her kneecaps occasionally bumped into each other.

"Nina, are you okay?" Cole questioned.

"I don't know. Brooke is supposed to be my number one priority, far ahead of my wants and needs. When I was younger, I used to be a hopeless romantic. I always fell in love with the idea of the happily ever after written at the end of the movie, where everything falls into place for the heroine. As much as I try to act like I'm over it, my life is in shambles, and I'm putting on the best show to pretend it isn't. There's the possibility that I may be alone until Brooke is grown up, missing my chance for the type of movie love I wanted so bad. But I know I have to choose Brooke, and in doing so, I lose myself." Nina sniffled, and when she blinked, tears flicked off the ends of her lashes.

Cole watched the tears rush down her cheeks, stunned. In a matter of seconds, Nina crumpled inward. His hands ran to her, pulling her face out of its hiding place before she began hyperventilating. Grief worked in mysterious ways, and he tried to understand how they ended up there.

Most of all, he worried about her.

He needed to be there for her. He wanted to be there for her. Nina deserved someone to lean on, and he was someone to step up. Whatever she wanted would be hers.

Cole cupped her face between his hands and ensured her eyes met his, "Hey, breathe with me. I promise you that your life isn't over. I can't buy into the idea that you won't find love from someone who accepts Brooke as a part of the deal."

"How are you so sure?" Nina's eyes watered hard, and the tears glowed along her lash line, unshed but still radiating such pain. She buried down her fears and pains, but the flood pushed them back to the surface.

So, Cole grabbed one of Nina's shaking hands with his, pulling their laced fingers to rest against his chest right above his heart, "Because I know you, Nina. You went on a whole description of me as the perfect package, but you can't give yourself even an ounce of that generosity? Let me show you what I see."

"Show me."

"You're tough. Maybe you don't think so because you've let yourself be vulnerable around me, but even reaching a place of such overwhelming hurt and continuing to fight shows how tough you are. You are braver than anyone I've ever met. You're bright, witty, caring toward Brooke, and genuinely fun. Hanging out with you and Brooke is the highlight of my day most weeks. Not to mention, any guy with half a brain would turn his head if you passed him on the street . . . me included."

Cole finished his tirade but didn't expect the conversation to go quiet either. But then, he realized the predicament of Nina pulled close into him where his knees brushed against her hip, leaving no space between them. Neither moved, not even after Cole noticed his closeness to her.

Nina's eyes dropped from his, but she didn't wander far when her gaze circled around his lips. She studied him with all the intense concentration of a lip reader waiting for a message, but his stomach tumbled around. *She doesn't want me to talk.*

Almost as if she knew his innermost thoughts, her eyes snapped back up, and a shaky breath hitched in her throat. Caught, the moment flailed around like a bird with its wing stuck in a trap, but no one rushed to relieve the tension.

As close as they were, Cole could feel Nina's breath on his face. Beyond the subtle warmth of the candle, he focused on the heat of her stare. Hell, he imagined he knew what she tasted like too.

So many bad ideas crossed his mind, but they fled in a blinding flash. All the lights inside the condo switched back on at once. Cole would've thought he and Nina had been struck by lightning with how fast they jumped back from one another.

Nina's lips parted open, and she said, "Um."

Wine and loneliness, not the safest of combinations, Cole thought while sitting on his hands, aware of the faint buzz underneath his skin.

Everywhere touched by Nina's skin on his exuded the same electricity, but he refused to linger.

Neither said anything before footsteps echoed into the room, and a half-asleep Brooke wandered into the living room, clutching a blanket. The lights' sudden return must've woken her up. "Auntie Nini."

"Right here," Nina bounded over to her niece and scooped the poor girl into her arms, pressing a flush of soothing assurances into her hair. Nina vanished into the other room to put Brooke down to sleep, but Cole didn't wait for instruction.

He collected the wine glasses and headed to drain his down the sink. He saw Nina's glass empty and assumed she had some when his attention wandered elsewhere. Cole washed out the glasses before he turned them over to the dishwasher.

He noticed a flash of blonde hair in his peripheral, and he remained calm when Nina appeared at his side. She grabbed the plates she abandoned on the counter at the start of the blackout, "Sorry about that. Brooke can't fall back asleep if I don't act fast."

"It's alright. I understand because I used to be the same at preschool naptime."

"Um, you don't have to handle the dishes. You're a guest in my house, and I don't make guests do chores."

Nina protested when Cole lifted the plates from her hand and flicked on the hot water. He picked up a sudsy, damp sponge from the counter to clean off the scraps of sauce and crumbs from their plates.

"I can handle a few dishes. It won't kill me to help clean the mess I made," Cole remarked, trying to keep his tone light. But those words carried along a separate meaning all their own. If Nina wanted to respond, she opted to grab a dish rag and help with the drying in total silence.

The two worked together to clean up, and the next logical step had Cole departing for the evening, going home for a night of rest before the Wednesday workday.

Don't get too attached to her. You and she are set on different paths, and it won't hurt as much when she finds the forever partner she deserves.

Chapter Eighteen
Nina

Nothing screamed 'fuck my life' more to Nina than waking up to unexplained agony. She started with her face buried in the nearest pillow, mouth tipped to the side so she could breathe, and the light smear of drool against the powder blue pillowcase. Then, she made the mistake of opening her eyes.

Everything hurt all at once.

Her vision blurred, too many things happening. She shut her eyes, finding some relief from the acute stabbing sensation pushing against her left eye. Darkness could do so little to help.

Even with the pressure hammering against her head and threatening to crack her skull open across the duvet—dramatic sounding but justified—Nina clocked exactly what ailed her. A migraine.

One that left her unable to see straight.

Nina tried to open her eyes again and faced down a sudden, overwhelming bout of nausea lumped in her throat. She shut her eyes, focusing on rolling over for more air. Light pressed hard against her eyelids, but Nina's chest thanked her with ragged gasps for air.

"Auntie Nini," a tiny sob beside her bedside had her struggling to open her eyes, or at least beyond a sliver. She pushed the duvet off her chest to pool around her thighs, too hot to think straight. "Wake up, please."

"I'm awake, bug. I promise. What's wrong?"

"I threw up on my bed and my nightgown. I'm sorry."

Brooke started to bawl, and Nina's already painful migraine descended to a new low, putting her on the fritz. Nina blindly reached for Brooke until she grabbed Brooke's hand. She ran two fingers along Brooke's wrist, searching for a fever. Unluckily for them both, Brooke's skin felt warm to the touch.

"It's okay, bug," said Nina. She couldn't open her eyes more than a sliver to find her phone. She imagined Brooke's wobbly lip and wide, tear-stained green eyes as she stood by her bedside, covered in vomit. "Can you grab my phone for me?"

"Okay."

"We need to call someone for help since I have a big headache. Maybe Miss Gloria or Mrs. Penelope can help us, so call one of them."

Brooke went quiet momentarily, and Nina strained to hear where Brooke disappeared to when Brooke let go of her. Nina swallowed hard when her migraine screamed out, causing her heels to dig into the rumpled sheets and the mattress.

Nina panted hard, "Brooke, where did you go? Brooke?"

"I'm right here," Brooke piped up somewhere to her right like before, but some distance echoed between them. "I can't find Miss Gloria's number or Mrs. Penelope's either. I'll call Mr. Cole! He told me to call him if I need help!"

If the migraine hadn't taken her out yet, Nina swore the thought of Cole finding out she and Brooke were ill would slam the final nail in her coffin. They hadn't said much of anything since the rainy evening when their almost kiss in the dark strained their easygoing relationship.

"Wait! No!" Nina tried to sit up and stop Brooke from calling Cole, but pain smacked her directly between the eyes. She yelped like a hit dog, and her hands covered her eyes, wishing she hadn't done that.

"Auntie Nini, Mr. Cole asked me to put the phone on speaker. What button is it?"

"The third one on the top. The right, top corner."

"Thank you!" Brooke followed through, and the soft, staticky background noise from her phone revealed Cole's presence in her morning of misery. "I put on speaker, Mr. Cole!"

"Thank you, Brooke. You said that your aunt has a headache? We should keep our voices down so her head doesn't hurt as bad," Cole remarked calmly, and his voice avoided agitating her further.

"Okay," Brooke whispered. Although her voice wasn't all that quiet, she tried her best, and Nina appreciated everything toned down. "Do you want to talk to my auntie?"

"That would be appreciated, sweetie. Thank you."

"Auntie Nini, take the phone."

Brooke put Nina's phone in her hand and she grabbed it. Her other hand helped push her off her back slowly. She heaved. "Hey."

"Hey. How are you feeling?"

"Not great. I would love to go back to sleep, but Brooke said she threw up, and she's burning up, so I assume she has a fever, too. That could be many different things like the stomach flu or worse."

"Got it, and what about you? Sounds like a migraine if you can't open your eyes." Cole stayed enviously calm on the other line.

Nina laughed weakly, "Ding, ding, winner, winner. Do you want a cookie for that big brain of yours?"

"How about we focus on you? Do you think you can get out of bed? I wouldn't want to leave you or Brooke stuck."

"I didn't mean to call you. I know it's probably early in the morning, and we haven't talked in a few days, but since I have you on the line . . . I could use the help. I'm overwhelmed and can't really open my eyes."

Cole's side of the conversation erupted with muffled movement, but Nina locked in on the jangle of keys. "It's alright. I can be there soon, but I'll stop at the store for supplies. Besides some saltine crackers, a couple of sports drinks for recovering electrolytes, headache meds, and maybe some soup for you and Brooke to keep down, anything else you need?"

"No. I don't think so," said Nina.

"If you need anything, call me right away. I'll throw in some clean-ing supplies for the sheets. Brooke, can you check your aunt for a fever? Can you tell me if she feels warm?" A starting engine from Cole's side underlined his words with urgency.

Brooke's hands, uncomfortably warm, pressed against the exposed skin of Nina's neck and her cheeks. She coughed, but the faint brush of her breath caused Nina to shiver. "She's warm."

"Okay. I'll grab some extra items to help break the fever. Don't worry . . . I'll be there soon." Cole ended the call, but Nina didn't slump back into the sheets and pillows like her throbbing headache demanded.

Instead, she set her phone aside in the duvet somewhere and scoot-ed until her legs hung over the edge of her mattress. Nina groaned. "Brooke, can you take my hand? Take me to your bedroom."

She hadn't opened her eyes, but she blinked a few times and held Brooke's hand. The two wandered toward Brooke's bedroom, and Nina squinted away from the early morning sunlight pushing through the open windows of the kitchen. She spotted the clock on the wall and balked at the time. *Six-forty-five.*

What a way to start the morning.

Nina pushed open the door to Brooke's room, trying not to gag at the smell, but she kept her composure together. Brooke's face pointed toward the ground, but Nina assumed she was embarrassed.

The sheets got the worst of it compared to Brooke's pajamas, but those would need to go in the wash. So, Nina kneeled before Brooke and smiled to soothe her agitated fidgeting. "We're going to get changed. Let me help you."

Brooke nodded and worked with Nina to get the soiled nightgown off. She crumpled it into a pile on the floor beside the bed. The pain left half of her face numb, but Nina focused on pulling Brooke's hair into a messy ponytail with the scrunchie she had kept on her wrist overnight.

"Shower?" Brooke asked, voice trembling.

"Shower. Let me grab it for you." Nina opened the bathroom, but Brooke waddled behind her into the room. Nina turned the water to lukewarm, waiting until the water reached the best temperature between cold to fight the fever and warm because Brooke liked her showers warm.

At the perfect temperature, Nina let Brooke remove her clean undergarments before the little one stepped into the shower. She adorned a baby blue loofah with lavender body soap and handed it to Brooke.

She sat outside the shower while the door stayed open, but Brooke was old enough to wash her body without Nina's guidance. She'd remain close until Brooke finished and wrap her up to dry.

The faint steam of the shower glossed over her face, and Nina inhaled, relieving some of the pressure in her head. She counted the time silently. *One Mississippi, two Mississippi, three Mississippi.*

Somewhere around *one-hundred-and-twenty-six Mississippi*, the shower water squeaked off, and Brooke's hand slipped through the crack in the shower door. Nina grabbed the hooded, ladybug pattern towel from a peg on the wall, passing it to Brooke inside the fogged-up shower.

"Take your time in there," Nina murmured and staggered out of the bathroom for Brooke's bedroom. She grimaced, staring at the fitted sheet with new stains all over the white sheets. "I can manage these sheets by myself."

Nina started at the head of the twin-sized mattress she pressed against the top right corner of the room. Her fingers tucked underneath the bed to find the first corner of the sheet and yanked it free, bringing black spots across her vision.

She dropped the first corner and walked to the lower half of the bed, kneeling at the corner on the same side. Her arms slid underneath the mattress and fumbled around for the corner, struggling to overcome a wave of dizzying nausea.

A slight tilt shifted her from kneeling to slumping against the side of the mattress, forehead pressed into the side. She heard a snapping sound, and the stretch of the fitted sheet underneath her forehead slipped away to curl on top of the twin mattress.

Gasping for air, Nina hadn't felt so winded in years. She closed her eyes for a stolen moment to recuperate as her migraine reminded her of its presence. She would get back up and handle the rest of the sheets, put them in the wash, and assess the damage before Cole made it to her place.

Nina had passed out.

She realized as much when she came to, hearing the door to Brooke's bedroom creaking open and the hushed whispers of two voices. Brooke and . . . Cole's.

Her eyes strained against the overhead light clicked on, but someone shut it off immediately upon hearing a groan. From across the room, Brooke whispered, "Is she okay?"

"She will be," Cole assured, his voice closer to Nina than Brooke's, and her eyes fluttered open. Kneeled in front of her, Cole's fingers touched her forehead and brushed away some hairs stuck to her skin from the sweat gathered there. His mouth dipped into a frown. "You're burning up."

"How'd you get in?" Nina coughed, ready to apologize for passing out and leaving him more to take care of. She pushed herself too hard and ended up in a pathetic heap on the floor, all exhaustion and sweat.

"Brooke let me in. Please don't be upset with her because she disobeyed the rules this once."

"I can't even be mad. Too tired."

"Well, let's fix that . . . the tiredness, I mean." Cole's other hand lifted to cup the side of her throat, gliding over her pulse point. Unlike her overly warm body, his hands carried coldness. She pressed closer to his touch for more of it, desperate for relief from the fever she couldn't sweat out. "Your pulse is steady if not a little fast, but the fever worries me. I brought medicine for it."

Nina shivered when he pressed a full palm to her forehead, taken by the cold she desperately craved. Through hazy vision, she paid attention to him for the first time. His hair hung damp, freshly showered if the faint scent of peppercorn and musk meant anything, and his eyes studied her with a softness that exuded the energy of a blanket fresh out of the dryer.

Cole's lips parted, but in his silence, Nina managed to whisper, "I also need my morning dose of meds. They're in my cabinet and marked for the day."

"I'll grab those for you. You and Brooke are in my capable hands for now."

"Mmm, okay. I trust you . . . and your hands."

"Oh, I'm glad to hear that," Cole laughed, and in the absurdity of it all—mostly the fog overtaking her mind thanks to her low-grade fever—Nina giggled. She caught Cole's eyes, and her laughter threatened to catch like wildfire, content to swirl about her chest in contrast to the pain in her head. "I need a few more things from you. Wrap your arms around my neck nice and tight."

"Around your neck? Like this?" Nina followed his orders, sliding her arms around his neck until her hands overlapped at the back. Concerned about squeezing too tight, she adjusted a few times until it felt right.

"Perfect. Keep those hands there. I need you to close your eyes."

"Alright . . . anything else?"

Nina closed her eyes to immense relief, killing a throbbing sensation against her temple. She wasn't sure if she slumped toward Cole or if her imagination had begun to play tricks on her, phantom sensations as side effects of the fever.

"Hold on tight and trust me." Cole's words flushed against the shell of her ear before everything happened at once. Weightlessness slammed into Nina's body, and cold hands glided from the exposed skin along her midriff from a ridden-up t-shirt. One hand slid up her spine while the other hooked underneath her knees, holding them together. "Keep those eyes closed."

Nina's arms tightened from their anchoring position around Cole's neck when she rocked side to side, still plagued by the weightlessness. However, she shut her eyes and let herself go limp beyond her arms. A realization dawned on her when her head slid against Cole's collarbone.

Cole was carrying her in his arms, bridal style.

The flex of his biceps moving so subtly kept her up while he stepped through Brooke's bedroom, probably dodging the soiled nightgown on the floor and the throw-up stained sheets. Nina nestled closer to Cole and pressed her forehead against his neck, finding relief in the colder touch of his skin.

However, he leaned forward, and she cracked her eyes open enough to see him toss the nightgown onto the fitted sheet curling into the center of the bed. Beyond the sheet, the mattress appeared untouched.

A silent observer, Nina didn't expect Cole to expertly yank the remainder of the fitted sheet corners out of their neat tucks. But he gathered the sheets and the nightgown with the hand angled beneath her knees.

"Which way to the laundry?" asked Cole.

Nina closed her eyes again, "The kitchen. You'll see a pair of sliding doors against the wall, and it's behind there. Washer and dryer." She nuzzled closer when he moved from Brooke's bedroom and ambled through the condo until he found the washer and dryer.

The rustling and beeps from the washing machine soothed any last pangs of worry, banishing them to a long-forgotten moment. Around them, Brooke's fast footsteps drew Nina's eyes open, and she spotted her niece in a brand-new nightgown patterned with fruit.

Brooke loved her patterns.

"Did you pick that out for yourself, bug?" Nina croaked, and Brooke spun in a circle before Cole eased her to a stop. Good thinking, unless they wanted another mess to clean up.

Brooke, not fazed, grinned, "Yes! You fell asleep again, so I picked out my clothes like a big girl. Mommy taught me how."

"Good. You did great."

Cole ushered Brooke silently, and Nina let him take them to her bedroom, darkened with the curtains drawn. She settled into the duvet when he lowered her onto her bed, and the mattress dipped underneath a petite body.

Nina's arms opened, and she let Brooke nestle in. She sank into the pillows, searching for comfort, before she opened her eyes. Cole scoured through the bags at the foot of the bed for some items.

He set a couple of boxes of medicine, in liquid and pills, on the foot of the bed. Soon, a box of saltine crackers and two bottles of a sports drink in blue flavor joined the medicine. However, he handled the last item carefully, and Nina needed to blink a few times to recognize it. Grocery store soup, hot and ready in a travel-sized cup.

"Alright, the saltines are for Brooke, and she gets her own drink," Cole opened a saltine package and handed them to Brooke, who tentatively crunched on one. But she took another relatively quick. "I wasn't sure what kind of soup you'd like, so I figured chicken noodle to be a safe bet to take alongside the sports drink. The medicine recommends having something in your stomach, but I didn't want to risk anything too rich or hard to finish."

Nina softened when he put the chicken noodle soup into her hands, "I used to love chicken noodle soup whenever I was sick as a kid. Thank you."

Cole winked. "I try my best." He vanished, but Nina focused on downing the chicken noodle soup. She hadn't realized how hungry she was until she blinked, and the soup cup appeared empty.

Simultaneously, Brooke managed to eat half of the first stack of her Saltines. She wiped the crumbs off her mouth and chugged some sports drink. Her eyes drooped a little, but she whined, "Auntie Nini? I'm sleepy."

"You can stay here with me. Lay on the other side of the bed." Nina gently moved her into the spare side, which had been empty for months. Brooke obliged and climbed into the spot, curling underneath the blanket. Kids had a funny way of sleeping easily, shown by how Brooke passed out within a minute flat.

When Cole returned to the room, Nina nursed her sports drink and opened the migraine medicine. She sheepishly held the bottle up. "A little help?"

"No problem." Cole read the instructions and put two pills into Nina's open palm. "Take those with something to drink, and they should kick in soon."

"Thank you again. I woke up so overwhelmed that I didn't know where to start."

"You don't need to thank me, I promise. Helping people is what I do for a living."

"Right, but we haven't spoken since Tuesday, and I feel bad calling in favors considering that I wasn't sure where we stand—"

"It doesn't matter what the circumstance is. I would've come regardless of any radio silence," Cole interrupted her, and he gestured for her to take the medicine in her palm. Nina appreciated the break and downed the meds with a side of her drink.

She shouldn't have mentioned the almost-kiss at the risk of making everything awkward again. Neither of them knew how to handle it, leaving it to be the elephant in the room.

Cole's eyes softened when she swallowed her meds. He entered the bathroom and returned with her labeled pill box, handing it to her. Nina popped open the Sunday box, and a third pill went down on a sip of sports drink.

When Nina pushed the box to the side, Cole reached for her hand. She let him take it with his and tolerated the stroke of his thumb along her palm. "Still friends?"

"Still friends," Nina whispered after a moment, startled. Most guys she knew would've done a humiliating talk about how she misinterpreted their interest, but Cole laid her anxiety to rest before it could flare up.

But she lied. Ever since that near-kiss, the memory replayed once or twice in her mind, and it took on a new life each time. She could never tell him that the lonely, desperate yearning for companionship blossomed from a tiny spark to something unsightly and unwanted. The sensation latched onto something more, and the hope Cole shrouded her in of a better man.

Nina found it in herself to let go of Cole's hand and reach for the duvet to replace it. Exhaustion caught up with her whirlwind morning, so when Cole helped tuck her in, Nina's defiant heart clenched in her chest.

Cole stood beside her. "You should rest. I'll be here when you wake up, and maybe I'll occupy my time with some chores."

"You're too good to me . . ." Nina's voice faded out when her eyelids started to grow heavy. Through it all, a slight dip in the mattress and a soft touch to her hairline by his lips were the last things she swore to recall before sleep carried her away.

Chapter Nineteen
Cole

Although Thanksgiving came and went, the commute into the city hadn't recovered yet. Cole left his apartment early but still ran headfirst into bumper-to-bumper traffic. He tapped the wheel with impatient fingers, always a beat behind the clicking of his turn signal, waiting to make a right into the parking structure by the courthouse.

He took another day from work at the request of Nina, co-signed by Rudy for the first time. Apparently, his presence unnerved Nina's family, and the thought brought him a twinge of glee, as bad as that sounded.

"C'mon, I can't be late," Cole mumbled while the cars around him crawled forward, but he stared at the turn ahead. His place in the turn pocket shortened when other cars drove into the complex.

He checked the clock with an obsessive eye, his mind counting down the minutes left, and hung up on seconds slipping through his fingers. Ten minutes until Nina's case started, at ten A.M. sharp, and she wanted him there.

He couldn't let her down.

Cole focused on the cars in front of him and, by some miracle, more began to move. Soon, he skirted past the white crosswalk lines and hit his turn right before the light changed.

A relieved sigh escaped him, but the issue of finding parking and getting through courthouse security on time loomed over his ticking clock. His head peered on a swivel for a parking spot for the slow trek up the ramp to the second parking level. No spaces jumped out at him, so he pushed to the third floor.

The third floor had open spots, and Cole turned into the nearest one. The car hadn't finished its lurch when Cole shifted into park and cut out the engine. Cole lunged out of his car and took off toward the stairs with a briefcase and a nice navy pinstripe suit to complement his Oxfords.

A few people in court attire waited in a small cluster outside the elevator, but Cole breezed past them for the stairs. He heaved in a deep breath as he sprinted down too fast for the tailored clothes he wore. But the clock kept ticking.

Skipping a few steps with precise agility, Cole cleared the stairs faster than any elevator ride and didn't wait around to pat himself on the back. He bounded through the ground floor of the parking structure and out into the overcast November morning.

He sped across the plaza outside the courthouse, sporting some holiday cheer in multicolored decorations displayed in the windows of nearby buildings and tinsel twined around nearby streetlights. People moved out of his way, and sheepishness found its way to the forefront, seated alongside the rush.

"Thank you! Sorry!" Cole shouted whenever he passed by people until he reached the steps outside the courthouse. He became too focused on his destination and deadline to pay much attention to the world around him.

His long strides propelled him up the stairs and through the front doors. The lines by the metal detectors appeared semi-busy, with people checking their items and clearing through security one at a time.

Cole swallowed. *Five minutes is enough time, right?* He eyed the watch on his wrist and, as he predicted, had five minutes on the dot until the session started. He slid into line, loaded his briefcase onto the conveyor belt, and counted the seconds with taps of his shoe against the polished floors.

The conveyor crawled through the machine, and when the security guard on the opposite side waved him through, Cole stepped under the metal detector. He grabbed his briefcase and beelined for the escalator, finding it surprisingly empty.

He climbed the escalator while it ascended to the second floor, where Nina texted him to be. He headed down the hallway and checked his watch for a final time check. *Three minutes left.* Even though he flew in under the wire, Cole continued briskly down the hall until he found the courtroom.

He double-checked his and Nina's messages, which resumed in fervor since the early morning migraine incident, and headed inside after confirmation. Cole spotted both tables for counsel filled up by Rudy, Mr. Francisco, and the clients.

Nina pushed out of her seat, and her eyes brightened when she spotted him in the doorway. She ran her palms down the length of her herringbone peplum blazer over a dark pair of trousers tailored to her shape. She flashed him a smile but glanced around at Vera, Maxwell, and Felicity to observe if they scrutinized her.

Cole, however, stepped forward regardless of whether the Byndels inspected him. He smiled at her and took her hands with his, turning her palms up. "Morning. I know it's close, but traffic had me worried I wouldn't make it."

"But you made it. That's all that matters."

"I promised you I would be here. Nothing would stop me from coming and supporting you."

A shy giggle escaped Nina, and she squeezed his hands, composing herself on the fly. Cole wanted to see smiles and confidence, not fear. Her family couldn't yank her down anymore.

He couldn't imagine the judge would award custody to the Byndels, especially after Brooke's psychological evaluation and how happily she returned to them. Rudy should've already submitted the wording of Naomi's will into evidence. All evidence supported the conclusion that Brooke was better off in Nina's sole custody and insulated from the toxic environment of the Byndels.

Cole guided Nina to her chair, and he pulled it out for her, ever the gentleman. Nina's gaze followed him while he took the chair to her right. He became a shield between her and her estranged family.

Underneath the table, Nina's hand sought out Cole's, and he laced their fingers together. Warmth pulsed between their palms, but so did a twitch of nervous energy. The sensation seeped into Cole's skin through touch, and he glanced at her.

Despite her faint smile, eyes riddled with anxiety glowed with un-spoken truths, and Nina's shallow façade crumbled under a second glance. Cole squeezed her hand in a soft pulsing motion until he noticed her jaw unclench, relaxing momentarily.

Cole leaned in, face tipped toward her ear. "Take a breath. I'll do it with you if you want."

"It's okay," Nina sucked in a rattling breath. "Can we talk about anything else besides where we're at?"

"Let's see . . . what are your opinions on the city setting up for Christmas already? I still haven't gotten past Thanksgiving yet."

"I never used to love Christmas as a kid, but Brooke helped me grow to love the holiday more. She adores Christmas and still believes in Santa Claus, which brings a little magic back to the season."

Cole chuckled. He imagined Brooke's wide eyes and open-mouth grin from sheer joy, squealing about meticulously wrapped presents from the jolly man in red. He might have to drop by their place with some gifts when the day got closer. He would deliver them before he went out of town; his family always celebrated Christmas at his parents' house. He couldn't ditch, even if he wanted.

He heard Nina murmur his name and leaned back in, "What about you? It sounds like you like the holidays."

"Who wouldn't? My family and I adore the festivities, especially my mom. She uses the holidays to try new recipes since she has a captive audience... but she's a great cook. We all let it slide," said Cole.

Nina's response would have to wait. Cole noticed the door by the judge's bench at the front of the room opened, and everyone scrambled to their feet without prompting. Yet, Cole and Nina's hands remained linked through it all.

Cole stared ahead at the seal of the state courts mounted behind the Honorable Grace A. Byrd, the presiding judge over the custody case, while she beckoned everyone to sit. Her hands picked up the gavel from behind the bench.

"Good morning, all," Judge Byrd remarked. Her dark curls bounced whenever she angled or dipped to look at notes hidden behind the bench. Cole knew plenty of judicial secrets from Dean, who loved to regale any poor soul in the immediate vicinity with courtroom war stories whenever he had too much to drink. "I have spoken with the court-appointed psychologist and minor's council about their findings regarding the minor's mental state and wishes. I am prepared to make my verdict."

At that moment, Mr. Francisco rose out of his chair with his hands gripping his notepad. "Your Honor, the plaintiffs wish to present one final segment of testimony regarding their personal experiences with Ms. Byndel."

If Nina knew what was to come, the shock on her face told a completely different story. The soft pinks wreathing her cheeks in a lively glow trickled out with the rest of the color in her face, leaving her almost ashen. Her lips tightened into a thin line, drawn taunt, pulling the rest of her features into the shadows.

Cole looked around her at Rudy, searching for a sign of protest or confusion on his face. He found none. In fact, Rudy appeared totally calm and stood up. "Your Honor, I had a chance to interview this witness, and they may take the stand for further questioning."

Some of the worry pent up between Cole's shoulders dissipated at Rudy's calm response. A good lawyer approaches every case with a varied strategy, some never revealed to the client before its execution. Nina needed to stay calm as it would be okay.

Judge Byrd stared between the two counselors, but any protest boiled down to the quirk of her brows and a sigh. "Very well, counselors. Since you two appear in agreement, I will accept the request. Call your witness, Counselor Francisco."

"The plaintiffs call Zachary Piker to the stand."

Nina's breath hitched, but the shaking seized Cole's attention. He let her hold onto his hands, even when her nails dug in. The grip threatened to break a finger or two. He whispered, "Nina, what's wrong?"

"Zach's my ex. The one we've talked about," Nina revealed, all startled eyes and bright red face compared to her ashen complexion moments before. She dropped her face toward her lap but couldn't hide from Cole. "What is he doing here?"

"I don't know. Your family called him as a witness."

"That doesn't make any sense! He's only met them twice through our relationship, and we've been broken up for months."

Judge Byrd's gavel knocking against the bench hushed Nina, but she struggled to stay quiet while hyperventilating. Cole's gaze turned when he saw a blond man in a suit amble to the witness box, posting up in the spot.

To him, he wouldn't be able to pick Zach out from a random guy off the street. With slicked-back hair and a plain black suit, nothing about him stood out. Not even the patchwork fuzz growing on the underside of his chin made him enough to remember. Cole wondered what even brought him into Nina's orbit in the first place.

Mr. Francisco meandered from around his table and approached the well, having obtained permission from Judge Byrd. He brushed off his blazer, gestured to Zach, and all eyes fell on him.

He cleared his throat, "State your name for the court, please."

"Zachary Piker. P-I-K-E-R," Zach announced clearly for the entire court to hear him, although his eyes focused on Nina. She, on the other hand, refused to look at him.

The bailiff stepped forward from his corner. "Thank you. Mr. Piker, please raise your right hand. Do you affirm that the testimony you are about to give is the truth, the whole truth, and nothing but the truth, so help you, God?"

"I do."

"The witness has been sworn in, Your Honor."

"Excellent," Judge Byrd remarked, but her tone implied a different story. The coldness of judicial impartiality weighed heavily on the room. "Counselor, proceed with the direct questioning of the witness."

"Thank you, Your Honor." Mr. Francisco paced around the well briefly before saying, "Good morning, Mr. Piker. Can you identify the respondent to these proceedings?"

"Yes, I can. You're pointing at Nina Byndel."

"And what is your relationship to Miss Byndel?"

"We . . . we were engaged until a few months ago. We had been together for years before then." Zach lay on the woe thick, causing Nina to quietly retch from beside Cole. The sound felt too real to ignore.

However, he noticed Rudy shift in his chair, and the once calm expression on his face vanished. He wordlessly tore off a piece of his legal pad and slid it toward Nina, laying a pen on top. Rudy's voice dropped, "Write me everything I need to know about cross-examining this guy."

He didn't know who Zach was . . . not until he revealed it on the stand.

Zach likely withheld that crucial information during the depositions, and Cole sensed disaster on the horizon.

Nina accepted the paper with shaking hands, and she refused to look up. She began writing down information as asked, but Cole's arm slithered around her shoulders to hide her from Zach's hawkish stare. He hadn't stopped looking at her, not once.

Cole glared at him, but his attention split between Zach and Mr. Francisco, who moved freely about the well between questions. Mr. Francisco had the floor, and like a trainwreck, Cole couldn't tear his eyes away.

"Mr. Piker, can you describe your relationship with Miss Byndel?" asked Mr. Francisco.

"Objection, Your Honor," Rudy stood up from his chair. "What's the relevance of that information?"

"Counselor Francisco, what is the relevance?"

"Your Honor, I merely wish to establish a foundation for the witness's testimony and his personal knowledge of Miss Byndel's fitness to be a guardian."

"I'm going to sustain the objection. Get onto a more relevant line of questioning, Counselor Francisco." Judge Byrd's quick reply may have shut down that one question, but Mr. Francisco moved on without complaint.

"Mr. Piker, how did you discover Naomi Byndel had passed away?"

"I was at work when I got a call from the hospital. They mentioned a car accident, but I was told that Nina, my fiancée, had been admitted to the hospital due to a severe anxiety attack. She had been inconsolable, and the doctors worried about her mental state. I went to visit her after work, but she was a wreck. For hours, she was unable to talk without crying.

"I see. Did Nina have struggles with anxiety before this point, to your knowledge?"

Zach nodded solemnly; if a jury was in the room, he would probably be playing on their sympathies. "She had been diagnosed with a generalized anxiety disorder since college and took medication for it."

"Objection, Your Honor! This information may cause undue prejudice on the fact finder," Rudy declared, but Judge Byrd shook her head.

"Overruled, Counselor Hawkins. Counselor Francisco, please continue with your direct examination."

"Thank you, Your Honor. Mr. Piker, once you and Miss Byndel discovered that Brooke—Miss Byndel's niece—would need a guardian, what was Miss Byndel's reaction to that?"

Zachary paused, looking at Nina like he wanted to see her face, and Cole's blood boiled. The heat started slow, but a sudden rush brought the temperature in the room to a simmer. If looks could kill, Cole wished he could scorch flesh off bones and leave Zach on the witness stand as ash.

He shook his head. "She broke down, sobbing. She said she wasn't sure if she wanted to care for Brooke. She wasn't ready to have children yet, and Brooke might hold her career back."

Nina's head snapped up, but no amount of composure could mask the hurt written all over her face. She clenched her fists into the table, and Cole's hands grabbed her waist, holding her in her seat. *Don't do it. Let him have it after the court adjourns for the day.*

An almost inaudible cry hit Cole's ears, and he knew Nina had to fight the urge to scream. In all the time he had known Nina, nothing about that statement sounded like her.

Mr. Francisco hummed. "Mr. Piker, what is your opinion on the Byndel family? Of Vera, Thomas, Maxwell, and Felicity?"

Zach managed to smile a little, "They seem like amazing people. A well-respected family, pillars of the community. Felicity and Maxwell are a lovely couple and honest people. I don't have a bad word to say about them."

"Conversely, what is your opinion of Miss Byndel after your broken engagement? Are you two on good terms?"

"Nina and I don't speak. Beyond the few times I've seen her, where she's blown me off, I can't say she's the woman I once loved. The Nina I knew would never rebound into a relationship so quickly after a loss."

Cole's hands on Nina's hips burned shamefully, but he didn't let go of her. He and Nina weren't dating, and the truth would be revealed. He needed a level head, which meant fantasies of cornering Zach and punching him at least once stopped then and there.

He needed to focus.

Mr. Francisco flourished his hands to the empty room and stepped to the back of the well, "No more questions, Your Honor."

"Thank you, Counselor," Judge Byrd wrote something down in the silence. "Counselor Hawkins, if you'd like to cross the witness, you may prepare for that."

Rudy nodded and rose from his chair, "Yes, Your Honor. I will be cross-examining Mr. Piker." He gestured to Nina for the paper with her debrief on all things Zach Piker, and she handed it over.

Cole read over her shoulder at the shaky handwriting, able to make out a few words here and there: *recently asked to get back together, and I said no. he might be looking for revenge. We were together for three years. He met my family twice, and I didn't sanction those meetings and wasn't comfortable with them.*

He glanced at Nina, who looked on the verge of tears, but she pushed the paper toward Rudy before he stepped to the well. She tucked her hands underneath her knees, bouncing erratically behind the table, and her melancholy stare eventually collided with Cole's.

"It'll be okay," he whispered to her, and she nodded, but neither embraced the notion with visible confidence. Cole's hands lifted to wrap a supportive arm around her waist, and Nina leaned into him.

"I want this to be over," Nina whimpered and hid her face when Zach stared at them again. Cole blocked Nina from his view and narrowed his eyes when Zach met his eyes instead. Cole knew better, but something guttural and angry wanted five minutes alone with Zach to remind him to stay far away from Nina.

Rudy rapped his knuckles against the podium set up in the well. "Good morning, Mr. Piker. Isn't it true that anxiety is a reasonable response to finding out a loved one was in a car accident?"

"I guess so," Zach mumbled, and his unruly eyebrows knit together like the idiot attempted to pinpoint where Rudy would be going.

"You guess so? Isn't it true that Miss Byndel learned her sister had passed away because of the car crash and thus became inconsolable?"

"Yes."

"Isn't it true that Miss Byndel was closer to her sister than the rest of her family, especially considering that Naomi Byndel was disowned by them?"

"I don't understand why that matters—" Zach started, but Rudy shook his head and spoke louder than him.

"Witness is being non-responsive, Your Honor," said Rudy. Cole swallowed the sickening, smug satisfaction of watching Zach's face freeze like a deer in headlights. Obviously, opposing counsel coached him to be evasive or simplistic in his answers, but Rudy tripped him up.

Judge Byrd tapped her gavel. "Answer the question, Mr. Piker."

"Yes." Zach snapped out, but Rudy paced a little closer to him. Cole leaned forward and caught Zach's attention, kicking off a stare-down between the two.

"Isn't it true that you only met the Byndel family twice during your relationship with Miss Byndel?"

"I can't say exactly, but I think so."

"Did Miss Byndel disclose her strained relationship with her family to you or the childhood traumas she experienced during your relationship?"

"Yeah, a little bit."

Rudy rapped on the podium again. "Do you think your brief acquaintanceship undermines any of Miss Byndel's sworn testimony about her harsh upbringing?"

Zach swallowed. "No."

"Did your engagement to Nina Byndel end because she wanted to adopt Brooke, and you didn't?" asked Rudy.

"... Yes."

"So, could Miss Byndel's statement in the hospital, which is hearsay, have been due to the overwhelming emotional stress of losing her sister, but she is prepared to be a caregiver when calm?"

"Objection!" Mr. Francisco exclaimed, but Rudy waved his hand. *Withdrawn.* The question would never reach the record, but Zach sat on the stand with shifty eyes. Cole smelled the blood in the water, and so did Zach.

"Mr. Piker, do you have proof that Miss Byndel is in a new relationship?" Rudy cocked his head, and Zach's lips twisted like he tasted something sour.

"No. No proof." Zach scowled, but the final question mounted before anyone could process it.

"Did you corner Miss Byndel at her place of work recently and ask to rekindle your relationship, only for her to say no?"

"... Yes."

"No further questions, Your Honor." Rudy stepped away from the well and flashed a thumbs up to Nina and Cole. Nina's shoulders trembled, but she mumbled soft cries and held onto Cole tighter.

Cole rubbed her back firmly. "Rudy handled the problem. Zach isn't going to ruin this for you." He wouldn't let that happen. Cole would climb into the witness box and testify if it came down to it.

Chapter Twenty
Nina

When Zach stepped to the witness box and testified, Nina swore she had forgotten how to breathe. He called her unfit, unstable, and unworthy to be Brooke's guardian, in so many words, on behalf of her family. She couldn't wrap her head around it.

Did he think she would collapse back into his arms without Brooke anchoring her? She wasn't some weak-willed fool who needed a man to prop her up and decide in her "best interest."

When Judge Byrd slammed her gavel down and announced the session adjourned, Nina rose from her chair and fled with a whispered "I need to use the bathroom" to Cole. His eyes on her back almost deterred her from running, but she wanted a minute to cry without shame.

She burst through the double doors, hobbling to the nearest bathroom. She spotted the sign on the way in earlier and beelined for the sanctuary of a stall. Every step in her shiny black pumps caused her to wobble and threaten to topple over. Nina tried to slow but straddled between a need to rush and the mounting anxiety of a nasty fall.

Nina refused to look behind her, toward the courtroom, knowing she'd see either Zach or her estranged family emerge from the same double doors she had. Seeing their faces would finally keel her over and knock her down.

They want to take everything. Despite what Cole promised her after the cross-examination, Nina's dread promised the unimaginable would come to pass. She couldn't lose Brooke. It would be losing Naomi all over again, but worse, knowing Brooke was alive and trapped with those people. *Their greed knows no boundaries.*

As graceful as a bird with clipped wings, Nina stumbled into the bathroom door and crashed inside. She spiraled as she locked herself into a stall, climbing inside. Nina's eyes skimmed the ground, and despite a thin layer of nylon stockings protecting her legs, kneeling on the bathroom floor prodded at that queasy feeling in her chest.

She tore one of the paper seat covers in half, one side for each hand, and she gripped the edge of the seat over the paper. Her legs wobbled as she bent her knees, hovering over the bathroom floor. A burn raced along the length of her calves at the awkward angle, but she dropped her gaze to the toilet.

She focused on the still waters in the toilet bowl, chasing a sense of calm while she counted the passing seconds. But the overbearing presence of bile gathered in Nina's throat, leaving behind a burning sensation in a slow crawl to her mouth. Hearing Zach's testimony on the stand made her sick.

She was a wreck.

Brooke might hold her career back.

The Nina I knew would never rebound into a relationship so quickly after a loss.

She couldn't bring herself to look at his face whenever he spoke, too busy hiding behind Cole. She didn't know what would've happened if he hadn't been there, stopping her from crying out.

Nina coughed hard when the bile kept pushing higher up her throat. The culmination of seeing Zach side with her family after knowing how they treated her for years solidified an unmistakable truth. *No matter how many times he said he loved her, he never meant it. He couldn't love her if he chose to help her family ruin her happy life.*

The death of the last couple of years of her life rode in on a burning, bitter current and left a sour taste behind in her mouth.

Nina closed her eyes, preparing for nausea to hit her hard and cause her stomach to turn over. But the push open of the bathroom door yanked her into a vice grip. The urge to vomit paused as a pair of heels stepped onto the tile flooring in the bathroom.

Her thoughts raced—*what if it was her mother or Felicity*—consuming every inkling of her attention. She faced forward and braced over the toilet, stuck in a prayer position where her arms began to burn from holding herself up. She couldn't bend and check the type of heels outside her hiding spot in the stall.

She would have to wait.

Sweat lined at the edge between her forehead and hairline, threatening to bead along her skin. Already in dire straits, Nina sucked in a deep breath in the silence while listening to the heels move through the bathroom. Two stall doors creaked like someone pushed them, causing Nina's arms to shake.

However, the heels quickly strode toward the sinks, followed by the audible flow of water. The crumpling sound of a paper towel and the creak of the sink eased Nina's paranoia a twinge. She needed an empty bathroom to cry and throw up in. Was she asking too much?

When the heels walked out the door and vanished, Nina gasped and promptly threw up into the toilet bowl. She buried her face in the rim and stopped fighting until the bile became dry heaving and not much else. She jolted between feeling light-headed and dizzy and spare moments of clarity, baffled by the uncertainty of what came next.

She burst into tears when the sickness lapsed, hopefully passing for good. Nina buried her face into the crook of her elbow as she pushed onto her feet, letting the tears dampen her cheeks and sting behind her eyes. She expected to look like a mess but would clean up once she crawled out of the stall with her pride intact.

Nina flushed the toilet and leaned her back into the door, holding herself up when her legs trembled. Her hand covered her mouth to muffle any sound threatening to spill off her lips. She needed to cry it out before she had to be brave for Brooke and everyone else around her.

"Pull yourself together," Nina whispered to herself, pulling her hand from her mouth. She closed her eyes, blinking through the tears, but words alone wouldn't save her. Zach's testimony prolonged the verdict another few weeks due to Judge Byrd's hectic schedule in December. Cole mentioned the week between Christmas and New Year's, but she lost most of what he said in a haze of dread. *This Christmas might be the last one she and Brooke ever shared.*

She nearly lost her stomach again at the thought but rode through the dizzying wave until her body settled. Nina stumbled out of the stall and slumped over the counter, hands frantically flipping on the cold water to the highest setting.

Despite the tremble in her hands, Nina managed to cup enough water and brought her lips to the water. Greedily, she drank the water and swished it to clean her mouth. She spat into the sink until her mouth was washed clean.

Then, she dabbed damp hands across her face and cleaned up any ruined makeup from her breakdown. The red tinge of her panicked eyes wouldn't disappear with any clean-up, so those would remain for everyone to see.

"Walk out like you aren't scared. None of them will prevail," Nina murmured at her reflection, and maybe if she repeated it, she'd believe herself. "None of them will prevail."

She crumpled a few paper towels into a wad and dried her hands and face off. Then, with nothing else holding her back, she headed for the bathroom door. However, she stopped in the doorway before colliding with Zach's chest.

Her heart bolted before catching herself, and she averted her eyes from his. "Excuse me."

She tried moving around Zach, but his larger frame blocked her escape. Her only option for refuge would be slinking back into the bathroom. Nina froze in the doorframe, unable to pull the trigger on any course of action. She could run, sure. But that required her to slam enough weight into Zach to bypass him, and she couldn't trust he wouldn't twist the encounter to suit his needs.

Her eyes jumped around him, hoping to glimpse Cole nearby. She'd even accept Rudy finding her in a precarious position and coming to her rescue. Cole would have to assume the worst if she didn't return from the bathroom and search for her. Could she stall Zach long enough for a rescue?

"Nina, we need to talk," said Zach.

"No, I don't think we have anything to talk about. Please move out of my way, or I'll—"

"You'll do what? Scream? No, you won't."

"I'll do whatever I have to," Nina yelped when he leaned toward her, but when she prepared to jump into the safety of the bathroom, Zach's hand snatched her wrist. She choked when Zach dragged her out of the bathroom and down the hall in the opposite direction from the courtroom. "Let go of me!"

Zach snapped, "Shut up. You owe me a talk."

"I don't owe you anything. You're hurting me!" When he pulled her into an off-shoot hallway, out of view from the main path and the other people in the court, Nina gasped. She wrestled for control of her arm, but Zach had the strength advantage.

Zach's eyes gleamed, and Nina couldn't shake how sinister he appeared in the dim lights of the side hall. However, when he leaned toward her until her back skimmed against the wall with his eyes fixed on her lips, she snapped out of it.

Her nails sank into the fleshy part of his wrist hard until he let go of her, backing away. Nina lifted her hand to warn Zach—*she would fight if necessary.*

"Do you always have to be so unreasonable and dramatic?" Zach snapped, rubbing over the nail indents she left behind on his skin. The sight of marks brought her a rush of pride.

Nina clenched her hands. "I'm the dramatic one? Me? I'm not the one who paraded himself into a court case to cause problems for my ex. You've got to be fucking with me at this point."

"Ah, there's that temper I remember." Zach's tone oozed condescension from every word, but Nina tempered a flash of anger with a breath. "You pretend to be such an innocent, gentle-natured person, but you have quite the explosive fuse."

"Newsflash, Zach . . . most people wouldn't be so nice if you treated them how you've treated me lately. So, excuse me for not licking the tips of those god-awful loafers you spend a small fortune on because they're designer."

"Whatever."

"No, it's not whatever! You walked into court and spewed a steaming pile of shit on behalf of my parents, asshole brother, and the witch he calls a fiancée. You know what type of treatment I endured because of them throughout the years, but me choosing Brooke over you pushed you to them, huh?"

Zach and she glared at one another. Suddenly, the thought that she ever loved him seemed painfully absurd. Who had he even become? Who had she grown into? Neither answer enlightened her.

Zach shook his head. "You want the best for that little girl? It's not you."

"How do you know that?" Nina scoffed. "You chose not to stay around and see how I've chosen to raise Brooke, honoring Naomi's memory. You put me in a position to choose with the ultimatum, but I chose the right path."

"You fucked up the good thing we had—"

"No, that was all you. Brooke needs a guardian who knows her and won't force her to change to fit a stereotypical image. My parents want her because she's biologically related to their golden son, but Felicity and Maxwell want a doll to sweeten their image. Brooke isn't a toy they can play happy family with . . . she's not some prop they can add to family photos and forget about later. She is every bit of Naomi left in this world."

Zach looked ready to slam his fist through the wall, which should've scared Nina more. But the fear had succumbed to a tidal wave of anger hotter than a blistering burn. No number of apologies could act as the salve and heal the rage. He was angry at her.

Tough. She was angrier at the world.

Nina's attention jumped toward the opening, but she snapped her gaze forward to find Zach's narrowed eyes. "Let me go. Screaming at me to change my mind won't have the effect you want it to. We're over . . . I don't know how many times I need to say it."

"We could've been happy."

"No, we couldn't be happy. Resentment would've built up and broken us over something else."

"I don't buy that. If you had let Felicity be a mom like she desperately wants, you and I would be living our best life. But I don't think you loved me all that much if you refused to meet me in the middle."

"First of all, you refused to meet me either. For someone who had once been so eager to have kids, the prospect of fostering a kid in need suddenly turned you off. I know why now. You were so turned off by the idea that Brooke wasn't yours biologically, so much so that you let your insecurities blind you."

Zach said nothing, but the dip in his Adam's apple conveyed everything Nina needed to hear. She had Zach by the collar, caught in his unspoken reasons for his staunch opposition to Brooke.

She resumed. "Second and more importantly, Felicity doesn't get to be a mom. She's not entitled to having a baby, especially not the baby of the woman she terrorized and got disowned by the family. Unlike the rest of the Byndels you aligned yourself with, I believe who we love will always be higher than who we share blood with. Brooke is both, and you are neither . . . it's not a hard choice to stand against you and the other demons in that courtroom."

Nina soaked in his heavy silence and tried to head for the exit. However, she didn't get far before Zach blocked her path again and leaned to keep her stuck. A twisted tangle of anger and the earlier fear locked in an embrace, holding Nina in place.

Zach scowled. "You never answered me the other day about whether you're seeing someone new."

"Because that's none of your business!"

"Did you think I wouldn't eventually find out the truth? I will only ask you once: are you in love with that stupid dweeb Cole Yearwood?"

Nina's heart lurched to a dead stop in her chest, and she stared at Zach, wondering if he snooped around on his own or whether her family happily supplied Cole's name to him. Regardless, she abstained from a damn word.

Cole, please show up. Things are about to go down.

Nina's silence stoked the brittle tension, which threatened to break under the next provocation. Aware of how things might go horribly wrong with enough anger, like detonating an explosion, she eyed the exit to the hallway.

"I saw the photos," Zach snapped.

"What are you talking about?" Nina stared at him with narrowed eyes. Her heart erratically slammed against her chest, trying to break out of her body with how hard it thumped. "Have you been stalking me?"

"No. Vera and Maxwell forwarded me some photographs of you and Mr. Perfect looking cozy with Brooke. You three have a little family going, huh?" Zach pulled his phone out of his pocket and flashed Nina his screen.

Horrified, Nina saw images of her, Cole, and Brooke taken at the fairground a few weeks back. The pictures blurred a little from the distance or the zoom of the camera that took them, but she and Cole wore unmistakable smiles and leaned close to each other.

Better than sticking around, Nina sprinted for the hallway and cleared Zach's larger frame, but his hands lashed out to grab her by her waist. Nina struggled against him, even when he spun her around.

She squirmed under his grip, "Let go of me! You're hurting me—" Nina pushed hard against his chest, but her shove wasn't enough force to break free.

"Nina, can't you see you're being delusional?" Zach's hold on her tightened, paining her. "You think that this Cole guy will stick around for you? When you get too much to handle, he'll leave. I'm one of the only people who would stay with someone like you as long as I had."

"You're such a bastard."

"And you're dodging because I'm right. Face the facts. If you act rational and give Brooke to capable parents, you may find a guy who can overlook the rest of your faults enough to be with you for the long haul."

Nina wished she could think of something more to say, a stronger comeback or a sharp-tongue jab. She wavered as her anger boiled over, rushing out of her body faster than she could collect it back.

"Let go of her *now*." She watched Zach's eyes snap over her head as an arm pulled her back into a chest, her back colliding with a firm wall of woolen suit and defined muscles. Nina's eyes wandered up when she tipped her head back, seeing Cole.

She studied him with wide eyes, but even at her odd angle, his anger shocked her. His usually soft hazel eyes darkened to pitch blackness, teeming with barely constrained rage. A vein popped along his neck, pulsing with every breath.

But his anger wasn't directed at her. Zach was his target.

Zach's hand had let go of her hips when Cole pulled her away from him, and they stayed far away when Cole looped his arm around her stomach, fashioned like a seatbelt to protect her from her ex.

"There he is." Zach slipped into a bitter laugh. "Mr. Perfect himself, here to white knight and sweep you off on some fantasy of happily ever after."

Cole gave Zach a once-over, and yet, the silent stare exuded disgust like Cole stared at a bug he might squash underneath the tip of his Oxfords. He had an inch or two on Zach and made the most of it.

"If you don't keep your hands to yourself, Mr. Piker, you'll find yourself on the receiving end of criminal harassment charges on top of a restraining order. I don't need to explain how the courts find hitting women the mark of a pathetic man, which you undoubtedly are."

"You wouldn't."

"I would do everything in my power to see you behind bars . . . consider that a promise," Cole remarked, deadly calm. "But both of us know Nina is more than capable as a guardian to Brooke, so you'll step off."

Nina winced hard. Zach's verbiage on Cole's tongue meant he overheard Zach's little diatribe or at least a part of it. But how much had he heard before his intervention? *Does he think of me as delusional, too?*

Zach decided to wise up and leave, but Cole shoulder-checked him hard when Zach tried to pass him. Nina heard the force of the bodily contact, followed by Zach's whine before her ex-fiancé vanished.

"Nina, are you okay?"

"Take me to my car. Please. I don't think I can be in this courthouse for another minute. I threw up in the bathroom and will bawl my eyes out."

"Okay. We're leaving now, I promise."

Cole eased her around, buried her into a hug, and moved with her slowly. They emerged from the side hallway, but Nina knew she couldn't go back to before the encounter. She was shaken, for lack of a better word.

She knew she should tell Cole about the lies her family fed to Zach about them and the stalker photos taken at the fairgrounds. She needed to speak up. Yet, it was like her throat closed, and no sound wanted to come out.

Tears sprung from the corners of her eyes. She sank into the embrace of Cole's body so close to hers and the protection she experienced with him there. The Cole she knew versus the Cole that came out whenever danger lurked seemed worlds apart, but she knew both sides to be equal halves of the same great man.

Her Cole brought a sweet, lighthearted energy, always knew the right words to comfort her when she hit rock bottom and cared so deeply. He made her feel like the most important person in the world. He treated Brooke lovingly and never let her go through troubled times alone.

The Cole that her family saw, however? He had a sharp tongue and plenty of malice to go around. He didn't fear any of them, which couldn't be said for her. He protected her like a shield from their attacks and intimidation, stoic and unflinching.

Those two sides merged into a great person; he stood as someone Nina was honored to call her friend. His companionship meant the world to her.

Zach and her family, by extension, insisted on knowing if she was in love with Cole more than she considered what they were. They seemed confident she loved him with an unbroken heart and coveted him for the future.

What if she did?

Chapter Twenty-One
Cole

Almost two weeks passed since the last custody hearing, and Cole sensed Nina's anxiety. But who wouldn't be anxious after an encounter like hers with Zach? True to his word, Rudy learned about Zach's confrontation and pulled some strings behind the scenes. Whatever he did, Zach hadn't attempted to contact Nina since.

Good. Zach could rot for all Cole cared.

Brooke had eventually fessed up about Vera's attempt to snatch her from daycare, which only worsened the context of the photos shown to Nina. The reveal strengthened Nina's reasons for why she was the best choice for Brooke's guardian. Since she retained primary custody, the court date after Christmas would be when they received a verdict.

The developments weighed on Cole as he watched Brooke sprint past him into her bedroom, her blonde hair loose and hanging around her face. She giggled at her green and white polka dot pajama set, spinning in front of her mirror.

Cole leaned in the door, biting back laughter when Nina moved past him with an exasperated sigh. She slipped a scrunchie off her wrist and pulled Brooke's hair back, "We don't want knots in the morning."

Brooke nodded. "Okay! No knots!"

"C'mere, bug," Nina squeezed her into a loving hug, peppering her forehead with a dozen kisses. Brooke's face turned bright pink, and she shied away from Nina's affection. "Let's get you ready for sleep."

Brooke glanced around Nina and blinked at Cole, "Mr. Cole, will you do my bedtime story?"

Nina turned to him over her shoulder and Cole shuffled out of the doorway. "If your aunt doesn't mind, I'd happily handle story duty."

"Are you sure?"

"I've got story time handled."

"Okay. I'll meet you in the living room." Nina passed Brooke to Cole and headed to clean up the leftovers from Tuesday dinner. Cole cooked that evening's meal—homemade chicken noodle soup—and ensured that Nina and Brooke had enough for the next week.

"Alright, kid. Time for bed." Cole let Brooke loose, and she dove onto the twin bed without hesitation, scrambling under the covers with kicking feet. Her excitement settled when she crawled underneath the fluffy duvet. He sat at the foot of the bed. "What story would you like tonight?"

"*Where the Wild Things Are!*" exclaimed Brooke.

"*Where The Wild Things Are?* I remember loving that book as a kid. Let me go find it."

"It's on the third level of the shelf."

Cole leaned over to the shelf and perused through the stacks of picture books and colorful spines, well-loved from the wrinkles and worn pages. Eventually, he eased *Where The Wild Things Are* out from its place sandwiched between *Goodnight Moon* and an illustrated collection of fairytales.

He thumbed through the pages with tenderness and settled back onto the bed. However, Brooke scooted over and opened enough space for Cole to sit closer to her. His legs would still hang over the edge if he sat at the head of the bed. But he accepted the spot anyway.

Cole opened the cover and cleared his throat, using the light from behind the butterfly-patterned lampshade to illuminate the page. He checked the star projector tucked into the corner across the room, decorating the mostly dim room with soft yellow stars across the ceiling and walls.

"Is there anything else you need before we settle for story time? Water? Stuffed animal?" Cole asked when Brooke cuddled into his side, already yawning. From the look of her droopy eyes, she would last a few pages before she fell asleep.

"Can I ask you a question, Mr. Cole?"

"Sure thing. What do you want to know?"

Brooke hesitated while playing with the long sleeves of her shirt, wrapping them over her hands and fidgeting shyly. Cole almost worried something had happened again, something Nina didn't know.

He sat up a little more, yet Brooke squeezed closer into his side, looking him in the eyes. "Mr. Cole, do you love Auntie Nini?"

Cole choked on his tongue but played it off like a cough. He needed a moment to figure out what to say, but Brooke stared at him expectantly, almost a little sassy with how she cocked her brow while waiting.

He faltered. "Your aunt and I are friends, Brooke. Where is this coming from?"

"I see you two staring at each other all the time," said Brooke. "I've never had a daddy. But a lot of my friends at daycare have mommies and daddies, and they always smile at one another the same way you and my auntie do."

"And what way is that?"

"With heart eyes, as Miss Gloria said. She always whispers that to herself when you come to pick me up from daycare with Auntie Nini!"

Despite the urge to crack a joke and change the subject, Cole knew a five-year-old outmaneuvered him with sharper insights and quicker wit than some of the attorneys he met. But it wasn't his place to confide in a kid the complexities of his relationship with her aunt.

"Friends can love one another, but it's a different kind of love than the one you're asking about. Your aunt is focused on raising you more than having a relationship with someone else. You probably remember her old boyfriend, Zach, right?"

"I didn't like Zach. My mommy used to say that he wasn't good for Auntie Nini and was stinky. But she pretended she liked him because Auntie Nini liked him. He never came for dinner or played tea party with me."

Cole frowned hard. Of course, Zach wasn't the type of man to befriend the people in Nina's life. If he asked, she'd probably tell him that her life revolved around his more than their shared life. He assumed the worst whenever Zach Piker got involved.

He fixed the duvet for Brooke, hoping the exhaustion would take over. Brooke wiggled underneath the blankets, likely drawn to sleep with the warmth of the layers pressing down on her. Her eyes fought to stay open, looking on the verge of shutting.

Cole closed the copy of *Where The Wild Things Are* and sighed, "I'm sorry he wasn't nice to you or your aunt. You two deserve better than that."

Brooke plopped her head against his chest, and Cole stayed still for her comfort. He glanced toward the door, expecting Nina to show up in the doorway to watch him regale Brooke with a bedtime story. She'd find him avoiding the topic of their relationship, constantly called into question by the people around them.

Maybe it was a sign.

He waited for her breathing to even out, but Brooke refused to sleep without answers. "So, you do love my auntie."

"I can't say that."

"Well, Auntie Nini likes you. She always talks about you, and she smiles big when I ask about you. She never smiles so big, not for ice cream or puppies!"

"Friends are supposed to like one another, so I hope she likes me," Cole mumbled, knowing what Brooke meant. But it was for the best if he didn't plant ideas in her head about him and Nina being something other than friends. That wasn't his place. "But if or when your aunt decides to meet someone new, she'll tell you when she's ready."

Brooke pouted at his answer, shifting her face away to stare at the wall, "I don't want Auntie Nini to like anyone else. I want her to love you."

"Well, we can't control who loves us or who we love. But I know your aunt is smart and won't choose anyone over you. Whoever she brings into your lives will love you as much as she does." Cole wished he could tell her something more comforting, but she was a perceptive kid.

After the silence persisted for a beat, Cole peered over at Brooke and found her fast asleep. Her pout melted into a more peaceful expression, even when Cole moved off the bed and the mattress jostled once released from under his weight. He pulled the blanket up to her chest and tucked one of her stuffed animals underneath it.

Then, he switched off the lamp, and the room darkened save for the star projector's splash of light across the ceiling and walls.

Cole set the copy of *Where The Wild Things Are* on top of the dresser when he passed, bummed he didn't get to read it. When he was younger, his dad read the book to him all the time. He remembered the book being his favorite for years until he latched onto Jules Verne.

He quietly shut the door behind him and listened for the soft click before heading for the living room. He expected the light rushing of water from the sink or the dishwasher when he passed through the kitchen, but neither was active.

Instead, he spotted Nina in the living room with their glasses of wine as filled as they were before Brooke's bedtime routine. Neither of them had enjoyed a nice glass of post-dinner wine meant for the two adults to unwind.

Cole intended to meet her on the couch for their glass of wine and some small talk before he headed out for the night or crashed on the sofa if the hour became too late.

However, Brooke's words rattled around in his head. *She wanted him and Nina together, like Dean and January.* Everyone assumed something existed between him and Nina beyond their stated friendship . . . even Nina's family, who wouldn't know the first thing about her.

Even if he wanted to, Cole knew forcing himself into Nina's life and playing house was wrong. She had an engagement fall apart, and he had no excuse other than his struggle to find the one. He wasn't looking for a passing fling or someone to be a maybe in his book. He needed to be undeniably sure of love after relationships fell apart or failed to start.

A pull existed between him and Nina, and neither jumped to claim it as anything other than friendship.

But the inevitable day would come when Nina would meet someone she wanted to spend her life loving. Knowing what she deserved, the guy would be a charmer and sweep her off her feet with sweet nothings and the honesty to follow through. Brooke would adore him and want him to be around every minute because he cared for her. Handsome, kindhearted, and devoted, that guy would waltz into her life and give her the happy home she longed for.

Cole should be happy thinking how she'd smile more often and have the help with Brooke she craved. Yet, his stomach churned when imagining another man doing precisely what Brooke wanted him to do.

If Dean and January were there, they might hit him with the one thing he continued to deny. *He had fallen in love with Nina Byndel, and she wanted him as a friend.*

Shit.

His revelation didn't open a can of worms. It exploded the can into a billion splintered pieces, leaving his thoughts in a scrambled mess. But shame was the first thought to prevail in the free-for-all taking over his emotions.

The last thing Nina needed in her life was a guy hoping for a long-shot romance when her responsibilities started and ended with raising her niece into a happy, healthy young woman. He needed to either shove those feelings back into the box and bury them or get comfortable with the fact that he and Nina weren't happening.

Cole would've lingered in the kitchen for much longer if Nina hadn't glanced over her shoulder and smiled when she spotted him, "I grabbed some cheese and fruit for the wine. You should probably have some before I steal it all."

The sweetness of her laughter acted as a vice grip around his heart, and Cole staggered forward, not wanting to keep her waiting on his internal crisis. He stumbled over to her and sat on the couch. A thin dividing line between their cushions marked the limited space between them.

He grabbed his wine and sipped it quietly. He nursed the wine instead of talking and caught Nina's quiet stares between sips.

"What's on your mind?" Nina set her glass down, but he clutched his tight in his hand, anchoring himself. "You seem far away."

"I'm thinking about how lucky I am to have our friendship. Brooke mentioned something tonight, and I can't wrap my head around everything."

"What did she say?"

"She asked me if I love you."

Nina's face flushed a wild shade of red, throat bobbing. She couldn't look him in the eye, but he was okay with that. He didn't think he could meet her eyes either, embarrassed to be spilling his guts without enough wine in his system to blame for loose lips.

She groaned. "Cole, I'm so sorry. She's normally not so nosy, and I know she's been taught not to insert herself into adults' business. I hope she wasn't persistent."

"She was adamant that we have feelings for one another and that she doesn't want you to fall in love with anyone else, even though I tried to explain that love isn't such an easy thing to promise to someone," Cole murmured, finally setting down his wine glass. "The only problem is that she's not the only one convinced."

"You mean Zach?" Nina's mouth twisted at the mention of his name, although relevant to their discussion.

"My brother and sister-in-law think so, too."

"Oh. I really didn't mean to cause you so much trouble. I don't know why they can't accept that you and I are . . . friends. Nothing inappropriate has happened between us."

Cole reached forward to grasp Nina's hand, catching her before she rolled away on a tangent. On his tongue, a confession threatened to burn down the stability he strove to keep with her—steeped in the platonic label he repeatedly defended—but the words were dying to come out.

He sighed. "They're right, though. I want your friendship more than I can explain, but I also want much more. Because the idea of someone else being the one for you makes me want to get on my knees and hurl."

Nina's face expressed every iota of shock from how fast she switched from embarrassment to bewilderment. The speechlessness on her features forced Cole to swallow a piping-hot ember of shame. *Way to go, genius.*

"I know that you're not looking for anyone since Zach, which I understand. I wouldn't want you to change your mind because of how I feel. I'm telling you all this because I still want us to be friends, even though I can't uphold the promise I made to myself that I wouldn't cross the line and fall over myself for you. If you want me to leave, I will—" Cole trailed off when Nina pressed her thumb against his lips.

"Stop," Nina remarked, and Cole's traitorous mouth obeyed, fixating on every intonation in her voice. He waited for her to be upset or angry at him for adding to her stress. Instead, she turned that thumb from his lips to his cheek and stroked gently. "Stop."

Evidently, it wasn't a warning to him.

Nina pushed forward until she sat on her knees, holding Cole captive with every movement from her. But the rough, sudden collision of her mouth with his spurred him back to life, releasing him from a trance.

He had fantasized about how Nina's mouth would feel against his, what she might taste like when he swiped his tongue over her lower lip, begging for permission to peek inside.

She tasted of wine, first and foremost, but the honey chapstick she carried in her purse slipped in there too. The whirlwind motions of her mouth against his left Cole dizzy when she pulled back from him, breathing hard.

She panted. "I'm sorry, but I hope that answer suffices."

Cole's mouth fell open at the boldness, but it worked for him. "Oh, yeah. I understand," he murmured while his hand circled her neck, thumb lazily stroking along her pulse point. Nina shivered and adjusted her position on her knees. With the slightest release of pressure, Cole brought her toppling down on top of him.

Their mouths met in the middle, making the first kiss feel like a sparkler instead of the roman candle of the second time. Cole swiftly pulled Nina closer by the swell of her hips, and his eager hand pawed over the material of her skirt. His tongue brushed her lower lip, and Nina let him in as he desired. Kissing Nina turned him into an almost unrecognizable person, driven up the wall by the sheer need to feel her skin pressed to his and run his tongue over unspeakable places like the dip between her thighs.

"Cole—" Nina panted into his mouth, eliciting a groan when she leaned back a little. But he pushed forward, chasing her mouth until their lips slid back together. Warmth swirled loosely in his stomach whenever her hands on his jean-clad thighs squeezed and gripped for leverage. "Let's take this to the bedroom."

"You don't want to get naked on the couch with me?" said Cole, although he meant it as lightheartedly as he could manage. With her permission, he would've taken her on the spot until he left a permanent indent of their shape on the cushions.

"Trust me, you make a compelling argument . . . but my room has a lock, and Brooke is sleepless sometimes."

"Lead me where you want me, sweetheart."

Nina grabbed his hand, lacing their fingers tight, and pulled him from the couch. Lovestruck, Cole followed behind her and left his mind in the living room alongside the unfinished wine and phone.

The urge to back Nina against the nearest wall and screw decorum out of her vocabulary hit Cole like a freight train. He hung onto his manners by the skin of his teeth as Nina pulled him into her darkened bedroom, diving straight for her bedside lamp.

Cole shut the door and flipped the lock closed, spinning around to see Nina silhouetted in the dim light. The lamp barely bathed a corner of the room in its faded, amber glow, but Cole watched Nina's rushed search through the top drawer of her end table. The scrambled movements of her hands as she rifled through the drawer became worth it when she slammed something down onto the bed.

A half-empty box of condoms peered back at Cole with some foils spilling onto the soft duvet like a promise of what would come. There went the last shred of his self-control, diving out the window and running off into the night.

Cole stepped forward, and Nina tossed him one, smiling when he caught it. Her eyes gleamed with the coy twinkle he spotted once or twice. She sucked in a breath, "I haven't been touched in months, so don't mind the cobwebs you'll have to knock off."

"I do love a challenge." Surging forward, Cole set his condom on the top of the end table, and in one fell swoop, he had Nina melting into his hands, gripping her hips with his mouth trailing the column of her neck. "May I take this off?"

One of his hands curled into the hem of the cute, heather gray long-sleeve she wore, itching to find it a new home on the floor. Nina's eyes fluttered half-open, and she nodded, but Cole whispered, "Verbal cues, sweetheart."

"Yes."

"Much appreciated."

"I live to please." Nina helped him peel the shirt from her body, but Cole had the next moves plotted out. The cute but functional bra needed to go. So, his hands slid up Nina's back and popped the clasp open.

Nina discarded the bra and smiled, staring up at him for approval. But Cole's attention focused on the shiny gold flash that caught the light. He swallowed. "Are those?"

"I got them done as a drunken dare at twenty-one and never felt the need to get rid of them since they're a hit. You like them?" Nina fixed the green heart charm dangling off one of her nipple piercings, golden bars catching on the light to glow.

"Now I wonder what other secrets you've been hiding?"

"Hmm, maybe I'll tell you."

"Your secrets are safe with me. I take confidentiality very seriously," Cole whispered against her ear, eliciting a gasp from Nina when he unzipped the back of her skirt. "Bed. Legs spread."

Nina collapsed back onto the bed, staring up at Cole. She kicked off her skirt to reveal a pair of lacy panties, nothing unusual. "You're still dressed. That's not fair."

"Oh yeah?" Cole leaned forward. His fingertips slid over the new wrinkles in the duvet made when Nina propped up on her elbows. At the first touch, when his fingers brushed against her sensitive inner thighs, a whimper slid off Nina's tongue. "You're free to take clothes off, too."

"O-okay." Nina's unsteady breaths got louder at the first contact of Cole's fingers through her panties. A light brush against her clit through the damp fabric elicited a few more moans, punctuated by the occasional *fuck* slipped in there. Cole's thumb wound small, tight circles over her clit, spreading her legs wider.

Meanwhile, Nina's hands fumbled for the belt looped around his jeans. She would whine whenever he slowed his fingering, especially when he hooked a finger or two to pull her panties to the side.

"You have the prettiest noises, sweetheart."

"Just for you."

"For me only? Mmm, I feel so special." Cole grinned hard. The clatter of his belt coming undone and the pull of leather against denim filled the space alongside Nina's whimpers. Cole brushed a finger from her clit down to her entrance, digit stained with slick.

His eyes wandered around the room when he noticed the mirror pressed against the wall and angled to face the bed. *Hello, good idea.*

The sound of a zipper captured his attention again, and he admired Nina, who appeared quite proud through all the heavy breathing and shallow upward thrusts of his hips. "I think I'd be faster with help."

Cole laughed. "You only need to ask." He smeared the slick on his fingers against her thighs before snapping each button of his but-ton-down open. Nina's eyes hungrily took in each additional show of his skin.

"I'm going to sue you for hiding all of this under those turtlenecks," she gasped, sitting up with eyes blown out. He prided himself on the chiseled ridges of his torso, from defined pecs to the deep indent of his

V-line decorated with a sparse happy trail vanishing into the waistband of his boxer.

"Sorry for holding out on you."

"I forgive you . . . as long as you put your whole body on me like a weighted blanket."

Laughing, Cole grabbed the foil off the end table when Nina's eager hands raked down and pulled his remaining clothes off. He caught one of her hands, kissed her knuckles, and helped her with his boxers.

He sat next to her on the bed, tearing the foil open. He rolled it over his aching cock, hissing at the contact of his hand. Nina had him worked up.

Cole patted his thighs, and Nina crawled over, throwing a leg over his lap and straddling him. Their eye contact thrummed with electricity, amplified by the arousal pitching a fit when Nina rubbed against his cock.

"Turn around," Cole murmured, earning a confused look in Nina's eyes. "Trust me, sweetheart."

"I trust you completely," Nina whispered but followed his instructions. With his help, Nina straddled his lap with her legs spread open wide and her face peering into their naked bodies reflected in the mirror.

Cole guided her hips to hover. He hid a smile into her shoulder as he tapped the head of his cock against her teased clit, drawing out pleading cries.

"Cole! You're such a tease!"

"I can't help it. You're so breathtaking. I want to take my time and savor you."

"You're going to kill me if . . . *please*," Nina whimpered when Cole rubbed himself against her entrance but stopped short of pushing inside.

Cole cooed and buried his face into the crook of her neck, still able to see himself and Nina's entire front. "I'll give you what you want, sweetheart, on one condition."

"Whatever you want." Nina agreed, words striking between a moan and a whine. Cole shuddered when a sharp pang of desire coursed down his spine.

"Someone's eager," he murmured into her neck, caressing the flustered skin with a stroke of his tongue. Nina's hips bucked in response, and the nipple-piercing charms twinkled from all the desperate, cock-hungry grinding she was doing. "Touch yourself how you would if you were alone. Show me how to worship your body."

At a loss for words, Nina nodded with how hard she bit down on her lip. One of her hands squeezed at her breasts, and a few breathy sighs coiled off her lips. Her other hand walked along her navel, leaving Cole to observe in silent excitement.

Two fingers teased her clit with practiced skill, and Nina's head leaned back to rest on Cole's shoulder, lost in her pleasure.

Using her distracted state, Cole finally pushed in and disrupted her rhythm. But her immediate moans of pleasure were met with Cole's hands settling on her hips.

"Keep touching," said Cole.

"I will," Nina promised while she rocked with the first thrust from Cole. "You're . . . stretching me . . . oh fuck."

"And you're taking my cock like a good fucking girl," Cole mouthed against her neck, barely audible over her pleasured moans. But his words spurred Nina's body to bounce on his cock, desperate for friction.

Nina grabbed one of his hands and laid it on one of her breasts. "Please. Don't. Stop," she panted out, whining since Cole hadn't moved yet. Well, her wish was his command.

Cole began to rock his hips upward, focused on deep thrusts rather than fast. He meant it when he told her he wanted to savor every moment. In the mirror, he watched her greedily take every inch of his cock in when he thrust up while he teased her nipples hard.

"Look at yourself, sweetheart. Do you see how good you are at this? I could watch you with those pretty eyes all day while you ride me."

"Cole?"

"Yes?"

"You think I look pretty?"

"Oh sweetheart . . . right now, you are the most gorgeous woman on the fucking planet. I love watching you be such a good girl for this cock. I'll bet you look even better when I get you close, where you're clenching around my cock and screaming for me to finish you off." Cole kissed up her neck, each kiss rougher than the last to leave his mark on her.

He wanted everyone to know he couldn't keep himself from her anymore.

Nina panted but smiled through all her noises. "It's been a minute, but I can feel it coming. My poor vibrator's probably collecting dust in the bottom drawer from inactivity, but it used to carry me all the way."

"I've never had a complaint," Cole promised and shared a laugh with her, nipping her earlobe between his teeth. "But a smart man uses all the tools at his disposal, so tell me if it'll make you feel good."

"I think you and whispering praises is enough," Nina promised, and her legs shook when Cole held her hips still. He began to speed up his thrusting without sacrificing hitting deep inside.

"Then, how about this . . . I don't think I can even do this with anyone else. I'll imagine your face and the feeling of your body, even when it's my hand."

"Fuck."

"You like how whipped you have me already? You had me before the sex, but this sealed the deal. Either it's you or no one, Nina."

Cole cheekily pinched one of her nipples, but it seemed to do the trick. Nina's pussy clenched hard around his cock, and he stifled a gasp into her neck when she came. *Hard.* Seeing her coming undone on his cock pushed Cole close to the finish.

A thrust or two later, he filled the condom with a few cries of his buried into her shoulder. The line between friendship and romance blurred more than his vision, but he wouldn't regret what came next.

Nina's voice strained a little when she asked. "Shower?"

"Shower. Let me take care of you," Cole promised. He held Nina in his arms, neither moving to leave quite yet.

Chapter Twenty-Two
Nina

Nina never wanted to leave her bed, not after last night's surprise developments. When Cole told her he had no complaints, she could see why.

That was the best sex she had in ages.

Stretching out in the askew sheets, her eyes blinked away the grains of sleep dusted over her lashes as her vision cleared. The room teemed with vibrance at the first strands of sunlight streaming through the cracks in the curtains, drawn tightly everywhere but the outer corners.

Nina sat up, letting the duvet slide down her chest and puddle around her hips. Goosebumps marked her bare skin, and the chill of December mornings seeped through the walls to tease her further.

She glanced to her side, a smile tugging at her lips when she spotted her companion. Cole Yearwood was a stomach sleeper. His face pressed into the pillow sideways, his arms crossed and tucked underneath. His dark hair without the pomade messily fell over his face, but Nina couldn't help the soft rake of her fingers to push the hair back.

She admired him while he slept. He looked at peace, not overwhelmed with the never-ending demands of his job. He didn't stir when her fingers grazed along his cheekbone.

Nina scooted toward the edge of her bed, careful not to wake Cole up. He needed more sleep before he left for work. Her legs hung over the side, and she slid onto her feet, watching Cole's face.

But none of her calculated moves stirred him from sleep.

Relieved, Nina walked away from the bed, but her eyes caught sight of her body in the mirror. A concentrated cluster of love bites marked her neck and shoulders, filling her chest with butterflies. She wandered closer to the mirror and leaned in, lovingly tracing her fingers over each mark.

Note to self, pick up some more foundation at the store today. Nina giggled at how her skin glowed. She ghostwrote enough articles about a post-sex glow to recognize it when she saw it. But with a shortage of foundation in the house, she'd use a turtleneck or scarf to cover the traces Cole left behind.

Her hands mussed her blonde waves in the mirror, and she smiled. For once, waking up wasn't hampered by dread about the day ahead. Debilitating, her anxiety led her through most of her life . . . but she had a chance to be happy once the court proceedings wrapped up.

She and Brooke would be happy as a family, but she could see a space reserved for one Cole Yearwood to stay.

Nina spun toward the bathroom and plucked her favorite robe off the peg mounted to the back of the door. The fuzzy, mint-colored fabric always brought a smile to her face, and her fingers tied the robe tight in muscle memory.

She ran warm water in the sink and unloaded the middle drawer's contents onto the counter. Five bottles of various skincare items, a mini tub of honey chapstick, her hairbrush, and her toothbrush with spearmint toothpaste.

Nina brushed through her hair, running into a few tangles. Her hair fell loose around her shoulders, with each knot undone after a few run-throughs with the brush. As she looked at her reflection, her eyes softened.

She hummed. "I need a trim."

She picked out a white knit scrunchie and pulled her hair back from her face. She lined up her skin care in order of use and slid her hands under the warm water. Nina dampened her face and applied a generous amount of cleanser onto her wet hands, slathering her face with the frothy white soap.

Nina leaned close to the bathroom mirror and scrubbed her fingertips across her face, not noticing movement in the cracked open doorway. However, the creak of the door drew her eyes up and she wasn't looking away, not when her eyes met the toned expanse of Cole's body.

Leaning in the bathroom doorway, Cole attentively studied her morning routine splayed out on the counter. Nina's attention landed squarely on Cole, standing there completely naked. She hadn't gotten enough of him the night before, oh god.

"Morning," Cole greeted when he noticed her stare, and Nina flustered at his boyish smirk and a subtle wink. "Did you sleep alright?"

"More than you know. I slept wonderfully." Nina cleaned the soap off her skin with a facial sponge, able to breathe a little better with cleaner skin. She turned off the hot water and turned around, greeted by Cole moving out of the doorway.

His hands boxed her hips in, and Nina lifted her chin, eager to feel his lips on hers. Cole dipped his face toward her, and their mouths brushed together, a softer embrace than either had experienced last night. The tenderness flipped something in Nina's brain, and she craved him more than the fevered rush to strip his clothes off.

"Yeah, I slept great, too."

"I thought I slept better alone than with a companion, but you proved me wrong."

Cole laughed. His hands rubbed soothing circles over the robe along her hips, but Nina swore she melted like putty in his hands. He winked again. "Happy to oblige."

"Are you going to keep flirting with me like this because I could get used to it." Nina fluttered her eyes and rubbed his chest. Cole's hands on her hips pulled her closer to him, which she never minded.

"If you'll let me, then yes," said Cole. Nina's grin matched his, and she could get used to them being not just friends. They were friends first, but love often blossomed from the most unexpected places.

"I'm inviting you to be as outrageously flirtatious as you want," Nina promised. "I don't know how we'll approach letting people know, but I'm in no rush."

"Good. Me neither. I'd like to keep you to myself for a little longer, or at least until everything with the court settles down. You have a lot on your plate."

"You read my mind. I want to enjoy my time with you without the world sticking its nose where it doesn't belong."

Cole quickly kissed her forehead and handed her facial sponge back to her. Nina saw him grab a small travel toothbrush, toothpaste, and mouthwash from the medicine cabinet. She might've purchased a spare of those items for whenever he accidentally spent the night.

Glad to see they came in handy.

Cole used the cold water in the sink before he flipped the switch to hot water for Nina to use. The two shared the sink with their bodies close enough for their fingers to constantly graze one another, exchanging soft smiles.

As Cole finished brushing his teeth, Nina walked through the motions of her skin care. Even in colder seasons, serums and creams on top of sunscreen kept her glowing. Caring for herself ensured she had enough energy to care for others—something she learned in therapy all those years ago.

Cole leaned into her with that boyish smirk, promising her a world of adventure. "Any chance you have an iron?"

"I'm afraid not." Nina squished his cheeks between her fingers and reveled in the soft crinkle of his nose, contradicted by the sparkle in his eyes. He liked it. "But maybe this is your suggestion to keep some spare clothes here for Tuesday dinners."

"Yeah, are you expecting to see me undressed on Tuesday evenings once Brooke goes to bed?"

"Maybe. That all depends on you."

Nina laughed when Cole whispered something incoherent against her jaw, but the blissful moment abated when she heard a little voice in the kitchen. *Brooke was awake.*

Cole seemed to hear it from how he let go of her waist and whistled. "I'll see you in there. I can handle the kid."

"Thank you." Nina meant for the love tap to his sculpted ass to be light when Cole turned to grab his clothes. But the smack had a little sound to it, enough force to make Cole jump. He glanced over his shoulder at her, eliciting a squeak from Nina. *Oops. He wanted payback.*

However, Cole stepped forward to drag Nina into a kiss, leaving Nina weak in the knees and swooning back into the counter. Memories of last night flashed into her mind about him and her on the bed, against the bathroom wall while the shower got hot, and under the steamy torrent.

Nina felt addicted to him.

Cole pulled back and vanished into the bedroom, followed by the rustle of clothes like his jeans and belt. Bewildered, Nina's fingers hovered over her lips like she wanted to confirm the kiss Cole planted on her.

In a daze, she grabbed her toothbrush and finished with her morning wash-up. She wandered into her bedroom and picked out some fresh clothes—a pair of jeans with a high-necked sweater and a plaid scarf—for the day.

Nina barely looped the scarf around her neck before a clatter from the kitchen shot her pulse into triple digits, skidding into the hallway in a pair of fuzzy socks. Worried something happened to Brooke or Cole, she scrambled into the kitchen and saw them . . . fine.

In fact, Cole had Brooke hoisted on his hip while the two searched the cabinets for something. Brooke's hand petted Cole's hair, which still boasted the post-sex look from their evening romp, and stared at him with critical eyes.

"Mr. Cole, did you wear the same clothes as yesterday?" asked Brooke.

Cole sighed, but nothing about the noise screamed exasperation. He always spoke gently to her, and Nina wished she had half his patience. "I did."

"Why?"

"Well, I didn't bring a spare change of clothes. I didn't intend to stay late. But your aunt suggested I keep spare clothes here for the next time. Sleeping in jeans isn't so fun."

"Auntie Nini is really smart," said Brooke.

"She is," Cole agreed. Somehow, Nina started to imagine the kind of PJs Cole Yearwood would wear to bed, and the idea of him being an *only the boxers* man stuck. She couldn't shake the feeling, which she identified as anticipation, causing her heart to do full somersaults. But she pretended her innocence when Cole turned toward her with Brooke. "Speaking of your aunt, good morning."

"Auntie Nini!" Brooke squealed, and Nina opened her arms to take her beloved niece off Cole's hands. Brooke jumped into Nina's embrace, peppering her face with morning kisses. As Nina gave her some back, her eyes met Cole's over Brooke's shoulder.

The secret gaze lit a fire in her stomach, but she focused on the wiggle worm in her arms. "What are you thinking for breakfast, bug?"

"Do we have waffles?"

"Actually, I just bought a new box of toaster waffles. They should be in the freezer. We'll add some yogurt and fruit on the side, okay?"

"Yes, please!"

Brooke wormed out of Nina's arms and pulled open the refrigerator. Cole, the closer of the two, grabbed the brightly colored waffle box from the freezer, and Nina grabbed the fresh container of sliced fruit and vanilla yogurt from the fridge.

She hummed. "Any chance you can stay for breakfast?" Nina expected a sheepish goodbye so Cole could retrieve some fresh clothes from his apartment, but he would text her later.

Yet, the twinkle in Cole's eyes gave her hope.

He checked his watch. "I have an hour before I need to go. I'd love some waffles, as long as Brooke doesn't mind sharing."

"I have a lot of waffles!" Brooke promised and grabbed his hand, dancing with excitement. Cole usually left before breakfast on Wednesday mornings on the rare occasions when he stayed. Staying for breakfast was a treat for Brooke . . . and a bigger one for Nina.

"Sounds good. Brooke, help Mr. Cole set the table for breakfast." Nina ruffled her niece's hair and watched Brooke drag Cole to set up plates and utensils for their cozy little breakfast. All the while, Cole and Nina snuck secret glances over the kitchen island.

Nina blew a kiss and watched Cole pretend to catch it, sliding it into his pocket. *For safekeeping*, he mouthed to her before Brooke giggled and jumped on his leg.

Nina softened, content to watch their interactions unfold like the epilogue of a movie. If she trusted anyone to keep her heart safe, it would be Cole.

Nina had trouble finishing anything once Cole left after breakfast. She thought she had lost her mind somewhere in her bed sheets last night with how much space he took up in her thoughts. But Nina wasn't rendered entirely helpless.

Years of discipline taught her how to carry on through the everyday chores, even when they were the last things on her mind.

With her focus, Nina managed to wrap up her first draft of her *Sunkissed* article for December, having secured steady work. The November article, meant to be about love and relationships, came together in the eleventh hour. Nina wrote about the forgiveness she needed to accept the dissolution of her engagement and how to heal from the heartbreak. According to Teagan, the article garnered a positive reception from readers, with people sharing their experiences in the forum and social media comment sections.

Something in the idea that her pain brought people some comfort and clarity through their own journeys touched a forgotten nerve. *She wanted what she wrote to mean something to someone.* However, for the moment, the sizable paycheck for November hit her bank account, and the leftover funds not meant for rent, groceries, or other necessities offered her and Brooke a golden opportunity.

"Auntie Nini! Look at that dress!" Brooke gasped loudly in her ear, gripping her oversized winter coat with one hand while the other held the peppermint bark sample she finessed from the sweet older lady at the local chocolate shop.

Nina followed Brooke's pointing with peppermint bark fingers through the large, shifting crowd at the shopping center a little way outside the city to see a sparkly tulle dress in the store window. The red fabric gleamed with layers of sparkles and a bow tied at the waist, meant for fancy Christmas pictures or church services.

Nina hummed. "That's a beautiful dress, Brooke. You're right."

"Who else do we need gifts for?"

"Let's see . . . we grabbed a yarn bundle for Mrs. Penelope since she loves to crochet. We picked out a nice charm bracelet for Miss Gloria. Mr. Rudy will be getting a nice bottle of wine, thanks to Mr. Cole's suggestion . . . I think we need a couple of presents for you."

Brooke giggled when Nina bumped their noses together, shifting the shopping bags loaded into the crook of her elbow. She would pick out a few things from her and the rest of Brooke's shopping list would be from Santa Claus. Nina insisted on keeping the Christmas magic alive for as long as possible.

She made Brooke draft a list hours ago. Two weeks from Christmas was already cutting it close for picking out gifts.

Brooke wiggled in her arms. "Can we go to ScentWorks? I like smelling their lotions!"

"Of course we can." Nina weaved through the crowd, careful not to jostle into people with Brooke perched in her arms. "I think they're having a sale, so you and I can grab an item or two, okay?"

"Yay!" Brooke, thrilled by the prospect of a nice-smelling lotion or soap, clapped her hands. The leftover smears of white chocolate and red dye streaked across her palms, and Nina's first stop would be finding a sink inside ScentWorks.

A short distance ahead, the orange logo of ScentWorks marked the shop, and ads for its annual holiday sale were plastered on every window, adding to the cheer of the Christmas season. Brooke continued to babble until she and Nina stepped inside the shop, falling quiet with a look of awe on her face.

Nina helped her onto the stool by the sink, "Let's clean off our hands before we touch anything." She washed her hands with Brooke's, noticing a few patrons glancing her way and smiling. *They would never know that Brooke wasn't her daughter.*

Although the thought of Naomi summoned the ache of loss still, her memory softened with flashes of the good times. She and Brooke would face their first Christmas without Naomi in two weeks, celebrating alone.

Before, she often went with Zach to see his family for every holiday gathering, and even though her space there had been conditional, Nina enjoyed knowing his mother and sister. She hoped they were well.

Blissfully unaware of Nina's pain, Brooke reached for the hand towel, which was too far out of her hands, and brought Nina back to reality. She handed Brooke the towel to dry off her hands and handled hers second, feeling the cold sting her wet fingers numb.

Nina focused on Brooke's broad smile and energetic wobbling through the store with her boots a half-size too big. Two employees in the ScentWorks long-sleeved uniform shirt couldn't help fawning over Brooke, who smiled at them.

She approached one of the shelves with a dozen different lotions in vibrantly colored bottles adorned by a cursive font on the labels. Brooke's approach was to study all of them before reaching for a deep green bottle labeled *Gingerbread Village* on the front.

Nina held the bottle to Brooke's nose and let her niece sniff the lotion while she scanned the shop. But her eyes caught on the *For Men* section on the opposite side of the room, drawn in by the dark brown patch compared to the pastel-colored walls everywhere else. It stood out compared to the rest of the room, and she scanned the shelves.

Cole crossed her mind again, striking that gorgeous grin whenever he had a joke on his tongue and in one of his court suits. Nina's face burned.

Part of her considered flagging one of the workers down and asking them for a recommendation for a gift. She couldn't recall if he had a signature cologne or a scent he preferred, so it may be best to table the thought.

When Brooke moved on to the next scent, one in a purple bottle aptly named *Sugar Plum Fairy*, Nina heard her phone ring from inside the pocket of her winter coat. She shifted the shopping bags around until her hand grabbed her phone tight and answered the call.

She hadn't checked the screen before answering, "Hello?"

"Hello, beautiful." Cole's voice caused her heart to skip a few beats and dial the warmth to a ten. The timing turned her downright bas hful."Mind if I steal a moment of your time?"

"Not at all. Did you call because you missed me?"

"Yes . . . but I was thinking about something and wanted to run an idea by you."

"Lay it on me. I'm all ears." Nina promised, even as she moved Brooke onto the next bottle of lotion. She eyed the *Miss Mistletoe* in a dark blue bottle for herself when she inhaled notes of a more earthy scent.

A squeak in the background caught Nina's ear, imagining his desk chair at his office cubicle with Cole in one of those gorgeous suits. He hummed. "So, I know you and Brooke don't have plans for Christmas this year."

"That's right." Nina agreed.

"Which is why I wanted to offer you an alternative plan. My family lives close to the city, maybe an hour's drive by car, and they have plenty of space for an extra guest or two. Would you and Brooke like to come home with me for Christmas?" Cole asked, stunning Nina into near speechlessness.

He wanted her and Brooke to come and meet his family?

"Are you serious? Cole Yearwood, are you asking me to meet your parents and the brother you talk about so often?"

"Yes, and my sister-in-law, January. This isn't me forcing your hand to out our relationship quite yet. As silly as this might sound, I don't think I could enjoy myself knowing that you're having your first Christmas without your sister, and Brooke's probably missing her mom, too. I hoped the trip might take your mind off it a little instead of being in the city. You're free to say no."

Nina's heart nearly tripled in size when Cole confessed, wanting to climb through the phone and wrap her arms around him. No one had ever been so thoughtful in her life.

She pressed the phone tighter, fighting the urge to smile until her face hurt or cried tears of relief. The loneliness of celebrating without Naomi might hurt less if she knew people wanted her and Brooke around.

Nina whispered, "I will agree . . . on the condition that you tell me what everyone there likes for Christmas gifts because I refuse to show up with nothing like a freeloader."

Cole laughed, but he couldn't hide the relief from her. "Deal. I'll drive us there the day of, and I promise you'll love it."

"I know I will. Brooke will, too." Nina cradled her phone and glanced down, seeing Brooke's curious gaze. She'd tell her later, after shopping.

Chapter Twenty-Three
Cole

B ehind the wheel, Cole admired the snow-covered landscape alongside the cleared roads and Nina's barely hidden nerves. The twenty-fourth of December had arrived with a full festive cry, evidenced by the white blanketing over trees and the homes they passed on their drive. Nostalgia reared its head at the sight of fresh snow in a perfect visage of holiday cheer.

In the backseat, Brooke's off-key babbling to the Christmas music playing on the radio filled most of the silence. Cole and Nina had their eyes focused on the road ahead, but Cole spotted a few smiles on Nina's face when Brooke hit a high note or clapped her hands along to the music.

Brooke would fit right in at his family's Christmas Eve dinner, and hopefully, Nina would see that she belonged there, too. She was his guest, and his family was thrilled to meet his "surprise" as he pitched it when asking for a guest room.

As Cole flipped his right turn signal while approaching a four-way stop, Nina's hands braced the pile of trays in her lap. Although Cole assured her his mom cooked a veritable feast in oven-roasted ham, mashed potatoes, gravy, and other Christmas dinner staples for the Yearwood residence, Nina insisted on contributing.

By her admission, she wanted to make a good impression. Cole didn't have the heart to tell her no.

Nina baked a giant tray of potato dinner rolls, stuffed pasta shells with a delightful ricotta and spinach mixture, and two full racks of chocolate and peppermint brownies. Her kitchen smelled heavenly when Cole came to pick her and Brooke up for their overnight stay.

"If you squeeze those trays any harder, you might tear the foil in half," he teased, hoping to lighten the mood. Nina had nothing to be scared of when it came to his folks. Even Dean and January weren't all that scary.

"I don't want anything to spill on the floor." Nina's face tightened when Cole completed the turn, a sharper angle than others on the way there, but relaxed once he proceeded.

"You'd tell me if there was another reason you're nervous, right?"

"Yes."

"Nina . . ."

"Okay, I've been overthinking my outfit choice for the last fifteen minutes," she admitted. Cole's brows shot up, and he checked out her outfit for the umpteenth time since he showed up at her doorstep. "Are you sure it's okay?"

"Nina, you look great. I promise you that Yearwood holiday gatherings aren't the Met Gala, and my family wouldn't mind a burlap sack dress as long as you're having a good time," Cole promised.

He watched Nina self-consciously pull the neckline of her long sleeve top higher as if a tiny flash of cleavage would offend his parents' delicate sensibilities. The rich wreath-green suited her, and for a moment, Cole wished Nina could see herself without the haze of worry blinding her.

"Okay." Nina swallowed and shifted the hot trays around on her lap, probably sweating through her black jeans from exposure to the hot meals.

Cole slowed down at the next stop sign intersection, empty except for his car, and leaned over the center console. He brushed his lips against Nina's ear and felt her still, arching closer to him. "First of all, you look gorgeous in your outfit. The green shines with your eyes. Second, and more importantly, my family is already so excited to meet you, and I don't think anything in this life or the next would ruin this. Be yourself because that's why I fell for you."

Nina's breath hitched in her throat, but she reached for his hand to hold. Cole gave it to her without hesitation. Whatever she wanted would be hers with a word.

"Thank you," Nina murmured, and her face lightened once the worry faded. There was the Nina he knew. The excitement finally winning out brought a shy smile and a delicate flush to her cheeks. "I needed to hear that."

"Any time. Tell me if you want anxiety to take a hike for a while. I'll give it a piece of my mind."

"I'll start taking you up on that offer."

Cole chuckled, but his hand remained laced with Nina's as he drove the rest of the way to his parents' home. The streets became more familiar the closer he got to his childhood home and the roads he used to run down with neighbor's kids during summer afternoons.

Brooke gasped from the backseat. "Are we here?"

"We made it. Good job, kiddo," Cole promised. Ahead, he spotted Dean's daily driver parked on the street, sidled next to the mailbox. The front yard and rooftop of the house boasted a visible layer of snow among the lights strung over the garage and porch and the decorations littered around the yard.

His parents hadn't skimped on the festive cheer. *Good. He wanted Nina and Brooke to experience the holiday cheer of his childhood.*

Cole pulled into the free space in the driveway beside his dad's car and maneuvered into park. He cut the engine, and Nina peered at Brooke in the backseat, guiding her to unbuckle and prepare to head inside.

Cole met her as she opened the door and helped Brooke out of the car, "There we go. Ready to go inside?"

"Yes." Brooke stretched her arms above her head, swamped by her oversized winter coat with the fluffy sherpa trim. Cole set her down, and she clung to his leg, even when he took the peppermint chocolate brownies off Nina's hands.

"Want me to take the others?" Cole asked, and Nina shook her head, smiling proudly. With that, he escorted Nina and Brooke up the porch steps and to the front door, knocking twice.

If he leaned in close, he might hear the echo of Christmas music playing in the living room or the sound of laughter floating through the house's hallways. But the approach of footsteps preceded the door swinging open, revealing his mom.

"Cole!" She crashed into his arms for a hug, and Cole, laughing, held her up without much of a struggle. "You made it!"

"I never miss Christmas with you. But I brought two lovely ladies to celebrate with us this year." Cole held his mom at arm's length but stepped back to bring Nina and Brooke forward.

"Yes! Please come in! I'll take those from you." His mom lifted the trays from Nina's arms and ushered the three inside. Cole let Nina and Brooke, who climbed into Nina's free arms, inside first and closed the door behind him.

He surveyed the living room with a quick glance at the tinsel draped over the mantle, adorned by patchwork stockings, and the gorgeous fir tree set against the wall by the fireplace. The warm brown walls gave the feeling of chestnuts roasting on an open fire, and flashes of red, green, and golden lights accented the room festively.

Through the connected doorway to the kitchen and dining room, Dean and his dad poured out two half-filled glasses of scotch. Behind them, January fixed the hem of her crimson cable knit sweater over her skirt while Socks pawed at her legs for attention, dressed in a holiday dog sweater.

"Cole!" Dean whooped and raised his glass to him as their mom returned from the kitchen, having taken Nina's contributions for dinner.

Cole tucked his hands into his pockets, "Everyone, I'd like to introduce you all to my guests for dinner. This is Nina and her niece, Brooke. They'll be staying with us tonight and tomorrow."

Cole noticed January and Dean exchange glances like an unspoken language made for them alone, recognizing Nina from the speed dating event. However, he hadn't expected his parents' eyes to flash with recognition.

Dean snitched on him. He had a feeling too strong to ignore there.

"It's lovely to meet you both." His mom stepped forward, wrapping her arms around Nina, who couldn't hide the startled noise she made. But she hugged back after a moment, eyes shut and clinging to Cole's mom. "I'm Sharon, but you can call me Shar or Mama S if you're comfortable."

His mom had a talent for taking even the most closed-off people and bringing them into her warmth. More shy than purposefully closed off, Nina melted into her embrace, and Cole's heart clenched. *She didn't have the same closeness with her parents as he did.*

"Thank you for letting Brooke and I come along. We didn't have other plans, and Cole promised a delicious Christmas dinner." Nina smiled, and the room lit up with small bursts of laughter.

His mom released her hold on Nina and squatted down to Brooke's level, offering her hands to the young girl for a high five. But Brooke eagerly jumped for a hug, and Cole watched his mom melt, face softened with joy.

But it was Dean who broke the silence and stepped forward, offering his hand to Nina.

"Cole can't say enough good things about you. I'm in awe of anyone who has him ready at their beck and call."

Nina laughed, but Cole scoffed. "Shut it, Dean. For old time's sake, I'm not above hauling you outside and whooping you in a snowball fight." He kept it PG for Brooke's ears, but this Christmas would hardly be the first time he and Dean had an expletive-filled, borderline violent snowball fight.

Dean merely laughed and hugged him briefly before he nudged Cole toward their dad, who clapped Cole on the back. The faint hint of cigar smoke and his dad's cologne reminded Cole of his childhood with a mighty swing.

"As my wife said, it's lovely to meet you. Please, call me Stephen," his dad remarked when he stepped past Cole and took Nina's hands in his. Cole observed how his dad gave Nina a charming smile with a twinkle in his eye, one he apparently inherited.

January bumped him with her hip and Cole pulled her into a hug, hearing her laugh when he lifted her off the ground a little. "I'm looking forward to getting to know Miss Nina Byndel over dinner tonight, especially since I can see the blush you're trying to hide."

"How on earth did you know her last name? Don't say Dean because I never told him Nina's last name for reasons," asked Cole.

"Ah, that was all me. A detective never reveals her secrets."

"I thought that was a magician."

"Regardless, that's for me to know and you to never find out. Don't worry . . . Dean asked the same and I won't tell him either." January patted his shoulders and elegantly stepped over to Nina, who had been watching their hushed exchange.

She smiled at January. "You must be January. Cole told me that you were his favorite."

January pretended to be surprised, even when Dean pulled a face and held his arms out while staring at Cole. *Guilty.* Cole may have declared January his favorite between her and Dean.

January didn't hesitate to wrap her arms around Nina, and the two women rocked in a warm embrace. "I'm so excited to have another two ladies around here. Shar and I are always outvoted on our picks for Christmas movies in the morning while we unwrap presents, and there are so many times I can watch *Die Hard* or *Elf* before I want to give up."

"January and I are big *Love Actually* fans," Sharon whispered, prompting a gasp from Nina.

"I love *Love Actually*!" Nina squealed, earning another embrace from Cole's mother and January, who joined her revelry.

Cole couldn't prepare for the whirlwind of activity when Nina accepted the peppermint chocolate brownies from his arms and his mom led her into the kitchen to add it to the feast. January squatted down to Brooke, who pointed quietly at Socks sitting at the front door, and she whispered something to Brooke.

Brooke grasped January's hand, and the two headed to sit by the front door, playing with Socks. The sudden departure of all the women wasn't lost on Cole, who eyed his dad and brother.

"Alright, you two." Cole spun to face them and crossed his arms, looking them over with a weary sigh. "I already know you're about to interrogate me. You can't use the playbook on the one who wrote the damn thing."

His dad shrugged. "Or maybe we'd like to learn more about our guests without making them uncomfortable."

"Yeah? I don't buy that for a second. Maybe from you, Dad, but Dean is too nosy for his own good." Cole snorted, ignoring Dean's huff.

"So, are you two dating? Because you haven't brought a girl to meet us since high school prom and some of your relationships lasted years. She's different, I know it," Dean argued.

"Even if I told you we weren't, you wouldn't buy it."

"Yeah, because clearly you two are dating, or you have a big bad crush on her."

"Or maybe it's early, and I'd like to preserve Nina's privacy, so I won't say shit without her permission. And you know better than to hound her for our relationship." Cole clicked his tongue, dancing around Dean's mildly annoyed but relenting twitch of his brows.

Stephen stepped forward, reaching for Cole's shoulders, and held him in place. "I respect that, but I know the look in your eyes. I could pick any photo from your mom and I's early college days, and I'd be wearing the same lovestruck glint. If I grabbed the wedding album and picked a random one of Dean, he'd wear the same look, too. Yearwood men always show it when we've found the one."

Okay, that was a lot to process.

Cole's jaw dropped open, and he stammered a half-hearted denial, but his eyes leaped over to Nina's return from the kitchen. She held a small glass of what appeared to be eggnog and laughed at something his mom said. *She's perfect . . .*

Brooke sprinted across the room, and Nina scooped her up, holding Brooke close while she enjoyed her first drink. It wouldn't be Christmas dinner without some eggnog or wine to sweeten things.

Cole hung back as January approached them, and the three women and Brooke giggled amongst themselves. Nina seamlessly fit into the group and even shined. What had she been so worried about? His family loved her.

He couldn't have predicted how she'd fold into the group, nor could he guess how his mom would excuse herself from the room, coming back with an extra pair of unlabeled, patchwork stockings in her hands.

"The mantle isn't complete!" she remarked, grabbing a piece of masking tape from the roll left by the tree, likely from last-minute present wrapping. His mom cut two pieces, stuck them onto the stocking, and wrote on them afterward.

She lifted them into the air with a grin, dangling the stockings on her fingers. Cole's mouth stretched into a smile when he noticed *Nina* and *Brooke* in his mom's handwriting.

"Now they are." Cole stepped forward and helped his mom hang the new stockings onto the mantle next to his on the far-right side. They had Dean, Socks, January, Sharon, Stephen, and Cole.

Nina and Brooke were perfect additions.

He glanced over his shoulder to catch her reaction and stopped. The watery glaze over her wide eyes and her lips fighting against a bittersweet smile struck him between the ribs, hitting the soft spot she had created.

She imprinted her shape on him, one too big to ignore or forget. Time would never force it to fade. Nina was there to stay, and he wanted them to last forever. Although, he might keep that little thought to himself for a while.

As he promised to Nina, Christmas dinner ended up a spectacular success. Everyone devoured the feast, including Nina's delightful contributions, with enough leftovers to last until New Year's.

Nina answered questions about herself, her career, and Brooke with such grace and ease, fielding them as if it were child's play. Her smile shone brighter than the star mounted atop the Christmas tree in the living room. Her smile stayed put after Cole hauled all the gifts he and she brought to set under the tree, hiding the *from Santa* presents behind the tree from Brooke.

So, when the evening wound down, peace blanketed the living room, much like the layer of fresh snow outside. Cole and Nina lounged on the loveseat closest to the fireplace, sharing half of a peppermint chocolate brownie between them.

On the nearby couch, Brooke slept peacefully. She and Socks, who took a liking to her when she snuck him a small piece of ham underneath the dinner table, cuddled underneath a blanket, sound asleep to the crackling from the fireplace and the jazz covers of Christmas classics.

Dean and Jan volunteered to clean all the dishes, and Cole swore he heard the occasional laugh from the kitchen, drowned out by the distance. On the other hand, his parents ran out to the store before closing for an errand his mom needed done before the following day.

Hence, he and Nina got some much-needed space to relax and talk. No more dancing around their words and playing dumb about their schedules for New Year's like the two hadn't discussed plans across the bed from one another last night.

"So, what did you think?" asked Cole, cleaning the last crumbs of the brownie off his fork. Nina's baking melted on his tongue; he wanted a whole tray, willing to beg for more.

"About?"

"My family? Dinner? Whatever's on your mind."

Nina set the plate on the coffee table. "Your family is amazing. I don't have words to explain how welcome I feel here instead of an unwanted tagalong. Besides his mom and sister, Zach's family never put in the effort to include me as one of them."

"Well, that won't happen here. If I don't bring you to the next family dinner, my mom and Jan might jump me. Dean and my dad, too, but they're more subtle about it," Cole promised, and he snatched up her hand. His lips skimmed over her knuckles, kissing each one with a tenderness reserved for her alone. No one came close to Nina, even in the short time he had her.

Nina scooted closer and wrapped her arms over his shoulder, content to stare longingly into his eyes. Her focus on him stoked the warm, fluttery sensation that seemed to roar to life whenever she was near, not unlike adding kindling to a fire.

"Good to know," said Nina. "I hope that they like me, though."

"Please, they love you . . ." Cole could espouse a million different signs to prove his point, but when the music shifted to the next song, his attention wandered to the twinkling tree and all its bright ornaments. Most of them, outside of the standard bulbs of varied shapes, came into the Yearwood family's possession during his childhood.

He closed his eyes, pulled back to years ago. Instead of hunting for Santa Claus, Cole sneaked out of bed and spied on his parents. When he and Dean were supposed to be asleep, his mom and dad would sneak to the living room and share a dance by the firelight.

He hadn't heard Nina's attempts to grab his attention until she grasped his hand and scooted close enough that their legs tangled together over the edge of the couch.

She whispered, "Cole? Where'd you go?"

"Dance with me," he replied. "Please?"

"Oh . . . okay."

Cole got off the couch and pulled Nina onto her feet, hands linked together. He stepped to the spot he recalled from childhood memories and brought Nina into a classic waltz position, one arm raised and the other wrapped around her waist. Her hand splayed across his back, and she waited for his lead.

Cole started with a shaky step, but Nina moved in sync with him, eyes brightened in the firelight. Each step pushed his confidence, and the two moved in a small circle, swaying to the saxophone and the fireplace in perfect harmony.

Nina nestled her face against Cole's chest and Cole's hand on her waist brought her closer to him, not wanting to be deprived of her body connected to his. How had he stayed away from her for so long? She felt like the answer to every question and the muse behind a million more.

Cole tipped his lips to bury into her hair, curled by hand that morning, and kissed her gently. Nina's head occasionally lifted, allowing Cole to mark her lips with a deeper kiss.

They kept a close eye on the kitchen door, a sleeping Brooke, or the front entrance to ensure their little secrets stayed theirs to hold. Sweetened by the taste of the season, their shuffling sway slowed to a stationary hold.

Cole held Nina close, and she burrowed into his chest. With the last few months of chaos and emotional turbulence stacked between reprieves, a moment like that one became sorely needed. For a blissful second, the world faded away for a sweet fantasy.

However, nothing stopped it from becoming something real besides them. Cole knew that much, and he promised one thing. *Nina's happiness came first, even if it ended with someone else's arms around her.*

A creak from the front door broke apart a final kiss between the two, and Cole noticed his dad carrying the shopping bags while shielding his mom from the cold with his frame. The sight inspired a bright pillar of hope.

"I grabbed some supplies! Cole, would you be a dear and grab me Nina and Brooke's stockings?" his mom asked.

"Of course, Mom." Although reluctant to let Nina go, Cole plucked the stockings off the mantle and presented them to his mom. She accepted them with a troublesome grin, and he didn't dare question her.

Instead, he spotted Nina swept away by January in conversation and the two getting along like they'd known one another their whole lives. He made the right choice to bring her home.

Chapter Twenty-Four
Nina

Curling underneath the extra blankets, Nina unsuccessfully chased sleep until her eyes fluttered open with reluctance. Beside her, Brooke mumbled in her sleep and drooled on the pillow.

Nina climbed out of bed as quietly as she could, not wanting to wake her niece, and walked across the hardwood floors of the guest bedroom. The heather gray walls, warm wooden décor in the armoire, and framed mirror hanging up should've reminded her of her childhood home, radiating suburbia perfection.

Instead, the home had a cozy quality that welcomed her in, not shunning for being an outsider. The family who lived in it had everything to do with making the house feel comfortable.

She plodded toward the door, okay with leaving her room in the fuzzy snowflake pajama pants and a matching midnight blue tank top. A shiver brushed down her arms when she stepped into the hallway and shut the door behind her, intending to be silent.

Nina's eyes checked the hallway; she spotted all the doors to the bedrooms and extra bathroom closed. *Everyone else must still be asleep.*

She inched past Cole's bedroom, noted by the little plaque on the door with his name written in a child's messy handwriting. With his door closed and seemingly undisturbed, Nina assumed he also slept in for Christmas morning.

A smile crossed her lips when she pressed her hand to the door, remembering how she snuck into his room the night before. She had tucked Brooke in for the night, and Cole suggested she come to his room to spend time with him. "Spend time" ended up being code for making out on his bed like horny teenagers and stifling each other's giggles so they wouldn't be caught.

She had never experienced such exhilaration before, but she considered that all a part of the "Cole effect." He changed her life in so many small ways, but the impact snowballed into something unstoppable.

Nina headed down the hallway and stairs, bracing herself for a creak underneath her feet to give her away. She took each step one at a time until she waltzed into the kitchen, expecting it to be empty. However, she ran into Cole's parents lounging in their little breakfast nook with the faint grind of the coffee machine working in the kitchen.

"Oh, good morning!" Nina greeted them when they spotted her lingering in the doorway from the hall. She inhaled the heady mixture of coffee grinds and the basket of pine leaves sheared off the bottom of the Christmas tree.

"Morning," Stephen tipped his head while Sharon nestled into his arms, reading something on her tablet. "How'd you sleep?"

"Excellent, thank you, sir."

"You don't have to call me *sir*. Stephen is more than fine, especially since any guest of Cole's is a friend of ours."

Nina nodded, but she leaned into the arch of the doorway. Her hovering pulled Sharon's eyes away from her tablet, and she pushed out one of the chairs, glancing between Nina and the empty seat. "Please, come sit."

"Alright." Nina slid across from Stephen and Sharon into the chair, twiddling her thumbs together. Stephen and Sharon straightened up and linked hands when she accepted the chair.

"Would you like coffee, dear?" asked Sharon.

"I like coffee. Thank you."

"We can grab you one when the pot finishes brewing. But my husband and I would like something sorted out before everyone else comes down."

Nina sensed a question ahead and knew what Cole's parents wanted to ask her. *Was she a friend to their son, or had she and Cole understated their relationship to his family?* Either way, she sat across from them for Christmas morning breakfast and presents.

"What would you like to know?"

Stephen cleared his throat. "We were curious about your intentions with our son. Cole may not seem like it, but he walks into relationships intending for the long haul. Is that something you two have in common?"

Nina laced her hands together. "When I choose to date someone, I date to marry. He and I are the same in that regard. But we haven't discussed anything as significant as marriage."

Sharon perked up. "So, does that mean you and Cole are together romantically? He didn't want to tell us without your permission."

"I appreciate his discretion. But yes. Cole and I wanted to keep our new relationship to ourselves with everything happening in my life. Our intention is to keep it between the adults for a while."

"How long has it been?"

"A matter of weeks, but Cole and I have been friends for months. I suspect our friendship blurred a while back, and neither of us decided to confront it until recently."

Nina's honesty stunned even herself. The words tumbled out without much coaching or prettying up, but the room hadn't given her reason to worry. Stephen and Sharon listened to her, interrupting only to ask another question. The silence felt thoughtful.

"Does our boy make you happy?" Stephen questioned.

Nina softened. "Yes, he does. More than anything, I've never felt safer in a relationship than I have with him. He cares for Brooke like she's his and supports my needs. He makes me laugh and is there when I need a good cry. We work well together."

Her voice wavered at the end, finally struck by the nerves she expected to hit her at the first question. But she held firm under Sharon and Stephen's unwavering gaze.

Sharon got up to grab some mugs when the coffee machine shot off a few chimes, signaling a finished pot. Nina heard the pouring of hot coffee into cups, and she breathed in the rich, specialty coffee blend wantonly.

She accepted the mug from Sharon when she returned with the coffee, holding the hot cup with cold hands to bring some life back into her fingers. "Thank you, Shar."

"Of course. You've been forthcoming, a quality we revere in the Yearwood house. But this isn't an interrogation. We wanted to know that you and Cole are on the same page because we like you more than most of his other girlfriends," Sharon admitted, and Nina thanked her lucky stars she hadn't taken a sip of coffee.

A warm flush heated her face and neck, unable to muster a response to such a high compliment. Stephen and Sharon exuded accomplishment, meaning they probably had no shortage of expectations for who their sons settled down with. She remembered her parents' insistence on the family image being heightened by marriage, not diminished.

However, a whistle interrupted the three, and Nina glanced toward the doorway leading into the hallway. Dean and January stepped through the door wearing matching black cotton pajamas, looking ready for a helping of coffee.

Yet, Nina picked out the knowing twinkle in their eyes. They overheard the comment by Sharon, and Nina thought about shriveling up. *How embarrassing.*

"My parents are right, though. I've heard plenty about some of his past girlfriends. Beyond maybe one of them, none of them have him quite as hooked as you." Dean hummed while he ambled through the cabinets for more mugs.

January slid into the seat close to Nina, rubbing her shoulders, "He speaks so highly of you. Even before you two started dating, he had nothing but the best to say."

"I hope I'm always as good as he makes me out to be. I'm sure that's a high bar to clear," said Nina.

"But you meet those expectations—exceed them even—without trying." January's face brightened with a smile when her husband handed her some coffee. "Cream or sugar?"

"Two sugar and one cream." When Dean passed them over, Nina reached for the sugar bowl and creamer pitcher. She filled her coffee with a taste of sweetness and downed half the cup before stopping for a breath.

"I hope we haven't scared you off with all our questioning. Our family can be a little much to someone unfamiliar with how close-knit we all are. Once you're in, you're ours for life." Dean chuckled, but no one else at the table corrected him.

Maybe if Nina were different, she'd find that strange or alienating. But without a tight-knit family, she craved closeness, and the Yearwoods represented everything she desired in no uncertain terms.

She shook her head. "You haven't. It heals something in me to see families who genuinely love one another instead of hiding resentments and jealousy behind a picture-perfect image. I've seen enough of that to last me a lifetime."

"Then, you're always welcome here." Sharon reached toward her and laced her hand with Nina's, sporting that motherly smile. Everything about the atmosphere planted an ache in Nina, but she ignored its pained cry. *Why should she resent when they offered her a place among them? She wanted to belong.*

Nina fumbled with a polite response to convey the magnitude of her gratitude, but the table's occupants turning toward the doorway provided a nice distraction. When she followed their lead, she spotted Cole entering the kitchen.

He appeared to have barely woken up, still dressed in his PJs of sweats and a tight long-sleeve top. When he yawned, the hem of his shirt rode up on his stomach, revealing toned muscles and the dark sporadic hairs of his happy trail dipping underneath the waistband of his sweats. Every additional expanse of skin revealed threatened to betray Nina's composure, struggling to not succumb to a bright blush.

His shirt rolled back down when he stopped his stretch, but Cole's eyes caught Nina's. He smirked. "Good morning, family. Morning Nina. Talking about me, are we?"

"Morning." Nina glanced around the table for where he would sit, but January scooted out of her seat next to Nina for one closer to Dean, leaving it open for Cole.

Cole glanced around the group and sighed. "Let me guess, you already gleaned the answers from my poor girlfriend while I slept? You all are evil."

"If it's any solace, she offered the information voluntarily . . . or at least for the price of one cup of coffee." Stephen chuckled as he accepted the tablet from his wife's hand.

"I'm only worth one cup of coffee? I should be more hurt, but coffee is delightful." Cole slid into the spot January vacated, leaning all over Nina. He pressed a warm, chaste kiss to her temple since they had guests, but Nina knew exactly how Cole's mouth could demand her attention.

He nuzzled closer to her, and Nina's hand rubbed at his thigh, happy to have him there. "At least your family was nice enough about it. I thought I would be more nervous for the shakedown."

"Ah, these guys? Besides January, they're harmless. She's the scariest one, but you two get along well."

"What a relief. Anyway, who wants breakfast? I can make some pancakes and eggs if that pleases everyone."

"That would be great, thanks!" January lifted her coffee in a silent toast, and the rest of the table agreed. Pancakes and eggs sounded more than okay for Christmas morning breakfast.

Cole helped Nina out of her chair and followed her to the kitchen. "Okay, you're officially going to be a favorite guest. You're the first to offer to cook breakfast."

"What can I say? I'm one of a kind." Nina winked, prompting laughter from Cole. His arms circled around her waist, and he nuzzled up behind her, chin resting on her shoulder. "Can you help?"

"I'd be delighted to help. Whatever you need, I'm at your service."

"Grab me a measuring cup, some oil, a mixing bowl, a fork, at least five eggs, and some flour or pancake pre-mix if there's any."

"Yes, ma'am." Cole let go of her briefly, on the hunt for her ingredients. She watched him scamper around the kitchen and pile the items into his arms until they looked cumbersome. But he delivered them all to her, kissing her when no one else looked.

Nina smiled and focused on the sizzle of the empty pan she had pre-heated on the stove. When she went to mix her batter, a soft "hello?" sounded off from by the stairs. Brooke.

She prepared to step away, but Cole patted her hips. "I've got her. Be back in a moment."

"Thank you."

"No worries."

Cole darted into the hallway, and Nina didn't have to wait long before he returned, carrying Brooke in his arms, half-slung over his shoulder to her giggles. She playfully hammered her hands into his back and kicked her legs, sidelined by peels of laughter.

"Good morning!" Brooke squealed to the adults at the table but raced over to Nina when Cole set her on her feet. She hugged her legs and whispered, "Hi, Auntie Nini. Merry Christmas."

"Merry Christmas, bug. Let's make some pancakes and eggs, but we'll focus on pancakes for you." Nina kissed her nose and set her on the countertop, far enough from the stove to be safe. She put the mixing bowl next to Brooke, supervising her mixing efforts.

Cole settled into the countertop a few inches down from Brooke, and Nina asked him, "Did you get any coffee yet?"

"Not yet, but I would love some." Cole grabbed a mug and passed it over to Nina, who served him a hot cup of coffee. She had a generous hand when it came to drinks.

"You'll need a cup before we start opening presents. You don't want to be half-asleep when this one starts screeching about the awesome toys from Santa Claus." Nina ruffled Brooke's hair to her whine. She laughed and focused on the full skillet filled with whipped egg yolks, turning the bright yellow into a fluffy scramble.

She hadn't been so excited for a holiday in years, even when it was her, Naomi, and Brooke. Deep down, a small part of her hoped the healing would soon come. She felt ready to step into the new chapter of her life.

For years, Nina secretly wished to hurdle past the Christmas season and put it behind her. However, that year, she hoped Christmas morning would go on forever. The impending deadline of her last custody hearing waited for her on the other side of the holiday, and nothing frightened her more than the prospect of losing Brooke.

The time between Christmas and New Year's snuck up on Nina fast, with the days speeding by compared to how slowly they crawled past before Christmas. She tried to rein in her anxiety about the situation but couldn't catch all her worries before they slipped through her fingers.

In the courtroom, wearing the gorgeous gray two-piece January picked out when Nina frantically texted her at five-oh-six that morning, Nina played with a loose thread hanging off her skirt. She wrapped it around her finger a few times, looping it equally across, until she pulled too hard and severed it.

"Nina, you okay?" Cole whispered from beside her, keeping his voice low since the other table appeared at total capacity. Her parents, Maxwell, and Felicity, showed up to celebrate their "victory lap" with their attorneys.

"I'm trying not to throw up. I wish we could skip through all the pretense and get to the verdict already."

"Hey, focus on your breathing. Drink some water. We're going to get there soon enough."

"Tell me everything is going to be okay."

"Everything is going to be okay." Cole grasped her hand underneath the table and stroked over her knuckles with his thumb. He knew what gestures to soothe her while she teetered on the edge of losing her cool. "I know Judge Byrd is a brilliant jurist who will do the right thing for Brooke."

Nina wanted to agree, but she struggled around the lump in her throat. Her eyes focused on the door leading to the next room. Brooke was supposed to be in there with her minor's counsel until the verdict determined the custody arrangement.

Her thoughts circled Brooke. She hoped her niece wasn't overwhelmed with all the strange faces and the possibility of their routine changing. Brooke needed a stable environment that wouldn't strip her of every last trace of Naomi for an artificial personality. That was the Byndel way.

All the noise in her head silenced hard when the door pushed open, and the room came to attention. Judge Byrd fixed her robe's collar and tucked it underneath her hair, surveying the room at all the people on their feet.

"Be seated," she declared before she settled behind the bench, reaching for her gavel. "I have a full docket today and want to render this verdict quickly after our last session. Unless there are any other issues before the bench, then I would like to address this court."

"Nothing from the plaintiffs, Your Honor," Mr. Francisco remarked, rising from his chair and paying his due diligence to the judge.

Rudy mirrored Mr. Francisco's body language when he rose out of his chair, too, "Nothing from the respondent either, Your Honor. We are prepared to proceed with the verdict."

"Thank you, counselors," Judge Byrd remarked, although she sounded on the verge of an exhausted sigh. Nina couldn't fathom how she handled cases day in and out without fail. One alone had Nina ready to keel over. "As I'm sure you know, this court operates in the child's best interest first and foremost. Both sides presented their versions of events and evidence of their capability to care for the minor, Brooke Byndel, from herein out. However, I have a decision to make, one I don't take lightly."

Nina tried not to be rattled by the judge's speech to the court, but her eyes wandered past Cole to the packed table of her estranged family. The confident, downright smug expressions swapped between her parents, Maxwell, and Felicity worsened the sickness lodged in her stomach.

"Therefore, I rule that, in the case of Byndel v. Byndel, I grant sole legal and physical custody of the minor to Nina Byndel. Additionally, no supervised visits shall be allowed by the biological grandparents, uncle, or Felicity. The testimony from the attorney who assembled Naomi Byndel's last will and testament on the credibility of her statements and the letter written before she passed proved compelling. A mother wants what's best for her child, and Naomi Byndel made herself expressly clear about who should raise her daughter. With no other issues before the court, this case is adjourned, and I remand the minor into the custody of Miss Byndel."

If Nina had been standing, her legs would've given out. Shock washed away under a flood of relief, covering every inch of her body in a buzzing sensation too vibrant to ignore. Nina covered her mouth as Cole helped her onto her feet, shaking Rudy's hand.

But Nina? Her vision tunneled when the door opened, and Holly led Brooke out from the side room. Brooke didn't hesitate to sprint down the ramp, rushing past the table with Nina's now angry family, and jump into Nina's arms.

"Auntie Nini, why are you crying?" Brooke cupped her face in her hands, and Nina hadn't realized she had begun crying. Her cheeks slicked damp underneath the stream of hot, unexpected tears. All the months of worry and stress were behind them.

"They're happy tears, bug," Nina promised, and she cradled Brooke closer. "We get to go home now. Mr. Cole will be coming for Tuesday dinner again."

"We also have movies for after dinner, so please clean up when you get home," Cole interjected, earning a nod from Brooke. He and Nina could debrief later about it all, but she needed to thank Rudy before she burst into more tears.

Brooke would be with her, where she belonged.

Chapter Twenty-Five
Cole

January sped by in a blur for Cole, where he and Nina's schedules acted like passing ships in the night. A sudden influx of clients at his work limited their windows to meet up, and Nina kept busy with Brooke. She started preparing Brooke to enter kindergarten when the school year came around.

But when the opportunity arose for Cole to switch one of his off-days to an evening Nina would be free, a Tuesday no less, he seized the chance to be romantic.

He walked down the winding path through the condo complex, carrying a bundle of flowers in his arms. He checked his reflection in the darkened windows of the condos he passed, pleased by the fit of the suit he picked out from his closet.

Cole stepped up onto the porch of Nina's condo, knocking on the door twice. He basked in the light over the porch switching on, and adjusted the flowers cradled in his arms. The locks and deadbolt on the opposite side of the door clicked loudly before the door creaked open.

"Hey," Nina gasped as her eyes roved over him, peeking her head out the door. She opened the door wider, and Cole glimpsed mint-colored silk caressing her body. Her dress brushed against her ankles, not counting the thigh-high slit. "You look so handsome."

"Me? Nina, I think you'll send me into cardiac arrest with this dress." Cole almost fumbled the flowers in his arms when he reached toward Nina. She met him halfway, leaning into his hands.

"You like it?" Nina grinned, fluttering her lashes at him. She turned from side to side, showing off the corseted back of the dress and the thin straps pulled over her shoulders. She smoothed the fabric bunched around her hips flat. "Naomi encouraged me to buy it a while back, but I never needed to wear it."

"Like isn't a strong enough term for how much I enjoy that dress. I did text you to pick out something nice to wear without other instructions. Oh, and these are for you."

"Thank you. You remembered that I love lilies."

"How could I forget? You always stop to smell them when we go to the store. But I have a small rose here for the other leading lady of the house. Is Brooke nearby?" Cole held up a pink rose, stem trimmed to remove all the thorns.

Nina hadn't turned to call Brooke before a little blonde blur appeared in the doorway, climbing onto Cole's leg. "Cole!"

"Hey there," Cole picked her up and offered the rose he had brought. "A rose for a little princess."

"Thank you! It's so pretty." Brooke accepted the flower, fiddling with the outer petals. Cole set her down, and she bounded back into the condo, singing the whole way down the hall. He and Nina watched her go, disappearing around the corner.

Cole leaned in the doorway and coaxed her closer with his hands sliding down her hips, "I can't spoil what comes next, but go get a nice pair of shoes and a purse. Then, we'll head out."

"We're heading out? I thought we were having dinner here tonight. I didn't hire a babysitter for Brooke," Nina stammered, but Cole fought the urge to smile. He took Nina's hands and eased her onto the porch, pointing toward the parked cars down the road.

A third car rolled up, a convertible with the top down, and Dean and January climbed out. The two were in the middle of a conversation, with Dean laughing loud enough to echo across the communal condo space. They waved once they got close enough to Nina's condo, noticing her and Cole on the porch.

"What are you two doing here?" Nina shouted as Dean and January approached, arms linked together. They wore comfortable clothes, and Dean carried a bag of takeout branded with the wrinkled logo of the Golden Elephant Chinese Buffet.

"We're here to babysit while you two enjoy a date night," January remarked.

"Wait? Seriously?"

"I owed Cole a couple favors, and he cashed one in for tonight. He's got some special plans, so you two should head out. We'll see you later." Dean helped January up the steps, where all four crowded on the porch.

Nina stared at Cole for a moment but headed inside and rustled through the small box of shoes next to the door. After a moment, she stumbled through the doorway with a pair of white heels on her feet and a miniature white purse in her hand.

"Bye Brooke!" Nina shouted down the hallway before she faced the others, "I grabbed my wallet and keys in case of emergencies. But Brooke usually is in bed around eight-thirty at the latest. She needs someone to supervise her brushing her teeth and a bedtime story, so she's a relatively easy kid. I'm lucky," Nina babbled, even when Cole looped his arm around her waist and escorted her down the stairs of the condo's porch.

Dean whistled and tossed his keys to Cole, which he caught. Cole handed over his in a trade. Cole held the sports car's keys up, "Thanks again, you two. I'll text you when we're heading back."

"Don't worry about rushing home. We've got everything handled here," January assured them and nudged her husband toward the condo.

Nina waved to Dean and January as they closed the door. She laughed giddily, "Oh, it's been a while since I've had a fancy date. Are you going to tell me where we're going?"

"It's a surprise," Cole said, but his girlfriend's immediate backlash of pleading encouraged him to further dig his heels in. A little surprise wouldn't kill her. "But prepare to be spoiled."

He swept Nina away to Dean's convertible and helped her into the passenger seat, focused on the princess treatment. Cole closed the door when she buckled in, jogging around the car to the driver's side. He switched the engine on and listened to the deep mechanical purr.

He flipped up the convertible top and drove away from the curb, speeding from the condos toward the open road. He memorized the directions to their destination several days ago so he wouldn't disclose his plans before he was ready.

Nina, lounging in the seat next to him, stretched out. She turned the radio a little louder and reached her hand across the center console. Cole snatched up her hand and kissed her knuckles, holding onto her as he drove. He only needed one hand on the wheel anyway.

With a few practiced turns, Cole drove them beyond the city's outskirts. The buildings started to fade away further from the heart, and eventually, they moved alongside the seaside road to salty air and crashing waves.

He slowed down when they approached the entrance to the city's marina, passing the toll booth with a lone security guard. He flashed the man a ticket, earned them entry into the marina's parking lot, and settled outside the docks.

"Okay, I'm stumped. What are we doing at the marina?" asked Nina when Cole started to leave his spot.

"You'll see," he chuckled and ran around the other side of the car, helping her onto her feet. He tucked her into his chest and locked the vehicle before escorting her to the rows of parked boats. His eyes moved ahead on the deck, searching for a sleek white boat tethered to the edge of the dock.

They checked down three rows before Cole spotted a sign propped up with an arrow pointing down the dock and strings of lights hanging between the different posts, blocking access to the other boats in that section. At the end of the pier, a sleek passenger boat on the smaller side bobbed on the calm waves with a crew standing at the plank.

Nina's face glowed in awe, and she glanced between him and the boat. "Is that for us?"

"Maybe. Let's head up to the passenger deck. Dinner is waiting for us." Cole let Nina climb the ramp first and stayed behind her, hands hovering over her hips. He nodded to the crew waiting for them to board, having shelled out a hefty fee for their services and discretion.

A short walk from the ramp led Cole and Nina to the small room inside the boat, a level below the wheel and the navigation software. The kitchen where their dinner was made sat below the passenger area. The crew had dressed up the room with ambient lighting, a candle centerpiece, and a gorgeous red tablecloth draped over the circular dinner table in the center.

Cole and Nina headed for the table, and Cole made sure Nina sat before him. He was a gentleman. He tucked her chair in and barely slid into his seat before two crew members, denoted by their all-white uniforms, entered with two large bowls and a bottle of unopened wine.

"Good evening," one of the crew—a smiling redheaded woman with a galaxy of freckles dotting her cheeks and blue and brown heterochromia—uncorked the wine and poured it into the two glasses on the table. "My name is Tara, and I will oversee your experience tonight. Cole has purchased a three-course meal package with us, including complimentary wine and bread baskets for a three-hour culinary experience. Is there anything you need before the first course?"

"Nina?" Cole reached for his wine, studying how Nina accepted all the attention. Under the candlelight, she glowed, and her smile rivaled glittering diamonds.

"I'm great. Thank you." Nina pulled her napkin onto her lap, and her eyes followed the bowls. A third crew member entered with a tray of oysters, placing them on the table.

"Very well. Our first course is locally sourced oysters caught fresh from the harbor. If you need anything else, please don't be afraid to ask. Enjoy." Tara ushered the two other crew members away, and Nina's lips parted.

"Oysters? Fine wine? I think I'm going to faint."

"No fainting. Tonight is all about us."

"I'll toast to that." Nina lifted her wine glass, and Cole did the same. "To us, because we've weathered through a storm and deserve to enjoy our calm waters."

"Cheers." Cole clinked the rim of his glass to Nina's, and the two took their first sips of wine, ready for oysters, more wine, and whatever else the night had promised.

Close to the one-hour mark, Cole wiped his mouth free of crumbs from the spiced pineapple cake he and Nina devoured. Nina cleaned the last bite of the spongey cake off her spoon, licking her lips clean. Neither spoke for a while since Tara set the cake on the table, too busy enjoying their dessert.

"Wow," Nina slumped in her chair, and Cole would be lying if he said he didn't want to flop back or loosen the buttons on his pants. "I'm about to split open this corset if I eat another bite."

"So, that's a no on another slice of cake?" he asked.

"No way. Cole, you've already spoiled me enough for the evening."

"Ah, that's not true."

Nina reached for her purse, revealing a tin box rattling when she shook it. "Would you like a mint?"

"Please." Cole accepted a mint from his girlfriend and slid it onto his tongue, awakened with the taste of spearmint. He let the mint rest on the tip of his tongue while he climbed out of his chair, converging on Nina.

Cole tipped Nina's chin up, pulling her onto her feet. Nina slid her hands up his chest, giggling against his lips when Cole leaned in close. The vibrations of her laughter drew him into her like a helpless voyager into her gravitational pull.

It was too easy for his mouth to slide with hers, and he, being a cheeky bastard, passed the mint with his tongue to her. Nina's eyes blew wide, and she pulled back to breathe, unable to hide the startled blush on her cheeks.

She covered her mouth. "Hold on, why was that so attractive?" Nina almost sounded offended at how his mint pass hit the teasing mark, but he knew better.

Cole shrugged; he went with what felt right when Nina was involved. Life became smoother sailing when he let spontaneity drive his romance. Being clinical never helped his love life before, so he decided to try something new.

Nina crunched on the mint with a small smile, face nuzzled into Cole's chest. He walked them away from the dinner table and planted them in front of the broad, ceiling-to-floor windows surrounding the inside deck.

The full moon's pale light shone over the darkened waters and cast a sparkling spell over the marina. Not a soul in sight wandered through the docks, and Cole glanced toward the boat's control room, not hearing a peep from in there.

They must've left as instructed. Cole leaned over to ensure he and Nina were the last people on the boat. He stepped behind Nina and started off slow. His hands moved with his palms pressed flush against her hipbones, rubbing the heels of his palms in small circles. *Alone at last.*

His mouth dipped toward her neck, hovering over her steady pulse with the urge to skim his teeth along her skin. Murmuring, he confessed, "So, I might have one last surprise."

"What's that?"

"I paid the crew extra to head to a restaurant a block down from the marina for the next two hours so we can have some alone time."

"You didn't," Nina gasped, peering up at him through her long lashes. When Cole nuzzled deeper into her neck, her face turned back to the marina, but her hand hovering above the window shifted to a splayed finger grip. "You're trouble, Cole Yearwood."

"But the good kind, I promise."

"Oh, definitely the good kind. Are you going to keep me here, tease me until I can't beg anymore?"

"And deprive us of a fun time? Never." Cole's wandering hands spun Nina around to face him, but he pressed her against the window's cold surface. He bent his knee and slotted it between her thighs, given enough room by the thigh-high slit of her dress. It was a perfect choice on her unwitting part.

Nina, as expected, clamped her thighs around his leg. Her hips rocked in a shallow rut, focused on the friction of her rubbing against his body. She didn't fuss when Cole captured her wrists with one of his hands, pinning them above her head.

Nina's eyes went from a sharp green, sparkling with clarity, to hazed over in a lustful stare. Her lips parted for a breath, but a moan pierced the room's silence. Beyond the rock of the boat on the waves, nothing moved or made a sound.

She pretended to strain against Cole's hold, pinning her to the window, but she stared at him through those lashes, and he soaked her pleasure in. With his other hand, Cole bunched up her skirt and pulled it higher, exposing her skin inch by inch. He heard a noticeable hiccup in Nina's breathing the higher his hands pulled the fabric.

"Have I rendered you speechless? Maybe I should pull back a little?" Cole mused and marveled at how his voice was loaded with teasing.

"Don't you dare stop," Nina demanded breathlessly while her hips pushed harder against his knee, hitting the right spot from how another moan exploded from her mouth. She clenched her jaw, and her hips moved faster. "I'm . . . I'm . . ."

"Close already?" Cole guessed, and he leaned in close, kissing her hard. He felt her nod, but she gave up halfway when their lips slotted together. The dampness of her arousal stained through the fabric of his trousers from all the friction, likely soaking through the flimsy excuse for underwear she picked for the evening.

Naughty.

Cole's mouth pried into hers, searching for all the answers to her pleasure. Hot breath, heavy and demanding, mingled with her pretty noises whenever her hips shuddered. She'd start and stop when her pleasure got too close, wanting to prolong her finish. He let himself be the instrument she used to tend to her arousal.

The foil he stashed into his pocket before he left his apartment burned hot, reminding him of its existence. He tried to ignore it and the almost animalistic urge to claim Nina up against the window. He planned to take his time with her but didn't know how long he could hold back.

Unbeknownst to his thoughts, Nina cried out as her thighs clamped around his knee. Her back arched off the glass, marked by her faint indent from fogged breaths, and her legs trembled. Her eyes rolled back. "Close."

"I know, sweetheart, let it all out. No one can hear us."

"I can't—"

"Let me help you." Cole pressed his knee harder against her when her hips slowed down, struggling to bring herself to climax. He wouldn't let her squirm or fail at another chance to get off.

His eyes connected with hers tethered to an undeniable sense of intimacy. The rest of the world vanished in his tunnel vision as he had only eyes for her. Nina stared at him as she gave her last thrusts, and he watched her crumble with an orgasm.

Cole's mouth quirked up at the corners, dropping his knee. He held Nina up with her hands still pinned to the window, and with the other hand, he tugged her panties down the curve of her hips. "Let's get rid of these."

Nina nodded and stepped out of them, face redder than the wine they shared over dinner. Cole stuffed them into his pocket, swapping the panties for the condom. He released Nina and opened the foil but didn't stop her eager hands from pawing at his belt and trousers.

She split open the belt, pulled down his zipper, and dragged his trousers and boxers to puddle around his knees. Nina wrapped a hand around his hardened cock, and the touch elicited a soft groan from the sudden contact.

"Keep touching me like that, and I won't be able to wait for a second longer," Cole said.

"That's the intention."

"Fuck. I'm going—"

Cole, startled by her forwardness, slid the foil onto his cock and backed Nina against the window. Her arms tangled around his shoulders and pulled at the hairs along the nape of his neck, goading him faster in her way. He couldn't be fooled by the innocent blink of her eyes.

He reached for her thighs and squeezed underneath them. Nina jumped up, and Cole caught her, holding her up against the wall. She loosely looped her legs around his hips, and Cole guided himself to brush against her. It took him a try or two before the head of his cock pushed into her entrance, eliciting panting in his ear.

He couldn't help his moans either. "You feel so good."

"You make me feel even better."

"Keep talking like that, and I'll be doing this for the rest of my life."

Nina gasped, but Cole wasn't sure if that was from her taking the last inch of him with her pussy clenching around him or over what he whispered into her ear. From where he stood, she would either be his forever or the heartbreak he wouldn't come back from, and he hoped she'd like to be the former.

Cole's hands roughly groped her hips, likely to leave behind marks for the morning, as he bounced her on his cock. He used her hips and met halfway with his upward thrusts, filling the deck with the slap of skin on skin. Their hips collided with friction in every thrust, and Nina took it like a champion.

Her eyes struggled to remain open, overloaded with pleasure from him fucking her. She tightened her grip on his hair and occasionally pulled. *Hair-pulling wasn't expected, but not disliked in the slightest.*

"Are you doing alright?" Cole whispered against her mouth, but Nina's lips hungrily chased his. Her legs flexed and pushed his thrusts deeper into her, hitting the sweet spot from how loudly she moaned his name.

"Don't stop," Nina begged. "Please don't stop."

"I won't."

"Keep talking to me."

"Yeah? You want me to tell you how fucking pretty you look when I fuck you senseless? Tell you how your eyes roll back, and your lips look kissable? You take every inch of me without fail and still beg for more. Greedy, my dear."

Cole felt Nina's fingers scrape down his scalp instead of pulling, and he barked out a grunt, feeling out of control. Drunk on her, he pressed her harder into the glass, and his thrusts became sloppy, rough to the touch, and desperate to have her.

"Cole, please!" Nina screamed his name in utter enthrallment, and her pleasure echoed off the walls. The dim lighting of the deck added to the unspoken, seductive ambiance while Nina and Cole chased their highs on dark, moonlit waters.

"I've got you, sweetheart. You're mine."

"I'm yours."

"Always?"

"Always."

Sealed with a kiss between them, their promise of forever carried them well into the night with the feel of skin-to-skin on their minds.

Epilogue

Two years with an energetic child slipped through Nina's fingers, but she wasn't alone. Cole, as he promised, stayed by her side through every milestone. To her, he was the perfect partner.

But to Brooke, he became her father figure.

"We're here!" Brooke cheered from the backseat, kicking her legs. She almost dropped the tablet in her hands onto the seat next to her, and that wouldn't be the first time her excitement caused a minor accident. Luckily, Brooke held onto it before she passed it to Nina.

"We're here." Cole parked the sedan next to the mailbox of the Yearwood family home, leaning into the backseat. "Stay there, bug. Either your aunt or I will get you."

"Okay, Uncle Cole!"

Nina caught Cole's eyes, and she nodded. He could grab Brooke out from the back, and she'd grab the gifts from the trunk for the in-laws. Although Christmas came and went almost three months ago, Nina refused to show up at her in-laws without something to share.

Ever since she and Brooke met them, the Yearwoods embraced them as family. But these days, the golden wedding band on her finger meant she was one of them.

She reached for the door handle, but Cole stopped her with a gentle hand on her face. Before Nina could ask what he was doing, his mouth chastely embraced hers. But even with its brevity, love radiated in every moment when their lips touched.

Nina sighed when Cole pulled back, too dopey to question him as he whispered, "Stay put." He cut the engine and bounded from the driver's side of the car. She observed as he sprinted around the front and opened her door for her, grinning like a devil.

"You're such a dork," Nina groaned, but she accepted his hand to help her out of the passenger seat. Her sundress fluttered when she stepped out of the car, hit by the early March breeze. An otherwise cloudless day made for a perfect outdoor dinner party.

"Yeah, but you love me for it."

"I do. My vows said something about that."

Cole winked and sidled to the backseat while Nina popped the trunk for the gift bags she had spent two hours assembling with goodies for the family. Through a tiny sliver, she watched Cole unbuckle Brooke and scoop her out of the car.

Brooke held onto his shoulders with the biggest smile. She kicked her feet with little white sneakers, "Do you think they'll like my ladybug dress?"

"I think your ladybug dress is beautiful," Cole promised but lifted one of her blonde pigtails. "But I think they'll like your hair even more!"

Brooke squealed and tried to hide her face while Cole pretended to chomp on her pigtail, grinning the whole time. Gentle was the best description for how he doted on Brooke, even on the challenging days.

Nina smiled, loading the gift bags onto her arm, and closed the trunk. "Alright, let's head inside."

She, Brooke, and Cole walked up the driveway when the side gate to the backyard swung open, revealing Sharon in a floppy hat and a striped shirt perfect for spring.

"Mama S!" Brooke wiggled out of Cole's hold, and he managed to set her down before she sprinted toward Sharon, who kneeled down and opened her arms. The two embraced in a hug with Sharon's incoherent cooing.

"My! You've grown some more! Soon, you might be as tall as Uncle Dean."

"Auntie Nini says that if I eat my veggies and drink lots of milk, I'll grow up big and strong."

"Your aunt is a smart woman. I'd listen to her."

Nina laughed when Brooke zoomed past Sharon at the first audible barks. Regardless of who she was talking to, Socks was Brooke's favorite member of the Yearwood clan. The two got along like two peas in a pod.

Sharon, however, turned her attention to her son and daughter-in-law. "Welcome home, you two. We saw one another a few weeks ago for dinner, but I still miss you." She wrapped her arms around Nina and Cole at the same time.

Nina embraced her mother-in-law to the sweet scent of her perfume, bringing a familiar comfort, but heard her husband's "Aw, Mom."

"I'm all sappy today. It's been driving your dad mad." Sharon laughed and held the gate open for them to follow her. Cole's arm looped around Nina's waist and kept her close to him, which remained her favorite place to be.

The short walk to the backyard was filled with happy barking and Brooke's squealing. Nina spotted her niece kissing Socks' wrinkled forehead and falling into the grass whenever he did. Two peas in a pod.

"There they are!" Dean cheered and raised his beer when he noticed Cole and Nina's arrival. He and Stephen hung out by the grill. Nina could smell the burgers already cooking with the fresh patties, melted cheese, and the distinct touch of char.

"We made it. Did you at least save me a beer?" Cole kissed Nina's temple before he strode toward the grill and chest of cooled drinks. Nina giggled to herself but headed in the opposite direction.

She fixated on January, reading something on her phone at the table, and plopped into the chair. "Is this seat taken?"

"Not at all. If my husband protests, he can deal with it," January and she embraced one another. "It's so good to see you."

"It's good to see you. How was the cruise?"

"I needed a break from work, seriously. We traveled around the Pacific Ocean and stopped at several islands like Catalina. Unplugging helped Dean and I focus on making memories."

"I brought everyone gifts, but I'll save those for after dinner." Nina rattled the bags and slid them underneath the table, obscured by the tablecloth.

January beamed. "See, this is why you're the best. So, tell me, how's Brooke doing in school? Has she made the adjustment well?"

"According to her teachers, Brooke is thriving. She's not developmentally behind the other seven-year-olds in the school and has a core group of friends she hangs out with at recess and lunch. Not to mention, she's quite an avid presenter during projects. A couple of the moms have mentioned to Cole that she would make a great lawyer someday." Nina knew Brooke would be a smart cookie, but nothing prepared her for how proud she could be of her niece.

"Oh yeah, I can see it. If she ever chooses the law path, she has four Yearwoods to help out."

Nina, in a conscious decision, enrolled Brooke as Brooke Byndel-Yearwood. When they first decided, she asked Brooke about it, and Brooke loved the idea. Naomi would be represented as Byndel, and she and Cole as Yearwood.

"All I want for her is to be happy."

"Which is what makes you a great guardian to her."

Nina smiled but spotted Cole heading over to the porch swing with a drink in hand and stood up. "Excuse me for a moment."

She headed from the table and climbed the stairs to the back porch, sliding onto the swing. Cole immediately curled an arm over her shoulder, bringing her closer.

"Hey," Cole whispered.

"Hey." Nina closed her eyes for a moment, enjoying the moment. She loved family events and never felt out of place. Meeting these amazing people taught her about true family. Family was what you made of it.

"Dean and Dad were talking about stocks, so I ditched that conversation quickly."

"Didn't you major in economics?"

"Precisely why I left. I decided to find my lovely wife so we could resume our conversation in bed this morning."

"Which one? Because one is inappropriate for a backyard barbeque," Nina teased but opened her eyes to see the earnestness on his face.

Cole's thumb stroked her cheek. "The one about expanding our family? Brooke seemed insistent about having a cousin to play with since one of her friends has a little brother, and she wanted one too."

Nina's heart skipped a beat. Even talking about it stirred up eagerness in her, which seemed like a good sign. She wanted to have a baby with Cole, and if he and Brooke were all on board, then she wouldn't waste more time.

"I'm all in," Nina said.

Cole's eyes brightened, and he squeezed her close. Nina buried her smile in his shoulder, hearing his soft murmur, "I love you. I love us. I promise that whatever I can do to help the process, it's yours."

"Your support is a good start. But I look forward to three A.M. pregnancy craving runs and all the crying you'll be subjected to."

"Bring it on. I know you're tough, and I aim to please."

Nina laughed, and she nuzzled. "You already have." She found herself fixated on his heartbeat dancing in his chest.

Cole kissed her hair, "You as a mom . . . Naomi would be proud of how far you've come. You and Brooke."

"I hope she is." Nina tipped her head to lay on Cole's shoulder, staring at the clear skies. The breeze carried dandelion fuzz and the aroma of barbeque through the backyard, reminding her of the summers she and Naomi spent hiding away from the world. But these days, she found solace in the family she created.

A little persistence to do right carried her out of the dark and handed her a lighter, more loving future. She found what it meant to be at home.

Cole turned toward her, and Nina leaned in, hoping for another kiss. But a sharp whistle from Dean interrupted their quiet embrace before they even started. "Dinner's ready, you two!"

"Perfect timing, as always," Cole groaned with a hint of sarcasm there. "Ready to join the others?"

"Oh yeah. I'm starving." Nina laughed, and Cole pulled her onto her feet. The two returned to the dinner table, where everyone gathered around, laughing and sharing food, underneath the spring sky.

Acknowledgements

Writing a follow-up story to *Love on the Docket* started as a daunting challenge for me. I knew Cole would be the male lead for the second book, but not much more than that. In his first incarnation, I sat down with his playful, instigator personality and his observant intelligence as the first threads to work with, knowing there would be room for nuance and hidden sides to him.

Nina surprised me. I wanted to continue the thematic trend I started with in January as a response to what society deems desirable in women. To the outside world, Nina would be considered a single mom. Compared to the books out there with "single dad" romances, single moms or solo female guardians never receive the same love. So, I decided to write my own.

Love Thicker Than Blood brought those two aims into a single book. When writing contemporary, I never wanted to sacrifice emotional depth or shortchange the intelligence of my readers. The romance genre faces many misconceptions, some self-perpetuated, that romance narratives are stale and supposed to be nothing more than an easy breezy read (full of hot air and no substance). That became the driving force behind my dedication in Love Thicker Than Blood, written after a discussion about the ideology behind what makes a good romance story with my mother.

But people embraced my vision with open arms, and I can't thank them enough. My biggest supporters in Bree, Hannah, Kit, and the members of the Writer's Guild Discord. These were the people who listened to me in my highs and lows, being the best sounding boards and sources for advice when I needed a second opinion. These lovely people are my closest confidants in the writing business, and everyone would be lucky to have at least one of these people in their lives.

Thank you to my family for their continued support of my writing. I dedicated this book to my mother half as an inside joke due to her love of cheesy, nonsensical Hallmark movies. She and I go back and forth where she gushes about whichever movie she plans to watch, and I crack off snarky comments and accurate predictions from the other room. My mother protests, but ultimately she can't argue with my sharp tongue and a keen appreciation for storytelling. Romance for her has to be a no-brainer, but for me, it has to be lively and three-dimensional. I appreciate being pushed to write the stories I want to see in the world.

Thank you to Christine of Christine Cover Designs for the job she did on *Love Thicker Than Blood*'s cover. Originally, I ordered the first book as a premade cover, but I wondered how the thematic elements would carry over into the next book. The pearls worked with the first book and a climactic scene there, but the diamonds for this cover added a subtle touch. She is someone I genuinely recommend for authors on a budget.

Thank you to Mads Arlow, Kelsey Gay, and Jennifer Speck, better known as the lovely ladies who worked as key beta readers and the proofreading editor for the story. These ladies devoted their time to appreciating and polishing up a story I've grown to love so much. Their contributions make the story stronger and more resonant than it would've been without their input. I look forward to working with them again in the future.

Finally, thank you to every reader who came with me on this journey. No matter how many times I put out a new book, I won't forget your flowers. The verdict is in... I appreciate you all so much.

-Cassandra

About the Author

Cassandra Diviak considers herself a storyteller at heart. Writing is her first love.

A Los Angeles native, the 22-year-old lives in the city while she attends law school. She is in her second year of school and has an interest in family law, specifically the representation of minors.

Besides schooling, which is highly important to her, Cassandra loves to read, play games like Stardew Valley, and spend time with the people who matter to her. With the continued publishing of new books, she hopes to travel more and see more of the world outside her beautiful state. *The Laws of Love Duology* is Diviak's first contemporary romance release, but there is plenty more ahead.

You can learn more at:
Instagram: @author.cassandradiviak
Tiktok: @author.cassandradiviak
Website: https://cassandradiviakauthor.weebly.com/

Also by Cassandra Diviak